VIXEN

Also by Rosie Garland

The Palace of Curiosities

VIXEN

ROSIE GARLAND

THE BOROUGH PRESS

The Borough Press
An imprint of HarperCollins*Publishers*
77–85 Fulham Palace Road,
Hammersmith, London W6 8JB

www.harpercollins.co.uk

Published by HarperCollins*Publishers* 2014
1

A catalogue record for this book
is available from the British Library

ISBN: 978-0-00-749279-4

Set in Minion by Palimpsest Book Production Limited,
Falkirk, Stirlingshire

Printed and bound in Great Britain by
Clays Ltd, St Ives plc.

MIX
Paper from
responsible sources

FSC
www.fsc.org   **FSC™ C007454**

Love is the longing
for the half of ourselves
we have lost

from *The Unbearable Lightness of Being*
by Milan Kundera

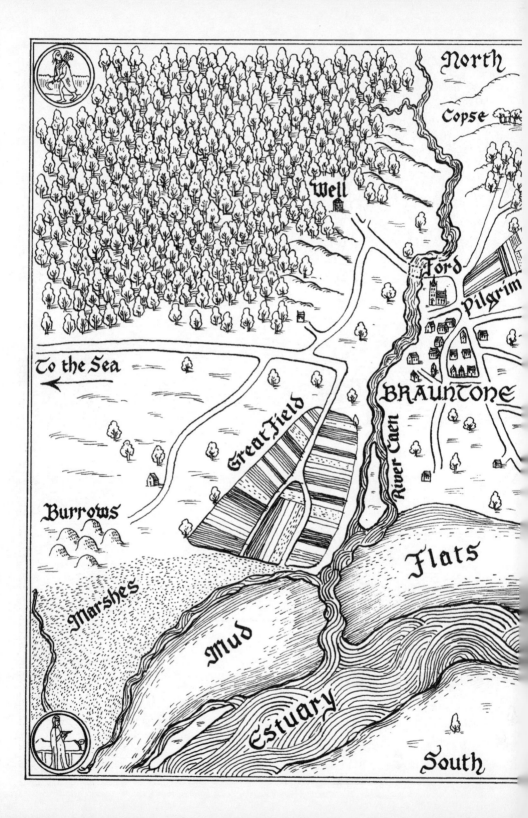

North

Copse

Well

Ford

Pilgrim

To the Sea

Great Field

BRAUNTONE

River Caen

Burrows

Flats

Marshes

Mud

Estuary

South

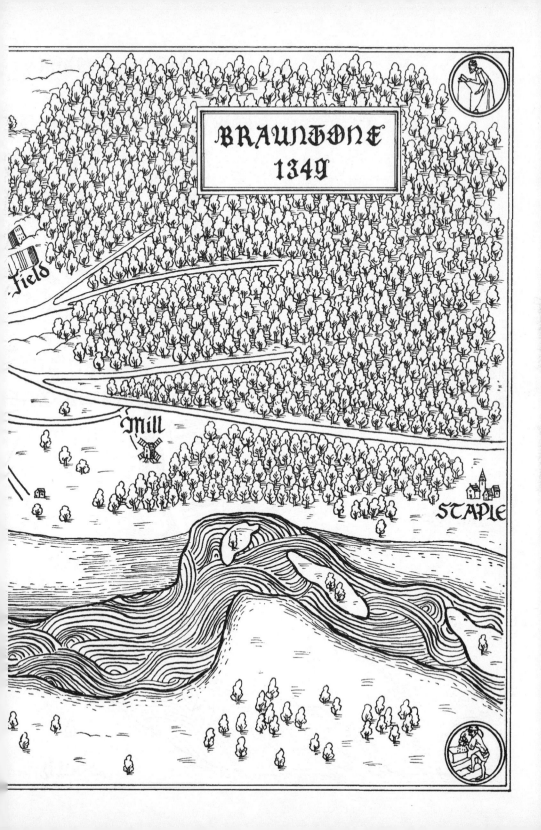

VIGILS
1395

ANNE

I declare at the start that I was muddle-brained and spoilt. There. It is out.

For all that, I shall have my say. I wasted years holding my tongue, and the older I grow, the less I am inclined to wastage of any kind, be it time, or bread, or affection. I have not been a particularly good woman, by the reckoning of men. Nor have I been especially wicked. I have been close enough to Death to rub elbows, and what I saw in His eyes did not affright me.

Before I go into His great sleep, I should like to see the village once again: walk along Silver Street, turn west at the crossroads on to Church Street, lift my skirts and paddle through the ford where the Caen runs shallow, pass the church and arrive at the house. There shall I pause, hand on the gatepost, and look up the path to the door. Memory preserves things as they were, not as they are: I see the windows shuttered, more oilcloth than glass in the panes; the thatch half-rotten; the raw patch on the door where the Maid picked at the wood. Therein I saw out my fifteenth and came into my sixteenth year. Such a scant number of months, yet they encompassed a lifetime.

I think of the child I was. I think of Margret, my beloved friend. What she had in prettiness I possessed in plainness,

3

although no mirror could persuade me of that fact. I was queen of my hearth, and carried that conviction into our games. I envied her and she bore the burden of my contrary nature with great meekness. I wish I had been a kinder companion. For does not Paul declare that the first shall be last and the last first?

I wish I could have seen where my feet were carrying me, the dangers of that path. If I had my time again – but here I go, twittering pointless wishes and dreams.

Perhaps my greatest foolishness was to think a grander fate awaited me: better than my sister Cat and her snot-nosed hatchling; better than my dam, planting turnips to feed us through hungry winters; at the very least, better than my brother Adam, gutted for some lord's whim on a battlefield far from home.

Adam was an oak given breath: as tall, as strong, as gentle. When I wept he was my comfort. He strove to make me laugh, made me his special pet, bore me on his shoulders in games of horse and rider where I was his little lady fair and he my sturdy palfrey. He brought me pretty morsels: a roasted pigeon's heart, marchpane from the Staple fair, a ribbon so blue I thought the sky should hang its head for being outdone in blueness.

He rose each morning, the sun of my life. The light he cast warmed the mud of my childish heart and I bloomed. I spent many an hour squeezing the muscles of his arm, transformed into rock by the rigours of drawing back the bowstring until the fletchings tickled his ear. How I cheered him at village contests, although he never carried off the prize. I could not understand, in my mind he was the best archer, the best brother, the best man at every task. He was my first love, my best love. I adored him with the innocent and all-consuming passion of a child, before she eats the apple and knows evil in the world.

Then, one spring, just after Candlemas, he was called to fight in France and we did not see him again. We lacked his body to grieve over, and mourned an emptiness that was without solace. I howled fit to tear the sky in half. I wanted God to tumble through the rift and fall to our patch of earth so that I could stick out my lip and demand, face to face, that He bring Adam back from dust. I was greedy with misery and believed none other felt it but me. No one slapped me out of my self-ishness, not even Cat. I wept and wept until, just as suddenly, I stopped.

I woke that morning and watched my soul quit my body, slipping across the sea to join Adam. I became a girl without a shadow, a half-girl. I ate, I slept, I crouched over the bucket and squeezed myself empty, but was as lacking of life as the wooden saints in the church. My hands made gestures, my feet moved when commanded, but I was stiff, carved from some tough material that was no longer flesh.

When I placed myself in the path of the new priest, Father Thomas, I reasoned that it was out of desire and affection, rather than a hunger for possessions to fill the empty place in my soul. I thought to find consolation. Not raising up to an estate I had no right to, but some peace. I wanted a mild man who lifted his hand only to bless me; a modest house to call my home; a son who toddled on fat legs to bury his face in his mother's lap. I did not start making sense of the world until much later.

I lost the better part of myself when Adam died and did not get any of it back until the Maid came to the village. My Maid, if I may make so bold – and I do, for I have grown courageous. Of all the folk who have burnished my life, she is the one I wish to see the most. She was flint to my iron. Dull as I was, she struck fire and I have burned bright since that first spark.

5

I think of her always; yet she comes rarely to my mind. It is a conundrum and I apologise. She was never fenced in, not with words and certainly not by any effort of man. I fear I will not capture her, either. But that part of my tale must wait a short while. There is more to tell, and there is time.

ADVENT
1348

VIXEN

Must I speak?

Must I stand here, say my piece? Make my words dance to the cramped tune of quill and ink? Must I squeeze myself onto the scored lines stretched tight across this page of parchment? I have no time for books – not that the likes of me can read them. Wear out my eyes squinting at scribbles when I could be lying on my back looking up at the clouds? I'd rather read their restless journey from lands where no man has set foot, and what they saw there.

I need no one, I want no one and no one wants me. That is the finest way to pass through this world, running so swiftly even the air cannot stick. I shake off everything as a fox sheds its tail when the hounds take hold. I'll skip through this world tailless rather than not at all.

I scratch my scars: the ones on my back, the ones between my legs, the ones between my ears. They itch, particularly when the wind has a mind to change. This year is such a wild turnabout that the earth creaks with the upside-down, pitch-and-toss of it all. What's at the end I know not, but a topsy-turvy world suits me. It opens new doors to slide through and leap out onto a different side.

Through it all I sing and dance and keep a step or two ahead of Death. Of course He is always there, but for the most part keeps His distance: playing His pipe on the roof-ridge of the next church but one, supping ale in the tavern I was in yesterday, banging on my neighbour's door all night. The rat-tat-tat keeps me awake but I do not care, for it is not my door.

This year He draws too close for comfort.

I'm the first to see Him. I'm on the quayside, watching ships come in. He stands on the prow of the largest, waving. I'm the only one to wave back. Even from this distance I can hear Him piping out the mortal tune that is playing across the world, from Jerusalem to Rome and all the way to this slack lump of muck.

A woman at my elbow, head bundled up against the winter, says, 'Who do you see? Who's there?'

'Don't you see Him?' I say.

'Who?'

'The pestilence!' I cry.

'Don't say that!' she hisses. 'What are you trying to do; bring it down upon us?' I laugh until she twists away, making the sign of horns with her fingers.

The moment the ships tie up, it begins.

I see three ships come sailing in with wine and glass, bolts of cloth and spices, things I may name but never dream of owning. Mooring ropes are thrown out: hands catch them, loop them tight, sew the hulks to the hem of the harbour. Rats skitter down the ropes and into town. The gangplank sticks out its tongue and the hold breathes out. I smell what's on the air. These ships are spewing out the taste of Death.

I know the truth as I know the lines on my hand: this is the Great Mortality come at last. I see Him: strolling down the walkway, trailing rotten robes, worms tumbling in his wake. He steps on to the quayside, licking His lips, for He loves the savour of man and woman, old and young, rich and poor. I look Him in the eye and He grins.

'Aren't you afraid of me?' He growls, and only I am shrewd enough to hear. 'Aren't you fearful of my bony fingers, ready to snatch and snuff you out? Of the smile that stretches to my ears? My wormy guts, the sores and scars and scabs I'm studded with? Doesn't it make you want to piss yourself and run?'

Of course I'm terrified. Only a simpleton would not be. But I fix His hollow eye with mine and shrug. I've seen worse painted on church walls: seen bloodier, blacker, harsher.

'Let others run, and scream, and fall,' I say. 'If it's really you, I'd rather dance.' I smile. 'I've heard so much about you. About the fever you bring this year.'

Oh, how He picks up his heels and rattles them along the street! Elbows clattering in and out, knees up, knees down, fingers snapping, clapping His great jaws together, arms a frantic windmill.

'All fall down!' He sings.

There's never been anything so fit to make you roar: we two capering fools, skipping along the harbour wall. I laugh until I ache. Of course, He falls in love with me and I have to dodge His kisses.

'Marry me!' He croons. 'I'll give you such a dowry as will snatch your breath away! Make you the richest bride in seven kingdoms!' He promises. 'I'll furnish a feast that goes on seven days and seven nights! Silk for your sheets! Wine till you burst!'

But dancing is all I want. So I dance, and watch others die.

The harbour-dwellers are first to sicken. They say it's foul air brought by the ships. The breath of a latrine may make me gag, but cannot kill me. I've cleaned up rich men's shit for long enough to know.

I see men die, and beasts live. Especially the horses: Death hates their odour, which makes me love it, purely to annoy Him. Then there are the rats, too small for men to notice. What is a rat? Of no more consequence than a girl. A girl who does not know her letters, but can read men. Who does not know her prayers, but knows what they are for. Who is tired of waiting for a saviour to turn stones into loaves.

I hear tales about punishment for sins, the wrath of the Lord. As for God's anger, I'll say nothing: not for fear of Heaven striking me down, but for the anger of men, who fear the fragility of their faith so keenly they would burn a child who spoke one small word against it.

I dance down the coast, from village to village. The first time, I tell the truth and say I am come from Bristol. They smell trouble and I escape with my skin, racing from hurled rocks and cudgels, only stopping when I am in the forest and they will not follow. I spit on the path that leads back.

The next place I am wiser, but still am chased off. I run: not only from their fists but also from the fever I smell on their breath, the roses blooming in their throats. I avoid villages, sniff out the stink of men and keep away. I use their fields for my larder; learn to move quickly. And all the while I keep one step ahead of the fearsome dancing partner whose breath rots the road behind.

We make a good pair, Death and I. As long as I can pique His interest, amuse Him with a merry expression and fancy riddles, He does not bid me stop. As long as I am more valuable alive than dead, He does not draw me into His most intimate and final of embraces. Each morning I devise a fresh amusement and play it out, ear cocked for His approving chuckle. Poised for dangerous silence.

I point to a man and say, *This one?*

He nods, and I start my game: steal a string of sausages from under the butcher's nose, piss on the blacksmith's fire, throw sand between the miller's stones, spit on my lady's poached halibut. I watch them fume and shake their fists, so consumed with anger they do not see the towering darkness behind them till He taps on their shoulder and there's no time for hand-wringing and pleas for mercy.

I boast, hoping he cannot hear my desperation.

See how light I can make your labour?

Did you ever have such fun before?

What diversions. What amusements! Do I not garland your workaday world with wonders?

It's a thin path to tread: I must not get so close that He gathers me into His arms and presses His stinking lips to mine. I must not strike a bargain, *their lives for mine;* nothing so dangerous as *spare me and I will make you laugh.* I am not so stupid as to spit on my palm and shake Death's hand. I'll keep myself well clear of His claw.

I am a jolly-man, a wooden-head; not everyman, but every-fool. I dance, I sing, turn cartwheels and weave my body into knots. For Him I flit between boy and girl, between dog and vixen; so fast that I lose sight of what I am, submerged in the swirling, glittering soup of my creations.

I am exhausted. So very tired of all this labour, this hanging on to life.

MATTINS
1349

The Feast of Saint Brannoc

THOMAS OF UPCOTE

Because I could not hear the voice of God, I went to the fields.

I woke early, hoping to find a small corner of quiet in my church, but there was none. Before dawn I knelt at the altar, straining to hear the Lord but instead heard some farmer bawling for his cow. By first light this solitary cry had swelled into a wild congregation of yawning and farting and belching and pissing and wailing and sneezing and hawking and cracking of stretched limbs and banging of doors and no chance to hear the boldest cock crow over the dreadful racket.

So I went into the meadow. The morning was brisk: crisp bracken, brown as crumbled horse-bread, curled into itself as though trying to keep warm. Holly thickened the hedgerow, beside thorn bushes and grey-skinned ash with its black fists of buds. Small birds fluttered alongside, keeping pace with my steps.

I strode to the centre of the field. The earth spread its cloak beneath my feet, prickly with barley stalks cut close as stubble on a man's chin. The breath of the dawn rose in a mist. Drops of water hung at the tips of the grass stems, catching the new light. Rooks splashed in the rutted puddles that lay athwart the fields. Over the sea to the west the sky was dark; the brightness of coming day showed itself to the east.

17

I shook my head of these distractions, pressed on, dropped to my knees. The dew came straightway through my hose and chilled me awake. I listened: nothing but my own happy breath. I pressed my palms together and spoke the beautiful words of the Office under the roof of God's sky. No one bothered me with, *Father Thomas, are you sick?* I did not have to snap, *No; I am at prayer. I am your priest. I pray. It is what we do.* It was delightful.

For a moment only. A crow cawed, emptying its throat of sand. Its fellow answered from three fields away, echoed by the clattering of magpies. A cow mourned for her calf, taken at the last harvest. Bullocks steamed, sheep coughed at the sparse winter grass. All I asked was a little peace. If Hell was unimaginable pain and Heaven was unimaginable bliss, then the bliss I sought was humble silence. I shook my head, tried to retrieve the silence I tasted when I first knelt.

But here was a fox crying with the voice of a whipped boy, the *dit-dit-swee* of the titmouse, the rattling chatter of robins, the *twee-twee* of dunnocks, the bubbling of blackbirds. Seagulls cackled at some private joke. I pushed away the thought that it was myself they found so amusing.

I prostrated myself upon the earth and inhaled the reek of its dark breath, rolled over and lay on my back, stared upwards into the bowl of the heavens: the half-darkness unrippled by clouds, the stars closing their bright eyes one by one as the approaching daylight spread itself across the sky.

Can you not pray, my son? Am I so difficult a master?

I groaned. My disobedient senses were drawing me away from God. I shut my eyes tight, shoved my fingers into my ears till all I could hear was the hissing of the fire in my head.

'Oh God!' I bellowed, to drown out the world around me.

My heart slowed. *Oh Lord, behold Your servant.* That was the

18

sum and total of my prayer, for the hour of the Office was done. It was time for me to spit upon my hands and labour for God. The pilgrims would come today and I would be ready.

I hitched my cassock and splashed through the ford into the village, slapping warmth into the cold meat of my thighs. Rain slanted down onto the thatch, gathering itself together for another busy day. There had been no frost all winter, only this steady river falling from the sky and making the fields swim. But the rain must stop soon: it was almost spring.

William stood at the lychgate collecting donations from the gathered pilgrims. He was a fine steward, and I could not fault him for the wholehearted way he displayed his stave of office with its clubbed head of brass. He stopped short of affrighting people, as a rule. Lukas stood at his side, arms folded, eyeing the crowd keenly for anyone who might try to slip in without payment. He grinned, tying up a sack of candles ready to be hauled away to the treasury.

'It is a good take today, Father,' he said, squeezing rain from his beard. 'There's two bags of tapers put by already and we're barely past breakfast.'

'The people turn to the Lord in earnest,' I replied soberly. 'That is what matters.'

'Numbers are up,' said William, gloating.

I would speak with him, another time. 'The Saint's intercession is most powerful,' I said. 'He has never failed us.'

'Indeed, Father,' he said. 'Very good to us, he is. And don't these folk know it,' he roared, sweeping his arm in a gesture encompassing the company. 'Come for a piece of his goodness, every one of them.'

'It's a fine thing he's so generous,' added Lukas.

Aline bawled a greeting and pushed a wooden mug into my hands.

'There you go, Father! The Saint's ale itself. Fresh this morning and I never brewed a better, if I say so myself.'

Her face was red. I decided to take it for hard work rather than hard drinking. I sniffed the pot, not discourteously, and took a mouthful.

'It is good, mistress.'

She grinned. 'Bless you, Father!' She turned round, took a deep breath and bellowed, 'He likes it! Good enough for the Saint's man, more than good enough for us, so it is!'

There was an answering cheer from the multitude, many a cup raised. I picked my way through the field of folk, spread thick as daisies upon the grass. They regaled me with tales of how the Saint saved them from drowning, healed broken arms and broken hearts, planted healthy sons in barren wombs, cured this sickness and that sickness till my head spun and my arm wearied from pumping up and down in blessing.

A man laid on the ground stretched out his arm and grasped my ankle. Though his shoulders were broad and muscular, his legs were so thin they could not bear his weight. The bones of his knees were as big as cabbages.

'Father,' he croaked. 'Can your Saint save us from the pestilence?'

With the speed of a bucket of water hurled onto a fire, the pilgrims fell silent. The burden of their glances heaped on my shoulders.

'My son,' I said, making the sign of the Cross upon his brow. 'Pray to the most holy Brannoc. God have mercy upon you.'

The man shook his head petulantly. 'The *pestilence*, Father. Are his relics proof against the Great Dying?'

The crowd hissed through their teeth at the dangerous words.

Inch by inch they drew back, clearing a circle of mud around him. One old female muttered under her breath and made the sign of horns with her fingers. I glared at her for indulging in such heathen tomfoolery. She ignored me and spat at my feet. I closed my eyes and called upon the Lord to plant the right words into my mouth.

'Only God knows the workings of His will.' There was a groan, and not a little sucking of teeth. 'The pestilence is His will. It is punishment for our sins,' I continued, gathering strength.

'God forgive me!' sobbed a man from somewhere in the mob.

He was hushed swiftly, and for once all ears turned to me with full attention.

'But,' I cried. 'But,' I repeated, for it was a good word and had captured them. 'The Saint is a strong protector. Not one goodman or goodwife of this village has perished since the Great Mortality came to this land.'

My words stirred up a hubbub of excitement: they hung on to my coat, pawing at my arms, heaping thanks upon my head and calling down the blessings of the Saint for some miracle they thought had taken place. I wriggled free of their clinging and hurried to the church, its hulk looming out of the drizzle like a monstrous bull. I patted its flank and let myself in by the small north door; laid my back to the wood, closed my eyes, stretched out my hand and brushed the plaster of the wall, warm and soft as a child's cheek. *Oh Lord, behold Your servant.*

What a dungheap you go to, John had said when the Bishop divided up the parishes between we new priests. He was given the Staple with its fine harbour and cobbled streets; its church with silver and gold and paintings on wood and wall. I had laughed then, and I laughed now, joyful in my heart to be amongst simple, unlettered folk. Did Our Lord not do the same? My church boasted no pillars, nor aisles, nor benches. A barn of a place rather, fit for gathering a harvest of souls who offer fruits of praise. I smiled at the neat thought: perhaps that would suit today's sermon. The Lord had not seen His way to giving me a theme as yet.

Besides, my church had its own prize: the shrine of the Saint, hallowed with his bones. My feet whispered a path to where it swamped the chancel, pinnacles piled up like sugar loaves nibbled by greedy children, pierced with windows through which could be seen the plain grey hulk of the tomb. I spat on my sleeve-end and rubbed at a thumb-mark, no doubt left by a careless pilgrim.

'Guide me, oh Lord,' I prayed. I heard God knock at the door of my soul once, twice, and I shouted, 'I am here, Master!'

'Father?'

I twisted about. A man stood at the rood-screen, banging his knuckles against the wood.

'Father!' he bawled. 'Shall I ring the bell? It is time.'

I blinked myself back into this world, waited until I was sure my voice was steady.

'Edwin, you do not need to ring the bell. I am content to do it myself.'

'I am the bell-ringer. Father Hugo chose me. I cannot be unchosen. Do I not do it well, Father Thomas?'

'Yes, Edwin, you do it very well,' I sighed.

He folded his arms. 'You have chosen no deacon yet, Father? You have been here this quarter-year.'

'No deacon, Edwin.'

'Not even a chaplain? A priest needs a chaplain.'

'I strive for God,' I said. 'It is my joyful duty to be about His work, however humble.'

'Father Hugo had a chaplain. And two church-wardens.'

'That Reverend Father was content to let others toil for him,' I said. *And he did many other things I would not,* I thought privately. 'I will not set myself above you.'

'But you've made William your steward. And Lukas. Do you favour them?'

'I do not,' I sigh.

I had had little choice in the matter, although Edwin did not need to know about those colourful discussions.

'You work too hard, Father,' he muttered; disappeared up the tower steps and the bell clanged out its welcome.

Soon, I must open up to the pilgrims. I propped the ladder at the west window and peeped out. Even through the glass I could hear them, buzzing like bees in a pot. Like bees to the hive for the honey of the Saint and his sweet miracles. Perhaps *this* was the right idea for my sermon. I let it bloom in the soil of my mind, planted there with God's grace. It came to me that a honeycomb with its many cells was like a psaltery, each of the cells a psalm dripping with the treacle of God's word. The hive was the community of this church, the congregation bees who laboured for their queen, bringing tithes of nectar and offering them freely.

I was delighted with these clever notions. Here was a fine Saint's Day sermon to instruct as well as dazzle the people. But a worm twisted in my mind: if the priest was the queen, then that made me a female. If I saw it, so would they. I imagined them snickering behind their hands and my enthusiasm stumbled.

I revived myself hastily; the remainder of the idea was sound, especially the part about the tithes. Then I remembered that bees had stings and used them on whoever tried to take the honey. Also, they were as like to desert a hive and fly to a better place if they had a mind to it. My idea, so clever, crumbled. Perhaps God did not speak to me after all. I shook off the prick of disappointment.

An idea would come to me. The pilgrims were here. They had heard of the pious priest who tended the relics. I would make them love me, would take the leaden blank of this day and stamp my impression upon it. I wanted them to carry away a clear picture of their new priest, not Father Hugo. I was tired of hearing how bold he was, how strong, how jolly, how wild. I wanted them to return home with my name on their lips and in their hearts. *Oh, that Father Thomas,* they would say round their hearths. *You should have heard him preach! Not like Father Hugo, and that's a good thing.* Next year, I would be greeted like an old friend.

I sighed. I could delay no longer. I climbed back down, pulled open the great west door and turned to greet the pilgrims with a broad smile.

Straightaway, they swarmed towards the shrine: clawing the stone, kissing and licking and begging to be cured of the itch, the flux, the ague, the earache, the falling sickness, the fever. All of them weaving their limbs in and out of the openings until the shrine could barely be seen for the bodies wriggling upon it, the onion reek of their breath so strong it heaved my stomach.

One man, very grandly dressed, approached the shrine on his knees. It was only when he passed that I noticed that the flagstones behind him were smeared with blood. Exhaustion had ploughed deep furrows upon his face. When he reached the chancel steps he paused and lifted one leg in an effort to climb the step. I approached and took his arm. He shrank from the contact.

'Don't touch me!' he growled, only then noticing my liturgical garments. 'I beg forgiveness, Father,' he moaned, balled his hand into a fist and clouted himself on the side of his head.

'My son,' I said. 'I offer succour. It is Christian charity.'

'I said, do not touch me,' he replied, only a little less angrily. 'I have vowed to undertake this pilgrimage with no help from any man. Do not thwart me when I am so close.'

Tears rose in his eyes and spilled down his cheeks into the grim stubble of his beard. I made the sign of the Cross over his head.

'The Lord forgives you, my son.' I spoke most earnestly, for his pain had moved me.

'How do you know?' he snapped. 'How dare you speak for God?'

I gasped at his intemperate speech, only to gasp louder when he tore away his tunic. The flesh of his back was raked with gashes. Where they had scabbed over they had been torn afresh so that new scars lay atop the old. Now I understood why the ground about him was smeared with blood.

'This is too much, my son,' I said gently. 'The Lord does not demand such—'

'Such what? Such *shows*? How do you know what God has demanded of me?'

The cause of his wounds was clear: about his middle was a girdle of iron, tight-fitting and barbed with teeth that pierced his skin every time he breathed in. Fresh blood soaked into his hose. As I watched, he removed this cruel belt and struck himself over the left shoulder: once, twice, thrice; then over the right, tearing fresh wounds. There were gasps of wonder from those standing around. He uttered not the smallest sound, teeth gripped together, face set like stone.

'You have no idea what sins I have committed,' he grunted. 'What God and my priest have ordered as repentance.'

When he finished flogging himself, he fastened the belt once more and put on his over-tunic. Without so much as a glance at the shrine, he turned and, still on his knees, dragged himself back down the nave. I walked at his side. No one else would stand close to him and I grieved for his loneliness.

'Absolution awaits all who truly repent,' I said.

'Do you presume to see into my heart?'

'I am a man of God,' I declared. 'Be careful how you address me, however noble you may be.' I strove to make my voice tender again, for he was a soul in torment. I had never seen one so undone by his sin. 'Surely you may stand now that you have completed your pilgrimage?' I said quietly.

'Completed?' he said, bitterness dripping from the word. 'I am but a quarter way through.'

'My son—'

He interrupted me. 'I am charged to visit every shrine in England, on my knees. Then Wales, then Ireland. Then Saint James at Compostela.'

'God grant you peace,' I said.

He turned empty eyes to mine and hauled himself away, huffing and puffing, swinging the stumps of his legs one after the other. All heads turned to follow him on his painful journey out of the church. Two servants awaited him, a grim-faced old man and one much younger of the same stamp: I guessed father and son. When they saw me they bowed their heads with the precise amount of reverence due an insignificant parish priest and not one whit more. It was difficult to tell if they succoured their charge or watched to see if he reneged on his vow.

'What did he do, Father?' said a voice at my shoulder, so unexpectedly that I jumped.

I turned stern eyes upon my questioner, a youth from the village whose name I did not remember.

26

'That is for God to know, and not for men to gossip about.'

'It must've been something very wicked,' he mused, as though I had not spoken.

I fixed him with a disapproving stare. He smiled, shrugged his shoulders and sauntered out of the church towards the great yew, where a clutch of young hatchlings gathered, lounging against each other and whistling at the girls who had flocked from the surrounding villages.

He pointed his finger at the retreating penitent and their heads drew close as they whispered who knew what sort of nonsense. I considered marching across and chiding them for treating this holy day with so little respect. However, when I raised my eyes to the west window, the Saint looked down with such loving kindness that I relented. I counselled myself that it might be better to bring them to godliness through mild words rather than cruelty. Perhaps kindness should be the watchword for my sermon.

The pilgrims were much affected by the agonising spectacle of the penitent on his knees. Their weeping increased in intensity, as if it was not already deafening. One woman fell to the floor with a particularly piercing wail. She was helped back up by her companions, but struggled against them, falling once more. They tried to lift her but each time were defeated.

I hurried to assist, for the disturbance was distracting the pilgrims from their devotions as they queued to touch the shrine. In the time it took to reach her, the woman had started to babble noisily and everyone was stretching their necks to get a better view.

'This is not our doing,' hissed one of her companions, before I had even had a chance to open my mouth.

'She has been moved by the spirit of repentance!' cried a stranger from a few yards away.

The noisy woman's friends looked at each other doubtfully, weighing up if this might be the case.

'Let me kneel!' the woman yelled. 'I beg forgiveness!' She tore at her coif and a long strand of hair tumbled out, a fat black worm sprinkled with salt. 'I am a sinner!' she gargled, sinking to the floor.

Her companions glanced at each other over her head and frowned.

'Come now, mistress,' I said sternly. 'The Saint does not demand that you shout. He can hear the quietest of prayers.'

One eye flipped open and peered at me. It looked me up and down, testing the weight of my words. Then it closed and she began to bemoan her sins even more fervently. I arched my eyebrow at her friends, who caught the significance of my gesture. They picked her up by the armpits and dragged her towards the shrine with as much grace as a sack of beets, her blubbering the whole while.

A number of pilgrims muttered complaints that she was carried to the front of the queue while they had to wait patiently. I made pious comments about the Saint's ears being dinned in by the screeching, and how it would be a shame if he grew deaf to the prayers of others as a result. They saw sense straight away and helped her up the chancel steps.

She had fainted clean away by the time they brought her down; exhausted by her exertions or some kind miracle, I could not tell. She was carted out of the west door with much flapping of kerchiefs in her face.

Her bothersome performance infected the pilgrims: some fell to their knees at the west door, some as far back as the lychgate. Most contented themselves with dropping at the rood screen and made the last few yards of their journey grunting and puffing. An uncharitable part of my soul wondered if they thought the Saint could only see them after they passed through its thick gateway.

I told the first ones that it was not necessary; the Saint did not demand it of everyone. I was given looks of disbelief that a priest should ask for fewer penitent gestures rather than more. In the end I left them to it and counselled myself that if God willed this, then so be it.

I wondered if word would get around and at the next festival the whole lot of them would approach thus. Perhaps leaden tokens in the shape of knees would be sold; perhaps Brannoc would garner a reputation as a healer of ailments of the leg and there would be a rush of pilgrims afflicted with diseases of the ankles.

These were distracting thoughts. What might happen next year was in the hands of the Almighty. I sighed and rubbed my fingers on the point where my brows met. The commotion was driving a nail into my brains. William strolled by.

'Why are you not at your post?' I asked.

'Clearing out a piece of rubbish,' he laughed, clapping his hands. He dipped inside his tunic and drew out a small leather bag. 'See?' he said, waving it in my face.

'What should I see?'

'The ties are cut,' he replied, slowly, and I had the strong sense he was speaking as you would to an idiot. 'I found a lad lightening a gentleman of his possessions. Scabby little snip of a – begging your pardon, Father.'

'Where is the boy? I must counsel him.'

'He doesn't need any more of that, Father. I've given him a right good counselling.' He laughed again. 'He'll not be back.'

He sailed out of the west door, tall and straight as a mast. He waved the money bag above his head and bawled for its owner to claim it. I leaned against the rood-screen to gather my tattered senses together. I still had no sure theme for my festival sermon and there was very little time left.

Two young women giggled and clutched their kerchiefs to their noses as they passed. For a moment I wondered if I was giving off a noisome smell, but it was only the silly shyness of girls when faced with a man.

'Do not jostle me so, Margret,' hissed one of them. 'Father Thomas,' she cooed, dropping a curtsey.

The female called Margret cupped a hand round her friend's ear and whispered something too quiet to overhear. Whatever it was, it earned a fierce glare from her companion.

'Father Thomas,' said Margret. 'We should like to welcome you to this parish. Shouldn't we, Anne?'

'Yes,' agreed the maiden named Anne, in a flurry of further curtseying.

'The new priest is a blessing, is he not?'

'Yes,' twittered Anne. Her cheeks flushed so pink it was little wonder she attended the shrine. Such an excess of choler was not healthy in a woman. Much as I applauded their modest blushes, I wearied of their chatter, so with a polite *God be with you*, I stepped away. But the encounter had not been without value: modesty in women was the perfect subject for a sermon.

Finally, I had my theme, and not before time, for I must be quick and deliver the Mass. I hurried to the treasury. A boy was there, William's son, I didn't doubt. He held up the festival cope with as much grace as you would a day-old herring.

'Higher, boy,' I said. 'I can't get into it if you drag it across the floor like that.'

He huffed, hoisted it and I poked my head through the narrow opening. I declare I staggered under the sudden weight, although I hid it well and he did not notice.

'You are an idiot,' I muttered. 'You may as well send your sister next time. She'd do a better job.'

He bore my terse words meekly, but his lips were tight, and angry spots reddened his cheeks. No doubt he would grumble about me to his companions.

'Go to, go to,' I commanded in a kinder voice, for he was not a bad child, merely untutored. 'Tell the choirboys we are ready.'

I smiled, but of course the lad did not understand such niceties. I wondered briefly if he might be worth instructing; he seemed attentive. He could hardly be worse than the previous boy, who sang in the bell-tower and was found in the churchyard with his hand inside a girl's bodice.

I wriggled inside the fussy cope. It was ballasted with gold stitching and pearls, heavy as a stack of logs. I did not hold with all this panoply. If I had the choice, I'd leave that to peacock priests. But I did not have a choice: the Bishop made that clear when he heard – I know not from whom – that I conducted my Christmas Mass in plain shirt and hose. I endeavoured to explain I meant no disrespect: I wished to emulate the simple dress of our Lord, not to ape my poor flock. He lectured me with some force that I had no idea how Christ clothed himself and I would dress as commanded. Grandly, as befitted my station.

He told me that I insulted my parishioners by pretending to be the same as them. *You're a priest, by God,* he thundered. *Act like one.* I could not believe he should so mistake my humble intentions. So today, I sweated in gold and garnets. I contented myself with the knowledge that God saw my inner humility. If men needed pomp to bring them to penitence, so be it. I was commanded, therefore I would obey, uncomplaining as a lamb.

The procession began. The choirboys tumbled in through

the west door, picking their noses and gawping at the pilgrims. They sang lustily, but to them the words were sounds only and they quacked them with as little comprehension as ducks. I strode ahead, robes trailing behind me. I tolerated their rude manners, their cracked voices that tore the psalms to shreds. I calmed myself with the knowledge that my reward was to read the Divine Office in solitude, tomorrow and every day after it.

I breathed relief. A high Mass such as this took place mercifully few times in the year. And at last, I had my sermon.

ANNE

For three days, we are a city. The world comes to our hamlet and brings its finery, its marvels, its smells, its terrors, its tragedies. For three days I stretch my eyes wide open and do not close them once, not even to blink. A handful of days, but crammed with a year's worth of new sights and sounds, fresh riddles and *do-you-remembers* unsurpassed. These days supply me with every tale with which I'll entertain myself for the remainder of the year.

The churchyard is too small to encompass these wonders, so the field behind Aline's alehouse blooms thick as daisies with tents, blankets, fires. Every trestle for five miles about finds its way there; tables spring up and are loaded with bread and cheese. The air is riotous with the scent of bacon, for John the butcher always has a pig fat and ready for the Saint. In return the Saint makes sure his purse is heavy afterwards, and the world carries away the memory of the best pork in the shire.

So tumble in the girdlers, purse-makers, skinners, tanners, cap-makers, smiths, pewterers, glovers and net-makers; behind them the scullions, reeves, nuns and shoe-makers, brewers, cooks, archers, glass-blowers, knights, goldsmiths, silversmiths and gem-polishers.

Next come in the ploughmen, the sailors, the sea-captains, fishermen, pig-men, shepherds, dairywomen, alewives, spinners, weavers, high ladies and low women. Here are the barbers, the saw-bones, men of physic and midwives, wise women and charlatans. We have fools, clerks, schoolmasters, pullers of teeth, bone-setters, knife-grinders, matrons, virgins, peddlers, tinkers and trench-diggers.

It is a small Heaven upon earth: a lion of a soldier fresh from the war comes to thank the Saint for his deliverance and lies down with the lamb of a carpenter come to pray for the soul of his son, who was not so lucky. The crook-legged man upon his wheeled tray prays for the straightening of his limbs. He slumbers chastely beside the beautiful young wife, who aches for her husband's seed to take root in the parched earth of her womb. For three days no one is troubled by lustful dreams.

Margret and I walk through the crowd. Heads turn, but I am grown enough to know that none of them turn for me. Margret is the lady now and I am the wench dragged in her wake. There is whispering also, and not all of it kind. I catch snatches of it, sticking to our skirts like teasels.

That is John of Pilton's woman.

A priest's woman is no goodwife, but a harlot.

You hold your tongue in check, Edwin Barton. You are the bell-ringer. Have some respect. This is the Saint's day.

Mama, what is a harlot?

I hear it; Margret hears it. When the sneering grows too loud to ignore, Margret stops and stares down the man who called her *harlot*.

'Why, Edwin,' she says, all kindness.

'Good day,' he mutters.

'How fares your mother, Edwin?' she enquires.

'Well, missus. Well,' he mumbles, tugs his cap so hard it slips over one eye. But there's no hiding from the press of Margret's courteous questions.

'And your brothers?' she continues. 'How fare they?'

'All well, to be sure, missus.'

'The Saint be praised.'

Margret's smile is so sweet I am surprised butterflies do not alight upon her head and lick her with their coiled tongues. But it is too early in the year for butterflies. 'Let me see,' she muses. 'Tell me if my recollection falters. There's Arthur?'

'Yes, missus,' he says.

'Bartholomew? Sam? Peter?'

He bobs his head at each name, declares each brother hale and hearty.

'I have forgot none, have I, Edwin?'

'Oh no, missus. None.'

'All of you so different in looks. By the Saint, who would have thought one father could bring to bear a redhead, a black-haired lad, one tall, one short.'

Her face is all concern for the welfare of Edwin's brothers. Yet I know the truth of their parentage, as does every man and woman here, their mother being an accommodating woman. Edwin grows red in the face, so dark a hue I think he might burst. Margret pauses for a long moment, her eyebrow lifted. Then she picks up the corner of her skirt and folds it over her arm. It is fine kersey, more shillings to the yard than I could hope to afford in a year, and exceeding beautiful. She bows her head politely and Edwin bows in response. She walks on without another word.

I pause for a moment, less time than it takes to pour a

cup of beer, but time enough to hear the giggles begin. I watch them, helpless with the need to keep respectful silence within sight of the church door, yet burdened with the equally pressing need to void their laughter at Edwin's expense. John the butcher chokes on his mirth and must be thumped on the back.

'She's got you there, Edwin, and right enough,' he splutters, to much cheerful agreement.

Edwin smiles as best he can. He is not a bad man. It is only his tongue that runs forward and escapes his mouth. I quicken my pace to catch up with Margret.

I find her within the church, gazing up at the painting of the Saint. He is planted on his knees before the Virgin and wears a look of avarice. Mary is the size of a child's poppet. She floats on a cushion just out of the Saint's reach, throwing sticks out of the ends of her fingers and aiming them at the Saint's head. I know they are supposed to be shafts of heavenly light, but they look like the poles you set up for beans. When I share these thoughts with Margret, she smiles again.

'Shh,' she whispers. 'That is the Virgin.'

'I do not insult our blessed Mary,' I hiss, curtseying as I say her name. 'I insult the hand of Roger Staunton, who imagines he can capture her on a cob wall. He is not as good a limner as he thinks.'

Margret heaves her shoulders up, then down.

'I hear those words wherever I go,' she says, and I know she speaks of Edwin Barton, and not the painting. 'Most of the time, they keep their foul opinions quiet, although I know what they are saying. It is like the sea: however far the tide is out, you can still hear it murmuring, waiting for the hour to turn so it may come back to land.'

Margret was always the poet. I have as much poetry in me

as a pound of pickled pork. She shakes herself, as a horse does when plagued by insects.

'The tide of harsh words is high today, yet I prevail.' She straightens her back and tips her chin at the wall. 'I thank you, blessed Virgin, for your blessings.'

'Blessings?'

'She has given me two. Greater than I could ever hope for. My dear son Jack, my dear John. He is a pearl of a man. I have not met a kinder, Anne, unless it be your father.'

I nod my head and do not disagree, for my father is the sweetest man ever to break bread.

'John serves God and man, and declares he does far better with me at his side. If God did not bring us together, then it must have been God's mother. It is to her I shall turn on Doomsday to pray for forgiveness. I have great hope for mercy,' she says firmly. 'John and I may not be chaste, but we love each other with a fidelity I defy anyone to condemn.'

My heart swells. At that moment, I would take up sword and buckler to defend her honour.

'It is strange,' she muses. 'They envy me my gowns, my furs, the cup from which I drink, yet they scorn me at the same time.'

'It is jealousy,' I say.

I do not tell her that I am envious also. Since she left for the Staple, there has been a hole the size of a door in the wall of my life. I guard that door. I did not know her love brought such comfort until she took it away and gave it to another. I see her seldom and the wind blows leaves into my empty heart. Today, she is by my side. For these few hours the breach in my soul is filled.

She clasps my hand and leads me through the pilgrims to a spot where we might have the best view of the Saint as he passes by on his wagon. He is carved from oak, face battered as a gate that has been swung on by a lifetime of rowdy boys. But he is ours, and we will have none other; not even the new one made of pear-wood and so beautiful he could make a cow weep. Our Lord Bishop gifted it to us, told us it came from Germany, and very costly too. But he's too pretty to be a man who yoked stags to a plough. So he stands on a pedestal in the north corner and bides his time, while our beloved tree trunk of a Saint protects us and favours us with miracles.

The new priest passes by, a hop in his step. He is nothing like Father Hugo, who could scarce pass through an alehouse door save sideways and whose voice could be heard in Hartland. His chin is unshaven and I wonder when he last took the razor to it. He takes his place on the chancel steps and clears his throat, which bobs with a sharp Adam's apple. We fall into a respectful silence, the better to hear the sermon. He lifts his arms.

'I speak of Solomon,' he begins. 'And the Queen of Sheba.'

There is a rumble of surprise, for we are expecting a tale of the Saint. Father Hugo always told a fine tale about one miracle or another and most amusing they were too.

'Wise King Solomon,' he continues. 'A lion amongst men.'

'What's this new man talking about?' murmurs Margret. 'Where is our Saint?'

She is not the only one to be asking that question. Some of the bolder lads shuffle towards the door muttering thirsty excuses, when Father Thomas raises his voice.

'Solomon had a hundred wives. A hundred to one man.'

Those halfway gone pause. Their heads turn: perhaps this sermon is not so disappointing after all. I look about. He has everyone's attention.

'Each as beautiful as a rose. But more beautiful by far was

Sheba.' His eyes shine as he describes her. 'Behold! She was fair. Her teeth were white as a flock of sheep fresh from the washing.'

The congregation nod their approval, for all men know nothing is whiter.

'Her hair was like a flock of goats that appear from Mount Gilead!'

My opinion is that goats are inclined to stink, but I keep my thoughts to myself. I look about. Every man is open-mouthed, every woman drinking the nectar of his words. More than one damsel raises a hand to her hair and smoothes it from the crown of her head as far as it will go, in imitation of Sheba.

'Her cheeks were like pomegranates.'

I spy one lass raise a hand to her face and pinch blood into her cheek.

'Her lips were like a thread of scarlet.'

Even I primp myself and nibble my lips to redden them.

'Her neck a tower of ivory, her stature like to a palm tree.'

At this, each girl stands up straighter, shoulders back. I have never seen a palm tree, but it cannot be very different from the ones in the forest. Father Hugo preached many a fine sermon, but not like this. I still recall his telling of Noah's flood and how we cheered when the rainbow appeared and all the dragons were drowned for ever. This affects me in a different way.

'The joints of her thighs were like jewels, her two breasts young does, feeding among the lilies.'

There is a drawing-in of breath. I appraise this new priest keenly. He must be very bold to speak thus. The blood of young men and maids needs little prompting to come to the boil, and he is stirring us as skilfully as a cook stirs batter for pancakes. He ploughs on, telling us of grapes and gazelles and temples and vineyards till I am giddy.

'Hear how she spoke to Solomon! A bundle of myrrh is my well-beloved unto me; he shall lie all night betwixt my breasts.'

I have never had a man lie between my breasts, let alone all night. It is an arresting notion. I catch Thomas's eye: it does not slide away in that way of priests who look at everyone and no one at the same time. He looks directly into my face and I hold his gaze, careful not to be too bold.

'Thou hast ravished my heart, my sister, my spouse; thou hast ravished my heart with one of thine eyes,' he says, chin bobbing, eyes bright with excitement.

My mouth drops open, and it takes a moment before I remember to close it. He does not look away, nor does he stop talking. His voice soars; as it does so it squeaks somewhat, but there are worse things of which a man can be accused. I flutter my eyelashes, venture a coy smile and am rewarded with a beaming grin that cracks his face open.

'How Sheba tempted the king!' he cries, spreading his arms, his gaze flying away into the roof. 'Come, she said. Let us go early into the field, she said. There will I give thee my love.'

I hear sniggering. It is hardly surprising. We all know what those words mean.

'But,' he says loudly, and cuts the merriment short. 'But,' he continues, and we hang on what is to come. 'Solomon was a clever man,' he says. 'He did not believe what he heard, nor what he saw. Our ears and eyes can be deceived, can they not?'

There is a murmur of assent, and not a little prompting from some quarters to say more of what went on in the field.

'He placed no trust in this queen's seeming beauty. Not for all her jewels and crowns, not for her fine robes, nor her flashing eyes and pretty smile. Oh no!'

I suck on my teeth, find a piece of pea-skin wedged there. I wiggle my tongue, trying to dislodge it, and when I fail, stick

40

my finger into my mouth and have another try at digging it out. It reminds me that I am hungry. As though it needed my permission, my stomach rumbles. I'm not distracted for long. What Thomas says next is enough to make a bawd catch her breath.

'Solomon has a test for this woman,' he cries. 'He commands: lift up your skirts!'

'Does he indeed!' I murmur in Margret's ear.

'The shame of it!' she replies quietly. 'I would not do that; not even for King Solomon.'

'Or King Edward,' I add. 'No king could make me show off my parts.'

There is a commotion of murmuring, like a hearth full of steaming pots, all of them boiling over at the same time. Matrons clamp their hands to their mouths. Goodmen blush, trying not to catch the eye of their friends for fear it will set them giggling. Only the bravest lads and lasses steal glances at each other and wink knowingly. This man is unlike any priest I have heard before. Even when Father Hugo came into the alehouse the worst I ever heard was the old joke about the new bride farting in her husband's lap. Still he is not finished.

'What does wise King Solomon see?' he cries, voice climbing further up its perilous ladder.

'What indeed?' I whisper to Margret.

She hushes me so piercingly I worry that Thomas will hear and look at me again, less smilingly this time. But I am not the only one to have spoken, judging by the waterfall of shushing. Either Thomas does not hear us, or chooses not to remark upon it.

'What does she do?' calls out a brave fellow.

Every head turns to discover who has shouted so disrespect-fully, even though all of us carry the same question on the tip of our tongues. I am pretty sure it came from the knot of lads leaning against the west wall. They display looks of the most sincere innocence.

'The king commands. The queen must obey!' shouts Thomas. 'When a man commands, a woman must obey, even if she is a queen!'

'Still, I would not,' declares Margret under her breath. 'It is a sin.'

I think briefly of her and John, and him a priest, and what sin means, but I say nothing.

'No woman can refuse the command of a man,' he growls. 'Certainly not Solomon. Did not the Lord ordain that God is the head of man, and man is the head of woman?'

There is another muttering of agreement, louder from the men.

'Sheba wrings her hands. Oh, she begs Solomon. Anything but this! But Solomon insists. He will be obeyed.'

The smaller boys are now sniggering openly, hissing coarse words at each other.

'The Lord guides him to find out her secret sin! The foulness she hides underneath her robes!'

I do not care for the direction this is taking. Yet again Thomas fixes me with his stare, wilder than before. For all his strange words, he is a man and is looking at me. This time I am daring enough to stare back, even if only for a few heartbeats.

'Lo!' he cries. 'She obeys! She grasps her skirt and raises it an inch so he can see her toes. How strange they look. But perhaps they are the outlandish boots worn by barbarians. Solomon must be sure. *Higher!* he commands. Weeping, she lifts her robe another inch. See how unwilling she is. Not from modesty. Oh, no!'

'How does he know it wasn't modesty?' hisses Margret, angry now. 'Was he there?'

As though he has overheard, Thomas glares at Margret.

'This is the Word of the Lord,' he says. 'She is *not* modest. She is ashamed. *Higher!* cries King Solomon and another inch is uncovered. *Higher!* At last her foul secret is revealed.'

He pauses and we hold our breath.

'She has the legs of a goat!'

There is a rumble of disbelief and amusement. I am not sure what I think. Relief that it is goat's legs and not her cunny that is revealed to us? Perhaps. Thomas rounds off his sermon quickly, thumping home the moral that the path to hell is up a woman's skirt, and that a great deal of monstrousness is hidden there.

Amen, we gasp, breathlessly. *Amen.*

I can only suppose that he means to horrify the lads, shame the lasses and thereby throw a bucket of cold water on licentious thoughts. But he holds up his hand against a tide, and the spring tide at that. Besides, by talking in such delicious detail about getting a woman to lift up her dress, he has stoked the fire of everyone's thoughts and thrown dry wood upon the flames.

A woman would have found a way to dissuade him from such a theme. That he is so gullible sparks a flame in my breast: it feels a lot like pity, and I dismiss it. Pity is not something I want cluttering me up if I'm going to set my eye on this man. I wonder if he can truly be that stupid: yet again, I wipe that word away swiftly and replace it with *innocent.* Which is no bad thing. Innocence is a state that wants only for education. I do not share these thoughts with Margret. I do not know why, for my habit is to tell her everything.

We stroll arm in arm around the churchyard. The younger children are racing up and down in a shrieking game of *catch me.* Plenty of older ones join in, adding saucy touches of their own when they capture their quarry. More than once we come upon a man and maid sitting in the lee of the wall, engaged in a grown-up pastime inspired by the recent sermon.

A brace of stout lads leap on to the path before us and push back their hoods. Their faces glow with the goodness of Aline's festival ale.

'Ah, it's you, Hugh,' I say to one. 'Good morning.'

'And you, Robert,' says Margret to his companion.

'Halt!' says Hugh, somewhat unnecessarily, for they stand in our way.

'We are not moving,' I say, waving my hand to indicate the truth of it.

'Good,' says Robert, and giggles. 'You are obedient, which suits our purpose.'

Margret snorts and this sets them both off, sniggering into their hands.

'We must examine you for goat's legs,' announces Hugh and makes a lunge for the hem of my kirtle.

'Oh no you mustn't,' I reply.

I step out of the way of his questing paw. It is not difficult, as his feet are unsteady.

'Or pig's trotters,' hiccups Robert. 'I'll wager one of you at least has pink trotters.'

'For shame, boys,' chides Margret. 'How much have you been drinking?' They find this an amusing enquiry, but she continues to tick them off. 'Go and play your silly games somewhere else. I am a married woman and am beyond such foolishness.'

Robert's eyes squint into crafty folds, making him look uncommonly like one of the pigs he seems attached to.

'Married?' he slurs. 'That's not how we hear it,' he adds, digging his elbow into Hugh's ribs. 'You might cover your head, but you're no goodwife. You're John of Pilton's woman.'

'What of it?' she says, tilting her chin upwards.

'A priest's woman,' says Hugh.

They are neither so drunk nor so disrespectful to venture further and they know it.

'Here comes Father Thomas,' I announce brightly. 'This would be a good time to see our ankles, don't you think? If you demand it, we must comply.'

'You *insisted*,' says Margret, smiling.

In truth, the man in question is not coming this way at all, engaged as he is in blessing pilgrims at the south door. Robert and Hugh are not to know this, as they are facing the opposite direction.

'Yes!' cries Margret, warming to the task. 'Please demonstrate to our new priest how diligently you have hearkened to his words.'

'He will be proud to have had such an effect on the two of you.'

The lads glance at each other, declare how thirsty they are and must be off, that we are very tiresome, and all manner of excuses.

'That's him,' says a voice at my shoulder.

It is my mother. She grasps my elbow and shakes me, jabs her finger in the direction of Thomas.

'Who?' I ask, even though I know full well.

'Him,' she hisses with great weight and portent. 'He is in need of a housekeeper. The village knows it.'

'I am not sure if I wish to be a housekeeper.'

'Don't play with me, girl. You know exactly what he wants. And you'll not get finer from any of these lads.' She raises her eyebrows at the throng of village boys.

'But a priest, Mother?'

'What of it?' she says sharply. 'You stand with Margret, do you not? You girls were always perfectly matched in everything.'

I look at Thomas. His chin is not so small, when you look at him from a distance. Mother purses her lips thoughtfully.

'I hear he lives on a diet of lentils, as though every day is a Friday. Gammer Maynard was there this week just gone, searching for her chickens, and she says the floor is strewn with old straw. Think of it. That big house, with him rattling around on his own. What a sin to let it go to waste. If you won't take him, plenty will. And quick.'

'Mother!' I clap my hand to my bodice and endeavour to look shocked. 'I am sure I do not understand,' I add with becoming coyness.

'That's my clever Anne,' she murmurs. 'We understand each other.' She smiles and touches her forehead to mine. It is a girlish sweetness I see in her rarely. Then her face crumples. 'My little babe! My Anne!' she warbles. 'Surely it was only yesterday you were at my breast and suckling there.'

She lifts the hem of her gown and wipes her face. When she is done, she is pink about the eyes, the skin puffed up. I lay my hand on her arm. It is a strange feeling to be the one soothing my dam, not altogether unpleasant. I feel important, a woman on my own account. I wonder if this is what it feels like to be a mother. I decide that I like it, and wish to have more.

'Look at me,' she says. 'I declare. I haven't got the sense of a pulled hen.'

She smoothes out her apron, all business once more, and is gone as briskly as she arrived. I continue my keen appraisal. Thomas: that is his name. Of Upcote: though where that place might be, I have no notion. Margret follows my gaze and examines him also.

'His nose is a little thin,' she says.

'Yet his teeth are fine,' I reply.

'His hair has been cut with a hay rake.'

46

'Then he must have a woman cut it for him.'

'His shoulders strain to bear the weight of his gown.'

'Then he needs good victuals to fill him out.'

So we prattle on in low voices, until Margret pauses. Her eyes are sad.

'What ails you, my sweet?' I say.

'Be careful, Anne. Have great care before you take this step. Once the road is chosen, there is only one direction you can walk, and that is forward.'

'Oh, Margret. How dour you make it sound.'

'Anne, you are as close as a sister. I speak as one who loves you as dearly.'

'Well?'

'Be sure of this man.'

'I am decided. I will have him,' I reply somewhat snappishly, for it seems she wishes to pour sand upon the fire of my happy plans.

'Anne—'

I round on her. 'What is it, Margret? Do you wish to deny me your good fortune? I did not think you so ungenerous. I took you for my friend.'

'I am your friend, and dearer than you know for telling you this hard secret.'

I will have none of it, and am angry with her. 'So, a fine bed and a heaped board are right for you but not for me, is that it?'

'Of course not.'

I know not whence comes my peevishness and spite. In my venom I hear an unhappy, jealous woman and I do not like her one bit. I would snatch back the words, but it is too late. The hag who has taken the reins of my tongue will not permit it.

'It seems to me that you want to keep all finery to yourself and fear a rival.'

'No, sister! How can you think this of me?'

'I can think it easily. Do you take me for a fool? Is this your revenge for our childish games, where I was your queen? Is this your plan, to pay me back?'

'Anne, do not speak like this.'

'Why should I not? Anne is below, and Margret is raised up. That's how you wish things to remain. You above me, now and for always.'

'Anne, no—'

'Anne, yes. You are no sister. A sister would rejoice.'

I see my words strike Margret, the poison of their cruelty mark her face as clear as the slap of a hand. She fiddles with her headpiece, a contraption of wire and linen that makes her look like a nanny goat.

'Perhaps I should return to Pilton,' she remarks. 'John and Jack will be waiting for me.'

Her face softens as she speaks. In a dark corner of my soul, a serpent flicks its heavy tail. Suddenly I am very tired of Margret prattling about her darling son, her precious John. Up spring more sharp words, and I cannot stop them from bursting out.

'Your son, your son,' I snap. 'The way you talk, Margret. It is quite tiring. I wish you would speak of something else.'

'Anne?' she says. Her face shifts, the gentle smile sucked back into her mouth. 'What do you mean by this?'

'You dare ask? How you crowed when you went to John. Me, the dunnock against your peacock. How very grand you have become.'

'I am blessed,' she replies, with dignity.

'I'm sure it is not sufficient. Not for a duchess like you.'

'I would not test the Lord by asking for more joy than is my portion.'

'You are no more a lady than I am, Margret. Be careful you do not climb so high you lose sight of the earth.'

At last I run out of nastiness. It is though I bore a sack of bile in my belly and had to spew it up. She stares at me; I stare at her. I have a great desire to hug her close and say sorry for my selfishness.

'Margret—' I begin.

At that moment the lady Sibylla, wife of our Lord Henry, approaches and enquires after our health. We fluster, curtseying and murmuring at being noticed by a person of such high degree. After a moment she moves on to make her gracious *good morrows* to the rest of the congregation, setting up a flutter like a fox in a chicken coop. The venom has been sucked from my meanness, but there remains a prickling unpleasantness.

'The Saint is truly powerful if he can make great ladies pass the time of day with peasants,' Margret remarks.

'Ah, Margret,' I say. 'Let me—'

'I declare,' she interrupts. 'I see Mistress Aline. I will greet her. God be with you, Anne.'

She tightens her mouth, turns and strides off. She does not glance back. I quiver with the desire to run after her, push aside the holiday crowds and beg her forgiveness. But shame and guilt have the governance of me and will not permit me to bend. So I stand and watch my friend walk away. By and by her sun sets in the distance and my world fades into a dimness of my own making.

I have said what I have said. I have set my eye on this Thomas, a man to hook and bring to shore. I must set my eye on ambitions greater than girlish friends. I tell myself I have no further need of Margret. I will see her at the next festival. But by then, everything has changed.

VIXEN

I strike south-west, outskipping Death. Only when I pause for breath do I realise how hectic has been my dash from the Great Mortality. My feet are worn out from dancing, my tongue a clapper of wood from all the jokes I've had to tell.

I stand at the gate of the forest and beg safe passage.

'Oh, grandmother, let me in, and I'll bring you the head of a charcoal-burner!' I cry.

She opens to me straight away, for wood-burners are her greatest enemy.

'Show me the path away from clever folk, and into the arms of simpletons,' I add, for it pays to be specific when asking favours from powerful persons. 'Do this, and I'll steal a hundred axes, and throw them into the sea.'

She shakes her branches and a swish of laughter ripples overhead. She knows it is a brazen boast, but my heart's-wood is behind it.

'Lead me away from Death,' I say, and she falls quiet.

I take it as a good sign. She makes no promises, nor does she make merry at my fear. It's as good an answer as I'll get from trees, so I content myself with it and press further into her labyrinthine belly. She draws me into her arms and I let her rock me. Death tries to follow, but her shadows conceal me from His eyes. I am safe under the swing of her cloak, for she is fearsome only to those who do not know her.

The forest is my song, the best kind: no words, but all manner of music. I tune my ear to her particular melody and she rewards me with all I need to know. I listen for clues, for knowledge, for information, for the sheer pleasure of it. Overhead, boughs rustle; dead leaves crunch underfoot and warn of pitfalls that can swallow your foot and snap it sideways. She guides me more clearly than any gazetteer, instructs me better than any primer, delights more than any gold-splashed psalter.

Most of all, she is peaceful. Where there are people, there is greed. Thievery. Falsehood. Murder. When beasts kill each other, they do so simply to eat. What I have seen of men is that they kill to clear a bigger space at the world's table for themselves.

I pick my way with the tiptoe step of a deer, so delicate that when I come upon a herd, they lift their heads without fear. Some of the does are heavy-bellied, flanks quivering as the fawn within stirs in its wet sleep. In me they see a cousin crippled with two legs instead of four, not someone come a-hunting. I am to be pitied and not scurried from, so they bend their necks and return to the more important business of grazing.

I almost trip over a fawn. He lies still as a stone dropped from Heaven and marked with the thumbprints of the angel who threw him. I stare at him; he stares at me, eyes bigger than my fist and blacker than the bottom of a well. His nostrils flare: he catches my scent and presses his nose into the fork between my thighs. If he is seeking milk, he finds nothing but the scent of the sea.

'You won't hurt me, will you?' I ask, and he trembles his answer.

His dam crashes through a bush and glares her jealousy. He droops his head, guilty for falling in love with another so fast, him not even weaned and her not gone five minutes.

'And you,' I say to her. 'You'll shake your head and stamp your hoof, but that's all.'

She answers by doing both. The fawn sighs and takes her teat. Her envious glare melts into satisfaction. She's not yet lost him to another female.

'There are arrows far more deadly than those of love,' I whisper, but she is deep in her trance of milk-giving and does not hear my warning. 'Rest easy,' I say. 'I'm away.'

I'm as good as my word. With beasts there is no need for lies.

I am safe here; safe as anywhere on this unreliable earth. There are rabbits to snare, raven's nests for my larder. Death cannot reach me. Perhaps I could hide in the trees and wait for Him to pass over.

But Death wants for amusement and so do I. I stuff my belly with eggs, laugh at the birds as they flap useless wings. Their blunt beaks cannot hurt me. What next for me? Who shall be my next fool? Where can I find me a dupe? So do I lie, sucking yolk from my fingers, head blooming with dangerous fancies. I ought to know better. I should be careful of what I wish for.

LAUDS
1349

From Saint Alphege to Edward the Martyr

THOMAS OF UPCOTE

'A man should not do the work of women.'

The man filled the mouth of my door, rain streaming off his woollen cloak. I scrabbled in my mind. Was this piece of wisdom a line from a psalm?

'Even less a man of God,' he continued.

'Indeed,' I agreed, wondering who he might be.

'You have let your needs be known, Father.'

'My needs?' Some agency sent heat into my face.

'A priest needs a housekeeper.'

'Yes,' I spoke hastily. 'I need a housekeeper.'

'Indeed, Father. My Anne would be a good housekeeper.'

'Anne?'

'I am her father. Stephen.' He rolled his eyes. 'The carpenter.'

'Ah, yes.'

'You know her.'

'I do?'

'By my head; you smiled at her on Relic Day.' Water dripped from his muzzle onto his clogs.

'I did?' Again, I searched my memory but found the face of each female as unremarkable as the next.

'Indeed you did, Father.'

'I smile at all my flock.'

'But her in special.' He gnarled his eye shut and I realised he was winking. He spat on his hand, shoved it into mine. 'I will send her mother.'

I opened the door to loud knocking. Three women shadowed the light: a matron and at her back two younger females who flicked at the ends of their braids. My face asked the question.

'I am Anne's mother, Joan.' She aimed a broad thumb over her shoulder. 'These two are her gossips, Alice and Isabel.'

'Greetings, Mistress Joan. Ladies.'

They pressed their way past me and walked directly to the hearth. They peered into the butter-pot one after the other, held up the frying pan and tested its weight, counted out the knives, the dishes, the pitchers and the pewter plates, banged their knuckles against the great pot on its hook over the fire.

The two maids sighed, scowling at each item as though it was wanting in some way I could not comprehend. Joan strode into the solar and stared at my bed awhile, mercifully without comment. She flipped up the lid of the chest as though it were only the weight of a penny, and straightway began filleting the sheets folded within.

'Good linen,' she clucked, 'what there is of it. Surely you have more?'

'It is stored. I have little need for—'

'Good, good.' She peered at me, from my uneven tonsure to my clogs. 'Your glebe, Father.'

I realised it was a question. I had the uncomfortable feeling of being a clerk standing before a strict schoolmaster and not knowing the answer.

'I have an orchard,' I gabbled. 'Apples and medlars, six cherry trees besides. Fifteen healthy ewes at the last count, tended for by Edgard. A tup-ram, a milk-cow and calf, many fowls for eggs. A mare in her own stable. My Lord Bishop is generous.'

She hummed and swept back into the hall, dragging us in her formidable wake. She kicked at the reeds on the floor, clicking her tongue at one of the maidens, who nodded and said *in need of fresh rushes* to her companion. She tapped at the oilcloth set into the window, tested the shutters.

'No glass?'

'It is warm enough. There is much vanity—'

'With the shutters open it is too cold. With them shut it is too dark,' she said as brisk as you would to a boy. 'How can a woman see clear to bake your bread?'

I had not thought that far ahead. One of the maids sniggered: Joan quenched the sound with a glare.

'I will pay for a glazier,' I gulped.

'And curtains?'

'Yes. I have some. Stored with the linen.'

'Fine?'

'Yes.'

'Good. A tapet for the bed?'

I had no idea why she wanted my bed to appear grander than it was. It was an indelicate question, but I let it pass, for rustic folk have odd notions.

'I shall not stint,' I said.

'That is a fine thought, Father. And for the feast?'

'The feast?'

'When she shall come to you. It is our way.' She patted my hand. 'There must be beer; the good brown, nothing sour.'

I felt myself suddenly in the sharp angle of a small room, its walls pressing hard upon my shoulders.

Ground almonds?

Green cheese and hard cheese?
White porray with saffron?
Wheat bread? Of sifted flour?
A dozen rabbits?

I quacked out agreement after agreement until I believe I could have given my assent to anything. *Raisins. Lemons. Hot wine caudle. Nutmeg. Mace. Custards. A sugar-loaf.* They were no longer requests but statements.

'Eels and herrings for yourself. Two new lambs to roast.'

'Two?'

'Two. You shall not stint.'

I was dizzy with talk of pies, and spices, and boiled chickens, and stock-fish, and clapbread and havercakes and so much honey my teeth ached. At last she stopped; held out her hand. I fetched coins from my safe-box and counted them into her palm until she clicked her tongue a final time and closed her fingers.

Anne was brought to my house fifteen days later, on the Feast of Saint Perpetua, her mother eager to bring her before Lent. There was a fine dampness in the air, as barely noticeable as breath. Maybe this was the day the rain would cease.

Just before Prime the women arrived with my dishes, now filled with the food I had paid for. They looked to be bringing it the whole morning, so I took myself to the church and did not return till after Terce. As I walked down the path I heard laughter, the bleating of a pipe.

Her hair was glossy as an otter. It had been combed through and sheaves of it looped up in plaited trenchers over her ears, threaded through with sprigs of mayflower. She fluttered with a girdle of coloured ribbons, wound about her so tight it was a marvel she could guffaw so loudly. As they reached the ford she was hoisted like a log and carried on the shoulders of two young men who hung onto her knees. She kicked out her feet and showed red slippers.

One of her bearers began to sing, 'I tell of one so fair and bright', and all bawled the refrain, 'Oh, bright and fair!' She grinned and swung her head about to be so praised; but I saw her slap the lad's fingers as he clutched her thigh too tightly, and knew her for a virtuous maid.

I was at my door to welcome them as they trod their last few steps. All were wet halfway to the knee save Anne, and there was much merriment as the women wrung out their underskirts and the men squeezed out their hose and came in bare-legged. They patted mud from their tunics, knocked dirt off their clogs. I resolved to be a cheerful host and not draw attention to this rudeness.

'Welcome,' I said. 'Welcome all.'

I barely knew my own house. While I had been in the church it had been wreathed about with ivy and may, as though the Feast of Saint Lucy was come round again. The trestle shone with bright linen, and a great heap of logs glowed in the hearth, the embers studded with seething pots of green and white porray. The very air was foreign to me, thickened as it was with tickling spice. There was a roar as the ale was brought in.

'It is the very finest,' said Joan. 'Made by our own Aline.'

The ale-wife dropped to her knees as I thanked her, drowned out by thirsty bellowing. Each man dug out a beaker from inside his shirt and polished it on his stomach, ready for it to be filled.

'Good Aline!'

'Happy woman and happier husband!'

The man spoken of cawed like a rook. 'It is the spring!'

'It is near!'

'It will be a good spring,' I said.

'It will, God willing,' a man declared, and ducked his head at me.

'God is good,' I continued, and they raised their cups in agreement.

'And so is Anne!' cried one voice, to answering cheers.

'My death I love, my life I hate,' sang one fellow. 'All for a girl so fair; she is as bright as day is light, but she won't look at me.'

'So fair she is and fine,' boomed another. 'I wish to God that she were mine.'

'Oh, Anne is a fine girl indeed,' whispered Joan, close to me.

'Fair was her bower,' cried a third voice.

'What was her bower?'

'The red rose and the lily flower.'

The company laughed.

'My turn now,' cried a voice thick with ale. 'When the priest comes in to pray, next day Death takes you away.'

'Best not get the priest in, then.'

'Hush now,' said Joan.

'No disrespect, Father.'

'I can sing too!' I smiled, and took a deep breath.

'Jesus Christ, my darling Lord, That died for us upon the tree. With all my might I do beseech, You send your love to me.'

They coughed and stamped, and said, *That is a good song, Father*, and I was warmed.

'We will be safe this year, Father,' said Joan.

'We are always safe in the Lord.'

'But here, in special.' She dropped her voice. 'Against the pestilence. Is it not true?'

'Our Saint protects us.'

I made the sign of the Cross over the victuals, and they fell to, picking at their teeth with their knives and spitting on the floor. The hours swam by in eating and drinking, and I began to wonder if they might stay the entire night. I could not leave them to go to the church, for it would show them less holy than myself. As I thought it, Joan left off gossiping and clapped her hands. The talking and laughter tumbled into silence.

'Good people,' she said, and I thought how loud her voice was, for a woman.

I had not yet heard Anne speak and I hoped her voice was milder than her mother's. Someone cheered to hear himself called good, and there was jostling until Joan lifted the spade of her hand and dug it into the air. The noise was struck down.

'Yes, good we are indeed,' she continued. 'And as such, we must be gone to our homes.'

The man roared again, wild enough to shout about anything. He stood up to assert his goodness, but his feet were unwilling to follow and he slipped to the floor. His companions hauled him upright and I saw his face made dark with ale.

'I am sorry, Father,' he said, the drink gone from him straightway.

The eyes of the room screwed themselves into me.

'It is nothing; you are merry.'

'Yes, Father.'

'It is a fine day to be merry, is it not?'

'Yes, Father.'

He rubbed his face. Someone slammed me on the back. I was pleased at my cleverness not to chide him, for the word would be about that I was a forgiving man. Joan smacked her hands together, and the room was hers.

'Let us say a good night to our priest. Our fine and right reverend Thomas.'

The people cheered and I burned with happiness. If I could pick out one instant in my life when I was entirely happy, it was then. A warm room; the company of innocents stuffed with food and smiling for me alone. But it was built of shadows. I did not know what was to follow, and when I look back, I cringe that I was so much a fool.

'Let me bless you before you go,' I cried.

'Yes. It would be a fitting farewell, Father,' said Joan.

There was a clearing of beery throats, the rustling of feet in straw. I must bid Anne sweep it out, for it was sticky with spilt victuals. It would wait until morning. Every chin dropped onto every breast.

'Oh God, who created the earth and everything in it, look upon our simple feast. Bless us in our humility. Grant us health on earth as it is in Heaven. Comfort our bodies.'

Ah yes, comfort us.

The room rumbled its thanks. Joan began to shoo the company out of the door, encouraging them to bear away what food was left. Anne's father grasped my wrist and gazed at me with a wandering eye.

'Father Thomas, you are a good man,' he hiccoughed. 'She is a fine girl, Father.'

'I do not doubt it.'

'Clean.'

'Yes,' I nodded.

'Willing.'

'Yes, good.'

'She could be meeker.'

'I am sure of it.'

'But bright in humour.'

'I wonder you can spare her; she is such a jewel.'

'My Joan fetches and carries well enough,' he beamed. 'I would rather lose a pig than send my Anne to a bad house.'

'She will be honoured under my roof, Stephen. Have no fear of that.'

'It is a good thing, Father.' His eyes shone. 'You are a better man than we thought.'

My heart leapt and thrust water into my eyes: at last they accepted me. I sheltered the thought in the soft nest of my soul.

Aline directed the steadier of the men to carry away the ale-pots: women wrapped roasted lamb in their aprons and men stuffed half-loaves down their shirts. I wondered how much would survive the crossing of the ford. I pressed them to take more, so they would also carry away the tale of my generosity. In the end it was Joan who stopped them, smacking the greediest of hands, and declaring that some must be left for the two who remained. She was the last to go, nodding a brisk farewell to her daughter.

The cloth on the table was stained with gravy and splashes of ale, the floor crunching with bread crusts and mutton bones. A bowl of pottage had been tipped into the fire: I noticed the smell of burnt peas only now. I held the door open to clear away the breathed-out air. The rain was now coming down steadily, but it seemed nothing could dampen my guests. I could hear them singing in the darkness, as though the heat of their happiness might dry up the downpour. I sucked in the clean breath of the night.

There was a small cough at my back. Of course, Anne was here. We faced each other, listening to the laughter grow fainter. When it was quiet enough to hear my own thoughts, Anne took her skirt in each hand and lowered herself to the floor in such a deep curtsey that her knees brushed the straw.

'No, mistress; there is no need to kneel before me.'

I grasped at her elbow to pull her upright, but she toppled sideways and I staggered with her: I would have fallen if I had not wrenched the both of us upright. Her giggle snapped off in a yelp.

'I am sorry, mistress. Are you hurt?'

'No, sir,' she said between her teeth. Her eyes wrinkled as she rubbed her shoulder.

'I am a gentle man, mistress.'

'Yes, sir. I stumbled. It is my fault.' She yawned, and a yeasty belch escaped.

'Are you tired?'

Her eyes sprang open. 'Oh no, sir. I have eaten well, that is all.' She looked about, as though seeing each thing for the first time: the hearth, the benches, the table still dressed with trenchers and dribbled ale. 'Shall I clear it, sir?'

'Yes, mistress. That would be a good thing.'

She looked surprised, and it came to me at last what she expected and feared. That I was a beast like other men; a corrupt priest who wanted her only to slave beneath me in my bed. I could have wept at her innocence; thinking herself trussed up and sacrificed to me. I started to undo the gaudy ribbons binding her waist; plucked out the wilting blossoms tucked into her looped hair. She panted a little.

'Do not be afraid, mistress.'

'I am not, sir. My name is Anne.'

'I know it.' I folded the ribbons neatly, for I understood and forgave the hunger of common girls for pretty things. 'There: you are free now.'

'Free, sir?'

'You owe me no debt, Anne.' I folded my hands together. 'You know I am a priest?'

'I do, sir.' Her breath furred the air between us.

'You know a priest can never be married to a maid.'

'I do, sir.'

'I am a chaste man, Anne. A kind man. I will never insult you.'

'Sir?'

I smiled at her virgin simplicity. 'I will never give you cause to rebuke me. You will never be dishonoured in my house. You will never be hungry.'

'Sir?'

'Our companionship will shine like a jewel at the heart of this community. We shall show everyone the meaning of marriage in Christ.' I leaned forward and pressed my lips against her cheek. 'Goodnight, mistress. I give you the kiss of peace. You are safe here.'

I went to the solar and closed the door behind me. The floor and bedcover were sprinkled with petals frilled with rust.

ANNE

I lie on my mattress in the outer room that night and every night after, listening to his snores shake the wall. The weeks pass, and every month my blood comes and goes also. Even the moon is less regular. I yearn for Thomas with a hunger that pricks me with wakefulness. Of course, I've seen rams tup their ewes and stallions cover their mares, but never guessed the eagerness to be about their labour. I burn for him: he should burn for me. He's no old dodderer, far from it. All young men have this fire: as the sun rises each morning, so men rise up with it. I do not know why he will not rise up for me.

In the meantime, I want for amusement and I take it where I may find it. Boredom is a dangerous estate for a woman, and I blame Thomas for thrusting tedium of the mind upon me. I cannot accuse him of sparing the labours of the body, for there is no end to the chores he discovers to occupy my hands. I scrub linen, bake bread, spin and a hundred other tasks. Not that any of this drudgery diverts me from wifely passions. But feeling sorry for myself will get me nowhere, nor will trying to fathom the workings of a man's wits.

I watch him in and out of the house, to the church and back. And most interesting to my way of thinking, he goes to his storeroom, tucked beneath the eaves. The way he scoots up the ladder fast as a weasel pricks my interest, and when he comes down he's carrying some treasure: a fine knife, a pair of embroidered slippers or a shirt so crisp I could shave his beard with it. More's the point, he has an air of guilt that fires my curiosity and sets it burning. I know a secret when I smell one.

He never permits me to go up there, even though I come up with plenty of reasons, from clearing out mice to opening the shutter and letting new air chase away the old. I bustle below, and the room breathes in and out above my head. As the tale says, there's nothing like the curiosity of a woman who is forbidden to do something. It is his fault. If I were not so bored, then I would have no need for distraction.

It is three weeks past Easter before I find the path up that ladder, and it is all due to his refusal to have good pots and pans. I clear my throat and begin with my latest stratagem.

'I was set to make you pikelets, sir. A recipe of my mother's, and very fine too. With butter.'

Despite himself, his tongue pokes out and draws a moist line along his bottom lip in anticipation of the treat.

'Go to, mistress.'

I sigh disconsolately. 'I would, sir. But I cannot.'

'Why so?'

I hold up the frying pan and peer at him through the hole in its bottom.

'Oh,' he says, for there is no denying a pan you can stick your nose through. 'Then you must fetch one from the upper room. Here.'

With the words, he unlooses the key from his chatelaine. It is as simple as that. I chide myself for not remembering a man's belly is the path to all desires. I bob a curtsey, fetch the ladder and try not to scramble up it too hastily. The key trembles in my hand.

A frying pan is the first thing I clap eyes on when I unlock the room. Although tarnished from lack of use, it is of the finest quality: one of four cooking pots, all new and in a heap behind the door. However, I have no intention of being done with my adventure quite so soon.

'Where do you think it might be, sir?' I call, making my voice as dull as possible.

The pots are the least of the wonders. When I lift the shutter and prop it open, a cave of treasures reveals itself: a mattress that feels like an angel's wing when I press my hand against it, a mountain of curtains, stacked wood with a fragrance so heady I am dizzy with the breathing of it. In one corner stands a fiddle, a crumhorn, a trumpet and a pile of tambours all higgledy-piggledy. Leaning against the eaves are half-a-dozen swords and a rusty pike, all surrounded by dust so thick you could roll it up and use it as a blanket. More enticing still than these wonders are two oaken chests, almost big enough for me to climb inside. I step towards them, but Thomas calls from below.

'What are you doing up there?' he shouts. 'A pan cannot be that hard to find.'

I kick at the swords and they rattle.

'I shall find it soon!' I shout. 'It's so dark I can barely see,' I lie.

'Foolish woman, I must help you,' he grumbles.

His foot thumps on the ladder.

'Oh, no sir! I have found it!' I cry, quick about it. 'I shall come to you this instant.'

I grab the pan, dash out of the room and wave it so he can see. 'There is no need to trouble yourself.'

'About time too. I never met a stupider female.'

'No, sir.'

If I dropped the pan, it would strike him on the top of his shining pate. If I threw it hard, it might crack that pate clean open.

'Make sure you shut the door and lock it properly. Ach, you are so foolish, you will not be able to do it right. I will come and do it.'

He takes another step.

'Do not worry,' I say, slamming the door. 'It is done.' I twist the key in the lock and it makes a terrific grinding. 'Can you not hear, sir?' I continue to turn the key so that as well as locking the door I also unlock it again. 'Am I not clever, sir?' I simper, pulling a rude face he cannot see.

'I can hear. I am not deaf. Come down.'

I descend the ladder and make a great show of pressing the key back into his hand. Next time he bothers to go up there, all I need do is make out that I am a silly girl who was sure she locked it, because of all the noise it made.

I make the pikelets, even managing to keep one back for myself, for he'd stuff himself with the lot if I did not. He makes what he thinks are kind remarks about how gifted I am to make such fine scones, and I seethe with the pleasure of what I have discovered. He will be mine, so will everything I have seen today. All it takes is time and patience. He'll share all, and gladly, too, when I've turned him to my way of thinking.

It is a few days after the Feast of Saint Bede when Cat pays a visit, along with our cousins and her new babe. Thomas is bustling up the path as they come to the door, and stalks past with a grunted *Good day*.

'Thomas,' I say, my cheeks pinking at his discourtesy. 'Sir. My sister is come from the Staple. With her baby. And Bet, and Alice, and Isabel.'

He peers at them as if they might be cows waiting to be milked. They bob and giggle.

'Good day, I say,' he repeats and passes into the house.

I dash after him and pluck his sleeve with enough determination to hold him still. 'Sir,' I hiss. 'They have come a long way.'

'The Staple? It is not so far.'

'Sir. May I invite them in?'

He pauses and narrows his eyes in the way he does when he thinks he is being crafty.

'Is this not the day you wash the linen?'

'I have done it all. It is dry enough to hope I may gather it in later. There is bread made, and a white porray simmering for you.'

'The Lord is good,' he mutters unhappily. 'Is there enough to feed them?'

'You do not need to concern yourself about food. Each has brought something for the board.' I eye him levelly. If boldness can't move him, softness might. 'Oh, sir,' I add, 'it would be such a charitable gesture.'

'Very well,' he says, grudgingly. 'They are welcome.'

'Thank you, sir,' I say carefully, and curtsey.

They enter at last, pretending they have not heard a word and each making a neat compliment about his benevolence. Cat waves her boy in Thomas's face and the infant stares at him with blank intelligence.

'God is good. He makes us fruitful,' he remarks.

Alice elbows me in the ribs. I busy myself with setting up the trestle so that I do not slap her. We drag the bench to the hearth, for in truth it is a cold day for May. We unpack the victuals and Cat offers Thomas a cup of ale. He refuses, as I guessed he might.

'You are not like Father Hugo,' says Cat.

'Holy Mary, how that man could drink,' said Alice.

'And eat,' adds Bet.

We know the tales, having had them since childhood. The French and Spanish wines, costly spices; how he bought in barrels of almonds and figs, even during Lent.

'But he did not forget his prayers,' Thomas reminds us.

'Oh no! He bellowed out the fame of the Saint,' agrees Cat.

'Ah, the crowds of pilgrims.'

'And the gold that came to the church.'

'How his stomach swelled!'

'Further and further!' I laugh, cupping my hands around an invisible stomach and blowing out my cheeks.

Cat raises her eyebrows and it occurs to me that I could also be imitating the belly of a woman with child, so I stop and tuck my hands behind my back. Thomas takes the action for contrition.

'To be a servant of the Almighty is not a cause for idle merriment,' he counsels. 'It is to be of sober and calm temperament.'

We point the tips of our noses at the floor. I hear Alice and Isabel stifling giggles with little snorts. If Thomas notices, he says nothing.

'Yes, sir,' I say, biting my lip.

Bet starts to chant rhymes to the baby and Thomas makes good his escape, scuttling away to the church. Free at last, we settle to eating and drinking and playing with the lad. He is so grown in the past two months I barely know him. He grabs for the edge of my kerchief and drags it askew. Alice and Cat wink and cast saucy looks upon me until I am vexed with their intimations.

'So,' drawls Cat. 'How is life with your man?'

'Quiet,' I grumble.

'But not at night, I'll wager,' titters Alice.

'Hush now,' says Isabel. 'See how she blushes. Be gentle.'

'Is that what you say to Thomas?' says Cat, and they collapse into raucous laughter.

'Thomas does not come to me,' I mutter when they've finished hooting.

'Why ever not?' asks Alice, face writ with disbelief. 'Do you anger him?'

'My Henry came to me quick enough after we were wed,' twitters Cat, with a salty laugh. 'A fine and upstanding man he is, too.'

'Oh, cousin!' snickers Alice, hiding her smile behind her hand. 'How you talk!'

'My Henry pays his marriage debt delectably often,' Cat continues. 'All our little Anne needs is a good firm man to take to hand, don't you?'

'Cat! This is a priest's house,' I say, hearing Thomas's priggishness in my voice and disliking it intensely.

'Perhaps we should not talk so boldly if you are still a maid,' she smirks, with a keen edge to the blade of her words. 'For you are, are you not?'

'Not for lack of trying,' I sneer.

'Maybe there is some fault in you,' chirrups Alice, enjoying every minute.

'You need a babby of your own,' declares Cat with great wisdom. 'That'll put a smile back on that sour little face of yours.'

'You are not ugly, my dearest,' Bet simpers. 'You could have any man.'

I nod at this morsel of flattery. I never before found their chatter annoying, yet today all I can think of is how I should like to smack the smiles off their faces.

'Oh, I don't know,' I demur. 'I am a cabbage compared to my beautiful sister.' I lift the heavy boy from Cat's lap. 'Aren't I, my little man?' I coo, tickling him gently. 'This is the way the farmers ride,' I sing and jiggle him on my lap.

He twists his square head round to gawp at me and vomits curdled milk over my bodice.

'What a lad!' crows Cat, patting me with a napkin and smearing the puddle in a broader circle. 'He does that if you bounce him too hard.'

Alice sweeps the child from my hands and cradles him on her lap, where he shrieks happily, seemingly done with spewing now that I am covered. He lets out a fart of such sonorous depth that he scares himself and begins to yowl, which of course only serves to make Cat and Alice laugh the louder.

'A true man,' crows Bet.

'My own little man,' adds Cat.

I know they do not mean to hurt me with their talk of adoring husbands and babes. I give myself a moment's respite by going to fetch bread. They have brought cakes, a jug of fresh ale and more besides, for which I am grateful. I am shamed by the empty cupboard I am housekeeper to. At least I have platters to spread before them, cups into which to pour the drink.

'Well now. It's early days. I'll bring Thomas to me soon,' I say, with a great deal more confidence than I feel.

'If it is help you need . . .' says Alice, a great deal more kindly. 'Even the loveliest of maidens needs a little—'

'Encouragement?' suggests Cat.

'Help,' says Isabel.

'Assistance,' adds Bet.

'Inspiration,' says Alice.

'Don't be cast down just yet,' murmurs Isabel. 'There are many ways to bring savour to your bed.'

'See, Anne,' says Cat, with unexpected tenderness, and pats me with a dimpled hand. How she keeps it so soft, what with cleaning up after a husband and her baby, I do not know. 'We are your loving friends. Isabel, show her.'

Isabel dips into her bodice and draws out a tiny packet wrapped in linen. She places it in my hand, still warm from her breast. I look at them in turn. Alice raises an eyebrow and Bet guffaws as though something very naughty is about to take place. I undo the folds to reveal a pinch of dark powder. Although a mere sprinkling, the scent of spices fills the room with delight. I lift it to my nose.

Cat glances about the room nervously. 'Careful!' she hisses. 'Don't sneeze over it. It cost more than you can guess.'

I hold my tongue. I must be polite, for she means well. Bet sniggers and I glare at her until she quietens.

Isabel pats my arm. 'Don't you mind her, cousin. This cannot fail. Put these spices in a glass of wine and Thomas won't be able to take his eyes from you.'

'Or his hands,' snorts Alice.

'Or his kisses,' says Bet. 'He won't sleep for dreaming about you,'

'Dreaming's not what Anne needs,' sneers Cat.

'There is no wine in the house,' I say. 'Thomas is not—'

'You mean he's a tight-fisted—'

Isabel's eyes widen. 'Cat,' she breathes. 'Kind words. We must help our little cousin.'

'Why must we?' protests Cat, raising her eyebrows until they disappear beneath the folds of her kerchief. 'Anne wants this, Anne wants that. It's all I've ever heard, from the moment the spoilt brat was born.'

'You're upsetting the baby,' says Alice, jiggling him up and down.

His fat features gather themselves together, lips pout. He looks on the verge of a good long squawk.

'Anne wants a man, Anne wants a baby, Anne wants a king and golden crown,' continues Cat in a sing-song voice, ignoring her son. 'Here we are, running around after her like we always did.'

I sniff the spices carefully. 'Delicious,' I sigh.

Their heads swivel like owls spying a mouse and I realise I've spoken out loud.

We set to preparing the drink, Isabel sprinkling the spices into the jug of wine, for she has brought that also. My eyes prick at her kindness. We chatter some more, and even Cat speaks warm words when we part. She kisses me and calls me her silly little goose, but not unkindly. There are lines drawn at the corners of her mouth and eyes, which I'd never noticed before.

I wait for Thomas to return. I unbraid my hair. I braid it again. I loosen my bodice laces. I tie them again. Never before has he been gone to the church so long. When he returns at last, I declare I am worn out with the waiting. His nostrils flare with the scents perfuming the house. As well as the wine, they have left a neat dish of food: lardons of pork, fried crisp; buttered peas with sippets; two honey-cakes so small you could swallow them both in one mouthful; a humped bun of wheaten bread studded with raisins.

'This is very fine,' he remarks, with a true note of pleasure.

I stand by the table, hands gathered behind my back so he cannot see my fingers wringing with nervousness. My face glows with the thought of him speaking as kindly from this day on.

'It is for you, Thomas. A gift from my cousins.'

'I must thank them.'

'They know you for a good man. They offer you this also.'

I heft a glass of the wine and hold it to his nose. The dark spot at the centre of his eye blooms with delight.

'It smells strong,' he remarks.

'It smells tasty. It is for sweetness in this household. Come.'

'Yes, that is a good toast,' he says, and once again his voice is soft. 'We live sweetly, do we not?'

He takes the cup and drains it off so fast that he coughs and water leaps into his eyes. I pour him another glass, and begin unwinding my coif until I stand before him bareheaded. He stares with his mouth open as I shake out the binding of my braids. I dip one of the sweetmeats into the wine and push it between his half-open lips. He pauses a moment, as though he has forgotten what you should do with a cake in your mouth, then begins to chew. I take the other and eat it myself, slowly. It is so luscious my eyelids droop.

'Are you tired?' he asks.

'No,' I say quickly. 'I am never tired.'

This seems to be a great jest for I start to giggle, then laugh and cannot stop. Suddenly neither can he. I pour another glass of the wine; he swigs half of it and offers the other. I smile and take a tiny sip, putting my lips over the wet spot where he laid his.

'No, I shall share all with you. You are my companion,' he says, pushing the cup into my face.

I take a mighty gulp. I am springing fire: throat tight, breath rushing and a stabbing, almost painful, between my legs. However, his eyes are closing and opening slowly. If my needs are to be met I must get him before he falls asleep, which won't be long by the look of him. I slip my chemise from my shoulders and draw his hands to rest upon the bare skin. He sucks in a sharp breath as I take his hand and guide him further down, to the breast. My nipple rounds into his palm and his head lowers as though he is about to suckle.

'Yes, Tom,' I gasp, and his head jerks up at the calling of his name.

He pulls his hand out of my bodice so quickly that he rips the laces; shoves me hard and I stumble backwards, falling onto the floor.

'No. No. It is not right,' he moans.

'It is. It is,' I cry, hanging on to his ankle as he walks away.

'I am not a fornicator; they couple like rats in straw.'

'Please, Thomas,' I beg. I cannot lose him now, not when I am so close to my goal.

'They fly from one woman to another like flies from one dungheap to the next!' he cries, his voice rising into a shout.

The room holds its breath. I pick myself up, smoothing down my apron.

'A dungheap?' I say. 'Is *that* what you think of me?' I raise my eyes and fix them boldly on to his. 'Am I so low in your estimation?'

'No, I do not mean that,' he mumbles. 'I am not one of those priests who think women filthy. Women are the mothers of boys who grow to be men. As such we should honour them.'

'Yes, sir.' I tuck away my breast and fold my arms, hiding the torn fabric.

'Would you have me bring the shame of a bastard child upon you?'

'My beloved Margret is a priest's woman, in Pilton. They have a boy; no one calls him bastard.'

'It is a sin. It is written.'

'Father Hugo sired a girl.'

'I know this. He was lecherous.'

'She married a merchant of the Staple with no shame.'

'Best she is gone there, and swept clean from this place!' His voice rises into a squawk.

'You do not need to shout; I am standing beside you.'

'Woman, show your master respect.'

I press my lips together and glare at him.

'Would you have me sin?'

'No, sir,' I sigh and give up the fight. There is no point trying to boil a pot of wet ashes. He lowers his voice and pats me upon the cheek, petting me as you would do a cat. Or a child. Something harmless, stupid and of no significance. I writhe beneath his touch.

'I shouted at you. I should not do that,' he says. 'I shall not talk of this matter again. I will never rebuke you for it. No one need know.'

I leave the house and am through my mother's door in moments.

'Mother, I must speak with you,' I begin, and the words parch upon my tongue.

She pauses in her chopping of turnips and raises her head. 'Come now, Anne. What is it? Tell your mother. I have a week's worth of work to do in an hour.'

'It is Thomas.' I whimper. 'He is – difficult.'

'All men are so. That's how the Lord made them,' she says, and returns her attention to the turnips. In an hour there will be a fine stew bubbling on the hearth. For some reason, the notion of eating turnips in my mother's house seems a feast.

'But,' I start again. 'He does not – things are not as they should be.'

She sighs, lays down the paring knife. 'By the Saint, girl. Can you not play him right?'

'I try, so hard. Nothing I do is enough,' I whine. She gives me a blank look. 'He moans, he complains,' I add, in case she does not understand.

'Daughter,' she says, and there is no softness in her voice. 'What did you imagine happens between a man and a maid?'

'Ma!'

'Not that,' she snorts. 'Did you have it in your feather-head that he would sigh, and weave you caplets of apple-blossom whilst composing pretty riddles praising your smile?'

'No,' I say uncertainly.

'It's hard work, and do not mistake me. If he's not what you hoped for, then make the most of it. You're not starved, you're not badly treated, and you're surrounded by more gewgaws than I could shake a stick at.'

'I have tried sweetness; I have tried meekness, cheerfulness, hard work, speaking, silence. He is wood. There is no pleasing him.'

'There is a way, daughter. There is always a way and if anyone can find it, it is my pretty Anne.'

I pause, so that she thinks I am meditating upon her words. 'Mother, can I come home?'

She gives me a long cold stare. 'You *are* home. And I am busy.'

'I mean, come home to stay.'

'You most certainly cannot,' she snorts. 'The very idea! That would be a fine business. First you're his woman, then you are not. The shame of it.'

'I want a proper husband.'

'You are spoiled, my girl. If I ever sinned, it was in being too soft with you. You wanted him; you have him.'

'It's not that simple.'

'It is. You shall stay where you are.'

'I don't want him any more.'

'A man is not a brass pot, to be tossed aside when tired of.'

'I am not tired. I—'

'Hold your tongue and listen, for once. What man will take the leavings of another?'

Never before did my mother speak to me so harshly. I feel tears rise in my eyes and am determined not to let them spill over.

'Thomas has never touched me!'

'So you say.'

'Don't you believe me?'

'I believe you want to be away from a house that half a year ago you begged to be in. You cannot change your man in the same way that you change the ribbons in your hair. I asked you if you were sure, and you swore you were. Heed me now. You will stay, and there's an end to it. I have done with this conversation.'

I do not know what shocks me more: the force of her words or that it is my mother who speaks them. She wipes her hands and wraps her kerchief around her head.

'I'm going to fetch your father from the alehouse,' she announces.

'But can we not talk some more?'

'You do not want to talk. You want to twist me to your way of thinking. It will not work any more. By the Saint, Anne, I thought you would have stopped hanging on to my skirts by now.'

'Mumma!'

'That is a child's word. You are not a child.'

I follow after her, for the last place I wish to go is Thomas's house. My house. She looks down her nose at me.

'Have you nothing better to do?' she says.

'Clearly not,' I growl.

She sniffs, but does not shoo me away. As we walk, she takes my arm.

'Come on, lass,' she says with greater warmth. 'If any woman can bring him round, it will be you. A man is an instrument and can be played. All he wants is to hear a sweet song, and a woman with her wits about her can sing it afresh every day. Even your father is this way, although I declare I am blessed with my Stephen, for he is the most agreeable of melodies. All you need do is find the tune to make this man dance.'

She pats my hand. I know she means to fortify me.

Stepping through the alehouse door is to enter a dream filled with delightful scents and sounds, and I am stabbed by a sensation that feels a lot like happiness. A cloak of laughed-out air lays itself soft around my shoulders, and I taste the moist kiss of Aline's brew on the halloas that greet us as we step under the lintel. Mother goes straightway to my father. They embrace each other and he clears a space for her on the bench next to him.

I sigh, imagining Thomas's sour expression when I return late to the house. It is hardly a sin for me to dawdle awhile and be merry for this one night. I resolve to stay.

The men are engaged in playing a game with a pig's bladder, which is already the cause of much mirth. Joseph the drover puts his lips to the hole and blows, then lays it upon the bench with a great deal of ceremony. He strolls about with his thumbs hooked behind his back, whistling, inviting us to sit.

'Come now, Mistress Aline,' Joseph cackles. 'Take the weight off your feet! You must be tired after a day making such a fine brew.'

He is interrupted by drinkers raising their cups and shouting huzzah. Aline nods her thanks and laughs.

'Oh no, not me. All these thirsts to quench and rushed off my feet already!'

She winks at us: we cheer at her clever answer. He scours the room for a suitable fool and this time points at me.

'You! Little Anne!'

'Me?' I squeak, and the folk roar at how tiny my voice is become. I clear my throat and repeat the word more resonantly, which, it appears, is even funnier.

'Yes, you, my chick. A pretty bird like you should have a comfy nest on which to fluff up her feathers. Look! Here's the very place,' he cries, and points to the bench.

I search for a smart retort or I shall have to sit down and lose the game. I find nothing, shake my head and shrivel into the wall. I wait for him to coax me out of my shyness, but when I raise my head he is gone to the other side of the room and is chattering to Alice.

I am more disappointed than I expect. I wanted him to cozen me, so that I could make a big show of saying how I was too busy to play his foolish game. I have been denied the opportunity and it irks me. Alice bats her eyelashes and preens her hair with dainty gestures. Every gaze is upon her and she fair wriggles with the pleasure of it.

'Oh la, sir!' she pipes. 'There are wolves in this very room.' She looks about, stretching her eyes wide. One old fellow starts to howl, to the amusement of those gathered. 'If I roost,' she smirks, 'one of them is sure to gobble me up.'

There is a thumping of cups and more huzzahs at her quick rebuff. My Da slaps me on the back.

'Why didn't you think of that?' he chuckles.

Alice is casting coy glances at Geoffrey the cheese-man. He returns the look with a grin that lifts first one side of his mouth then the other; a smile that cannot believe its luck. I remember

82

how he once set his cap at me; a short while only, for I looked down my nose at him and made no secret of it. I set my eye way above the head of a man who smelled of curds.

'We should have Father Thomas here,' declares Joseph. 'He's a man on his feet all day, wouldn't you say so, Anne?'

At the sound of his name my heart drops.

'He is not a man who takes much rest from his labours,' I say as respectfully as I can manage.

This answer makes them roar lustily and I wish it did not.

'I'll bet our little Anne keeps him busy!'

'Now now, he's a man of God. Let's keep it clean,' chides Aline, to a volley of sniggers. 'Haven't you told him how good my ale is?' she continues. 'Father Hugo was always front of the queue.' She gives me a look that has an edge of hurt.

'Eager to get a bellyful, so he was.'

'Father Thomas is not like Father Hugo,' I say.

I look at her, raising my eyebrows and praying that she can hear what is behind my words, for I dare say no more. But Aline was never much good at riddles and does not understand my meaningful glances.

'He's a lot scrawnier, that's for sure. Peaky, I'd say. You should feed him better, Anne. I'm not the only one thinks so. Have you got a headache, screwing your forehead up like that?'

'Aline's right,' adds Joseph. 'Fatten him up and tell him how good this ale is.'

'You can't keep him to yourself the whole time.'

'What?' I gasp.

'A honeymoon's a honeymoon, but you've had him cooped up over two months.'

'You only let him out to go to church.'

My mouth falls open. 'I do not—'

'No need to be abashed, my love,' chuckles Aline and plants

a kiss on my brow. 'I couldn't let James out of my sight for a quarter-year, could I, now?'

The man in question grins lopsidedly as his companions slap him on the back and snort their congratulations.

'That's right. Let him out for a bit of fresh air.'

'Bit of colour in his cheeks.'

'And a pint in his belly!'

I consider explaining to them that Thomas would no more sit on a pig's bladder and pour ale down his throat than he would bare his backside at the high altar. However, Aline would sooner believe that than believe in a man who does not drink beer. It occurs to me that I do not understand Thomas either.

I am surrounded by folk I have seen each day of my life, as much a part of me as my hair and my hindquarters. Yet it is as though I am hovering above their heads like a hawk. Like a glamour wearing off, I see them for the first time, small and terrified as voles, swilling ale to drown out their fear of the pestilence, which prowls around the village like a starved wolf.

I wonder if this is how Thomas sees us, and if he has made me like himself. Perhaps I am becoming used to him, and his coldness is rubbing off on me. It is not a pleasant idea. I shake myself like a dog shakes off water. Ma is right. I need a bit of fire in my belly. I have been doused far too quickly. Alice can have Geoffrey and his dripping cheeses. I have a man and I shall bend him to my will.

As I leave, Ma presses a jug of ale into my hands. 'This'll set Thomas right,' she says, and winks.

She links her arm through mine and accompanies me back to the house. We splash through the ford, lifting our skirts and giggling like children, for the ale has made us clumsy.

'That's better, my little Nan. A smile on your face and this good brew. That's all that's needed.'

She squeezes my cheek. We reach the door, although it takes longer than it ought, and the latch is slippery in my fingers. At last I get it open and we tumble inside with much hushing of each other, so as not to waken Thomas.

'What a quiet place!' Ma says, in the sort of whisper that can be heard three fields away.

We kiss goodnight and she bustles away. However carefully I try to close the door, it slams so hard the house shakes. After she has gone the room seems emptier than it should. When I turn, Thomas is there, fingers laced over his privates.

'I did not see you, sir,' I say for lack of better greeting. 'Were you asleep?' I add, rather weakly.

'I was,' he says, with considerable weight upon the second word.

'I beg pardon, sir. My mother saw me safely home.'

He makes a harrumphing sound, as though the idea is a foolish one. 'Mistress,' he says. 'Must you have visitors so often?'

'Often, sir? It was my mother. Not a visitor.'

'Comings and goings. All hours.'

'I beg pardon, sir. It is a little late—'

He continues as though I have not spoken. 'Every day my house is . . .' he ignores me and purses his lips, '. . . overturned.'

'Every *day*?'

He raises his hand and flaps my words away. 'Day, week.'

'Or month, perhaps?'

'Too often. I am a man of God. If it's not your mother, tramping in and out in the middle of the night, then it's your – sister, friends, silly women filling my ears with bothersome chatter. I have had enough of it.'

Dear Lord in Heaven, I think. *Here he goes.* I bow my head and let the sermon roll over the top of my head. To help pass the time I consider how I shall get up early tomorrow morning and set myself to sifting the barley to make a white porray. Every now and then I mutter, *Yes, sir*, to keep him happy. I swallow a yawn.

'So we are agreed.'

'Sir?' I say with a start, for I was a long way off.

'You will give proper notice of visits and seek my permission.'

'Shall I?'

'You shall.'

'Very well.' I bob a curtsey. I think quickly. 'Sir, may I be permitted a visit from my mother in one week's time?'

'No.'

'Then,' I begin carefully, 'in two weeks?'

'No,' he says, more loudly.

'What of my sister?'

'No!' he cries.

'Please, Thomas.' I hear the plaint in my voice and hate it.

'I said no, woman. And stop calling me Thomas.'

'It's your name, you fool.'

'I am *sir*. Don't you forget it.'

'Little chance of that, *sir*,' I sneer. 'You can't cut me off from my family. My sister has a new baby,' I add desperately. 'My nephew. I am his godmother.'

'Very well. At the feast of Saint Eadburga.'

'That's past next quarter-day! He'll be pushing a plough by then.'

'Do not exaggerate. He'll still be spewing up all over your clothes, I'm sure.'

'What of it? I'm sure the blessed Virgin had her fair share of baby sick to wash out,' I growl.

His face turns so pale I declare I could knock him over like a ninepin. I leave him to his spluttering and go to my pallet before he can gather his wits and call me a blasphemer. When Christ was a child he'll have puked like one. And farted like one also, although I do not press my luck by drawing this to his attention.

'Mistress,' he calls after me.

I raise my eyes to the roof, for he is not done with me. I wait for the accusation of speaking against God, but instead he looks me up and down.

'Why is your head covered?' It is such an unexpected question that I gawp at him for a long and silent moment, wondering whither his brains have taken him this time. 'You are unmarried,' he continues. 'You do not need to do so.'

I hold his gaze and say nothing. I stare boldly enough to earn a slap, or words of caution at the least; but after a while a red spot appears on each cheek. He lowers his head and scurries back to his bed. Perhaps if I had chased him then, if I had asked him why he blushed, demanded to know what he felt for me, perhaps things would have been different between us.

However, nothing is different, and everything is the same. I thought I would grow fat on meat in the house of a priest. But porray is my portion, day in and day out: green, white and red I eat it. I am not starved. I have enough to satisfy hunger, but nothing more. I am no glutton, but I ache with the tedium. So many turnips my belly aches for an onion to brighten my plate, let alone a bit of bacon, fried crisp.

A few days after the Feast of Saint Boniface, John the butcher brings a rabbit.

'For Father Thomas,' he says. 'Once he tastes this he'll send for my wares more often, eh?'

'I wouldn't set too much store on it,' I sigh.

He coughs. 'Thirsty morning, is it not?'

I bite my lip. 'There is water,' I whisper, my face so heated with embarrassment I can barely look at him.

He snorts. 'Well, there's a welcome. Have you been telling tales against me, Anne?'

'Tales? Of course not!'

'Then why does he not send for me?'

I have no answer. John stands on tiptoe, tugging his hood forward to hide his eyes and trying not to show how greedily he scans the room for goodness knows what stories of riches. His gaze swallows up the old rushes, the hard benches without so much as a cushion to ease your way, the plain walls, the single side of pork dangling from the roof beam, the dark embers on the hearth.

'Well, now,' he says and scratches his head. 'Ah.'

I see the dismal interior through his eyes, as unkempt and unloved as every other thing of Thomas's. This is not the house wherein I was toasted a handful of weeks ago. No table set for a feast, no bunches of herbs to sweeten the air, the door opened to him by a goodwife as dreary as the sodden reeds which should be swept out.

He holds out the rabbit, grinding its ankles together in his fist. My fingers brush his as I take the dead beast, less than a second, but it is enough to make my flesh quicken. For no good reason I see my braids caught in his firm hand, tugging my head back as he plants a kiss upon my lips. I slam the door in his face with a muttered word of thanks.

I set about skinning and drawing the coney. The aroma of cooking meat calms me. As I catch my breath, I talk to myself sharply for entertaining such brutish imaginings. I set up the trestle and spread a clean cloth. By the time Thomas returns from visiting a poor widow out beyond Saint Michael's chapel, the stew has fragranced the whole house. Mother always told me that a good cook feeds her husband's heart. Today might be the day I succeed. His nostrils flare as he steps over the threshold.

'A fine smell, mistress,' he says.

'For you, sir,' I grin, with a pretty curtsey. 'John brought a rabbit.'

'Another visitor?' he asks darkly.

'A gift, sir. A kindness from our butcher. I have made a stew.'

He grunts and kicks off his boots, scattering dried mud across the floor. It does not matter. I shall sweep it away later.

'You may take it to the miller and his family.'

'The miller?'

'Yes.' He snaps his fingers. 'Nathaniel? Simon? Martin?'

'Simon.'

'Yes, yes. I hear he is taken sick and I am tired out from walking all the way to the far side of the marshes,' he mutters. 'With God's blessing,' he adds quickly.

'I could spare a bowl,' I say, wondering if he truly means me to give away the whole lot and have nothing to eat myself. 'But I made it for you.'

'Then you have wasted your time, mistress,' he says, shrugging off his cloak, which smells like a wet ewe.

It sprawls across the bench. He stares at it until I pick it up, shake it off and hang it on its hook.

'Does the scent of rabbit displease you?' I ask, knowing it does not. His eyes are glued to the pot, even if he thinks I am too stupid to notice.

'Of course not. Your cooking is quite sufficient. But it is Thursday evening.'

'Yes?'

I must sound truly confused, for he smiles. He always smiles when I do not understand what he has said. I wonder whether he does it on purpose.

'So I cannot eat flesh.'

'Thursday is not a fasting day,' I say, a little uncertainly, for the good Lord may have changed His mind this morning and added Thursday to the dense thicket of days when meat may not be eaten.

'It is past Compline. I did not think to be so late. But the widow would keep me . . .' He draws in a steadying breath. 'May the Saint bless her and keep her. So it is the eve of Friday. As a man of God, I must fast.'

I look at him. He looks at me. I am not convinced: he looks far too pleased with this act of piety for my taste. But there is nothing I can say. I return to the hearth and set to heating the porray left over from this morning. I consider adding a piece of the rabbit to it, but he would notice and I would get another sermon. I stir the mush so angrily some of it flies out of the pot and lands on the rushes.

I watch the spilled oatmeal dry out. I could scrape it off the floor and put it into his bowl. It is hardly a sin. He says neither a word of praise nor condemnation about the food I cook, whether it is the best dish I ever made or something I hurled into the pot without thinking. I doubt he'd notice if I seasoned his victuals with sheep dung. I know these thoughts come from the Tempter and I should pray, but today I am not in a prayerful mood. I continue to stir, feeling very sorry for myself.

When I first came here, I prepared victuals with the shy hand of a maid who loved and hoped for it to be returned. I thought my store of affection was enough to last many a lean winter, but I was wrong. It has shrivelled away so quickly. I look into the pot. Steam rises off the surface and warms my face with its gentle touch. I hover there a while longer, feel water pool beneath my tongue.

I shape my lips, part them slightly and watch spittle fall in a silver string. It rests on the surface of the pottage, the size of a small coin. I could pretend it is a mistake, one I did not intend to make. But I intend every bit of it. One movement of the ladle and it is gone. No, not gone: hidden. How I will smile if he praises his supper, tonight of all nights! Only I know it is there, and I will watch him eat.

VIXEN

I am sitting in the arms of an oak, picking shreds of rabbit meat out of my teeth when I see them: a flight of starlings moving as one bird, a banner turning the morning dark. I watch the play of their flight. I never tire of the tales they write upon the clouds: marvellous stories of where they have been and the wonders they have witnessed.

I feel that mix of wistfulness that I have no wings to spread and join them, yet happy that my journeys are conducted in solitude and not subject to the squabbling whim of birds. I am so wrapped in the drowsy distraction of a full belly that it takes me a while to realise that something is amiss. Their flapping is troubled, unlike their usual joyous dance. They cast themselves raggedly across the sky, first one way and then the other.

Their cries fill the sky and in them I seem to hear: *Come close; follow and we will tell.* Half-words, half-news and I must know the whole. The last thing I want to do is venture from the safety of the forest and any closer to the village squatting a stone's throw away. But something pulls me, like iron to a lodestone.

I slide from my perch, scrambling down fast as a squirrel. My attention is so fixed on the birds that I almost trip over the body stretched across the path. I leap away shrieking, and hear a dry chuckle above my head. Some would say it's no more than the rattling of rook's beaks, but I know better.

'Very funny,' I grumble. 'I suppose that's your idea of a joke?'

The man's arms are stretched out as though nailed to the earth; back arched upwards, his body a bow that Death pulled back and never released. I don't want to look at him. I cannot take my eyes away.

His scrip is gutted, any coins long gone. His boots must have been fine, for they too have been stolen. His cap bears a leaden badge and just out of reach of his clawing fingers is a tiny book: face down, wings spread, prayers melting into the dirt.

Don't you want to step a little closer? whispers my old friend. *Smell the roses I have planted in his throat?*

I don't need to be a clerk to read this riddle. His flesh is swollen, eyes thrusting from his head, mouth gaping in its final shriek and gagged by the thick tongue bloating between his lips. The pustules at his throat broke open long ago and are congealed with black ooze.

I am muffled in silence, as though the forest is stuffing her fingers into her ears. I wonder if this is what the birds want to show me. I squint through the branches, a dart of disappointment that I have lost them, then spy the flock heading west. The call to be away is clear. I set my shoulders straight, leap over the pilgrim's carcase and follow them out of the trees.

I keep pace as best I can: running alongside streams and ducking under hedgerows in case I should meet some worthy peasant who takes it upon himself to ask difficult questions of a strange girl wandering where she shouldn't.

The starlings reel in the direction of the sea, a bowshot distant, chattering, *We know what's coming! Follow us and we'll tell all!* I skirt the village and chase them into the saltmarsh, a scribble of whip-grass and vetch heavy with the brackish reek of sedges. There's not so much as a bush to provide cover. My feet itch to be back in the forest, my neck prickling with the fear some man is watching. But curiosity drags me forwards. I must know.

'Come on,' I growl. 'If you've got something to say, be done with it.'

The mere is raked with drainage ditches, digging their talons through the mud. Weak sunlight catches the surface of the water, turning them from black to silver, silver to black. I jump into one, scuttle along out of sight.

After a few minutes I meet a water rat dashing in the opposite direction, fur sticking out in a shock of frizz. The only thing they fear are dogs, and where there's a dog there's a man soon after. I crouch low in the cutting, sending silent thanks to the fleeing creature for its warning. My ears are cocked for barking, for the snuffling of a wet nose on the scent, the encouraging shouts of its master; but there's nothing save the racket of birds heading further into the marsh.

More water rats bounce past on tiny paws, then a pair of otters, all running inland. The hindmost otter pauses and hops onto her hindquarters. She peers at me and sniffs.

'What's afoot?' I ask her. She pats her broad paws together. 'That's right. Tell your old friend. What's all this business with the birds? I've never seen such a commotion.'

For answer, she ruffles her whiskers and dives back into the waterway. With a flick of her tail she catches up with her mate and is gone. I can't help but laugh. I have always found the beasts of the field far better company than men. The breeze stiffens and I curse myself for leaving my over-tunic in the fork of the tree. I press on, shivering in under-tunic and half-hose.

The starlings continue to swirl, crashing into each other

with such force that they tumble to earth in a sprawl of feathers. I trip over snapped bodies: beetle-wing eyes already dim, the tips of their beaks pointing in the same direction, towards the sea. They are not alone. A wild parliament of birds is gathering there.

Lapwings brush the earth with their bellies, curlews flipping over like cakes on a hot stone. A pair of swans thrash their necks so furiously I think they will snap. Even rooks have joined the throng, drawn from the forest as urgently as myself. The air roughens with the *okokok* of geese, the clattering of oyster-catchers, the booming of bitterns, a hubbub of squawking and screeching. In the melee, more and more collide and plummet, raining down until the earth is pillowed with plumage.

'What do you want?' I shout. 'Why have you brought me here?'

At my words, the company falls silent. They stretch their wingtips and pause, hanging in the thickening air. It is the matter of a moment. Then, as if by some unknown command, they draw together like the fingers of a giant hand, from the greatest to the smallest, till they are one flock. Not one touches the other, not by so much as a tail-feather.

With stately grace they form a circle the breadth of the heavens: no haste, no sound, even the beating of their wings muted. They glide round and round in a dizzying arc, the maelstrom so thick as to make the morning dark as evenfall. I watch open-mouthed, and in the silence I see what is coming. To the west, massing over the sea, is a mountain of cloud, black as the bottom of a well and greater than any I have ever seen.

'A storm?' I yell at the birds. 'Is that all? You dragged me out of my warm, comfortable tree to tell me it's going to rain?'

I shake my fist and a bellyful of seagull shit lands on my head. I run my hands through my stinking hair, cursing shitty-arsed birds the world over. My fingers tangle in filth.

'Why me?' I yell, dripping with half-digested fish. 'What did I ever do to you?'

The gulls laugh, a raucous rattle like a stick dragged along a gate. A black-faced bird unpicks itself from the whirlpool of wings and dives so close to my head that I have to crouch to escape its attack. It swoops away without striking. Another does the same, and another, buffeting my head with salt air. I have seen birds mob a cat before, and have laughed mightily at the sport. Now the tables are turned and it is not in the least amusing. Drops of rain strike my shoulders, save it is not rain, it is more bird shit. All join in, pelting me with muck.

'I hate you!' I shriek. 'I'll kill every one of you! I'll set fire to every nest and burn your hatchlings to cinders! I'll burn down the forest and you in it!'

Egg-killer! they shriek. *Murderer of our children!*

I see the empty nests, all their generations gulped down my gullet. 'I was hungry!' I whine.

They make one more turn of their grand dance. The smallest are the first to leave: sparrows and wrens head back to their hedgerows, followed by the larks, the thrushes, the blackbirds, the plovers, the fieldfares, the magpies, unravelling themselves one by one from the tight-wound skein of quill and claw until only the gulls remain, chuckling at the joke I am beginning to understand. I was the fox. Now I am become the quarry.

I look up at the jaundice-yellow sky. I'll have to take to my heels if I'm going to outrun the storm back to the forest, for it is coming in fast. I hear the cracking of a distant tree, pulling up its roots and crashing through the frail arms of its brothers as it falls to earth. But there are no trees: it the sound of approaching thunder.

I take no more than three paces before the rain begins in earnest. At least it'll wash off the muck, I think. I race along and soon come upon the drainage channel, now churning with orange water. I can't believe it is full so quick, for the downpour has barely started.

It is too dangerous to crawl within, so I crouch and run alongside, comforting myself with the knowledge that no other person will be so mad as to venture out in this weather. I am a fool to be so caught, and counsel myself over and over never to follow the flight of birds again, for they bring nothing but trouble.

'You bastard birds!' I shout, and am rewarded with another splat on my arm. 'Ha! Missed my head!' I cry, and a volley lands on my shoulder.

The marshland is a blur, rain pouring so heavily that I swear it goes up my nose. I am grateful for the straight line of the ditch, guiding me back inland, but the next step thrusts me into mud up to the knee. I sink further and only just manage to drag my foot out. Somehow, I have followed the ditch in the wrong direction and am at the sea's edge. Rusty water spews into the estuary.

I throw myself backwards and gasp on the quaking edge of the morass. I shove down the shock and remind myself that I have made a simple mistake and gone towards the sea rather than away from it. All I need do is retrace my steps and all will be well.

I turn about and make my way as swiftly as I can, which is not that fast, for the ground sucks at my feet as though unwilling to release me from its grasp. I fortify myself with the thought that soon I will come upon a hedgerow that betokens solid ground. But the ditch is met by two more: one leading to the right and one to the left. It is impossible to see further than five paces in either direction. I hop from sodden foot to foot, the earth softening dangerously as I loiter.

I set off to the left but go barely twenty paces when I am knee-deep in sludge again. I head back, bent beneath the downpour, but all is mud this way also. I have no choice but to strike out across the wasteland and pray that I can hold a straight line away from the sea.

The earth quivers like a haystack soaked by a week's rain. The wind leaps in front of me and slaps my face; I turn and it flings mud into my eye, tearing up clods of earth and hurling them past my ears, twisting me round and round in a game of hoodman blind. Bulrushes uproot themselves and fly past, lashing my body in wet rope.

The storm gathers itself and howls. I am so drenched that I do not know where the rain ends and I begin, my eyes so thick with dirt I've no idea which way is up or down. I trudge, half blind, through marshland that is indistinguishable from the estuary mudflats. I no longer know if I am walking into the sea or away from it.

The wind gives me a final clout, knocking me face-forwards into slime. I give in to it. The land was here before me and will be here after I have gone. I have done less than stir the grass upon its face. Of the one hundred deaths I imagined for myself, not one of them was in a filthy puddle in the middle of a swamp.

PRIME
1349

From Saint Alban the Martyr to Saint Mildred

THOMAS OF UPCOTE

When Anne told me a storm was coming, I chastised her, for the spring gales were long past. She raised her eyebrow, quit the house and I lay awake the whole night listening to thunder boom like a sail.

At last the night seeped away, but the dawn was so stifled with cloud I needed a rush-light to find my clogs. Anne came through the door, head bundled in a shawl.

'I am here, sir. I was with my mother. She was sore afraid. I beseech you, forgive me.'

I smiled at her childishness. 'I am not angry, mistress. I am glad you are returned safe.'

She fetched me ale, chattering about the weather while I prepared myself for Lauds. The wind had dropped and the sky flapped with mewing gulls tossed inland. The track beside the church slurred with mud, and my heart sorrowed to see the cottages torn so cruelly. I feared for the people, but they were as merry as kids, thronging the path to the fields.

'Did you see the moon last night, Father? How swollen and red it was.'

'It presaged a calamity.'

'No, good luck.'

'I have never heard such terrible thunder.'

'I thought this world was brought to an end!'

'You seem very merry,' I remarked. There were so many names for me to remember.

'We are safe, Father.'

'The Saint protected us, did he not?'

'We were spared. Not one of us lost.'

'May God in His mercy send us a good world!' declared another.

I consoled myself in their faith, and resolved to be cheerful with them. After I had said the Office, I followed them to the Great Field, striped with water like rubbed pewter. The common paths were blotted out, and trees turned their roots upwards as though terrified. Stinking mud lay over everything. Above, clouds strung tidemarks across the sky.

I thanked God for the calmness of the morning: thus did He reward Noah after his stormy journey, granting him peace and fruitfulness afterwards. I stored this neat idea in my mind, congratulating myself that it would serve as a theme for my next sermon.

'I hear the cart-way between Bideford and Appledore is nearly swept away,' cried one fellow, dragging a hay sledge after him.

'The causeway at Crow Point also.'

'Many acres of country are drowned.'

'But no men.'

I praised the Saint for this miracle. I had feared greatly for souls caught at sea, for their boats would have been chewed to pottage.

The whole village was there, eager to see what wonders had been delivered in the night. I ploughed in their wake through tangled marsh-grass. A great quantity of fish had been cast up, still gasping and leaping upon the earth, and the people rushed about, gathering them in baskets.

They were as happy as children on a feast day, men and women alike stripped of their lower garments. But they were unabashed: the slime was thick as winter hose. All the while they ran to show me some new wonder: a piece of broken wood of great size, an iron bucket with its side broken in by the force of the waters, a strange quaking fish with a mouth wide as my foot.

I ventured further, inspecting the ditches and broken hurdles, but the dykes had held in most part. The water sucked and swallowed, gargling between the piled mud banks, which men were already repairing. I took a shovel and leapt down, and began to dig out the channel with the rest of them.

'You should let me do that, Father,' said one. 'It is not work for a man of God.' He grasped the handle of my spade.

'Let us labour together,' I smiled.

He pulled at the handle; I pulled back.

'No, Father,' he whispered. 'Rather, strengthen us with your prayers.'

'Yes, I will pray. After this!' I shouted. We stared at each other a moment; then he let go and I continued my work. 'I will offer indulgences to all who help in making good the damage,' I cried. 'We will be holier men!'

I tired quickly, but felt no shame, for I was a priest and not a peasant.

Then it began. A shout went up from the direction of the sand dunes, followed by a murmuring like water running over stones. I heard them before I saw them: a tangle of men the colour of mud. At first I thought they were coming to thank the Saint for their deliverance from the storm; waited for their mutterings to shape into prayer, but as they approached what I heard was the pipe of nesting birds with a cat in their sights.

They moved slowly, side to side, as though carrying a filled sack. A sack that struggled, striving to be free. They let it down before me, but hummocked about it, hanging onto its arms. It moved as wildly as a dish-clout shaken in a woman's hand.

'Look at the fish we have caught, Father Thomas,' said one.

'Is it a fish? It does not have scales, but is slimy, like an eel,' remarked another.

'It stinks like a fish.'

'It is a mermaid, like sailors tell us.'

'Not a *maid*, you fool. A maid has breasts, and it has none.'

'What do you say, Father Thomas?'

I looked closely at the writhing creature. It was so piled with filth it was hard to tell where its limbs ended and its body began. But it did have limbs: two arms and two legs.

'It is no fish; it is a child,' I said, to make an end of their chatter.

'It is black as a Moor.'

'Or a devil.'

'Or a Jew.'

'It is no Jew,' snorted one. 'All Jews are rich. Where is its fine clothing?'

'The Jews have brought the pestilence to the world,' said a solemn-faced fellow. As he spoke, he crossed himself, smearing mud upon his brow. 'The Pope tells us so.'

'No. It is the gypsies have brought it down on our heads. Everyone knows this.'

'The Jews.'

'The gypsies. For their thievery and filthy habits.'

'The Jews murdered Christ,' replied the first with slow

emphasis. 'That was the greatest sin that ever was. Am I not right, Father?'

'What?'

I had so long closed my ears to their bickering that I realised too late he addressed me. I wondered if Eve's sin was the greater: at some point in my studies I had been given a clear answer, but what it was, I could not remember.

'There are no Jews in Brauntone,' I said confidently, but my hesitation cost me dear. They glanced from one to the other and I heard their thoughts, loud as if spoken. *He does not know. He is a fool.*

'There are no gypsies, either,' I continued, hoping to win them back. 'Our Holy Brannoc will hold back all those who would creep in and poison us.'

They chewed on this notion awhile, until one of them gave the child a shake.

'All the same, Father,' he said. 'What if it is carrying pestilence? Will we be so foolish as to let it in?'

'It will breathe on us and we will die.'

'We should burn it, as they have burned all the Jews of Germany.'

'Just to be sure.'

They nodded, hopeful that I might say the word and let them cut the child's throat and be done.

'The Saint will protect us from all ill,' I declared.

'Will he, Father?'

'Did you not see miracles of healing? At this very Feast Day just passed?'

If I hoped for agreement, I was disappointed. I looked into their faces and saw the darkness in their eyes, the wolfish blades of their teeth, how they would rend this pitiful wight into shreds if I turned my back for but one moment. I cleared my throat and raised my hand.

'Enough!' I cried sternly. 'It is clear. He is a child. Nothing more.'

'Is it a boy, Father? He has no pizzle,' cackled one, waggling his finger in the space between the creature's legs.

I looked closely. It seemed to be true, although it was difficult to tell. By God's good mercy there was a puddle at my feet. I dipped my sleeve and wiped it over the child's brow, though it struggled mightily and would have torn itself free had not the men's hands become used to catching fish on dry land. The dirt sloughed away and the skin showed pale.

'See,' I said, and very loudly so all might hear. 'Girl or boy, these are no devil's scales. It is dirt. Look at your own legs. Are they not the same colour? You are muddied just the same.'

'Yes, Father,' they muttered, looking at their knees and sighing their disappointment.

'The Saint has always protected you. He will not withdraw his protection now. Unless we fall into sin,' I added heavily. 'Remember what our Saviour Christ said unto the people. Suffer little children to come unto me.' I pointed at the creature. 'Like this child,' I declared, hoping that my voice did not shake overmuch. 'It has come to us by the grace of God, so we will treat it well. God protect us!' I cried.

Protect us, they mumbled.

I did not know if they understood me fully, and was too tired to care. One man, less contentious than the rest, smacked his hands together, and all turned to him. Anne's father. His name came to me after only a few moments: Stephen.

'Very well,' he roared. 'We shall spare it. We have many of our own children,' he continued. 'So we shall give this one to you. He – or she – will be safe in your house. And if he turns out to be a bag of sickness, then he will burst under your roof. You are closer to God, and He will hear you pray for healing a lot faster than He will hear us.'

They accompanied me back to the house, dragging their prize. The rain was full of splinters that dug through my cloak. Only yesterday I had been cudgelling my wits for a way to divert Anne's womanly desire into a more befitting direction. I was no fool; I had noticed her female leanings and far too many of them leaned towards me. Of course she desired a mate: it was the function of woman. Woman was the field, man the plough and seed.

The Lord had answered my prayer: a child upon whom to heap her motherly affections. I rubbed my hands together, pleased with myself. Not only had I done a charitable act, but had found something to bring peace to my household. And if it turned out that this was no more than a runaway thief, then the Sheriff would deal with the matter, not the villagers. I would prevent murder, and provide food and shelter until the law took its course.

So were my thoughts that first day. I was a fool for thinking the course of my life would run so simply. God had other plans.

ANNE

'What have you brought?' I sigh.

'A child,' Thomas replies, looking proud as a cat that's dragged in a dead pigeon.

'Sir, I can see that.'

'Mistress, do not be ungenerous. A child sent out of the storm. By God, perhaps,' he adds hopefully. 'A girl-child, I believe. Would you have her sent elsewhere? William would be most welcoming.'

The creature writhes, desperate to be away, but Thomas's hand is clamped firmly round her wrist. Her struggles grow more and more hopeless until she droops, worn out.

He lowers his voice to a pious purr. 'It is our duty.'

'Sir, indeed.'

Thomas loosens his grip and the girl falls to her knees, gasping. I hold out my hand to set her aright but she shrinks away. Her gaze bucks and dives about the room, resting nowhere. She is so covered with mud as to be more beast than girl. And she stinks. Thomas watches as I drag the wooden tub from its corner.

'Will you help, sir?' I pant. 'I shall need more water bringing from the well if I am to get her clean.'

'Me?'

There is a brief silence.

'Sir,' I continue, patiently. 'If I go, the child will run away. Unless that is what you wish. Perhaps, on this one occasion, you can help.'

'I am always willing to labour for others,' he replies primly.

He picks up the bucket, after I have pointed out where it is stored, but still does not leave, staring at the girl and myself.

'Sir. The water.'

'Yes, yes.'

At last he is gone. I dip a towel into the pot on the hearth and drag it across her cheek. At first she struggles, but with gentle cooing and murmuring I bring a semblance of calm. Each swipe makes her wince, as though to be touched causes pain. I stroke more and more gently until I barely brush her skin with the cloth. By and by her frame undoes its knots a little.

'You see?' I murmur. 'No need to fight. Whoever your enemies are, I am not one of them.'

She mews and tucks her fingers into her chest like a squirrel. From the size of her, anyone would be forgiven for thinking her a child. Anyone save myself. I am a small woman too and I know signs men do not. There's a sprout of hair under her arms and a feather between her legs, so pale as to be almost white. Her breasts are no more than a whisper of skin, but the swollen nipples betray her womanhood.

I can count every bone in the basket of her ribs. She is gap-toothed, her teeth ridged with brown stripes, her nose cracked by some hand long ago. And there, running up the centre of her back, across her shoulders and chest is downy fur. So pale it can barely be seen, it is the silver-grey you find on the inside of a beanscod.

'If you were a dog, I'd say you'd been beaten, chained up and starved half to death,' I remark. 'Fur or no fur, you're no pup, and I'll not treat you as such.'

She glares at me, eyes big as oysters, and lets out what sounds a lot like a warning growl.

'Don't you worry about him. What I've seen here is none of his business.'

In my mind I see Thomas discovering her dusting of hair. How he'd straightaway declare her a wonder, the same as when the Saint transformed a wolf into a man to be his servant. He'd make her his miracle: dress her in golden robes and parade her round the church. She's been in this house for less time than it takes to boil a cabbage, but he'll have to put me in the pot and boil me along with it before I let him do any such thing.

'What passes between you and me goes no further,' I declare, and surprise myself with the fire in my voice.

I am so carried away that I think I see the cloud of unknowing lift from her expression for an instant. But it is nothing but my fancy: her mouth droops, lips gleaming with spittle, her eyes pond-water dim.

As the days lengthen into summer, so does my delight grow that I am blessed with this maid. When I first came to Thomas's house I chattered away to myself, but the sound served only to remind me that I was on my own, and I stopped. My voice no longer dribbles into emptiness, now that it has another pair of ears to pour itself into. It is an unhoped-for pleasure to have a companion, even if she neither understands nor answers.

I begin to recognise the sounds she makes: mewling when she hungers, only quietening when I feed her. I learn her odd ways: how she looks in my direction, yet not quite at me. The

110

moment her gaze and mine meet, she slips away, as though her eyes are greasy in their sockets.

And by the Saint, how she runs: wild as a vixen. She starts the day in the stable, for she beds with the mare and will tolerate no other cradle. It was sufficient for the Blessed Virgin and our Lord so I have no complaint. As soon as she wakes, she's off, I know not where, nor can she tell me. She could race to Jerusalem and back again for all I know.

I tell her not to stray too far; tell her the forest is full of bears. She heeds me not. I could speak in tongues for the difference it makes. In my heart I know the selfish truth of it: I wish to keep her beside me. But you can't tell a fat baby not to fart. In the end, I let her flit to and fro. The easier I let her go, the faster she flies back to this little ark. By and by she stops longer, departs less and I believe I learn a lesson about love.

The weeks go by, and the feast of Saint Etheldreda is passed by that of the holy martyr of Canterbury. It is the season to fetch laver from the beach.

We tramp through the dunes: Bet, Alice, Isabel and myself. And of course the Maid. She sniffs at every clump of gorse, wrinkling her nose at its sweetness, only to leap away with a wail when the breeze whips thorns into her face. I too was caught out as a child, thrusting my hands into the bushes to pick those yellow flowers. Her scrapes are soon forgotten. She stoops, pawing at the bones of a rabbit picked clean long ago by a fox and scoured bright by the sand. She lets out a small whimper.

'One of your four-legged brothers ate him,' Alice tells her, and laughs.

'Ah, she's hungry, that's what it is,' says Bet. She cries, 'Here, Vixen!' and pats her thigh.

The Maid scampers over and is rewarded with a scrap of cheese. We trudge up another sandy hillock and at last catch sight of the sea.

'Still a fair stretch,' sighs Alice, with an air of great suffering.

'Hardly any distance,' scoffs Isabel.

'We'll be there in no time,' I add brightly.

I set off down the slope, ploughing through the soft ground, the Maid yipping and turning somersaults. Alice puffs the hindmost, red-faced with the effort of remaining on her feet and not on her backside. She trips and falls: I reach out my hand.

'Can I help you, cousin? You are quite out of breath.'

She shades her eyes against the sun, unsure if I am laughing with her or at her. But she takes my hand in any case. I haul her upright and we set to beating the sand out of our skirts. I pound her gown energetically. The Maid hops around us on all fours like a giant hare; arse in the air and kicking out her heels.

'I declare,' says Bet. 'I can't tell what she is sometimes: coney, vixen, girl.'

'She is a girl,' murmurs Isabel, but neither Bet nor Alice pay any attention.

'Maybe she's a swan, for she came from the marshes,' muses Alice. 'Or a fish, for she came out of the storm.'

'Fish don't fall out of the sky, silly.'

'My uncle says he heard of a shower of fish in Ireland.'

'You believe that gobshitery?'

I let them rattle on while we climb the next dune. When they have tired themselves out with disagreements, they fall back into accord with one another. Bet tugs my sleeve.

'What do you think she is?' she asks, shyly.

'The Maid?' I ask, pretending I don't know what they've been bickering about.

She nods. 'She lives in your house.'

'And has done since my father found her,' caws Alice.

'It was my brother Richard who first laid hands on her!' declares Bet.

They look set to start a fresh round of squabbling, but Isabel calls silence. She's a head shorter than me, but burns with a fire brighter than the rest of us put together. I always found her unremarkable as a child. I wonder when she changed; what else I missed along the way.

'You know her best, Nan,' she says to me, using a pet name I've not heard for a long while. 'Whoever was the first man to find her,' she adds, casting a stern glance at Bet and Alice. 'What *is* she?'

The Maid is leaping from tussock to tussock of marsh grass, yipping surprise when she finds each is as full of spikes as the last. I regard the serious faces of my companions and it strikes me how far I have grown from them.

I turn and look out to sea. The sun pierces the clouds and throws down beams onto the waves. Adam once told me that this was God pushing the clouds apart for a better look at His people. I used to love the idea of God watching over us. Now, as I look at the shafts of light moving over the face of the waters, it is as though He is seeking me out for all the wrongs I have done.

I turn about quickly and look back towards the safety of the village: smoke curling from thatched roofs, a pot of peas bubbling on every hearth, the forest stretching away to the north. In a sudden fancy I see the Maid standing on a treetop and beckoning. I stand between land and ocean, neither at home nor away from it.

'Nan?'

'I'm sorry,' I say.

'You were miles away,' says Isabel, gently.

'Careful now,' snipes Alice. 'The Vixen is making Anne addle-brained too.'

I sigh. 'She cannot help how God made her. Father Thomas has instructed me to care for her.'

Alice giggles at the mention of Thomas's name, but I fix her with a glare and she swallows the laugh.

'Come now, you must've seen more. Is she always like this?' Alice points at her, where she is digging with the furious passion of a dog that's scented a rat.

I smile. 'She is unlike anything I have ever seen. Anyone I have ever met.'

'Oh,' gasps Bet. 'A marvel, then. Is she—' She lowers her voice 'An angel? My brother said his hands went right through her when he grabbed her. Like she wasn't really there.'

I laugh. 'She's flesh and bone, all right,' I say. 'No more celestial than the shoes on my feet. Maid!' I shout. She cocks her head, leaves off her burrowing and comes barrelling pell-mell, rubbing her face into my apron. 'There's my clever lass,' I coo, rubbing the straw of her hair affectionately.

'She comes when you call,' says Isabel, impressed. 'I thought she didn't understand anything.'

'Everyone calls her a halfwit,' snickers Alice.

'No more than you or me,' I laugh. Alice pouts. I might be insulting her or myself: she cannot tell.

We come at last to the beach, a wide tongue of sand with barely as much as a shell upon it. We ignore the barren strand and head for the rocks, long dark fingers clawing the water's edge. The tide has brought up enough laver for us all to fill our baskets twice over. The salt breath of the sea makes us lively and we set to with a good will.

As I gather the sea's harvest, I think again of Adam; how he used to carry me on his shoulders when Ma sent Cat and him to collect laver. He told tales of the great dragon who lived under the dunes; how the cliffs were its shoulders, these rocks its talons. We spent far more time playing games than collecting seaweed. He chased me up and down the beach, roaring how he was the dragon and was coming to eat me, while I screamed with terrified delight. I remember also how Cat grumbled that she had to pick the laver on her own.

Thinking of Adam makes me melancholy, so I concentrate on finding the tenderest pieces I can. I push away the uncomfortable thought that I am the one who is now left with all the work, while my childish self runs laughing along the water's edge, chased by the memory of her brother.

In my search I come upon a broad mass of seaweed caught in a shaft in the stone. I open my mouth to call the others, but some force holds a finger to my lips. It is spread thick as a meadow, a rich green splashed with purple, glittering gold where the sun strikes. I cast a glance over my shoulder, I know not why, then shove my fingers into coolness.

I mean to draw out a handful, but instead thrust deeper until I am halfway to the elbow. Still I have not touched the bottom. I churn it about, and it stings my nostrils with the smell of the shadows at the bottom of the sea. It should be terrifying, but I revel in its moist cling, its heavy odour. It is as though I can plumb the ocean and touch the bottom with my fingertips.

There is a giggle behind me and I spring back.

'I am filling my basket,' I say loudly, before turning to see the Maid grinning, head on one side. 'I was about to call them over,' I add, blushing at being caught in such whimsy. Not that there is any reason to feel shame, for the Maid understands nothing.

115

I pick till my fingers are dazed. When we're done, we share our cheese and bread, tossing morsels to the Maid. However high we throw, she catches each one and this provides much amusement. For a short while even I forget the hard-working woman I have become.

'Still no sign of one of your own?' says Alice, taking me by surprise. 'A babby, I mean,' she adds, for my confusion is writ clear.

'I have the Maid,' I reply.

'Of course you do,' says Alice, and chuckles.

It is not a kind sound. I make a silent pact that if she continues to look at me so pityingly I shall smack her face sideways. She turns to Bet and raises her eyebrow: Bet ignores the mean gesture and for that I could kiss her. I think of the smug voices of the village women when they wave their infants in my face and ask if I want one like it, filling the room to the eaves with their boasts. *Isn't he fine, the best boy in the shire, the best boy who ever drew breath?*

'She is no baby,' I say. 'But the Saint in his goodness has seen fit to deliver her into my care. Who am I to question his gifts?'

There's no arguing with this, not even for Alice, so we all cross ourselves and give thanks to the Saint and the mysterious ways of God. The Maid rubs herself into my skirt and purrs with deep contentment. I smile despite myself.

We make our farewells at the edge of the Great Field and I continue homewards, the Maid at my side. I see no reason to hurry her along. Her clumsy frolics add bright splashes of colour to the afternoon. I knew there was a blackthorn at the turn of the path, but never noticed how it spread its branches just so. I never looked at the way sunlight glances off puddles, transforming them into silver plates laid along the path. The hedgerows are thick with old man's beard. I sigh.

116

'It flowers in spring. By autumn its beauty has fallen away. The story of men and women down the ages.'

She pauses in her games and peers at me, tongue lolling out of the corner of her mouth.

I laugh. 'Listen to me! I'm quite the wise woman, doling out her proverbs. For all the good it does,' I add less cheerfully, for what will I become other than another old gammer with hair sprouting from her chin.

Her hand reaches out and I take it without thinking that this is the first time she has touched me willingly. Her fingers are so bony it is more like catching hold of a chicken's foot. She gurgles, the strings in her neck clenching and loosening, and barks a single word. It might be *Anne*. It might be *ham*. Or *hen*, or any number of words. I crow with delight and clap my hands. I am sure Thomas would give me a sermon about sober comportment, but he is not present. She has spoken her first word, or half-word, to me. Not him.

'Yes, *Anne*,' I repeat, for I decide that is what she meant. 'What a clever girl. You warm Anne's heart, so you do.'

I throw my arms around her and squeeze. For an instant, she softens. But just as swiftly she is transformed into a block of wood.

'I'm not going to hurt you,' I croon. 'Won't you give Anne a little cuddle?'

She holds her breath and does not yield.

'You'll go blue in the face,' I say, tickling her ribs to make her laugh.

She does no such thing. Teeth clenched, eyes clamped shut, hands balled into fists, arms rigid, stiff as a plank. Wherever she has gone, it is a long way off. Her face is frozen in a rictus of misery and I am making things no better. I release her.

'There now. All gone,' I coo. She cracks open an eyelid. I waggle my hands, to show I have let go.

117

The eye opens completely, followed by the other. Her shoulders relax a little, but she is still as taut as a bowstring and would fly if I touched her again. My heart swells with the desire to cradle her in my arms. It takes no small effort to resist.

'Come now. Have a bite to eat.' I untie the corner of my apron where I've kept a crust, pinch it between my fingers and hold it to her lips. Her face remains stony. 'Thirsty?' I try. I mime drinking, complete with glugging sounds, but to no effect.

'What is it you want, my chick? A star from the sky?' I stretch my hand upwards, close my fist around a handful of air, lower my arm and hold it under her nose. Slowly I uncurl my fingers. 'Look. A star. For you.'

Her furious stare melts away and she gives me the oddest look. For the space of an eyeblink I am looking at a woman as clever and sinful and peevish and lonely as myself. Then it passes and all is as it was: her face shuttered, eyes blank as those of a sheep.

I cannot read the words in Thomas's books, but I can read her broken body. She reminds me of the trees around the coast, roots clinging to the brackish soil yet determined and unbowed. Kindness never touched this girl. I catch myself: this woman.

'I am sorry,' I say. 'I shall not cuddle you. Nor coddle you, for that matter. You are no babe.'

I do not know if I feel sorrow for her alone, or for us both.

Even I know I have made a good batch of laver cakes. For once I succeed in rinsing out most of the salt and neither burn nor undercook them. I set the plate before Thomas and watch him screw up his mouth at the first taste. He forces himself to take two more small bites, pulling a face like a pickled walnut.

It is a mercy when he lays down his knife and declares himself full; although he proceeds to sniff around my ankles for the remainder of the hour, asking if there is any pottage left over from breakfast, and is morose when I say no.

'There is plenty of laverbread,' I say mischievously, for I have a great desire to press him into admitting what he truly feels. 'It will do for tomorrow, also,' I add.

'I wonder,' he says, wrestling with politeness and honesty. 'You have not had leisure to visit your mother recently, have you?'

'Not these past three weeks, sir,' I say, being careful not to let my rancour show.

'No,' he muses. 'Perhaps I could spare you this afternoon.'

'But there is wool to be carded . . .' I let the words trail off and wait for him to pick up the dropped thread, which he does.

'Plenty of time for that tomorrow. You can do twice the carding then.'

'But I must scour the pots,' I continue.

'They will wait a few hours for your attentions, I believe,' he smiles, thinking himself very clever.

'Of course, sir,' I reply, with exceptional sweetness.

'It is meet and right for a girl to visit her mother. We must honour our fathers and mothers, must we not?'

'Indeed we must.'

'Then go to, with my blessing.'

'Now, sir?'

'Now.'

'Thank you, sir. They will be much fortified by your kind words.'

I am partway through the door when he adds, as if an after-thought, 'Your mother relishes laverbread, does she not?'

'As do all my family,' I add.

119

I know where this conversation is headed, but I have no wish to make his path any smoother.

'Why not take it with you? As my gift.'

'But I made it for you. What will you eat tomorrow?'

'I am sure you will prepare something even more tasty.'

'*More* tasty?'

'Yes,' he says, nervously. 'Of course.'

'Are you certain?'

'I am.'

'You are too generous.'

It matters not what he stuffs into his mouth. There's enough laverbread to feed Ma, Da and the neighbours, I tell myself as I pack the cakes in a basket. I wrap my shawl around my shoulders and am out of the door before he changes his mind.

What I hear at my mother's hearth sparks me afire with indignation. She counsels me to say nothing to Thomas, but I cannot hold my unruly tongue. All the way back to the house I bear the weight of the injustice done to him. I stamp up and down, waiting for him to return from Vespers. The words flame from my lips as soon as he steps through the door.

'Sir,' I say, as he kicks off his clogs. 'I must speak with you.'

'Now? It is late,' he grumbles.

'Now. It concerns Edgard. Your shepherd.'

'I know his name. You do not need to tell me what I already know. What of him?'

'I have heard troubling words against him.'

'Indeed?'

He shakes rain off his cloak and drops it to the ground. I look at it and fold my arms. He looks also, irritation spreading across his features. We stare a good while longer, the silence grinding its whetstone. In the end I pick up the discarded garment and hang it on its hook. He makes a grunt of satisfaction that the world is set back in order.

'You should not listen to tittle-tattle. Or spread it,' he continues, sharply.

'How do you know it is mere tittle-tattle if you have not heard what I have to say?'

'Be careful how you address me, woman.'

'Sir.' I stand my ground.

He sighs. 'Well, well. What nonsense is buzzing around your head?'

'Edgard is not honest with you.'

'How so? Let me tell you what a pearl he is, mistress. Edgard cares for my sheep as tenderly as his own. They overwinter with his beasts: he feeds them, tends to their every need, tells me which ones have died, which have come into lamb, how many lambs are born, how many survive. I am blessed to have such a diligent man.'

I chew the inside of my cheek. 'He does all this for the love of God?'

'I believe he would if I asked it. When he first suggested the idea, he declared he would not take a penny.'

'He brought the idea to you?'

'Yes, and it took me some time to persuade him to take any payment. I had to remind him that his family would go hungry if he did this out of charity. At last I was able to make him agree to a reward.'

'I'm sure you were.'

'Then there is the winter forage. Of course, I must pay for that. Last season it cost more than expected. When he told me the price I thought he would break a rib, he pounded his breast with such grief.'

'Thomas, you are a fool.' His mouth falls open. 'Edgard is laughing at you when your back is turned. Plenty of times when it is not, but you do not see.'

'What evil is this you speak?'

'It is not evil, Thomas. It is sense, and of the common sort. He is cheating you – the whole village knows it.'

I will not name my mother as the bearer of this news.

'This is a lie,' he says haughtily. 'You speak of a stranger, not the obedient and humble man of my acquaintance.'

'Then wake up. How many lambs did he tell you were born?'

He considers the question. His eyes roll up a little and his lips move as he recollects. I tap my foot. A man either knows how many lambs he has or he does not.

'Seven,' he declares brightly.

'Seven?' I cannot hold back the shock.

'Yes, seven. What ails you? Why do you insist on questioning me so? I have fifteen sheep. Ten were in lamb.'

He smirks, proud of his memory and how he is able to rattle off the figures. I do not point out that I could have baked an oatcake in the time it took him to remember.

'Fifteen sheep, ten in lamb?'

'That is what I said. You do not need to repeat everything I say. I'm not a simpleton.'

'Yes you are!' I cry.

'Woman,' he growls, his voice dark with warning.

I do not, or will not hear its knell. I snort and fold my arms. 'You have twenty sheep. This is the word in the alehouse, what-ever he tells you.'

'That cannot be. I *had* twenty. They were Father Hugo's before me. But there was the murrain—'

I wave his words away. 'Did he tell you only your sheep were

122

unlucky enough to fall victim to this disaster? Did you ask how many of his were carried off?'

'Why should I ask? His sheep are of no concern to me.'

I ignore him and his stupidity. 'In truth, you had sixteen lambs this spring. I have heard it.'

His mouth falls wide again. Then his eyes grow crafty. 'You heard these stories in an alehouse. How do you know they are not the wicked words of his enemies?'

'Because the words come from Edgard's own mouth. He boasts of it to anyone who will listen. And your congregation do listen.'

'No! The people would tell me if anything like this was afoot.'

'Would they? Edgard grows fat on your mutton, Thomas. He makes sure he gives enough away to still wagging tongues. No one likes you enough, respects you enough, or cares about you enough to tell you the truth and put an end to his cheating. Until now.'

It is the first time he strikes me.

I only know it has happened when I find myself on my arse, halfway across the room. Only then does the pain wake up in my cheek and flare its hot insistence. I touch my fingers to the bone, but he does not appear to have broken anything. I prod more deeply and lightning forks into my flesh. With great care I move my jaw from side to side. Slowly, cupping my chin as though it might fall to the floor, I stand.

I look at him. His face flowers scarlet and I consider telling him that excess of choler will upset his stomach. But I do not trust my mouth to make such complicated movements. His breath swells in and out between us, and sour it is too. I continue to stare at him; but there is nothing to be gained so I shrug, none too energetically as it engenders another stab of pain, and turn to leave.

'I have not dismissed you, woman!' he shrieks, voice shrill as a piglet when you cut off its nakers.

I stop and move no more, not even to turn around and face him. My chin grumbles. I stand a while longer, listening to him wheeze. Now he has arrested my departure, he seems to have forgotten what he wanted to say. I begin to wonder if I'll be here at Judgement Day when he barks: 'You have plenty of work. Go to it.'

I walk away with studied slowness. As I pass out of the room I find the Maid crouching in the lee of the doorpost, eyes wide. I say nothing, nor need to. She chews her lips as though deciding what to do, then bolts from the house with the wind behind her. Thomas is not long after, railing about collecting tithes from his loyal parishioners. I listen to him kicking stones down the path.

My jaw aches. If I do not set a cold towel upon it quickly, the whole world will see the scarlet banner he's slapped on my face, but the only dishclouts I can find are filthy. Then it occurs to me how much clean linen lies unused in the attic room.

The ladder is up in two breaths, and I am up it faster. I believe it eases the sting to know that I am going to use something from Thomas's precious store to soothe the hurt he has caused. My hand trembles on the door. I wince with a sudden fear that he crept up here while I was at my mother's and locked it: but he would have been unable to keep that morsel to himself.

I lift the latch: the door swings back with a creak. At first I think the room is a void, for it is dark as the inside of a mouth. I am seized with the even crueller idea that I only dreamed the treasures. Slowly, my eyes accustom themselves and I see that all is exactly as I left it, down to my footprints in the slut's wool on the boards. I pick up one of the swords and lunge at a heap of curtains, imagining it is Thomas's scrawny backside that I am piercing, but it reminds me of Adam and how he may have died. I throw the sword as far from me as I can and wipe my hands on my apron.

I lift the lid of the nearest chest. It brims with fine garments, both men's and women's. I smirk at the reason why Father Hugo needed to clothe a woman, and so beautifully. Thomas would no more dress me in such finery than wear the gowns himself. But these thoughts curdle my excitement and I have no desire to feel more resentment towards the sapless goat than I already do. Besides, smiling hurts.

Beneath the clothing is sheet after sheet of linen, each with folds sharper than the sword I was playing with. I'll wager not one has ever been spread across a mattress. I lift out the upper-most piece and press it to my throbbing cheek. Its coolness is almost enough to soothe the pain away. It is of such a tight weave you could carry water in it. If I took it – just this one – I could lay it upon my narrow plank of a bed and wrap it round me, brushing my skin from neck to ankle.

Thomas would notice. Even if I stowed it under my skirt he would discover it somehow. I do not know how I can be so sure, but I am. I return it to its nest, close the lid and move to the next chest. It is even more stoutly built than the last, and is locked. This fills me with a passion to uncover what is within. My jaw is forgotten. In my mind's eye I see pearls, rubies, a king's crown, gold coins. Not that I would have the slightest idea what to do with any of them.

I consider kicking the lock, but have no desire to break my toe, whatever the reward. The sword I discarded is a better choice. I wedge it into the narrow slot where the lid bites down, but only succeed in snapping the blade in half and cutting my thumb, though not deeply. I suck on the wound while I search

125

for a stronger tool. Amongst the pile of weapons is the head of a pike. It is a fierce-looking thing, even without its shaft, which either broke away or was fixed to a rake in more peaceable times. It splits the lock as easily as if it was made of cheese. The lid flies back.

Pale grey fur fills the interior. At first, I think a wolf is crouching within and jump back, a cry escaping my lips. The beast does not stir, and I recover my composure. I stretch out my hand and lay it upon the creature, half expecting it to stir with warm breath. But all is quiet.

It is the softest thing I have ever touched. Softer than the down on a day-old chick, softer than my mother's breasts, than the breath of my sister's babe upon my cheek. I plunge my fingers deep and am lost up to the wrist. I haul it from its resting place.

It is too small to be a wolf, yet too large to be any fox from hereabouts. Its head is gone, but the tail is still attached and bushy as a heap of teasels. The colour is unlike anything I've seen: pale as the moon, a misty grey save for a darker stripe down the spine. My mind spins with the notion that somewhere, far away from here, live white foxes.

I stick my face deep into the nap and it tickles any remaining pain into sweetness. I drape it around my neck. It is supple as velvet and possessed of a fresh scent despite the long sojourn in its oaken prison. I parade across the boards, making a broad trail through the dust, grand as a duchess.

I turn it over so that the hair lies against my skin. As I do so, heat springs between my shoulders as though a bonfire has been lit at my back. I let it slip from my shoulder to the wrist and my body sparkles with the fire of a hundred tapers. I examine my arm, half expecting it to be singed. Every hair is pricked and upright, my dreary flesh called to life by this pale beast.

I do the same with my other arm and experience the enchantment afresh; a tingling so delicious my knees quiver. I want to sit down, but the floor is so dirty I'd cover my skirt in smuts, yet another thing to conceal from Thomas. So I return to the first chest, drag out the topmost sheet and spread it over the floor.

I lie down and hug the fur close; draw it to and fro across my limbs, trembling with each caress. Never before have I felt so encumbered by my clothes. They chafe, they itch, they demand to be off. I obey the command and unfurl my body across the sheet, naked except for my beastly cloak, animal fragrance rising around me like a mist.

I take the fox to my breast and writhe beneath the press of its body, my belly lifting and falling. It melts me as surely as a flame melts a candle. My flesh cries out and for the first time I hear its call. I do all I can to draw closer to its promise, pulling the pelt firmly between my thighs. The fox rubs me, teases me, smoothes me, tempts my body into flight. My legs quake like those of a foal wet from the belly of its dam, knees knocking together. I never tasted anything so wonderful, so strange.

Yet it is not enough.

However tightly I grip the fur, however loud I pant in the race towards my own body, I fall short. Completion dangles out of reach from my groping fingers and I am left empty.

VIXEN

I'll not stay in this village a moment longer than I must.

But I have scrapes to heal, a belly to fill and their money to lay my fingers upon. I see clear enough how things are between her and the priest and my task is to reason out how to use that knowledge to my best advantage. So I hold up my paws, loll my tongue, and act the goat. Dear God and all the saints, how it chafes. It is the same every day, and I wonder that neither of them are driven out of their meagre wits with the tedium of it. Time passes and I itch with the desire to go, the present need to stay.

He blesses me so often I am surprised that angels do not fly out of my arse. At first I'm happy enough to trot behind him, for all priests are rich and he must have a barrel of coins squirrelled away somewhere. I can sniff out gold like a dog can sniff out meat. Or so I think. While he's away in the church whining for God's attention, I hop about, peering into every hole I can find. I might as well use the time to pick my nose. He keeps nothing of use or value under his roof.

But I have eyes, and soon enough I see that she knows far more than she lets on. She gets as tired of his blether as I do and sends him scuttling off, only then letting out the laugh she has been hiding.

'Don't pay any mind to that fool,' she says. Her smile does not live on her lips more than a moment. 'Listen to me,' she sighs. 'Calling him the simpleton, when it is topsy-turvy.'

I roll my eyes. She is prone to prattling, but I prefer it to his incessant holiness.

'I thought I was so clever,' she continues, twirling the spindle.

She is spinning wool and a poor job she is making of it too, for the yarn breaks every other moment and she must start again.

'Imagine, that, my chick? Even you, mud-brained as you are, can see that I'm the most wooden-headed of women. What a choice I made in this man!'

She laughs again. It is a sound that has been plucked naked. The yarn snaps and she sighs.

'Look at me. I ended up with a skinned reed of a fellow who keeps a meaner table than a beggar. I sleep on a straw mattress the mare would turn her nose up at. I spin wool that is more knots than good thread. That's the tale of silly Anne.'

She hurls the spindle to one side, claps her hands, chanting *silly Anne, silly Anne*. I slap my knees and honk like a goose. She tickles me under the chin.

'My little bird. You make this dried-up pullet merry. We make a fine pair; silly Anne and silly Maid.'

I point my fingers at my open mouth, mewing piteously, and finally she leaves off her cooing.

'You're hungry? Bide there and I'll fetch something good to eat. Or what passes for good under this roof.'

She bustles away. I sigh and stretch my cramped legs. All this lurching about bent over like a hunchback is making me ache. I wager she'll bring back a bowl of gruel. Not that it's bad – it's hot and I've eaten far worse – but my belly groans for a bit of meat. The salt pig hanging from the roof beam is driving me to thoughts of climbing the wall and biting off a chunk or two. I'd even eat a plate of eggs, though the thought of anything out of a bird's backside still turns my stomach.

She returns all smiles. I contort my body into its twisted shape and not for the first time curse myself for choosing such an uncomfortable disguise. Not that I had much time to think up anything better. She pokes porridge into my mouth and I slurp each spoonful. I wonder if I could trust her. If she was in on my deception, I could tuck into a trencher heaped with bacon and gravy. The thought makes me groan, and she peers at me closely.

'Gulping it down too hastily, are you? Slow down.'

I do just that. I'll not let my belly be my god. You can't trust these people, even when you think you've got them round to your way of thinking. You imagine you're safe, then bang: middle of the night you're running for your life with all the hue and cry of a village at your back. Not again. A kind hand makes a fist in a moment; a kiss is waiting to turn into a bite.

Yet all I have from this woman is affection. It is a trick; it must be. Her caresses are to make me lower my guard. She is waiting for me to slip up. There is no other reason for such sweetness.

When I see him strike her, I feel – pity? Anger? I know not what, except that I feel and I hate it. I've seen hundreds of men raise their fists at hundreds of women and have not even blinked. I have no idea why this small beating should affect me, but it does. How dare she do this to me? How dare she slip under my walls so? I must get away. Money or no money, I must be gone.

It's time. I've let her feed me up a bit. My bruises have healed. I've strangled all I can out of these pullets. This is a priest's house, and if the best household in this flea-ridden hole offers nothing better than a dish of lentils, then there's no point looking anywhere lower. I steal a cloak, a tunic, and pull on a pair of hose besides. I learned many years ago that a lad travels this world safer than a lass.

I race to the forest with a clean pair of heels, my shirt stuffed with bread and cheese. I left money, clothes and a good knife in my comfortable tree. Not much, but enough to carry me as far as the next purse I can cut from some man's belt. I must head westwards, along with everyone else who has a mind to living, and that costs money.

Each step I take away from the village and towards the forest weighs less. At the head of the path, just before it climbs past the well and into the trees proper, I turn about and see where I've come from: the squat cottages thatched with sodden reeds; the squelching filth between them; the church, graceless as a toppled cow. The priest's house might be grander than the huts surrounding it, but it is still a yokel dwelling for a yokel priest of a yokel flock. I think of the woman, her milk-whey face simpering. She does not matter, no one ever has. The day I respond kindly to kindness is the day hell freezes over so hard the Devil himself can go skating.

I spit on the ground.

I slide into the forest and feel her shield me. I am grateful as a boy falling into the arms of his lover. I breathe in her scent and she sparkles in my lungs, heady as a draught of powerful cider. Hoof-prints of sheep the size of stars light my way, coupled with the two half-moons of goats, dwindling as I press deeper into her shadow. Birches embrace me with their clean white limbs; even the oaks bend creaking backs to brush my hair as I pass. A crow hops ahead, tempting me from the path. When I grow tired of its misleadings, I shoo it away. It flaps

131

awkward wings, flies into the branches of the nearest tree and glares.

'Don't think to fool me twice, you blackguard,' I shout, and laugh.

I find myself skipping, and only reel in my giddiness when I come upon my particular tree. I scramble up the trunk. It is empty.

I know the scabby hands of thieves when I see them, being acquainted with thievery myself. I slide back down and sit at the root, considering my next step. No money, no clothing other than what I have on my back. Everything is gone and I have nothing. I can go on and starve, or return to the village and run the risk of bumping into Death. It takes far longer than it should to reach a decision.

It is only while I am berating my lack of choices that I hear them. A deaf man could do so, for they are making such a commotion: singing, crying out to each other; that and the smell of roasting venison and the tangy smoke of their fire. No attempt to hide themselves; no skulking from the Sheriff and a swift kick and dangle from the nearest oak.

They're as filthy as ever: hands and faces greenish black with ground-in dirt, their clothes of a matching hue so that they look like earth-men, shaped of the heavy clay they lounge upon. They might have a doe fat enough to feed four families roasting in their midst, but their belts are notched tight and their faces betray long famishment. They gobble the meat, tearing it off the bone and cramming it into their maws as though they fear someone will take it away from them.

I saunter to the fire boldly, as though I belong there. One man begins to rise, but is pulled back. I see the glint of blades drawn. The only sound is the crackle of deer fat dropping into the flames; that and my thundering breath. I tear away a small

132

piece of the meat and shove it into my mouth. It is tough, for the idiots do everything too hard and too fast, but I nod my head and hum with appreciation.

'My compliments, gentlemen. You keep a good table,' I say.

I must not look at them too closely, or they will read my fear and that will never do. I place one hand on my hip and suck grease from the fingers of the other. A laugh rumbles from somewhere to my left.

'Good day to you, young sir.'

I turn slowly in the direction of the voice. A tall man, his beard twisted with red ribbon into a stiff horn that sticks out from the end of his chin. It's him, of course, and the less said about him the better. I smile companionably and sweep away my hood. They'll find me out sooner or later and this way I am the author of my own revealing. They're at my throat in an eye-blink, waving knives under my nose and growling all kinds of imprecations. I affect an air of boredom. It is the best part I have ever played, for I swear my bowels are water.

'You little bitch,' roars Knot-Beard. 'I swore if I ever saw you again I'd split you down the midparts like an apple.'

'With good reason,' I say, and incline my head. 'I left certain debts.'

He shoves the point of his weapon into the coat and I am glad of its thick folds.

'I'm going to kill you,' he grunts.

'Then how shall I pay you what I owe?' I sigh, being mindful to skate away from the ice of sarcasm. That would not be a wise move with a skewer between my breasts.

'I'll take it out of your liver and lights,' he grimaces, hoping to frighten me, which he does not. He is far more terrifying when he does not try.

'Wouldn't you rather have gold?' I enquire.

133

The pressure of the knifepoint eases a very small amount.

'You, cough up money?' he cries. 'You never handed out a penny unless you were strung up by your ankles.'

His companions snicker at the engaging picture this presents. I spread my hands to take in their camp. I smile also. It seems polite.

'You're bold enough to roast a deer within a bowshot of a village. I'm bold enough to pay a visit and settle old business. These are interesting times.'

Knot-Beard withdraws the knife a quarter-inch and slackens his grasp enough for me to see the handle and recognise it for the one I stowed in the tree. I nod towards it.

'Besides, I'd say from that knife that you found my belongings. Let us call it a small down payment against the settlement of what is owed.'

'Or let us not,' he replies. 'What's to stop me gutting you now and nailing your hide to that tree?'

'Nothing,' I shrug. 'Then you'd have the shabby cloak off my back and not one whit more.'

'I'll have the bird in my hand.'

'Maybe I can bring you two in the bush.'

'Why should I trust you?' he drawls. He squints his eyes half-shut, as men do when they wish to show themselves sharp-witted. To my mind it looks more like they are straining to void their bowels.

'No reason. Save these are changed times.'

'And?'

'And I need to get through the forest. Safely.'

'Which will cost you dear.'

'I'm sure it will.'

He sheaths the knife in his belt and I breathe more easily. I take off the cloak and hand it over. It may be undyed murrey, but it is a great deal cleaner than anything they've seen this side of Candlemas. In his vast paws it looks particularly threadbare. I'm about to remove my hose, when he stops me with a laugh.

'You can keep your arse covered. I've no desire for a skinny rump like yours. I like my women shapely.'

He waggles his hands in a memory of curved hips and bulging breasts and his followers take up the game, slapping their thighs and cackling obscenities. For all the bluster, it's a long time since anyone here tasted a woman and when it's dark there'll be a lot going on behind these trees. I'll wager they've all felt Knot-Beard's bristles tickle them between the shoulder blades.

'What else have you got to offer?' he guffaws when he's finished.

I think of the rubbish in the house: pots, pans, her straw mattress, his prayer book and cross. No use unless you live under a roof. And I can't see these men taking up holiness any time soon. There's no point promising them church treasure I can't lay my hands on. I squeaked through on falsehoods with these men the once: I'll not be that lucky again.

The answer comes so clear and bright it is as though the branches draw back their curtain to let the sun shine in. In my head I see them taking each other to satisfy lust. The silence they keep, the shame they feel.

'I have a gift of unusual and unexpected value,' I say.

He snorts disbelievingly.

'A woman,' I say, and let the word rest awhile. 'Pretty, too. She'll come willingly.'

'Some hobbling old crone,' cackles Knot-Beard, but his eyes are bright.

'You can test the truth of it for yourself,' I reply, casually. 'But this I declare: she's ripe, she's young and she's a virgin.' The knob of his Adam's apple bobs up and down. 'When did you last have one of those? Take me to the coast and she's yours.'

135

'Bring her,' he croaks. 'And some money. Then we'll see.'

I walk away with the heat of their eyes branding holes in my tunic. I have never been one to return to a place I have left, and I want to go back to the priest's rat-hole less than any. But with Knot-Beard barring the way forward, I have no choice.

Perhaps I shan't have to give Anne to them. Perhaps it won't come to that. But if it does, so be it. I could coax her here with no trouble, for she follows wherever I lead, like a lamb after its dam. Besides, she'd do the same to me. Many have done, all smiles and then a change like the weather: sunny, then rain with plenty of hailstones thrown in for good measure. She is like the others. Or would be, if I granted her the smallest opportunity. Which of course I shall not.

Yet she is the only one in this crippled world to have dealt with me fairly. A chill settles upon me, greater than the fear of Knot-Beard and his men. A rushing of waters begins to roar between my ears; green stars dance behind my eyelids. I stagger, lose my footing and fall to my knees. Rooks rattle their beaks, and in that sound I hear an old friend clattering His jaws.

'That's my girl,' he chuckles. 'You only sell the good ones, and so cheap.'

My stomach rocks like a kicked gate and I hurl its contents on to the path, spewing until I can do so no more.

I will not let myself be tangled in her sticky net. It will hold me back, hold me down, hold me under until the bubbles cease to rise. I shall get my blow in first. That'll teach her to show me kindness. I can't be trusted. I am cruel. I shall not soften, not for her, not for anyone. If I soften, I am lost. She shall not be my undoing. I shall stay hard and harsh, and live.

TERCE
1349

From Saint Swithun to Saint Neot

THOMAS OF UPCOTE

'This is the House of God,' I declared, pushing open the south door and shaking the water from my shoulders.

I held out my hand to the girl, but she hunched her wrists into her chest. I was not concerned: it was fitting that a maiden should shrink from a man's touch. It would be different when she learnt the depth of my chastity. I walked down the nave and heard her feet slap the flagstones behind me.

'This is the font,' I said, and was seized with a fine idea.

However often I said a blessing over her head, nothing seemed to bring her any closer to the Lord. But if I baptised her, the holy water was bound to soak into her soul and lighten her load of witlessness. I did not know why I had not thought of it before. I smiled and winched up the cover: the bowl was full. The water threw my face at me; her features swam alongside as she peered over my shoulder. I plunged my hand within, lifted it over her head.

'I baptise you,' I boomed, 'in the name of the Father, the Son, and the Holy Ghost.'

At first I feared she might bolt, but she licked at the liquid trickling down her face, uttering small exclamations of surprise. I dipped my hand once more, and sprinkled her a second time.

'The blessing of God be upon you,' I roared. 'May He bless you and keep you.'

I trembled, awaiting a sign from the Lord. She could make sounds. All that was needed was to shape those sounds into words. Surely I would be the one to do it. With God's grace. Today might be the day when the light of comprehension broke through the darkness swamping her mind. I snapped my fingers and she looked at them, drooling slightly. I pointed to myself.

'I am Father Thomas,' I said. 'I am a man of God. A priest. Thomas. Yes?'

Her eyes danced about the roof-beams. I would not be dismayed so easily. I clicked my fingers again.

'Now, listen,' I said, with firm intent. 'Thomas.' I slapped my chest. 'Say it. Thomas. You have heard it over and over.'

She gulped a great throatful of air, and threw it at me in a rough bark. It was as though the noise came from a great distance and she was in fear of it, for she started back and looked about her, wondering whence came the racket. I sighed and made my way to the altar to say the Office. It was not much of a miracle, but it would have to do. She followed me into the chancel, her feet leaving damp prints on the steps.

'This is the altar,' I said, for perhaps the presence of the Lord would awaken this beast. 'Here I bless the bread and it becomes the body of our Saviour Jesus Christ, who died for our sins. Bread? Bread?'

I pointed to my mouth, chewing the air, for all men understand what it is to eat. I rubbed at my stomach, shoving it out through my cassock. She tipped her head to one side, features smooth.

'And this is the shrine,' I continued, feeling a little embarrassed at my antics. 'Here lies the body of Saint Brannoc. He worked many miracles. He made animals lay aside their savage way of life. His wolf became a man.'

You could do that, also. If God willed it.

My words were silent, but she cocked her eyebrow so knowingly it was as though I spoke aloud. Heat bloomed in my face as we stared at each other, man to beast.

The light slanting through the east window stippled her with colour, but it could not hide the plumage of scratches feathering her arms and legs. Who knew what malice she had suffered. She would know no cruelty in my house, I thought, most determinedly. I left her in contemplation of the shrine and stood at the altar, where I said the Office of Sext.

I thought of the scars upon my own flesh from my father and brothers, the injuries left by the clerks at Exeter that no man knew of but myself. I had survived all of that, and worse. I had been born into famine, watched the wasting of my little sister. Mother would take the baby upon her knee, holding its tiny paw and shaking it up and down, whispering. The arm hung like a strip of unbaked dough, the wizened fingers swallowed up in my mother's fist.

She took a long time to die: such is the way of slow starvation. She squalled at first, as we all did, confused by the lack of food in her belly and being too young to understand. My mother pressed her breast against the tiny mouth, watched it gape, too exhausted to suck. She would never stop crying; that small noise you get when you squeeze a kitten about its throat.

My brothers and I were sent into the woods to hunt for food. I picked amongst the beech mast to find scraps of nuts left behind by others, for we were not the only ones searching. I chewed shelves of fungus from trees, plucked snails from under stones, berries from hedges. Devoured all of it, swore to my father I could find nothing, pinched myself to make tears come.

It was filth and creeping stuff in my belly, but it was something like fullness. Each night we ate grass boiled into gruel. I did not die.

Still my sister mewed. My mother tried to spoon some porridge into her mouth, but she swung her head from side to side, fists clenched, eyes spitting tears. I had not eaten anything that wholesome for as long as I could recall.

'I will eat it, Mother,' I said, 'if she does not want it.'

My mother struck me on the side of my face with the spoon. I felt blood settle about my cheekbone. A smear of oatmeal lay across my face and I wiped it carefully away, licked my fingers. I can still recall the sweetness.

Mother placed her back against me. I pressed myself into the wall, but did not leave. The hearth smoked. The pot sat at its edge. Mother rocked backwards and forwards, groaning like an old door. I wanted to ask why my sister would not eat when we were all so hungry; wanted to know why there was no food; when food was coming; why father was so angry. But I was already six years old and had learned that the answer would be another beating. I stayed silent.

I took a step towards the pot. The rushes under my bare feet were soft and made no sound. The rocking continued; forwards, back. I took another step and felt my face flare, although I was not close to the fire. I could smell the simmering oats: it was the savour of kindness, of nestling in the crook of my mother's arm, the memory of her kissing me, singing *lullay* and kissing me again.

These days she was angry all the time. Any fear was smacked aside by my hunger. Not caring if I made a noise, I stuck my hand inside the pot, swept up a palmful of porridge and sucked it into my mouth. Mother did not turn around. I stole another. I ate this more slowly, letting myself delight in the taste. I sucked my fingers clean and drew them out with a pop. I froze. My mother continued to rock the baby, keening softly, unable to hear me.

I took more, feeling it warm my gullet, reaching deep into my centre. I peered into the pot. There was very little left. My mother might forget how much was there, but she would remember there was something. I must not empty it. I paused, staring at the pale glister at the bottom, then at my mother's swaying bulk. I dropped my hand and scooped out the last of the gruel. It would be worth any amount of thrashing not to be hungry. I was warm inside and out, my right hand pink from its labour. I closed my eyes and belched.

My father flogged me first; then my brothers took their turn. Mother cheered them on. I was able to stand upright again by the time my sister died. Mother would not leave the grave and I was sent to find her there.

'Mother, you still have me,' I said.

She stood up and came back to the house, hands tucked into her armpits. I held onto the side of her skirt, rubbing the fabric between my thumb and forefinger, and sniffing the musk of the lap where I was no longer allowed to sit. When I was seven they gave me to the clerks in Exeter. I was now a man.

The Office was over, and I realised I could not recall one word I had said. It did not matter, for the girl had noticed nothing amiss. She was rattling the door to the inmost part of the shrine, grunting with frustration as if she wanted to break into it. Perhaps she was nothing but an idiot abandoned by its mother. I did not want to believe that. God had sent the storm. Surely He sent her also.

'You are no demon,' I roared, loud enough for God to hear

and take note. 'You are a daughter of Eve.' She screwed up her nose and sneezed. 'You do not understand what I am saying, but it matters not. If you are a sign from God, and I believe you are, then must I find out why you have been sent to me. To us.'

She raised her eyebrow once more. Then she was off, galloping out of the south door.

There was something in this child to read of God's glory. She had to be part of God's plan and vouchsafed to my safe-keeping. Yet despite my confident declarations, my soul remained perturbed. If the Lord had delivered this child into my keeping, then why could my wits not find out the godly part of her? I must not fail Him, and refuse to learn His lesson. I would learn from her. God would teach me. I knelt and locked my hands together.

'Oh Lord,' I prayed. 'Cast away all doubt. Guide me aright with this girl. Lead me.'

I laid my face against the flank of the shrine and as I breathed my prayer into the stone, the stone breathed back. I stopped, and it stopped. I breathed again, felt holy air brush my cheek. My flesh shivered. At last, I was answered: God was with me. A breeze began to stir the carved leaves and branches, setting all into a quiver like true greenery. From a great way off I could hear the piping of birds.

Out of this heavenly forest the girl came towards me, light dancing about her head like the wavering of air above a pot of seething water. Through her flesh her bones blazed with gold.

I am what you seek, she hissed into my ear, and I knew she was the answer to all the questions I had dared ask God. She touched me and my limbs swelled with divine fire, peeling away gross humanity. She pushed her hand into my belly and stirred me, faster and faster until I churned into buttermilk.

144

I will be your beast made tame. Your wolf made miraculously into man. Just like the Saint himself.

'Oh Lord!' I panted. 'Oh, Holy Maid, yes!'

I returned to myself gasping. It was true: the Lord had sent her to this place, at this hour of need. I saw His light about her. This, then, was God's message: if we took this rough creature to our hearts, we would be spared the scourge of the pestilence. Just like the Saint himself, she was come to preserve, to heal, to lead us back like lambs into God's fold. Only a fool could not see it and I had been that fool, until now.

'I crave pardon, Lord, that I did not perceive Your glorious gift straight away,' I cried.

I knew I was forgiven. The vision was proof. Throughout my life, God had tested me, and sorely too. Now I was rewarded and it tasted sweet, far sweeter than any earthly honey. I alone would guard the child's holiness. I was chosen: she was to be my relic, my creature, my possession.

I carried the flame of my revelation out of the church. Rather than go directly to the house, as was my habit, I felt the Lord guide my feet past the stable. I paused at the door. I did not hear God's voice telling me to be away, so I stepped inside, balancing on the tips of my toes. The Maid lay stretched out beside the mare. I prayed again, and God bade me approach.

'You are safe with me,' I said. 'You are my miracle. None shall harm you.'

Although I spoke very softly, she raised her head at the sound and grunted. I knew she wanted me to stand some way off. I obeyed.

'God sent you,' I breathed. 'A miracle to preserve us when we most need it. He has revealed this to me, for I am a man of God.'

She stretched out her arms and legs and yawned. Then she

145

stood and slid her arms about the mare's neck and licked the nap of its nose, nibbling at the long whiskers. Its nostrils gawped. I feared she would be bitten, for the animal was contrary; but it shook its spit-stringy muzzle and they whinnied together in pleasure. The girl rubbed the mare from front to back, and back to belly; tickled the fur within its ears, all the time humming a wordless lullaby. The black square at the heart of the mare's eye gaped and clenched, and it swung its head to and fro.

The girl continued, fisting its belly and sniffing the sour-bread reek of the beast's breath. The mare swayed, slowly turned its backside to me and raised its tail, showing the velvet twist of its arse. The Maid placed herself between its legs: I worried afresh that she would be kicked. The flanks quivered, and it commenced pissing. The girl crouched in the thunderous flow; rubbing herself from wrist to shoulder, unpeeling her soaking shift and waving it like a flag. She sopped her head, washing her armpits, belly, thighs; all the time hopping from foot to foot.

At last the mare twitched shut and the downpour ceased. Its head drooped slowly into a drowse. The Maid threw her shift over a roof-beam; drops from it punctuated the dirt. She stood before me naked. I watched, unable to move. She smiled, fists on her scrawny hips and shoved out her chest. I could see the buds of breasts beginning to show themselves. I should leave, but God would not permit it.

She cocked her leg and showed me the place between her legs. Even in this I told myself that the Lord was revealing more of His wonders, for she was not like common women, rank with estuary smell and slack breasts after child after child has taken suck. The Maid was clean and whole, smooth as a piece of pork fat, her slit the shallowest of knife cuts.

146

I swallowed, loudly. She let out a series of harsh coughs that might have been laughter. Then she shook herself, turned on the earth in three small circles, curled up beneath the horse, and closed her eyes. I left, my feet staggering all the way back to the house. She could not have been laughing. Blessed creatures sent by God do not laugh.

I went directly to the solar, fell to my knees before the Cross, and prayed again. Was she godly or godless? She seemed entirely animal. But God had vouchsafed her to me, so this could not be so. My vision happened in the church so it must have been from God. Surely it was not the work of the Tempter. Yet I had looked at her naked flesh; I had not looked away. But God prompted me to observe: it could not have been lasciviousness on my part. I quaked at these doubts. My chest was a barrel of fish pulled freshly from the sea. I felt my faith waver. No. This way of thinking would not do. This was between God and myself. I did not need to tell anyone what I had seen. My belief in the Maid would prevail.

The next morning, I was calmer. Since we had fished her from the marshes, her only human company had been myself, and of course Anne and her gossips. She should be with maids her own age. That would coax her out of animal darkness and into the light of humanity. My soul breathed relief.

The next morning after Terce, when I reasoned that the morning chores would be completed, I called on some half-dozen cottages I knew to have daughters of a right age. They came willingly enough when I said it was not for any labour that I wanted them, but for play; and I smiled at the brood of maids that followed me to my orchard.

They were much alike, in that way of unmarried girls; hair

bothered with ribbons, and giggling at every second word I spoke. I clapped my hands as we walked, and sang *Maris stella*. They laughed to begin with, but noticed that they soon joined in the refrain. A grey sky washed over the meadow, and the grass was pearled with daisies. I prayed earnestly it might not rain.

'Here,' I said. 'See what I have for us.'

I waggled the fingers of my right hand while my left dug into my shirt and drew out a rag-ball of twisted scraps from one of Father Hugo's discarded vestments. I tossed it skywards, heard their breath catch as the gold thread sparkled.

'It is pretty, is it not?'

'It is, Father,' said the boldest.

I threw the ball to her and she caught it neatly. Our faces bloomed with smiles. They were nimble, and devised many clever ways of throwing high and low, with handclaps, and hopping on one foot or the other, and never dropping the ball. I made a valiant attempt to copy them, but I was a poor pupil and the source of much merriment. I cared not, for Christ instructed men to become like children to enter His Kingdom.

'Wait,' I said, after a few rounds. 'I shall return right quickly.'

I ran to seek out the girl. She was in the stable, scooping at the dirt with the flat of her hand and examining the sweepings very carefully.

'Come,' I panted. 'I have a more pleasurable pastime for you.'

She blinked, lifted one side of her mouth into a half-smile, but raised herself from her haunches when I pointed out of the door. The girls stared as we came through the gate; the ball fell.

'See, I have a new friend for you,' I smiled. 'She would like to play.'

She twisted up the hem of her shift, revealing bony knees.

One of the girls gasped, another hid her mouth behind her hand. I picked up the ball and threw it gently to the nearest lass. She clutched it; casting her eyes about as if unsure what to do.

'Come now,' I said. 'Throw it. You were clever enough before.'

The ball passed slowly around the circle until it came to my girl. She made no attempt to catch it and it rolled between her ankles.

'Let us try another game,' I piped, trying to remember any.

I undid my hood and pulled it up and down over my eyes, playing *I can see you* until I had coaxed them back into cheerfulness.

'Ah, yes,' I said. 'That is better. Let us play hoodman blind. It is merry. And simple.'

I shoved my hood over the head of the nearest. She squealed at first, but did not cast it off. She staggered about, hands patting the air before her, laughing at each tree she came up against, each pinch her companions dealt her.

The Maid did not stir, watching them as a cat observes chicks. Soon she would understand our pleasure and join in. At last the blindfolded lass stumbled into her and held on to her arm, squeezing hard.

'I have you!' she squeaked.

The girl sprang back, slapping at the small hand.

'No! You shan't escape me! It's your turn now!' her captor laughed, dragging off the hood.

It happened quickly. The Maid's jaws opened, clamped about the girl's wrist and stayed there. Suddenly everyone was shrieking and squalling; battering her with their small fists, calling her *vixen* and *beast* and all manner of cruel names. She unlocked her teeth and began to howl, clawing and kicking against the assault.

149

'Stop,' I said. 'Now. This is unseemly.'

There was the crack of tearing linen, and blood sprang up across my girl's cheek.

'Stop!' I roared.

They did not hear me. Then Anne was at my side, quick as if she had formed out of the air. She hurled the girls aside.

'Get away from her,' she growled. 'Go. Before I show you the meaning of a beating.'

She flourished my staff at them. The Maid hawked noisily and spat, then lifted her leg and aimed a stream of piss at her attackers. They melted away until the orchard was empty save for the three of us.

'What were you doing?' Anne barked.

'The Maid should have companions.'

'And fine ones you chose. Look at her.'

The Maid dug into Anne's skirts, grizzling.

'They were foolish,' I said. 'They did not understand.'

'They were foolish? Girls have a right to be so. Priests do not.' Her breathing slowed. 'Here is your stick. Sir.'

She took the Maid, and left me in the orchard. I searched for the ball, but one of the lasses must have taken it. I noticed that the storm had blown away a lot of the blossom. There would be little fruit this year.

I returned to the house on my own. I was not to blame for this: if I erred, it was to expect wisdom from young females. I should have known better. Woman is the seat of unreason, unwilling or unable to perceive godliness even when it is as clear as the sun at midday. I would not be turned aside so easily. No more games. The Word of the Lord would establish the Maid in the minds of the villagers. I knew what must be done.

* * *

150

'We must have a procession of the holy relics,' I said to Anne the next morning. 'And the play of the Saint's Miracles. With the Maid. To show the people she is sent from God, and must not be harmed.'

'Yes, sir,' she said meekly. 'I shall prepare her.'

'I can do that.'

'You have many duties, sir. There is the church to make ready. The men to carry the Saint's bones. The costumes to prepare. Edwin must ring the bell.'

By the time I was returned, Anne had cozened the girl into a fine dress. She glowed within the crisp cleanliness of the linen, and I hoped she would not take it upon herself to roll in the dirt before I presented her to my flock.

'We are ready, sir.'

'Then we will go to the church. I will take the Cross.'

I led the way around the bounds of the village, announcing the play and the procession as we went. The cottages emptied out their store of human souls, men ran from the plough. All the world followed me, and I delighted in it. By the time we trod the track back to the church, the whole congregation was gathered there, bustling in and out of the churchyard, chattering excitedly.

'We are to have a play!'

'The Saint is coming out of his house.'

'Surely that is earlier in the year?'

'No! This is a special celebration!'

They were very merry and it cheered my soul to see them so, until it occurred to me they were far more interested in dusting off the players' outfits, dressing up and smearing grease all over their faces than engaging in sober meditation upon the miracles of Saint Brannoc. I strove not to chide them, and dedicated an hour to drawing them back to more devout prayer and contemplation. It was like trying to fold cider.

151

It took me from Prime to Sext to gather together sufficient men to carry and boys to sing, for they all declared they would prefer to take one of the parts in the play. In the end I persuaded enough. I gladdened to see them dressed neatly in their cottas and copes, so much more becoming than the rustic pomp of the costumes. I took every taper out of the treasury and found hands to bear them; commanded Edwin to ring the bell to announce the beginning of the procession.

I unlocked the heart of the shrine, and bade the men haul out the iron coffer containing the sacred bones. *Help me, Holy Brannoc,* I prayed. *With God's grace, send me the strength I need.* They mounted him on his oaken sledge, hefting it onto their shoulders and bore him, staggering, down the nave.

'Careful, he is sliding off!' I cried. 'Lift up the back there.'

After the time it would take to say the Pater Noster, he was steady, and the boys swung the censers without spilling very much incense. I raised the Cross and led the way with Anne directly behind me, the girl hanging onto her hand. We came out of the west door and I led the way through the mob, smiling. Their twittering washed its tide against my ears.

'See! The Saint!'

'And there's that wild maid, pulled from the marshes.'

'The Saint, yes: but why the Vixen?'

'We need all the help we can get.'

'I still say she's a gypsy.'

I heard the muttering against her, but would not let it cast me down. Rather, it served to strengthen my resolve to conquer their doubts. God lifted my voice in song; we passed once around the churchyard, entered the church and the folk followed. The men returned the Saint to his dwelling place and I locked the door. The people began to leave, eager to start their play, but I called them back. I raised my hands in prayer and God rushed to fill my mouth as soon as I opened it.

'Who holds the thunderbolt in His hands? Who chooses to cast down the rain, or hold it close? Who sent the storm?'

I waited until I heard them give the correct response, *God.*

'Who protects us?'

God. God protects us.

'Who also? Who?'

The Saint protects us.

'And who sent the girl in the storm?' At this there was a hesitation. I filled the gap. 'God!' I roared. 'Say it again. Who sent us this Maid?'

God. God.

They spoke agreement. Yes. This was God's answer. For the first time my words harnessed them truly, and I was made giddy.

'Will she not also protect us?' Again they paused. I would brook no disobedience. 'Answer the Lord!' I cried. 'Will she protect us?'

Yes, amen. Yes.

God planted fire in my soul: I burned in my desire to honour Him.

'When God sent His only begotten Son amongst men, did He wear satins and fur? Did He feed upon honey-cakes and wine? Did He?'

No, oh God, no.

'No. Christ came amongst fishermen; farmers. Common folk. Like you. Not merchants or kings. And is Christ to be prized?'

Yes, oh yes.

'Were there some who reviled Him? Spat on Him?'

Yes!

'Tore His clothes and beat Him and crucified Him?'

Yes!

'Are they not damned?'

Yes!

'Now God has sent us this Maid. At this time of need.'

There was a flurry of hands as they crossed themselves. I pointed to the shrine where Anne stood, holding on to the girl's wrist. All turned to stare. I prayed she would not run, and God rewarded me yet again.

'He has sent her to humble farmers. She does not wear fine clothes. She eats plain food like you. Must we not prize her?'

Yes, they said, still a little uncertainly for my liking.

'Will we revile her, spit on her?'

They moaned, *No.*

'Let there be no more harm done to this girl. This jewel at our heart. Forgive us now.'

I glared at a clutch of girls by the south door. I was not sure if they were the ones who had attacked my girl, for they looked the same as any young females, but they served my purpose. They dropped their heads, blushing. The people twisted in their direction and hissed.

Forgive us, wailed the girls.

'Bless and forgive us, oh Lord!' I cried, and my flesh sang. 'We must tend her, love her, protect her. Then shall she keep us safe.' I had meant to say, *God shall keep us safe*, but the words spilled out differently. 'When she was pulled from the marshes, she was dirty. But she is not foul. This maid is fresh and innocent. Not a beast. Not a vixen.'

It came to me as I spoke. I would not let them continue to call her Vixen, nor any other beastly name. Nor would I name her, for there was none to give. I would not pen her in with common words. I was not Adam, instructed by his Maker to name all creatures. For Adam fell, and I would not fall. I smiled at my new cleverness.

'She is our Holy Maid,' I cried. 'Let all call her such. God has spoken.'

Amen, amen.

I had said enough. I gave the kiss of peace with a good heart, and said Pax to share with them the joy of God's gift to us. They shouted *Deo gratias* and my heart turned over. My whole body was wet beneath my garments. Outside the church they clasped my hand, one after the other, so much that I thought they would shake it asunder.

'Ah, Father. We shall be safe.'

'Now we have the Vixen,' said another. 'The Maid,' he corrected himself swiftly.

'We are always in God's care,' I replied.

'But especially now, is it not so? With the Great Mortality so close upon us.'

'Death is ever waiting for us,' I replied.

He frowned. 'But never more so than this year.'

'The fever is come to Hartland,' said another.

'The wind blows it up and down the coast.'

'I hear that in Bristol the bodies rot in the streets for lack of men to bury them.'

I shook my head to clear out their bothersome words. 'There is nothing to fear. Do not despair of the Lord. Are we not healthy?'

'Yes, Father.'

'We were nothing,' I cried out, for it seemed I was inside the church again and preaching. I must turn their minds from such dreadful imaginings. 'We were cast down. Now we are raised up. Filled with hope, for God has smiled upon us. This Holy Maid has come to succour us.'

'I hear the Virgin has come to the Staple,' said one fellow with great eagerness.

My words dried up. 'What is this?' I asked.

The man stared at his thumbs. 'I mean no disrespect, Father. All are talking of it. They pulled the Blessed Virgin out of the harbour.'

'Not the Virgin, fool,' said William. 'Her image.'

'Yes,' breathed another. 'The picture painted by Saint Luke, the very one.' He crossed himself, and his fellows did likewise.

'What is this foolishness?' I said.

'It is no foolishness, Father. The storm sent us this Maid; it sent the Virgin to the Staple.'

'She swam up the estuary.'

'Right to the harbour.'

'It is true. I have seen it. Her.' He pulled a scrap of lead from inside his shirt and waved it in my face. Crudely stamped with the face of a woman.

'Do you desert your Saint?' I rumbled.

'I do not.'

'Do you believe the Maid is sent to us by God?'

'You have told us it is so,' he said carefully. 'Then it is so.'

'Yet you take yourself away from your rightful labour and dance to the Staple.'

He lifted his chin. 'I work as hard as any man here, Reverend Father,' he said. 'I am not the only one who has gone.'

'The road is deep with ruts for carts go back and forth in such number.'

'There are miracles already, as I hear it.'

I waved away their buzzing voices.

'Father,' said William. 'We have such need of protection. From wherever we can find it. Against the fever.'

'The fever, the fever. All this clucking about fever. I see no

156

sickness here. Put your faith in the Lord. And the Maid. She will protect us. We need nothing else.'

They bowed, and turned their attention to the play.

Never before had I received any sign that the Lord noticed me. He had always been detained on more important business than the travails of a poor parish priest. I knew myself to be unremarkable before God, and indeed man. I had seen the yawning during my sermons, had heard the emptiness of my prayers. All that was changed. Like Job, God had tried my faith with seeming indifference; now He blessed me with the Maid.

My faith, so tossed about and storm-battered, stood firm and shone its light into my soul. My piety lifted its strong hand, holding back the tide of the pestilence. I would not fail; I could not, with the Maid at my side. The people would love her. They would love me. The Maid was Jonah come out of the whale, Margaret springing from the belly of the dragon, sweet as the honey from Samson's lion. I had won.

ANNE

For once, Thomas is right. His words establish the Maid in the people's hearts, and I pray he can hold her there. The miracle play is a welcome diversion: a rest from toil, and not merely scrubbing and spinning. For an afternoon I forget how dull I am become, how cramped the life that pens me in.

Although I dash from the church, I am too late to join in the carole. Men and maids are holding hands, circling to the left then skipping to the right. Alice stands in the middle, quacking the words and pounding out the rhythm with her foot. Very pleased with herself she looks, too.

Everyone joins in the chorus and I sing also, even though I stand on my own. Bet catches my eye as she swings past and reaches out her hand, breaking the ring for a moment. I grab her with more gratitude than I care to admit and am drawn into the dance. I catch up quickly. It is a simple pleasure of the body to lift my feet, fill my lungs with sharp breath and sing.

I am surrounded by smiling faces, cheery voices in my ears. This is where I belong. I am reminded how easy a thing happiness can be, and how tangled up in misery I have become. I am tired of being so.

Bet is to my right and Michael the miller's son to my left.

He grasps my hand, glances at me long and slow as honey poured out of a pot. I gaze back. He is stripped to his under-tunic, the hair on his chest showing crisp through the slashed neckline. His hose are rolled down to the knee, revealing the hams of his thighs. I wonder if I couldn't have made a better match with him. In faith, I could have made a better match with a barn door.

I shake my head. Today I will not dwell on considerations of what might have been. Still, my desire quivers that he has looked at me. However sinful, I think of Michael's handsome face, his long clean limbs. Even though he is humble, he has two arms to clasp about me, a mouth to gasp my name, and between his legs that thing I burn for.

The dance reaches its end, and it shocks me how swiftly my heart begins to plummet back into unhappiness. But I am saved by a shout going up at the lychgate.

'Prepare the way! The Saint approaches!'

The players stride into the churchyard, the Saint leading his beasts. I glance over at Michael, who has placed himself where I can see him, by the church wall. I wonder how easy it might be for us to slip away to the forest without anyone noticing. I am alone: Thomas is busy bothering God, the Maid with him. Michael tips his chin. It is as though a thread tugs me, for my feet carry me to his side.

'Well, pretty Anne,' he smirks.

'Well, Michael,' I reply.

'Do you remember how I carried you over the ford to the priest's house?' he smirks.

'I do.'

'Remember how you gave me a fair old kick when I pinched your thigh?'

'I do.'

'You wouldn't look at me then. But you're looking at me now, and hungry enough too.'

'Hungry?' I say, but fail to make it sound light and uncaring.

'Yes. And so am I. Let's be about it, then.'

He starts to untie his braies, which show bulging evidence of his haste.

'Here? Against the church wall?' I swat away his groping fingers.

'Why not? You let the priest up there – the Bishop too, for all I know. I'll have a piece of the pudding as well.'

'You will not.'

I slam my heel down upon his foot. He yelps and hops about, the linen drooping off his bare backside. I don't loiter to laugh at the sight, although I'd be merry enough if it wasn't happening to me. I straighten my kerchief, shake out my kirtle and am back in the crowd in less time than it would take to pour a cup of ale. I am sticky with a feeling like wasps crawling over marchpane. I glance about to see if I have been missed, but everyone is applauding the players. My breast is heaving and I watch the play while I wait for my blood to settle.

Roger the blacksmith plays the stag, a fine set of horns upon his head. He rushes into the crowd, roaring at the maids, and the Saint has to call him three times before he bends the knee, receives the yoke on his neck and pulls the plough. It is no mean feat, for the ploughshare is heavy. The ropes in his throat stand out hard and stiff; he grunts with the weight and when he succeeds everyone cheers.

I join in the applause as he drags it around the church, shake off the dirty memory Michael has smeared over me and concentrate on the spectacle. Next, wicked King Magnus steps out of the west door, face painted red, and we boo and hiss and shake our fists at him as he steals the Saint's favourite bull, played by

160

Aline's man James. I know him straightaway, even though his face is blackened with charcoal and he has a cow's hide slung around his shoulders. As he steps into the pot, he makes a pretty speech about how he is not afraid because the Saint will save him.

But the Saint does not come in time, and we gasp when King Magnus chops off the bull's head and blood spurts out. It is only a bunch of scarlet ribbons fluttering on the breeze, but it is most chilling. The smaller children cry, which of course upsets the babies, who bawl with one voice till we are all weeping, one way or another.

The Saint appears! *Too late*, we moan. King Magnus cowers, throwing his sleeve across his face to shield himself from the Saint's stern words. We pelt the king with cabbage stalks until he falls to his knees, wrings his hands and begs the Saint to pray for his soul. He repents all wickedness, thumping his chest with many exclamations of contrition, not to mention telling us to lay off with the cabbages, for they hurt him.

The Saint strides about, rubbing his chin. We shout encouragement and our cries persuade him, for he raises his hands and calls upon God to look down on the sinful king with mercy. There is a rattle of tambours, which sets the babies off again. Even I jump, though I see this play every year and know what is coming. An angel appears, Aline's eldest boy, in a tunic I'll wager his mother washed three times to get it so clean. He speaks his celestial message and almost gets it right. We do not care if he trips over the words, because King Magnus is saved from the pit.

'But what of your bull?' wails King Magnus. 'I have slain him! He is in a hundred pieces!'

At this moment James sets up a fearsome groaning from inside his pot, enough to turn a man's blood to gruel. 'I am murdered!' he moans, in case anyone has forgotten his fate in the excitement of King Magnus's repentance.

We turn our attention to the pot and King Magnus slips away, his part completed. I see him dragging off his crown, which is wood and not the gold it seemed to be. He wipes a cloth over his face, the paint comes away and he is once more William the steward.

The Saint weeps and beats his breast. 'Was this not the most wonderful bull ever known on this earth!' he yells. 'It could spear a barn door with its horns! When it stamped its hooves, trees toppled and fell! Its bellow could tumble walls! Its balls were fat as barley sacks! Its pizzle thick as a tree trunk!'

At this, James can be heard chuckling inside the pot. The Saint gives it a kick to make James shut up but does not have much success, and we join in the mirth. More than one lad throws a hopeful glance at a maid, to receive one in return. I glance in Michael's direction, but he is gone from his spot. After a moment searching the crowd, I spy him beneath the yew with Alice, who is twiddling the end of her braids between her fingers. If I gave her hair a good hard yank, she'd crack her skull against the trunk. As if she can hear my thoughts, she slides a look in my direction and the corner of her mouth lifts in a half-smile.

The drums sound again, there is a mighty squawking of shawms, the Saint calls upon the Lord and James leaps up, restored to life. He bellows so wildly I wonder if the church walls might not crumble a little and fall on Alice's head. They stand firm.

The crowd clap and cheer. The Saint leads us in a prayer that God might bless us now as He did then and a lusty *amen* echoes the sentiment. With that, the play is done. I wander about, thinking how empty the path seems without the Maid trotting alongside, when Mother grabs my hand and hauls me into the lee of the wall.

'I have warned you, girl.'

'What?' I say with true surprise.

'I see you. Making cow's eyes at Michael. And Geoffrey. Anything with two legs and a pintle.'

'Ma!'

'Do not imagine for one minute that you are free to do anything about it.'

'Of course not. How can you think such a thing?'

'I think it very easily, for I know you better than you know yourself.'

'I am a hungry woman, and still a maiden,' I growl. 'Thomas does not come to me as a man should. I told you.'

'Don't presume to chide your mother, girl. I know you when you're thwarted, but you'll not get your way this time. Leave off mooning after the village lads. Or any other, in case you have some wild scheme to skip off to the Staple fair. You got the man you whined for. One is all you get.'

She sweeps away, her gown snapping like a sail in the freshening breeze.

Thomas appears from the west door, hand raised in blessing and extolling the virtues of the Maid, who totters at his side. She stands upright, almost graceful. He has draped her in an altar cloth so white it dazzles the eye. How he managed to make her so biddable I have no idea. I am pierced with a dart of jealousy that she obeys him and not me.

The people gasp, for this is no painted creature from a mummers' play. She raises her arms and the people drop to their knees, hug their caps to their breasts, muttering prayers. All it took was his words in the church and the Maid is suddenly their darling. I wonder at how fast things turn around: not so

163

very long ago they'd have skinned her like a rabbit and been quick about it.

Thomas shoves forward the lasses who teased her. They hang back, eyes puffed up from weeping over who knows how much chastisement. They proffer a posy of milkweed. The Maid takes it, bites the heads off the flowers and spits them in the girls' faces.

That's my Maid, I think.

The people bob around her, waggling their fingers and feeding her scraps of cheese and bread. She squeals hungrily, which serves only to prompt more exclamations of delight at their new treasure. I push through the crowd and their bothersome coddling, grasp the Maid by the hand and start to lead her away. She whines, but I have a firm grip on her paw.

'What are you doing?' asks Alice, who is dangling a piece of bacon fat in front of the Maid's nose.

'She's tired. She needs to rest,' I say, none too politely.

'So say you.'

'Look at her. She doesn't want to go,' adds William.

The Maid moans.

'What a girl wants and what a girl gets are two different things,' I grunt. I tug her hand and she stumbles after me. 'She must learn to honour her elders. The Lord said so to Moses. If it was good enough for him, then it's good enough for her.'

They can't think of a retort to that one, but as I heave her away there's a lot of muttering and none of it complimentary. I even catch the word *whore*, but when I spin round to catch the culprit, they are all wearing innocent expressions. *This is what Margret has to cope with*, I think. *It is not so bad.*

'I hear you,' I growl. 'Don't think I've gone deaf. Whatever you say, God's chosen me to look after her, not you. So you can stick that up your backsides and squeeze tight.'

164

I turn my back on the lot of them, hold my head high and stalk off. The day is done and I am done with it also. There is drizzle in the air and the folk bustle away swiftly, bearing the masks and costumes. Mothers drag their snivelling children homewards, telling them there is no need to make such a fuss; the bull was not dead for long.

I think I'll have to fight to bring the Maid away, but she trots along obediently. If I was given to fancies, which I am not, I'd swear I hear her chuckle.

'Listen to them,' I mutter. 'The miserable bean-splitters. The clapper-heads. The dried-up herring skins.'

So I grumble. I am still seething with bile when I splash through the ford and up the path. Thomas is at the door, looking very pleased with himself. I shove him aside, make straight for the hearth and peer into the pot. There is enough porray to feed the three of us, if I have a small portion. At my shoulder, Thomas sucks his teeth loudly.

'It was a fine show, today.'

'Yes,' I grunt.

'The people take the Maid to their hearts.'

'Hmm,' I mumble, dividing the food as carefully as I can.

He would gobble the lot if he had half the chance, and then look surprised if I pointed out that the Maid and I had empty bowls. I don't know why he is such a spindle-shanks, the amount he shoves down his gullet.

'I said, the Maid—'

'I heard you. Isn't it time to say the Office? God wants to listen to you; I do not,' I snap, far too quickly and far too rudely.

His eyes blaze, and I wait for the clout I know is to come, for he has already balled his hand into a fist and raised it above his head. It is the only part of him he does get up with any regularity, I think sourly, and place my arms over my head in their accustomed position, ready to shield myself from the pummelling.

'How dare you speak to me thus?' he starts. 'A man picked out by God?'

His voice is shrill, the song one that I have heard many times before. I know the tune so well that I can time with perfect precision exactly when and where the blows will fall, how they will grow in intensity from waspish slapping to the climax of kicking. I know how much pain to express: too much excites him to greater efforts and too little makes him go on for longer.

I play my part, groaning where I must make a sound, and biting my lip where I must not. The whole while our dance is accompanied by his chorus of sayings from this saint or that saint, on and on. I am set for it to continue as usual when an unfamiliar sound joins Thomas's ranting about the disobedience of women.

Thomas leaves off his sermon and looks in the direction of the interruption. The Maid is perched on the hearthstone, chin pointing at the roof-beam, mouth wide open and making the stretched-out howling of a faithful dog that finds its master slain by bandits. The sound rings in my ears, bounces off the walls, swells the room to bursting.

'Ah-oo!' she whines.

I am astonished that such a piercing sound can emerge from such a small frame. By the look on his face, Thomas is equally stunned. And worried. His eyes dart towards the door. It is closed, but I know what he is thinking. He is not worried about passers-by hearing my cries, but the Maid? If the villagers think he is mistreating the miraculous gift of the Saint – for that is how he has placed her in their minds – it would not be such a simple matter to explain away.

'Quiet!' he hisses.

'Ah-oo!' she yowls, even more disconsolately.

'Obey me!'

At this, she tosses her head back and shrieks so loudly I do not know whether to ram my fingers in my ears or join in with the yowling. Her screams curdle my brains. It is impossible to think, impossible to escape the racket.

'The woman is disobedient!' he whines and I almost laugh at his petulance. 'She must be punished. It is God's law.'

The Maid snorts, spraying snot over his boots. He takes a step in my direction, ignoring the noises bubbling up from the girl's throat.

'Don't hurt me, sir,' I whimper, making my voice piteous.

He draws back his foot and I curl my knees to my chin in case he should take it upon himself to kick me in the stomach. The Maid howls. He lowers his foot, and the moment he does so she stops, panting happily, tongue hanging out of her mouth and glistening with moisture. He lifts his foot and she starts to shriek once more. It is like the miracle play, and as much of a wonder to observe.

'You cannot stop me!' he shouts.

Very slowly, I get to my feet. I ache, but only a little, for the Maid brought an end to this beating before it truly began. I look at her; she looks at me. Thomas's gaze flits between the two of us, unable to settle, unable to decide what to do.

The Maid sidles across the floor, clutches a handful of my skirt and hangs on with furious determination. She opens her mouth wide and I think she is about to vomit, for she retches like a cat trying to spew up a fur-ball. She screws up her brows, shaping and unshaping her lips. Eventually, after much gagging, she lets out a bark, loud as a clap of thunder.

'Good!'

As she speaks, she thumps my thigh with great enthusiasm.

The word sounds a little like *goot*, but I hear it and so does Thomas.

'Good?' he says, all disbelief. 'Did she call *you* good?'

For answer, she strokes the rough weave of my skirt, turning adoring eyes to my face in case he should be in any doubt as to her meaning.

'It is her first word,' I say. 'Perhaps she is not so unreachable after all.'

Thomas frowns. I watch the creaking wheel of his thoughts turn in a most unwilling revolution, seeking out the many reasons why I am not good. Before he can discover them, the sound of the church bell reaches us.

'Why, sir,' I say. 'It is time for the Divine Office. Edwin is there before you.'

He scowls, and I see how dearly he would like to tell me I am mistaken. But there is no time, and I am right. He is away quickly. I watch him grow smaller as he disappears down the path to the church. I know he will find some excuse to call me worthless and deceitful and strike me again. No doubt I will give him good reason, for I have run out of the patience it takes to speak to him courteously.

The Maid gawps at me, huffing and puffing in that puppy-like way of hers.

'So,' I remark. 'I am good, am I?'

She smiles. Not in the halfwitted way I have observed till now. Her eyes are clear, and for that moment she is no more a fool than I am. I tell myself it is nothing, but struggle to believe my own counsel. I have glimpsed this before.

By the Saint, I am not good. My bodily desire grows until it is fit to burst out of me. I am wakened and there is no chance of sleep. My mother is right: I ache to quench my heat with another. Any other. Every word Thomas says, every cold gesture, should throw a blanket on my conflagration. But I smoulder. I cannot be put out. I am banked up like the fire of a charcoal-burner, a man who knows how to tend flame and bend it to his will. And as simply as that, I know what to do.

Lust calls me to the forest, clear as a bell.

I could tell Thomas I am off to dance naked with gypsies, he takes so little notice. The charcoal burners come to the village but once a year, so I have no fear of my escapade becoming the subject of salty tales told in the alehouse. I settle the Maid by the hearth and shove a piece of bread into her hand. The fire is low and she is seated far enough away not to fall into the embers.

'Be a good lass,' I coo. 'I'll only be gone a short while.'

She watches me prepare to leave, sucking on the crust and rocking backwards and forwards. She gives a squeak of curiosity and stands, so I shove out the flat of my palm and tell her to sit. She understands either the word or the gesture and squats upon the rushes.

'Good girl,' I say.

Her face carries the look of concentration it wears when she is considering a shit, but I decide to take the chance. Besides, if I am unlucky, I can sweep up her turds and the rushes with them when I return.

I race to the well and keep on walking into the forest. Birds call to each other in their different tongues, remarking upon the stranger come among them. Wind moves the trees, so that the leaves speak with their own voice also. But it is the barking of a dog that guides me to the spot I seek.

His turf hut is surrounded by a large circle of brushwood; I pick my way carefully and although I make little sound, he is there to meet me. His face is smeared with oily ash, skin dry as the bracken heaped over the kiln. Sharp lines crease his eyes from peering into the stack.

'Good day,' I say.

'Ah,' he croaks.

'I am here,' I say. 'Not for burned-up wood.'

'Ah,' he repeats.

He rubs his hands together, warming them at the fire of what we both know is to come. They are black from shovelling charcoal and I think of my kirtle and kerchief. Easy to explain away a little mud about the hem, but not the dark prints of this man's paws. For all that Thomas is a fool, he is not blind. Even he will notice his housekeeper dirtied from head to foot. And if he does not, then I can be sure that every soul from here to Hartland will remark upon it and their tongues will flap like dishclouts in a gale.

The charcoal-burner moves forward, his eagerness to begin plain as the stick pushing out the front of his leather apron. I hold up my hand and he grins, revealing teeth the same colour as his hands and face.

'Not a time to be changing your mind, missy,' he cackles, and takes another step. He busies himself with the rope binding his apron, frowning at the knot.

'I've not changed my mind. But I'll not go home as black as you.'

He laughs, the *ack-ack-ack* of a magpie. 'Lift your skirt and be done with it,' he caws, laying his hand on my hip.

I shrink away from the touch. 'I said wait.'

I am all busy-ness, all fire. My kerchief is off far quicker than it took to fasten it about my head; my kirtle away in a moment, for I did not lace the sleeves. It's an easy matter to find a bush on which to hang them. He hops from foot to foot, smiling

170

wider with each garment I remove, until I am down to my under-shift. As I hoist it to my armpits, he gloats at my body hungrily.

'Well then, man?' I gasp, for I am famished also. 'Why do you wait? A moment ago you would have nailed me to that oak.'

'It is a long time since I saw a woman,' – he waves his grimy fingers – 'thus.'

'Eyes give no satisfaction. Come now. Give me what I need.'

I squeeze my breasts, lifting so that the nipples poke their pink noses through the slashed neckline. The ache between my legs is so piercing that I fear I may cry out. It is a heavy full-ness, yet at the same time I am empty and yearn to be filled.

I need, my body moans, *I need.*

I choose a patch of ground that is neither cruel with stones nor filthy with bird droppings. I lie down while I still have the choice and am not thrown into thistles or shoved against a tree. Finally, he is done with unfastening himself. I spread my knees and point at the wet place where I want him.

'In here,' I pant, in case he does not know what to do with the maypole that's waving its purple head at me.

But he does know, and is on me, and at last I am full. He rams home and my body cries *yes* with the relief and rightness of it. He pulls half out and I moan, 'Oh, do not go!' But he is straightway in again, again and again. I throw my legs around him, drum his ribs with my heels as though he is a mule and I must spur him to more vigorous action. I yell for more. He pounds harder and still it is not enough. I want more; what, I do not know. Then he shudders: once, twice; drops his weight upon me like a sack of flour and is done.

I roll from beneath him, pull my shift past my knees, collect the rest of my clothes and climb into them. I return to the village without another word, nor a backward glance. I should feel shame, but I do not. Mother said it would hurt, my first time; that there would be blood. If there is blood, I do not see it. If there is pain then it reminds me I am alive. I am not merely a pair of hands to prepare food or a pair of feet to run back and forth. I know my monthly courses well enough to know I shall not be taken. And if I am: so be it. I do not care. That night I sleep better than I have since I was a girl. That child is gone and I am free of her.

I observe the Maid privately, hoping to catch that look or hear her speak again with comprehension. But for the few days following she seems more witless than ever, even pissing where she stands. I am not so easily put off, however. I act the innocent, prattling on as usual, but secretly watching for her to make some slip that I may leap upon. I do not have to wait for long.

So it is that I catch her on the fifth morning, a day of unrelenting rain, sniffing around the corner of the room and pawing at the floor. I grab her just as she cocks her leg: it is a particular annoyance that she always chooses the freshest reeds to relieve herself upon.

'No you don't,' I growl.

I drag her towards the door. She falls like a stone, just as a small child does when hauled away from a game by its mother. She whines in irritation, but I'm having none of it.

'Stop this,' I say. 'You are not an infant, so stop behaving like one.'

Her answer is to squeal the louder, a thin sound that shreds the air into sharp pieces.

'You can stop that, too. I'll not have you pissing all over the floor. As if I haven't got enough to do, chasing after him.'

172

She is a dead weight, but I've lifted far heavier. As I pull, her body clears a path through the reeds. I tut. It'll make her shift filthy. Yet more work. But I shall finish what I have begun. If a dog can be taught tricks, then I shall teach this pup to piss out of doors. She grabs hold of the bench as we pass and drags that behind us also, thumping and bouncing.

'Do what you will. You're going outdoors and there's an end to it. You're no more a dog than I am.'

I pull. She pulls back, barking as if to disprove what I have said.

'You little—' I mutter.

My kerchief is working loose. Strands of hair droop across my eyes and stick to my brow. I gasp wildly: it's like dragging a full-grown sow away from her wallow rather than a skinny girl. I haul the Vixen to the door and step over the threshold. Of course it is still raining. It never seems to stop. She wraps her free arm around the doorframe so that I am without and she within.

'I don't care if it's wet,' I grunt. 'You are going out.'

I take a deep breath and give an almighty tug that I hope will dislodge her, but my palm is so sweaty our hands slip apart. I fall backwards out of the house and land on my arse with skirts rucked up to the knee. I have lost my kerchief and the rain pelts down upon my bare head. We stare at each other for a few surprised moments. She looks frightened, full of know-ledge that she's taken things too far. It is an expression that is the opposite of animal. She tries to wipe it away and resume her dull stare, but it is too late. I have seen what I have seen.

I tip back my head and laugh; whether at the ridiculous spectacle I am making, or because I know for sure that she's not as daft as she makes out, I cannot say. I am filled with the delicious realisation that I have uncovered a secret and Thomas knows absolutely nothing about it.

'Look at me!' I crow. 'The great lady of the house, soaking her backside in a puddle!'

I throw my arms around myself, rock back and forth, hugging myself with glee. The Maid gets to her feet and stands in the doorway, one toe making circles in the dirt.

'Trying to work out if it's me who's the madwoman, or you?' I giggle.

She gives that familiar tilt of her head and I dismiss the gesture with a flick of my hand.

'I know you understand more than you appear to, so you can leave off the dumbshow. It's wasted on me. Keep it for him.'

She eyes me carefully.

'You don't have to worry,' I continue. 'Whatever you're hiding, I'll not go gabbing it to all and sundry.'

Her eyebrows rise.

'I know, I know. You've no reason to trust me. But you've seen how it goes under this roof.' I make my voice gentle. 'I may live in a priest's house, but I am no priest's woman, nor his slave, nor his whore.'

She regards me with such grave consideration that it sets me off again, laughing so hard I get a stitch in my side. The rain is coming down in streams and I must look a fright.

'Well,' I say, slapping my sodden thighs. 'Enough of these games. The gobbling gizzard-neck will be back sooner than you can say knife, and I have no desire to greet him like this.'

I roll to one side and start to scramble to my feet, hampered by my kirtle, for it is laden with water. I look up to find her hand hovering before my face. She nods and jabs her fingers at me in case I am too addled to understand the gesture. I grasp her hand

and she pulls me to my feet. Despite the thinness of her frame, she draws me up as easily as a feather bolster.

She rests one hand on her hip, leans all her weight on one leg. The easy way she does so sweeps the last scrap of foolishness from her and in the relaxed stance I see a woman no different from myself. We stare at each other for the length of time it would take to sort stones from a plateful of peas. Neither of us speaks a word, nor needs to.

'Well,' I say.

It is not the most engaging way to begin a conversation but I can stand the silence no longer.

'Well,' she says.

With that, everything changes.

'I knew it,' I say.

'You did,' she answers.

We go back into the house and dry ourselves by the fire. Things are different from this moment on, but not always in the way either of us expects them to be.

VIXEN

I cannot believe Anne is as good as she appears. More importantly, I must not believe. I don't know why I am getting caught up in all their sticky business. I ought to stand aside and let him get on with beating the breath out of her.

It's a game. All of this is a game, and I've never lost one yet. Not one of them will get the mastery of me. Especially not her. I have her wrapped around my finger. She thinks she's found me out and for now I am content to let her ramble down that path, me dancing ahead, for I do love to lead folk a dance. I'm glad to be able to lay off acting the idiot, with her at least. It is an exhausting part. Of course, I must keep it up with him, at least until I choose otherwise. And I will be the one to choose.

She thinks she's seen the whole of me. Not so. She's peeled one blanket off the bed. Now she is looking at the one beneath, for I am heaped with them: I am sheet after sheet and each a different colour and weave. I have a hundred faces to show and not one of them is my own. It occurs to me that it is so long since I wore my true face that I do not recall who that person is. The thought slides a claw down my spine, so I thrust it away and stop thinking about it. No one sees my face and that is how it shall stay. Not even Death's seen that.

176

I am still on my guard, more than ever. I sleep with one eye open, waiting for the mob at the door. I am affrighted by dreams. Always the same one: Anne, crowing, *You fool. You trusted me? Ha! I shall close my eyes and count to ten. We want for sport. Run. Be the Vixen you are.*

I fall to my knees and beg, just as I begged my mother in my other life. Begged for kindness, for mercy, for my small body to be given back to me. She throws back her head and laughs, Anne or my mother, I cannot tell. If it's not Anne in my nightmares then it's Knot-Beard, hanging over me. *Where's my virgin?* he leers. *I grow hungry.* I start awake, heart thundering so wildly I am sure it will break free through my breast.

Knot-Beard will forget my bargain. I'll take someone else. If I can't find someone else then I'll take her, be done with it and feel nothing. I'll work out something. I always do. Anne doesn't matter. Of course she doesn't. No one has ever mattered. But there's a thrumming within my belly as though some hand has plucked a string deep inside my gut.

As for the priest, he never lets me be. He spies on me through the stable wall, worming his fingers into the daub and picking holes in the plaster, the better to gawp at his miracle, for that is what he has decided I am. If he gets some shrivelled-up pleasure watching me, then I am content, for I've had far worse.

It amuses me to throw crumbs in his path and watch him dive at them like a famished crow. I give him a fair old show. One day I coo as sweetly as a dove when he reads me a passage from the Gospel, the next I strip off my shift and caper naked. One moment I kneel and force my features to match those of the angels painted on the wall, the next I howl like a pup, and how I keep from laughing out loud at my own antics, I do not know.

By God, it makes me merry to see the dolt bounce in my wake as I frolic through the village. He doesn't even have the excuse of being an *old* dolt. He's young. Considering the efforts I go to, he ought to throw pennies to thank me for the entertainment, the tight-fisted lizard. Poorer folk have done as much and more.

He is not entirely stupid, for all his stiff neck and pretence at a limp pintle. Perhaps I should not test him so. I might slip and make a mistake: the birds proved I am capable of error. I shake the thought from my head. No. By Saint Peter's fishy farts, that was no mistake. I was duped. Anyone would have done the same. I'll not birch myself for something that was not my fault.

If he didn't force the wizened stick of his faith down my throat, maybe I'd be kinder, though I doubt it. I have so many baptisms I have the cleanest head this side of Bristol. He drones the same words every day at the same hour and everything he says sticks in my throat sharp as a fishbone. Perhaps angels are comforted by this day-in, day-out repetition. If I were the Ear of God I should be mortally bored.

The closest I get to his money is the shrine, for saints love nothing better than to rest their bones on golden beds, but it's locked fast. He lets me poke about in the cupboards, for he takes my curiosity as one of his interminable signs of godliness. My nose twitches, but all I find are books and more books. He's so proud of his psalteries and gospels and legendaries it makes me want to choke. I watch him lift them off the shelf gently as a first-born son, kiss their furrowed covers and gabble on about the word of the Lord. I can fill neither my belly nor my pockets on a diet of words.

'You called her good,' he says. 'The female,' he adds, dragging the word out to breaking point, for in his eyes I am still too stupid to understand. 'That was generous,' he says, and sourly too, for he makes no secret of his jealousy that my first word was for her. 'But there are things far more worthy of praise. We must praise God above all, must we not?'

I blow a raspberry. He marches me to the church wall, grabs my ears and twists my head in the direction of a painting of Christ.

'You know who that is, don't you? He is our Saviour.'

You could have fooled me. This creature has a nose like a turnip and a halo the shape of a failed pancake, drawn with all the skill of a sow clasping a brush in her trotters. If that is our Saviour, then God help us all.

'Yes?' he warbles hopefully.

No, you fool, I think. It's not Christ. It's a painting, and a shameful one at that. I waggle my tongue at it.

'Come now. You said *good* about that woman. Won't you give me the same? Do it.' He jabs a stubby finger at the wall. 'That is Christ your Redeemer. He is good. Good, damn you. Good!'

His arm falls, his chin falls. He claps his hand over his eyes.

'Dear Lord,' he croaks. 'Forgive me.'

He drops to his knees, wringing his paws together. With a lurch, he heaves to one side and cracks his head against the plaster. I see stars even if he does not. It'll do me no good if he splits his pate open. I'm the only one around and will end up charged with murder as likely as not. That'd be a pretty pass: accused of something I had no hand in for once.

I pat his sleeve and whine piteously, careful not to say a word. I don't think for one moment he's crafty enough to snare me thus into speaking, but trickery comes in all shapes and sizes.

179

'Mew,' I say. 'Mew.'

He groans and clasps his head. 'God have mercy! Forgive my pride!'

So that's it: he is penitent only, not mad. He gives his brow a second whack for good measure and resumes his usual prattle about pestilence and miracles and what have you. His skull must be as solid as a keystone to withstand the battering he's just dealt it. Which explains a great deal, I think, and chuckle. He is out of his remorseful daze in an instant, hands gripping my shoulders. I twist my chuckle into a gurgle.

'Yes?' he asks, bruised noggin forgotten. 'A word for Father Thomas?'

I feel sorry for the poor sap. Not that sorry, however. I think of how quick he'd turf me out if I wasn't his celestial toy. I gag, and gulp, and swim my hands about and by-and-by he sighs and lets me go.

I have had enough. Enough of being tossed to and fro on the churning seas of this man's need, self-pity, envy, greed, pride and who can guess what else: more deadly sins than you can shake a stick at. Now that it's clear he has nothing worth stealing, or at least nothing I can get my paws on, I'll waste no more time in this church.

I turn about, flip up the hem of my shift and bare my arse at the wall. Wrinkling my brow, I make a drawn-out groan and squeeze out a turd. He watches, unable to stir. When I'm done, I rub my buttocks against the plaster and race out of the door into the sunlight, turning cartwheels as I go.

Kindness is always a trick. I must not trust Anne. If I do, what then?

I know mouths opened only to curse, hands raised only to

strike me down. I am so used to cruelty that I do not know what it is to taste sweetness; so used to running that I do not know what it means to stand still. It is not a skill I have ever had to learn. I can lie, cheat, cozen, simper and act a hundred parts, and not one of them is real. My heart has grown as crooked as this disguise I wear.

Now I am faced with a truth of feeling and it terrifies me more than Death. In Death there is familiarity. With Anne, there is the chance that I might live. A different life.

SEXT
1349

From Saint Sidwell to John the Baptist

THOMAS OF UPCOTE

The mare gasped her surprise as I slapped her side and tightened the belly-strap. Anne filled the empty page of the stable
door.

'Why do you not speak?' I grunted.

'I am not spoken to, sir.'

'You are now.'

She folded her hands before her apron. 'It is raining, sir.'

'It has been raining since Easter.'

'You are riding out?'

'I have the horse. I am riding out, yes.'

'I must prepare a meal. When do you wish to eat, sir?'

'I do not know. I do God's work in the Staple. Bread-making
is not my concern.'

'Yes, sir.'

She did not move away. I stuck my foot into the stirrup and
hoisted myself onto the saddle.

'Well then, mistress. I will go now.'

'Yes, sir.' She gazed into the eyes of the beast. It shook its
lips and rubbed its nose in her armpit.

'I shall visit Father John at Saint Petroc's.' I would not say,
And the icon also, for that was of no significance.

'Yes, sir.'

'Will you wish me Godspeed?'

Her face turned up to mine. 'Godspeed, sir. And a safe return.'

My heart loosened and I smiled at her. 'I shall not be gone long, Anne. I shall be back by evening, to be certain.'

'There will be food waiting for you, sir.'

She unwrapped one hand from the other and I thought she would reach up and take mine: I flushed beneath my shirt at the thought, even leaned forward to receive her touch the more easily, but she patted her smooth apron even smoother and turned away towards the house.

I twitched the reins and the mare plodded to the gateway. I turned and saw Anne waving. I waved back, but it was not meant for me. Quick as a breath the Maid sprang across the yard to Anne's side. I watched a moment: even at this span of distance I could see Anne smile as she took the girl's hand. In my fancy, I saw the Maid return the smile. My heart turned over inside the cage of my ribs and I counselled myself it was gladness to see Anne so affectionate a mother.

As I reached the edge of the village the rain slowed to a drizzle, and I was cheered by this good omen. The blessed Maid was safe under my roof. I had given the people a miracle. Now, I saw respect in their eyes when I passed one or other of them as I walked about. Sometimes I wished she was a little more – saintly. But the Lord's gifts are sent to edify and instruct, not to satisfy selfish desires. Wishing her meek and pious was the easy path, and my path had never been easy.

My clothes began to dry as I clucked the horse up the high road to the Staple. At last, the sky was unfettered by hills and trees: to the south was the broad sweep of the estuary; to the west the Great Field, beautiful and varicoloured as any tapestry. Beyond that spread the dun-coloured marshes, all cut about

186

with the steel blades of water channels. Beyond that, the banked sand-hills; and beyond all, the sea. To the north was the forest, stretching more leagues than I cared to count.

Clouds piled up over the estuary, high as bales of wool on the quayside. But to the east there were breaks in the grey, with streaks of blue and white to be seen. Some small light struggled through these chinks, sprinkling itself upon the water below. Lapwings stood up to their knees at the water's edge, beaking the mud. I drew in a draught of air and felt it clean and bright as water from the well, enough to make me tremble with delight at God's creation. I was so caught up that I discovered my voice raised in song:

O Lord, how excellent is thy name in all the earth!
The heavens declare the glory of God;
And the firmament sheweth His handiwork!

This took me as far as the vill of Ashford, straggling along each side of the highway. I thought to greet its people, for I knew many of them from the Saint's holy day. Strings of smoke crept up from gaps in the frayed thatch, so I knew men were within, but each door gaped dumbly. A cow moaned to be milked. There was a thick smell of hog's lard, and laid beneath it something darker, as of flesh sickening.

'Good day!' I cried, pulling in the reins to slow the mare, glad enough to drop her head and snuff about for blades of grass. I lowered my head and shouted through the window of the closest hut. 'God's blessings upon you!'

There was a scuffling within, and a face swam into the dark square. I took it for a woman, for a dirty kerchief was bundled about its head.

'Greetings, mistress,' I said warmly, so all would hear and be comforted. 'Be of good cheer.'

Her mouth opened and closed and she made the sign of the Cross.

'I am the priest in Brauntone: Father Thomas. You know me.'

Her lips continued to pop open and shut, without speech.

'Brauntone. The shrine of the Saint and healer, Brannoc,' I smiled again.

'Healing?' she cawed, and her voice snapped in the middle. 'You are too late,' she moaned, and the room ate her up.

I raised my head to see if anyone else had come out. There must be someone to greet me: I had spoken loud enough. Nothing. There was little to do but continue to the Staple, so I clucked at the horse and we made our descent into the town. I reflected on the coarse manners of some folk, and thanked God for the friendliness of my parishioners.

I would have known myself at my destination even if my cap had been pulled over my eyes. The stink of the tannery brought me rudely to my senses. The air was threaded about with smoke from uncountable cooking fires and I wondered that men did not go about coughing the whole while. I wrapped the tail of my hood round my mouth and it gave me some respite.

The way was clotted with all manner of carts, the potholes so deep I had to guide the mare with great care. At last I was at the church, and it seemed I came at the time of some great event, so thick was the huddle of people about the door. I tried to reckon what it might be. I grasped the shoulder of the man closest to me.

'Greetings, good man; is the Bishop come here?'

He looked at my boots, my cloak, my cowl. I was strangely glad it covered my tonsure.

'You're not from about here, are you?'

'No, from Brauntone. The shrine of the Holy Brannoc.'

188

'You all come here,' he snorted. 'Sooner rather than later, and all. Doesn't say much for your Saint, does it?'

'Ours is a holy and blessed healer.'

'If you say so. I am going now; I want to get a good place.'

'Where?'

'In the church, fool. They show us the icon this morning. God's Bones, why else are men here?'

He shook off my hand, and the mob swallowed him whole. I hugged my hood close and entered the church with the rest. We shuffled forward one tiny step at a time. I could not understand why those at the front did not walk more hastily, and opened my mouth to say so. Another stole my words.

'Move your feet, I say! We are kept standing at the back here.'

He was hushed straightway and I was pleased I had held my tongue. At last I passed beneath the arch of the door and came into the nave, the walls and roof falling away from me. There was such a quantity of men that the stone pillars seemed to be growing out of a field of human flesh. I wondered how we might all fit into the church, for there was still a crowd eager behind me.

My eyes squinted against the darkness. There was whispering to my right and I twisted my neck to discover what was happening. The wall of bodies opened, making a narrow path that a man strode down. Although he looked too coarse to be one of God's servants, he brandished the deacon's staff of office and pushed us back like dogs.

A child's voice squawked once, and was throttled into silence. More people came into the church and we were rammed closer and closer together. I could have lifted both of my feet from the floor and been held up. Then, the west door slammed shut. We swayed quietly together, a sheaf of human cornstalks reeking of garlic and stale beer. No one coughed, or spat, or chattered.

When I endeavoured to look about and admire the painted glass, I felt fingers pinching the flesh of my arms.

'Be still,' wheezed an onion voice in my ear.

I was motionless. But I wondered why were there no candles, no lamps. The window shutters were drawn together. All was shadow and unnecessary dimness. Then I heard it: the voice of a boy, singing:

He bowed the heavens and darkness was under His feet;
His pavilion around Him were dark waters
And thick clouds of the skies.

I could not believe it was an earthly voice chanting the words: I must be dreaming such sweetness. My throat bunched into a fist and my eyes leaked water. The man next to me sniffed loudly, wiping his nose on his hand. The psalm curled over and about our heads and too soon it was over. I had a great hunger for more.

At once the light of Heaven shone out. A host of lads in white filed in through the north door, carrying tapers. At their head walked John of Pilton, swathed in a cope that glittered like blood in the candlelight. I crouched behind my neighbours, though it was foolishness to think he would spy me in this horde. I had not spoken to him since we were ordained. He climbed the steps to the chancel screen, turned and lifted his hands in prayer.

'Oh sinners!' he bellowed. 'You have chosen to scorn God's laws. Disaster is at hand. The Great Dying is fast upon us. Your sins have brought down this calamity!'

A terrible groan swept through the church. I staggered and would have fallen were it not for the multitude of bodies pressed tight about me.

190

'Who can say that he is clean of sin? Is there one amongst you?'

There was a stopping-up of breath straightaway. Even the infants quietened their customary squalling. I gulped. It was as though he sought me out especially and found me lacking. But it could not be so: God had chosen to send the Maid to me. Surely He would not charge a common sinner with this great task. John continued to bluster.

'Who are you to presume that you may drop your pitiful words direct into the ear of God? To whom may we pray? Oh brothers and sisters, to whom can we turn in this time of travail?'

My neighbour began to weep; it was picked up by the man at his shoulder, and the next man, and the next.

'Who has always held sinners in Her lap? Who intercedes for us, unworthy as we are? O Star of Heaven, who bore the Lord, and rooted up the plague of death that Adam planted! O Mother of Mercy, save us from this Pestilence! Shelter us under Your cloak!'

John swept his hand through the air as though turning a page of the Gospels.

'O most blessed Mary, O Consolation of the Desolate!' he cried.

I was clustered about with souls wailing repentance, their rapture so passionate that even I was drawn into its toils. 'Forgive me, Mary,' I keened. 'I am steeped in sin. Forgive me.' I was helpless; tossed about on a torrent of fear and hope and sorrow all mingled together. Suddenly, John's voice dropped from entreaty into gentleness.

'We kneel before You. We beg at Your most holy feet.'

At that moment he flung his hand towards the north porch: a boy raised his candle; a curtain fell away. Out of the darkness the image of the Virgin flared into life. The light wavered the

191

shadows and the face of the Woman wavered also. Although I knew it to be the agency of the flame, I saw Her lips move. I could not stop my hand from making the sign of the Cross on my brow.

A man to my left shrieked, 'Look at her mouth; she speaks!'

A fearsome moan tore from every throat at the same instant. My neighbour fell to his knees and cried out, 'Blessed Mother forgive me!' I wondered if he called upon the Virgin or the woman who bore him, for his voice was as desperate as a child's. He was not alone. All around me men and women tottered and were struck down. I stood firm, despite the hissing of, 'Kneel, man!' in my ears. John let the uproar continue a short while, but after the time it took to say the Pater Noster he shouted out again.

'Yes! Let us pray to our Holy Mother! Only She is our shield against death. O Gentle Mother of God, turn Your gaze from our sins; wash away our iniquities and make us clean so that God may show mercy to us at last.'

John paused: slowly the snuffling and snorting ebbed into something approaching quiet. The people struggled back to their feet, helped by their fellows. He waited for us patiently.

'Oh, most dearly beloved, let us not be like beasts, but let us rather hold up our hands and beg for mercy from our tender Mother: for who else will have mercy on Her stumbling children?'

He paused again: waited until the mob murmured *Mary, O Mary* with one voice.

'The coming pestilence is just payment for our sins. Let us embrace prayer so that God's Mother might spare us from this evil death. Whatever you seek with prayers, believe that you will receive it, and be it done for you. Amen, I say to you. Amen. O, praise and glory to our Holy Mother for ever, amen.'

192

For an instant there was peace, and then the weeping began. I felt wetness upon my own cheeks, and heard my own voice cry out for forgiveness, and I was angry.

I was still angry when I found my way out of the church, for it took as long to come out as to go in, however hard I shoved. It was raining once more, and I felt water inch its way down the back of my neck. I was making my way to find the horse when I heard the pounding of footsteps behind me.

'Brother: stop.' A man's breath sounded heavily. 'Did you not hear me calling you?'

I turned to face the voice I knew so well. We had been clerics together; now we were priests, and apart. He was still a head taller than me, still built like a cattle-drover, though softer about his belly. He panted a while longer, then raised his arm. I flinched from the blow I thought was coming, but he slapped me on the shoulder in friendship.

'Dear Brother in Christ. My dear Thomas: welcome. It gladdens my heart to see you here. It has been too long a time. Were you in the church just now?'

I nodded.

'You came to hear me preach.'

I watched his face glow: with pride or exertion, I did not know. He patted his breast, gathering himself into calmness. Raindrops sparkled on his naked scalp.

'It has indeed been a long time,' I said. 'Brother John, greetings.' My arms hung from their hinges.

'A hearty good greeting indeed. You will come to my house. You are getting wet; so am I. Let me refresh you.' He laughed at the pleasurable thought.

'My horse is tied up.'

'Then let my man untie it and bring it also. There is plenty of hay in the stable.'

'I cannot stay long.'

'You labour as hard as you ever did, Brother,' he grinned. 'How do you keep?'

'Well, by the grace of God.'

'And Anne?'

My tongue shrivelled. What did he wish to imply about the chastity of my house? How had he heard about her?

'My housekeeper is well also, thank God.'

'Good. Good.' His eyebrows lifted and he grinned, although I had said nothing amusing. 'You are the same man, Thomas.'

'I am the same man, Brother John. Steadfast and true, as ever. And you?'

'The Lord blesses us daily.'

A smile flowered in his face. It came to me that he was a happy man. He laid his arm across my shoulder and hugged me to him, and would not release me until we walked over the threshold of his house.

A man opened the door to us and took John's cloak and mine, shaking away the shower and greeting us cheerfully. As he laid off his outdoor clothes, John revealed himself dressed as grandly as a lord in fine blues and russets. I was clad in homespun cape and cassock. I praised my judgement for wearing my old boots. It seemed no one in his household could keep from showing their good humour: neither John, nor his servant – not even his dog, which flapped up to welcome us and thrashed its tail against my leg when John bent to tickle its ragged ears.

I was led, with much good cheer and stroking of my upper arms, questionings about my comfort, and *was I warm enough?* into the solar. I struggled to stop a gasp escape my throat, and I believe turned it skilfully enough into a cough.

The room was almost the size of my whole house. Tapestry draped three of the walls, and the one without boasted a window of many lights, each of them glazed with the clearest of glass. The rain tapped politely at the panes. Woven mats of straw covered the floor from side to side; but the greatest wonder was the fireplace set into the wall, all smoke sucked up a sturdy brick chimney. The hearth was littered with fire-forks, and tongs, and bellows, and andirons, and a heaping wood-basket.

I could not help but thank God for my poorer dwelling, secretly pleased for the fire in the centre of my own home. Everyone knows a smoky room is the best medicine to keep a goodman from the quack. I must have become lost in gazing at all the worldly riches about me, for the next thing I knew was John plucking at my arm again.

'Please, drink with me, dear Brother. You must be thirsty. I know I am after all that speaking.'

His man brought us each a cup and into them he poured an inky liquid that smelled of spices. I wrinkled my nose, yet tasted it for civility's sake. There was such a delight about it that it melted my tongue straightway, and cosseted my shoulders into restfulness.

Then the female came into the room. I had heard talk of her, of course. How they lived as a man and wife do; and not one man in the Staple judged them for it, not even for the bastard child they had between them. Her long skirts brushed against the rush matting, so that she approached as a breeze through trees. Her under-dress was fitted tight as a second skin over her breasts and arms, and the loose over-tunic was of some deeply figured yellow stuff that caught the light and flickered as if those trees were shedding their leaves in autumn. A fist of keys swung from her girdle and the kerchief of a wife enveloped her head. She walked directly to John and he took her hand in his great paw.

'My dear Margret, let me welcome you to my Brother in Christ, Thomas of Upcote, who is priest at Brauntone.'

She arched her body in brief courtesy.

'I am as joyful as John to be in your company, Brother Thomas,' she said. 'John talks of the time you studied together with happy recollection. I pray you have brought news of my dearest friend Anne.'

'News?' I croaked, throat parched.

My cup was unaccountably empty. When I drained it I did not know. The woman raised her eyebrows at my continued silence, but I could not think of a response. At last she sighed, turned from me and seated herself at the window. She drew out a piece of fabric from beneath the bench, and commenced sewing.

'Another cup for our dear brother,' said John. 'Please, Thomas, sit. Sit. I beg you be comfortable.'

My head bounced like a spindle. My backside found the nearest bench, which was so loaded with cushions and coverings there was no bare wood to be seen. John's man poured more wine. *I must drink more temperately,* I thought.

John placed himself upon the chair at the head of the room and rested his elbows on its arms. It was so carved about with vines and flowers that I had a great desire to kneel before it and run my fingers over the fanciful work, counting all the different varieties of plant: rose, lily, primrose, violet. But I gripped the edge of the bench and gazed into the dark eye of my cup.

'It is an honour to receive you into our home, Thomas,' said John. 'It is so many months since I saw you last. Your company is most pleasing to us.'

The mud on my boots was beginning to dry. I knocked my heels together and lumps of it fell onto the mat. I nodded my thanks: my head seemed to take a long time to stop bobbing up and down. At last I was steady.

'We do not see you in the Staple, Thomas. You are always welcome at our board.'

I bent my neck again: once, twice.

'I sent diverse writings and messages,' he said. 'But never had an answer back.'

'It has been a busy time. I do not keep servants to wait on me.'

'Ah. Yes.'

I raised my cup and took a small sip; another, larger mouthful, then dragged it away to rest at my knee before I could swallow the lot.

John coughed quietly. 'You are pleased with the wine?'

I wanted to cry out that my senses had never been so enraptured, that my eyes swam, that my belly rejoiced. 'It is good,' I said carefully. 'Very pleasing.'

'I have it from France,' he said, as though France were as near to him as his shoe. 'But it is Margret who mixes the spices so elegantly.'

I was astonished that he talked of her so boldly, with no embarrassment. She lifted her head and smiled. Their mutual tenderness was as apparent as a delicate ribbon tying one to the other. I could not believe John insulted me by parading his whore. I thanked Christ he had enough shame to hide his bastard lad.

'I have had enough wine,' I grumbled, hearing the ashes in my voice.

'Come, Thomas,' said John. 'Be merry. We have not talked as brother to brother for so long. There are only six miles

197

between us. My heart is glad that you crossed them to come to me this morning.'

'I did not come to see you. Or your woman.'

His eyebrows jumped. He darted a swift glance at the female where she sat in the light from the window, embroidering a long strip of watery fabric. She winced, no doubt from shoving the needle into her thumb. When John returned his gaze it seemed as though his eyes were darkened with fear; but it was gone so swiftly I must have been mistaken, so dazed was I by drink. I sucked at my cup. I did not wish my words to pinch, but it seemed I could not blunt the edge of my sharpness. Maybe the wine would cozen my angry humour into something more loving. Many men are snared by women. God is the Judge; I am not.

'I came to see the icon, as it is called,' I said more reasonably.

'Yes, it is so called,' John sighed. 'The people are terrified. Every day I watch for signs of this pestilence: at the quayside, in the men who come off the ships. How we have been spared, I do not know. Bristol has been scourged, and all the coast running south. I hear it is as close as Combe Martin. Perhaps closer.'

His voice quaked. He ran his hand over his new-shaved head. My own scalp prickled. I should have commanded Anne to shave me before I left. I did not know why I had forgotten such a simple task. My cup was nearly empty. I tipped what was left down my throat. At a distance, I could hear John's voice asking me a question. I tried to remember what he had been talking about, and how much of his conversation I had missed, but all I could think of was how neatly his hair was trimmed.

'Yes, indeed, it is true,' I mumbled, for I reckoned that every man desires agreement.

198

He seemed surprised. He waved his hand and my cup was filled once more. This would be my last draught, I said inwardly. I was not a carouser.

'I am glad to hear it,' he said. 'I took you sometimes for a harder man.'

I wondered what I had agreed to. I laboured to draw my thoughts together. 'John: this painting of the Virgin. It is why I am come to the Staple. What of it?'

He peered at me closely as a woman examines her yarn for breaks. 'We were just talking of it. I thought you heard me. Unlettered men need to throw their hopes upon something they can see; we bring them thus to God. This picture satisfies the hunger of unlearned men. You agreed.'

'I did not. I do not.' A little of my wine spilled onto the floor. 'You break the Commandments, John. It is idolatry.'

'Thomas. Brother. Calm yourself. Men do not worship the picture. They are comforted by the Virgin, and Her great power to work miracles. It is succour for fearful men.'

'Are you saying there is no holiness in it? Did you paint it yourself?'

The room was suddenly quiet. John and the woman flicked their eyes at each other.

'No, Brother Thomas.' His voice was tight. 'The holy icon of which we speak was found on the banks of the river after the storm on the feast of the Blessed Augustine. It was brought here straightway by William Godeby the carter, and the carrying of it cured him of a bloody flux he suffered this past six months. We pray daily that the power of our most Blessed and Holy Mary may protect and save us from the coming storm.'

The female stabbed tiny holes in her embroidery.

'But the storm passed,' I said. 'Surely we shall have no other.'

'I mean the storm of this foul corruption.' He raised his

hands and let them fall. 'We hope for miracles. We have never been in such great need for them.' He took a deep breath. 'God is punishing the world,' he whispered.

'Then the sinless have nothing to fear,' I said, and smiled at my clever reasoning.

'Brother Thomas, I fear you are not listening to me. Have you not heard the tales of this Great Dying?'

'No.'

I kicked my heels together and showered dried mud onto the floor. I must bid Anne clean my boots and oil them on my return.

'You must have. The whole world talks of little else.'

'In the Staple, perhaps. In Brauntone we are poor village folk. We are not distracted from wholesome work and humble worship of the Lord.'

'Thomas; men are dying.'

'Then we must hold fast to all that is godly,' I cried. 'Not the vanities of the world.' I pointed my eyes at the tapestry hanging on the wall opposite me. Two men on horseback pursued a stag through a forest. 'Or idol-worship,' I added, hoarsely.

'Do you dare call the Mother of God an idol? The Bishop has given us his warrant. I am your Brother in Christ, but have a care that you do not blaspheme.'

I chewed upon my lip, the better to fence in my words. 'No. She is not an idol. But I observe that her image is treated as such. And I note that you are dressed and fed better than you ever were, John.'

'The better to serve God and my flock. Do you fall into the sin of covetousness, Thomas?'

'I covet nothing of yours. I never have done.' I spoke with a heart that waxed ever more fiery, his words serving to fan the flame. My breath came in gasps. 'You have a thing of wood,' I continued, my soul blazing with faith. 'We have been sent a miracle made flesh.'

John leaned on his fist and smiled at me. 'The green girl?' he said. 'Ah, Thomas, do not be so out of humour. The whole Staple talks of her. There is not one cott, one vill between here and Exeter that has not heard of her. Is it true she is scaly, like a fish?'

I swallowed hard, my mouth suddenly packed tight with stones. 'No, she is not. She is bright as an angel. She came up out of the marshes on the night of the great storm, just as your icon did. God sent you a picture; how much greater to send us an angel.'

'Out of the marshes? Her feet are webbed like a goose, then?'

He was smirking, and I could see the woman's mouth turn up at the edges. I would not let them mock me.

'This is God's work. At first she displayed the behaviour of a beast, but turned miraculously into a girl, just like the story of our Saint. He turned a wolf into a man. It is as though the Holy Brannoc is among us again.'

As I spoke the words, I felt their truth fill me with certainty. My body sang.

'So, Thomas,' said John. 'Is she miraculous?'

I could not understand how my cup was empty again. I looked about my feet to see if I had spilled any, but the mat was dry. He twitched his hand and the serving-man appeared at my elbow and slopped liquid into my cup. It had been refilled three times. Or was it four? John held his hand over the mouth of his glass. I could not understand why he did not drink with me; it was unmannerly. I would drink with him if he came to my house. And I would hide Anne away; not parade her like an object to be admired.

My throat was packed with straw. The wine soothed it and

my faith glowed again. I strove to seek out the words to explain to John what she was, what I had witnessed in my vision.

'Yes! God sent her to us. You say men are dying all over the earth? Well, our village is not sickening. Not one man or woman has died since she came. Is that not a miracle?' I sighed.

'I do not doubt it,' murmured John. 'So: you have informed my Lord Bishop of this great marvel?'

I stared at him.

'You have not? We had a commission in the Staple to examine the icon; it was deemed holy by the Bishop himself. I would not dare to claim powers for something which might not be from the Lord. Has no one examined this girl? My Lord Bishop has not given his approval?'

'I have been very busy.'

'Of course. The Lord's work is labour indeed. Let me help you, then, Brother. I shall collect together some goodmen of this parish and we shall visit you presently. We shall examine this creature and send a report to my Lord Bishop. He will then decide what is to be done. He may well attend you himself, and test these miraculous happenings with the full rigour of his office. As he did to the icon.'

Once again, words fled me. I should welcome his help, but a dark bundle of fear hung suddenly upside down in my head, slowly unfolding damp wings.

'I must . . .' I began. Must what? I wanted to say, *Ask Anne*. I did not know whence came such a thought.

'You must?'

'I must open the door of my house in welcome. When shall you come?'

'I do not know.' He rubbed his chin. 'I will ask Master Nicholas Fuller the physician. And Master William Sneaton, from the school. They are as vexed with hard work as we are.

When I know the date, I will send word to you. I would not have you inconvenienced.'

'No.'

John stood, and patted away the wrinkles in his lap. Margret continued to prick at her sewing. I noticed she wore a tiny stall of silver over the end of her finger, and with the help of it she pushed the needle through. Some fancy from London, no doubt. John cleared his throat.

'I must go and say Terce. I am sure you are eager to return and do the same.'

I stood quickly. The cup fell to my feet and lay there.

'You are a godly man, Thomas. A lucky man. Be sure you convey our warm greetings to Anne.'

At first I thought he raised his arm in farewell, but saw that he was merely directing me to the door. My boots crunched the reeds. My cloak was thrust into my arms. Before I was two steps down the path, the door closed.

As I came to the outer door of my house I heard low whispers: two voices, one of which I was sure was Anne. I knew the flow of her words from overhearing her babble many a time.

The other voice I did not know at all. I wondered if it was butcher or baker or simply one of her gossips, for which I most certainly had not given permission. But I had heard this voice before: it hissed and crackled like green wood thrown on a fire. I stepped forward quickly. However urgent the matter, I had not given Anne leave to invite guests. I must chide her. We had spoken of this and I did not relish disobedience.

I laid my hand upon the wood and paused. It was as though I heard my sour thoughts for the first time and was taken aback at how little I liked them. Was I truly so unbending? Did charity have so precarious a foothold in my soul? My hand trembled. Was my wrathful and unforgiving nature the cardinal vice which might bring down the fury of the Mortality upon my flock?

I stood rooted to the threshold, quaking like a whipped pup. I would not chastise Anne. She was lonely and no doubt affrighted by the chattering about this pestilence. It was rumour made the people sick, not the fever, I counselled myself. We would stay healthy. We had the Saint, and now the blessed Maid.

I lifted the latch, pushed open the door and stepped into a silent room. Anne was seated quietly beside the hearth, sorting the stones from a dish of dried peas. She looked up as I entered and bade me good day, eyes meek as a lamb's. I looked about. The door to the garden was open and I fancied I had seen it swinging as I entered; now it was still.

'Is the Maid in here?' I asked.

Anne made a show of looking about with great curiosity. 'No, sir. She is not,' she said, after a longer search than was necessary.

'I heard voices.'

'Sir?' She stretched her eyes so wide that the arch of her brows was lost beneath her coif.

'Were you talking to someone?' I continued.

'No one is here for me to talk to, unless it be myself.'

I snapped my fingers. 'Do not address me thus, woman. I heard whispering. There were voices. You and another.'

'Sir, there is none other,' she said politely, then brightened, seized with the answer to the conundrum. 'Perhaps it was this you heard?'

She dug her fingers into the peas, lifted a palmful and dropped them. She scooped up a second and a third, the beans swishing against each other.

'Was it like that?'

'No,' I grunted. 'It was not like that at all.'

She wore a look of such innocence that I was not able to be angry for long. I stood a while, observing her pick out pieces of grit so tiny I could not see them, although I would notice them soon enough between my teeth. I complimented her on her careful work and, rubbing my hands together, said I must say the Office. I had no need to tell her of what had passed in the Staple. There would be plenty of time for that.

'God be with you,' she said, not looking up from the bowl.

I forgot this incident, caught up as I was in the Lord's service, and the misfortunes that were to befall the village, but I had cause to reflect upon it later.

ANNE

'You know I can't stay here,' she blurts, voice rough round the edges.

'Oh?'

I lay the carding paddles in my lap where they lie, knotted with lumps of wool. The Maid stands at the door with her back to me, scratching at the threshold with a grubby toe.

'You have found out what I am. It is never safe when that happens.'

There is a pause. I consider picking up the combs and resuming my task, but my hands are as motionless as wood. The pile of fleece sags at my feet, exuding its particular odour of wet sheep. When I think the silence cannot continue a moment longer, she lets out a long exhalation and turns. The light is behind her and I cannot read her eyes.

If she's half the girl I think she is, begging her to stay will be like pouring water down a rat-hole. I command my hands to move and they obey. I pick up the paddles and scrape them one against the other until the oily scent rises to my nostrils. Only then do I speak.

'Where will you go?' I ask.

She draws close enough to see her face clearly. 'The next

place,' she says. I see a flicker of uncertainty, stamped out before it has a chance to set a fire. 'I never know where that might be until I am there.'

'It will have to be a long way off. Somewhere folk have not heard of the Holy Maid of Brauntone.'

'That won't be difficult. I won't be this Maid when I've gone. I'll be someone else.'

'Ah. That is indeed clever.' I pause to pluck out a leaf trapped in the wool.

'You've been combing that same piece for a long time.'

'Since when were you the expert? The fleeces delivered to the reverend Father take twice the coaxing to deliver half the yarn. Full of breaks.' I scratch the pins roughly to prove my point. 'Have a care when you leave,' I continue. 'You'll be dodging a lot more than curious folk. There's the pestilence to consider.'

The nervousness tarries on her features for the space of a breath.

'It surrounds this village like the iron collar on a mastiff,' I muse. 'That's what I've heard.' I lift the comb to examine the wool more closely. It's as good as it's ever going to be. I scrape off the pad, set it aside for spinning and scoop up the next piece. I have to pick out a dead beetle and even a few pellets of dung before I can start. I do not look at her. 'Then again, I rarely step an arrow-shot from this village. You'll know the truth of it better than me.'

I draw the paddles back and forth, back and forth. The rhythm of brush and pause and the shushing of the pins reminds me of waves upon sand.

'You've already run away, or tried to,' I continue. 'You came back, but my wits tell me it was for lack of money, not love of this place. If you must go, you must. My heart will be heavy, more than you know. But I can't hold the wind in my arms.'

Her mouth hardens. 'What? So now you're saying you want me to leave, are you?'

'I do not need to. You are telling yourself, so loud you cannot hear a word anyone else is saying.'

'You can't wait to be rid of me,' she mutters, as though I've not spoken.

I slap the combs into my lap. It occurs to me a game is being played here, one she has played before.

'By all the saints, the Virgin and the Babe besides. Now you put words into my mouth. I do not know who spoke thus to you, but it was not me.' Her face reddens. My arrow has found its mark. I speak more kindly. 'Who was it?'

'I don't know what you mean,' she grumbles.

'Who *did* say that to you?'

She glares at me, angry at being found out or at the recollection, I cannot tell. 'Everyone,' she snaps. 'Every person I have ever met. You'll do the same.'

'Will I now?'

'You all do. You'll betray me. You'll swear on a heap of holy bones to stay quiet, but you won't. The secret will sear its way into your heart like you've spilled a bowl of porridge down your bodice. It'll slip out in front of Thomas. Or you'll gabble to your ma, your sister.'

'We shall see. I shall not waste my breath swearing if you have already decided not to believe me. But I tell him nothing. Nor do I have streams of companions to while away the hours over cups of ale and sweetmeats.'

She throws me a wide-eyed look and chews her lip. 'I must leave. But I cannot,' she says in a small voice. 'I have nothing, save the shift I stand in. Which will get me precisely nowhere.'

My smile grows, slow but strong. 'Then I believe I can help.

Come. I shall furnish you with what you need to quit this place. The rest is up to you.'

She watches as I set up the ladder to the upper room and beckon her to climb after.

'Well? Are you coming or not?' I say from halfway up the rungs.

She laughs. It is not a pretty sound, but in its creak I hear a door squeak open and let in a crack of light.

I never met a wight who wasn't dazzled by treasures: I've spent my life observing folk gawp at the shrine. The delights in the attic are not as grand as those belonging to the Saint, but they caught my attention quick enough and I'll wager they'll capture hers. I throw back the door and show off the treasures as proudly as though they are my own possessions and I am displaying them to impress a wife.

She is on the first chest like a starving man on food, tossing back the lid. She picks up each item and examines it minutely, working her way through with the efficiency of a sheep that will crop a meadow bald if left to itself.

At first I think she is enraptured by the sheets, for she takes out each one, shakes it firmly and runs her fingers along every seam. I realise that she is searching through the folds for items of greater value. Whenever she finds a copper coin she grunts with pleasure, until one by one they grow into a small heap. She selects hose, tunics, caps and any number of men's garments, turning up her nose at the gowns and kirtles, although some of them are very fine. I'd wear them fast enough if it wasn't for the fact that Thomas would know where I found them and lecture me on women's vanity.

She is deft, confident, nimble. Everything about her is so different that I can hardly believe this is the girl who dribbled and hobbled only a few days ago. I was completely hoodwinked.

209

If she can dissemble so well before the world – and that included me – am I a fool to trust her now? A chill creeps down the back of my neck.

She opens the second chest and picks up the fox. I wait for her to hug it to her breast as I did, but she wrinkles her nose and hurls it at the wall. It sprawls in the dust, patchy and balding.

'Have a care,' I snap. 'All these things must be put back. Thomas may be a fool, but if he comes up here and finds this disarray, he'll work it out.'

She looks surprised: either forgetting that I am there, or that I am able to make a good suggestion.

She shrugs. 'Go to, if you would have it tidy.'

With that, she returns to her search and I am dismissed. My anger flares. I grasp her arm and squeeze tightly enough to make her squeal.

'So. I have your attention,' I growl.

Her mouth forms a slack circle of shock. 'Mistress?' she squeaks, and arranges her lips coyly.

'You can stop calling me that,' I say. Her false smile is replaced with something far craftier. 'Make cow's eyes if it pleases you,' I add. 'You may think I am one of a hundred women who can be wrung like a wet rag. In my case you would be making a mistake.'

'Anne.'

It is the first time she speaks my name. The way she breathes it softens me a little, but I am determined not to bend so fast.

'You are a clever girl, I grant you that. How you've made your way here, and whence you came, I know not. But you are under this roof for now. You shall not address me like that again.'

'Or you'll do what? Gather the goodmen of this parish and drive me into the sea?'

She tries to speak as though she does not care, but I've smelled fear on plenty of pilgrims and I smell it now. It is my turn to smile.

'No.'

'If it is civility you desire, then I shall bow and call you mistress,' she sneers.

I laugh, and it is slow and easy. I gather up one of the discarded sheets, shake off as much dirt as I can and lay it in the chest.

'What are you doing?' she asks.

'Folding linen.'

'It is still dusty.'

'Indeed it is. He's not *that* observant.'

'Shall I help?' she says uncertainly.

'No.'

'But you said—'

I flap my hand and laugh again. 'You know what you're searching for. I am a good housekeeper. I am better at this task.'

'I do not understand. I thought—'

'The clever maid has something yet to learn.'

She returns to her search. At one point she finds a shilling sewn into the binding of a blanket, and her mood lightens. She examines the rest of them more carefully, shaking out flurries of moth wings like so many flakes of grey snow. But no more coins are served up. At last she is done. She sits in the dust, face smeared and surveys the haul. By the number of coins I know better than to ask if there are sufficient.

'You have only taken men's clothes.'

She raises an eyebrow. 'It is easier and safer to travel as a boy.'

'But you are not a boy. You will simply look like a girl in hose.'

211

'Here. I will show you.'

She hops to her feet: pulls a tunic over her head, drags a pair of hose to the knee, holds out her hand and draws me upright. To my surprise, I am looking at a strange young man half a head taller. But the Maid is shorter than me: of that I am sure. She sees my astonishment and grins.

'Is that better?' growls this lad in a voice deep as a millpond. I laugh. 'How do you do that?'

Her eyes glitter. 'How do I do what?' she asks.

'You know very well.'

'Close your eyes and I will show you more.'

It seems I have little option. I obey with an exasperated sigh.

'Now, open them again.'

The youth is gone. In his place stands a priest. Not any priest: Thomas. She sings a scrap from a psalm, intoning his reedy warble so perfectly she sounds more like him than he does himself. She captures the tremor of his head upon his neck, has the particular shuffle of his step. I never remarked on these things before, but now she has drawn them together I wonder how I ever missed them.

'Do I not amuse you?' she asks.

'You are far more than amusing,' I say. 'You are remarkable.'

'Close your eyes,' she says again, grinning.

The next time I am commanded to look, I am presented with a one-legged beggar, his face a squeezed mass of wrinkles.

'Alms, mistress?' he croaks. 'Bless me and receive blessings yourself!'

He hops towards me, and I shrink from his claw.

'You do something when my eyes are closed,' I say. 'You are cheating. No one can do this without magic tricks.'

With a shake of the shoulders, the cripple is cast off and the

Maid returns, laughing. I am relieved she is herself again, even though I know the beggar was her also.

'There is no trickery,' she says. 'Something cleverer. Keep your eyes open this time. It will make no difference.'

She pauses, breathes. In her hands a tablecloth becomes the bump of an unborn babe a wife bears before her, huffing and puffing. She twists a sheet into a beggar's hunchback, milady's over-mantle, an angel's wings. With the slightest curl of her body she is a tumbler doing handstands; she dons a cap and is a sailor fresh off his ship, purse bulging with coins and lusty desires.

With another twist she is a drunken woodcutter who cannot strike the tree without falling over; a crone with a wall eye and a withered arm. When she retrieves the discarded fox fur and places it on her head she is straightway a true vixen, all snap and snarl. I swear her bones are water and she can pour herself into any vessel she chooses. The garments obey her.

I clap delightedly at the show, like nothing I have ever seen before; so exciting it makes me catch my breath for fear of losing it. Next she is a harlot, I her customer, and she prowls around me like a cat. Then she is a lovesick boy who drops to one knee, begging a favour from his beloved. He is quite the esquire and I play along, holding out my hand so that he may take it and prance about, bowing low and praising the gold of my hair and rose of my cheek.

On and on she leaps from person to person, body to body, and it comes to me that each one is the reflection of someone she has observed. Across this land are folk lacking a portion of themselves and they know not where they might find it: a beggar who has lost his misery, a tumbler his balance, a priest his faith, a harlot her heart. She has stolen a piece of their souls and taken it into herself.

If she can be so many different people, how do I know that my girl is the true Maid? Perhaps that is another of her fabrications. I try to shake the thought away, but it sticks, nipping at my insides. Faster and faster she goes, man after woman and woman after man, till they blur into each other and at their heart I see the same face shining through them all: an angry face, twisted, screwed up, monstrous with terror. I stop laughing.

'Wait!' I cry. The play stutters to a halt. Her body melts the final time and she is the Maid once more. 'Who is that?'

'What?' she pants.

'Who is at the heart of these disguises? Where are you in all of this shadow-play?'

'Me? Nowhere. I am nothing.'

'Anything but,' I snort. 'Tell me who you are, in truth.'

Her eyes darken. 'If you knew the truth, you would thrust me away.'

'Would I now?'

'There's nothing to me but disguise. It is safer to be a different person.'

'Are you so unacceptable that you do not wish to be yourself?'

'Anne,' she growls, with warning in the sound.

'Trust me.'

'No!' she snorts, as though I have asked her to cut her own throat. 'I am not worth trusting, Anne,' she adds, voice smaller than a cockle. 'I am evil.'

'Are you? To me you sound frightened.'

'Enough. Do not press me. Please.'

I don't know what possesses me, but without thinking about it, I lean across the space between us and kiss her on the mouth. Her mouth is soft, surprisingly so, for everything else about her is as brutal as bent wire. She freezes, stares at me from huge eyes.

'Yes, you are frightened, if a kiss can make you stone.'

'Anne—'

'Come. Let us go downstairs. I shall steal nothing more from you. Until you have enough money to go, you're safe here. And from more than the pestilence.'

Despite the delight with which the Maid sweetens my life, still I must endure daily battle with Thomas. Every morning we take up arms: I demand he send grain to the miller along with every other woman in the shire; he grumbles about the cost and bids me get on my knees and grind his oats into meal. He tries to sweeten his obstinate behaviour with flattery, but I do not for one moment believe he prefers the taste of home-ground oatmeal. He savours the labour he must load on to my shoulders.

One afternoon shortly after the Feast of Saint Lawrence I am in my accustomed position, at the grindstone. Thomas hops around, finding fault as always. His barbs have lost much of their sting, for I harbour a secret companion and he knows nothing about it.

'You should rub the grindstone to the left,' he snipes.

'Widdershins? That is bad luck, sir,' I say, seemingly without guile.

'Superstition is the work of the devil,' he grunts.

I stretch my eyes wide. 'I say it only because the bad thief was hung on the left side of our Lord. You said so in the Easter sermon. Of course, I might be mistaken. That is altogether possible. Am I wrong, sir?'

'No,' he grumbles. 'You are correct.'

'Your sermons are very memorable, sir,' I simper.

His eyes examine me for impertinence. Finding none, he turns to go.

'Sir?' I call, pointing at the grindstone. 'You are leaving? I thought you were going to give me proper instruction.' I make my expression so helpless I am sure even Thomas will see right through to the scowl behind. But he does no such thing. He purses his lips and I dare even more. 'Please, sir,' I trill, pattering my eyelashes against my cheek. 'You could show me, I am sure.'

I give him my most beaming smile. He mumbles his usual excuse about *the work of the Lord* and scuttles away. The Maid appears beside me. One moment she is not there; the next she is.

'I don't know how you do that,' I gasp, fanning myself with my apron. 'One day I'll faint clean away, so I will.'

'I'll teach you sometime,' she says softly. 'It's not so difficult.'

I give the grindstone a few more turns, aware of her bright presence at my elbow.

'What are you doing?'

'Don't you start. I get enough of that from him.'

She laughs: it is such a delicate sound. 'I have something to help.'

'A spare pair of hands?'

Her laughter continues, so thin as to be near invisible. 'That's better,' she says. 'I like it when you are prickly.'

She holds out her hand and uncurls the fingers. In her palm is a mound of sand, dry and yellow.

'Where did you get that?'

'The dunes.'

'They're three miles from here!'

'They are.'

'Very pretty. Now let me get on with this, or he'll have no oatcakes with his supper and oatcakes are what he wants.'

'Lift up the stone.'

'Maid,' I say. 'Leave me be. We can play after.'

'No. *You* listen,' she snaps, sharper than I've ever heard her. 'Learn something, Anne.'

I am so taken aback that I open my mouth to give her a piece of my mind. But it's not her that's vexed me: that's Thomas's doing. If I shout at her it would be unfair. So I hold my tongue. Whatever she wants to do, it won't take long. I can indulge her. I sigh with the air of one martyred to their patience and lift the grindstone onto its side, revealing the half-ground meal beneath. Before I can stop her she sprinkles the sand onto it.

'What was that for?' I cry. 'My work, ruined! I'll have to start all over again.'

I go to slap her skinny calves, but she hops out of the way.

'No you won't,' she giggles. 'Drop the stone. Turn it a few times and you'll be done.'

'But it's full of sand!' I moan.

'Do it,' she commands, takes my shoulders and shakes me. I am always surprised by how much strength there is in that whip of a frame. 'Christ's bones,' she growls. 'You say *I* am witless.'

Grudgingly, I give the grindstone a yank. After two revolutions, she holds up her paw.

'Now. Look. Test it.'

I roll back the stone and find finely milled flour. It is a miracle. A moment ago it was half husk.

'That's all very well,' I grumble, to conceal my surprise. 'But it's still got sand in it. Unless you have a clever plan for getting it out.'

'Can you see the sand?'

'No. That's the problem.'

'Is it? You can't see it: neither will he.'

'He'll feel it soon enough, the moment he bites into the cake.'

'Exactly.' She watches my face as the sun of comprehension rises. 'Yes, you got there in the end. He gets his bread. I take it he gobbles the lot and you have to content yourself with the porray left over from this morning?'

'Yes.'

'I thought as much. Here is your answer: half the time to grind it, twice the pleasure in serving it up to the swag-bellied bastard. He'll never know what you've done.'

I think of the Maid calling him *swag-bellied* and smile, hiding my amusement behind a straight face as I set up the trestle, spread the cloth and lay out the trencher of salt pork and bowl of oatcakes. I am careful to proceed with not one whit greater or lesser pomp. I must do everything just as I always do or the conniving dog will be on my scent in a flash.

The Maid and I seat ourselves next to the hearth. I take the stool and she crouches at my side, leaning against my thigh in the way she has done since she came to me. At first I thought the gesture of no more consequence than a cat rubbing its body against my leg to get attention. Now that I know her for what she truly is, her flesh warming mine through my skirt is oddly thrilling.

As I heat up the pottage, I wonder what it would be like to place my thumb beneath her chin, tip her face to mine and kiss her as I did before, right here by the fire. Would Thomas even notice? She pats my knee and I jump. I have meandered so far away that I have forgotten to fill our bowls. As I do so, I reflect on how these delightful wanderings have kept me from staring at Thomas and gloating over his coming discomfort, and that is no bad thing.

I make a dumbshow of reminding the Maid how to hold the spoon so that the gruel does not slide off. It would not do to have her be too skilled too quickly. Besides, I like to have some excuse to be close to her. These days, I feel empty when she takes herself away, even for a moment. We play our meal-time game of spills: I wipe her mouth and praise little successes with kind words and pecks on the cheek, and Thomas is almost forgotten.

'Anne,' he says with a choke, drawing me back to the room.

I start: he seldom calls me by name. Perhaps something in my manner with the Maid has given us away.

'Sir?'

'This bread—' he coughs again and pounds his chest.

'Yes, sir?' I keep my face sober.

'What is *in* it?' he rasps.

'Oatmeal, sir.'

'Nothing else?'

I pause and consider the question. 'Water,' I say, after a long moment's reflection.

'Did you do anything different?'

He holds up a piece, peering at it as though it is sprinkled with thorns. I rub my chin thoughtfully. The Maid lets out a squeak and I lay off the philosophical brow-wrinkling. She is right: there is no point overdoing things.

'I ground the flour differently.'

It is the plain truth. Putting sand into his bread is one thing; telling a falsehood before God is another thing entirely.

'How so?'

'You remember, sir. You instructed me to turn the stone the other way.'

'The other way?'

'That's right, sir. That is what I did.'

I smile obediently. The Maid rattles her spoon around the inside of her bowl, scraping up the last morsel and making slurping noises, for all the world ignoring our conversation.

219

With a grunt of achievement she elbows me and holds up the empty dish for my inspection.

'All finished!' I coo. 'What a clever girl you are.'

I never spoke more truly. She continues with her distractions, hopping about and pointing to the door.

'Sir. She wishes to ease herself. She is getting so much better at letting me know, isn't she?' I simper. 'Permit me to take her outside, if you will.'

I watch him wrestle with the desire to skewer me with sharper questioning and the prospect of her baring her arse and squeezing out a turd in front of him.

'Go to,' he says reluctantly.

I lead her outdoors as slowly as I can manage. Once we are clear of his prying eyes and ears, we run to the far end of the glebe and throw ourselves on to the ground, rolling on the grass and laughing like children.

Thus are my days lightened of Thomas's burdens. A touch of her hand, a smile given willingly, however swiftly she swallows it afterwards. The hearth grows cold, for I neglect to keep the fire lit. More and more often my feet carry me to the stable, for the Maid is there, and Thomas is not. When I look at him now, all I see are her gestures aping his. He is lost to me: not that I ever had the smallest portion of him.

At the Feast of Saint Bartholomew, the charcoal-burners descend from the forest and pass through the village on their way to the Staple to sell their wares in preparation for the colder days of autumn. Thomas sends me to buy some, and hands over a shilling as though it is a bag of silver as big as my head.

The whole company of villagers bustles about, making what

meagre bargains they may. I can hardly see the donkeys save for their spindly ankles poking out from beneath the knotted rope nets. The charcoal-burners pretend to have none put by for us, hemming and hawing and rubbing their chins at how pressing are the demands of the burghers at the Staple. They say the same each year and each year there is enough for our needs. It is their game, and we take part with a good enough humour.

My mother plucks at my sleeve. 'You look a lot happier,' she says.

'I am.'

'It gladdens my heart to hear it. So, you finally found a way around him, eh?' she winks.

I consider how insignificant Thomas is to my present happiness. 'I am content, Mother,' I say, when the pause stretches out its ribbon too long.

She nods her head. 'If God preserves us, I will see grand-children?' she adds hopefully.

Once again, a silence hangs on to the tail of her words.

'I pray for the Saint to keep us in his care,' I say, for lack of anything better to drop into the space.

'Of course, of course,' she mutters. 'Thomas is a fine and wealthy man.'

'Not that I see any of it,' I remark in a voice sharp as horse-radish.

She grunts, strides away and starts to harangue one of the charcoal-burners. As I look about, I see the man I lay with amongst them. He smirks in my direction, baring his teeth.

'I've got a couple of good fat sacks for you, missus, if you should care to test them for quality.'

He slaps the bulging nets and the donkey staggers. I eye him as boldly as I am able.

221

'I've no need for your goods, sir,' I say primly. 'I have plenty of wood set by for winter.'

'Those dry twigs of yours,' he cackles. 'Snap in two as soon as look at them. Set a flame and they'll be gone in a moment. Now, a nice hard bit of charcoal will see you through the longest night.'

'Aren't you going to tell me that all your wares are promised to the Staple?'

'Maybe they are. But I can always find some to spare for the right person.'

He winks. The Maid yanks at my skirt so hard I topple slightly.

'Behave,' I say.

'So, this the idiot child I've heard of, is it?' he enquires, jutting his chin at the girl. She growls at him. 'How'd you like a piece of what I've got, girlie?' he leers, and tickles her under the chin. 'I've never been fussy about the face.'

'I wouldn't get too close, if I were you,' I point out.

'Why not?' he says.

For answer, her head snaps forward, quick as a viper, and she sinks her teeth into his hand. She lets go at once, but he springs up and down, making such a fuss you'd think he'd stuck his fingers into the heart of the charcoal pit. I'm not the only one to find it comical, for everyone looks in our direction, always happy for fresh sport. Even the Maid laughs, in that odd way of hers which is more about honking and spitting.

'The bitch has bitten me!' he moans.

'Stop complaining. It's barely a scratch.'

'Should have the little bastard strangled, if you can't control it,' he mutters.

'Now, now,' says William, wading in. 'That's our Maid you're talking about. She's sent from God, she is.'

'I found her,' adds Richard, joining our little crowd.

'I was there, too,' says Michael.

'And I,' declares Roger.

While they are engaged in their usual argument about who was first to set eyes on her, I tug her hand and we walk away, the charcoal-burner glaring after. It's the matter of a few moments to reach the stable. As soon as I bolt the lower half of the door and half-close the upper, the Maid stretches, gasping with the pleasure of easing cramped limbs.

'Every day I wish I'd chosen a more comfortable disguise!' she says, and casts a sly look upon me. 'So, tell me, Anne. What was your business with him?'

'Business?'

My face burns. It is as if she knows what I did. I have a sudden vision of her in the body of a bird, flying over the trees and seeing me grunting beneath that man, crying out my need.

'I've made mistakes,' I mutter. 'I'm no saint and you may as well know it.'

She raises her eyebrow but says nothing, nor has she any need to. She laughs at my shamefacedness, and its weight lifts from me as easy as a lid off a pot.

'I am right glad to hear it.'

'I am a woman,' I continue. 'I hunger. It is as natural as the sap rising in a tree in spring.'

'And he satisfied that hunger?'

I shrug. 'For a while. It was—'

'Brief?'

'Yes,' I mutter. 'Something was – missing.'

She steps to my side, lays her fingers upon my arm and skims her hand from wrist to elbow and back again.

'Like this?' she asks.

'Yes,' I say, and hear an unaccustomed cracking in my voice. 'Something like that.'

'Something?'

'Permit me to demonstrate more precisely.' I untie the ribbons at my wrists and roll back the sleeves. I take her hand and press it to my naked flesh, and once again she strokes my arm. Every hair pricks to attention.

'Indeed, that is better,' she says.

Her face swims close to mine, pale as a moon floating in the dim light of the stable. I do not fully believe she is going to kiss me until she does, but my body is straightway warm with the fire that is ever smouldering. She slides her fingers under my coif, finding the warm spot at the base of my neck.

'Your hand is cool,' I rasp.

She draws back a little, regards me carefully. 'Too much so?' she asks quietly, and takes her hand away.

I let out a sigh of frustration, for her touch has thrilled me deeply. I am not disappointed for long, however, for she busies herself with drawing out the two pins that hold my kerchief tight. She is about to toss them away when I pluck them from her fingers and stick them in my apron.

'Do not discard them,' I whisper. 'I will need them later.'

'My careful Anne,' she murmurs, smiling.

She lifts away my scarf, uncovers my hair and with tantalising slowness unrolls the coiled braid around my left ear then that around my right, combing her fingers through the strands until the tresses spread in a loose shawl across my shoulders.

'You are the sun, and your hair its rays.'

'A dull brown sun,' I mumble.

'Bright and warm enough for me to warm my hands. What use do I have for a lamp to light the whole world? All I need is a candle to brighten my small patch of earth.'

224

On any other occasion I would snort at such a ridiculous avowal. But I do not feel inclined to laughter of the scornful sort.

I take a deep breath. 'Who are you being at this moment?' I ask, for I must know.

She pauses, and runs her tongue across her upper lip, left to right. 'No disguises, Anne.'

'None?'

'No.'

I ask no further questions. She takes a sheaf of hair and lifts it to her face and smoothes it across her cheek, her lips, her brow, burying her nose in its folds. She runs the tip of her tongue around the whorled flesh of my ear and I let out a strangled gasp that has been building up in my breast. At the sound she pulls away and at first I am afraid she will stop her delightful caressing, but her face is soft, softer than I have ever seen.

'My legs are unwilling to stand,' I breathe. 'It seems foolish to disobey them.'

She laughs, very quietly. I take her hand and lead her to the back of the stable, where the straw is heaped, a mattress made especially for this moment. The mare raises her head and snuffles as we pass, nodding her head in approval. I do not know whether the Maid draws me down or I draw her, but all that matters is that we are in each other's arms.

I never felt so languorous, so loath to move. I wonder if we might lie here safely until this dying world has passed away and a brighter one has been born. I speak none of this foolishness: I am far too caught up in the enchantment of her embrace. Her lips begin an intimate exploration, pressing their warmth into my throat. Her teeth nibble the fruit of my flesh, and the more hungrily she devours, the more I need to be tasted.

225

Suddenly, I am burdened with far too many clothes. My fingers tangle in the laces of my bodice, and I never had so much trouble trying to undo them. The harder I try, the tighter the knots become.

'Let me,' she breathes, and the ribbons unravel beneath her fingers. She lifts up my skirt, heavy as a stook of wheat. 'How do you bear such a weight around your legs?' she says, grinning. 'You may as well be hobbled. You cannot run.'

'I never have any reason to run.'

'And now?'

'At this moment, the thought of running has never been further from my mind.'

She unpeels me from my garments and it occurs to me I have never been this naked with another, not even with the charcoal-burner in the forest; not since I was a child and was too young to know what it meant when men and women lay together. My fingers search her out, brushing her face, her shoulders, her arms, rubbing and squeezing her flesh so frantically that I am unsure where she begins and I end, so do we melt into each other. I draw her shift over her head and devour her; ready, so ready for this banquet delivered into my hands. I think it is a hunger that can never be satiated.

She is all smoothness; different from the broad and bristled bodies of men I thought were my portion. Yet for all she is a woman, we are nothing alike. I trace the curve of her breasts, so small they are almost not there, stretched tight across the basket of her ribs. Only her nipples betray her sex: brown and the size of cherries.

She watches me watching her, my breath halting as her hand brushes against some part of me that is particularly sensitive. Especially my nipples: it is as though all passion and tenderness are concentrated in those two points. She takes them between her teeth and pulls, gently to begin, but more fiercely as my demands to be so used grow fierce.

'This sharpness pleases you?'

'Pleases?' I gasp, voice strange in my ears as though I am speaking a foreign tongue. 'More than that. It stirs me to life. But no words. You have stopped what you were doing,' I frown. 'Go to.'

My body soars into the heaven of her hands. I am soft and wet as though wounded, but there is no pain, only pleasure. She presses her fingers into the folds of my quim, moving faster or slower in time to the urgency of my breath, giving greater rapture than I thought existed in this world. It is like running down a hill, faster than my feet can go, and I cannot slow down because if I do I will tumble head over heels, face first. I cry out almost angrily, as though I am delighted against my will. As though this is a shameful thing. With that thought, all delight crashes about my ears like an old wall.

'No!' I whisper. She ceases her wonderful stroking. 'This is sin,' I hiss, wishing it were not so. 'It must be. It is too—'

'Pleasurable?' she snorts. 'Is that so terrible?' She cups my cheek and smiles very gently.

'If this is not shameful, then why are we hiding?'

'There is a world of difference between private and sinful. Your prayers are private, are they not?'

'You're telling me this is a prayer?'

'Why not? Do you not feel closer to heaven than ever before?'

All the blood in my heart presses itself into my face, for I am reminded how wildly I cried out. She grins, and tickles me under the arms, where I am very ticklish. I try to bat her hands away, and we collapse into giggles. She kisses my brow.

'Listen to me prattle on. Here I am sermonising when there is kissing to be done.'

'Let us pray,' I answer.

With that, she makes good as her word. Under her hands I reach into the heavens with my whole body and shake down the stars with my cries. I soar into myself at the insistence of her touch and further still, lifted into rapture I never thought to taste because I did not know it existed. Higher than the summit of a hill, the air crisp as an autumn morning when the world shimmers and sparkles.

I lie gasping in her arms. The stable is the same as a few moments ago: straw tossed about, the mare stamping her foot. But a change has been wrought. I do not know what it is, but it has been waiting its chance to spring up in my soul. Now I understand what the charcoal-burner could not give me. His was a brief satisfaction of the flesh, a hammer pummelling the anvil. She is the furnace, coaxing me to melt into who knows what shape.

It is only afterwards, when I am putting on my gown, that the shilling falls out of the folds and I remember that I bought no charcoal.

Whenever we can steal a moment, the Maid and I dash breathless to the stable, passing secrets on our tongues as we embrace. We have our daily game of seeking each other out away from the eyes and ears of Thomas: a grasped moment amongst the apple trees, another few moments when he goes to the church. We find more and more reasons to go to the well, falling into each other's arms under the dripping arch of the trees, mouths and hands ravenous. I am so filled with the savour of her flesh against mine that I can think of little else but when I may next clap my arms about her and squeeze her close.

I must have money, she says and I reply *Yes, yes*, although I know not whence it might come. I do not understand her hurry and determination. I have no desire to hasten this delectable time away. Nothing can dampen my cheer. The sweetest being ever to draw breath is mine. If this is a game, then it is the best I have ever played, for I have already won.

It is only afterwards that I realise this game is in earnest, and of the deadly sort.

VIXEN

I am more naked with her than I have ever been. I am alive. I have not felt alive before. I hate her for making me desire her. I love her for making me melt. But this cannot be love. This is the grinding of flint, two bodies striking sparks.

Anne sees through my disguises and asks who I am: the question I cannot answer, will not answer. Asks to see *me*, as if that girl exists. I'd like to see her face if I let her in on the wreckage that is my life. See the smile fall away and be traded for fear, her so-called love turned to loathing in the blink of an eye.

I hide in the stable. The mare tosses her head in greeting. I rub my palms along her neck and she blows air through soft-bristled lips.

'You ask me no questions,' I murmur, and she snorts once more.

I find a tick under her mane, bloated with blood. I tiptoe to the house, which stands mercifully quiet, take a half-burned stick from the hearth and carry it back to the stable, blowing on the ember to keep it aglow. I touch the red tip to the creature and it sizzles, falling away. The mare stamps her hoof, but I tell her all is well and she quietens, making no more to-do.

I inspect every inch of her, tracking down and killing every tick that I find.

I'd be a horse any day. Four legs to carry me away, nothing to do but eat, fart, sleep and serve a stallion when the time is right. I jump on to her back and wrap my arms and legs about her. Her heat sends a shiver through my thighs. I cannot put my arms all the way round her belly, however far I stretch my fingers. My stomach tickles with her rough hair, nostrils prickle with the scent of her hide.

As I drowse in the dip of her spine it occurs to me how dimwitted I am, for the means of my escape is stirring beneath me. I grasp her mane in my fists, press my knees into her flanks and we trot from the stable, out of the yard, through the ford and in a moment are on the road to the sea. It is that easy.

I spur her into an unwilling canter and will not let up, kicking pitilessly until she begins to gallop, faster and faster till the fields are a blur of yellow, brown and green; till we barely touch the earth and she is flying me from this cramped rat-hole, wings on her fetlocks.

We thump along, my backside bouncing on her broad back. I feel the flex of bone and muscle, taste the snort of her breath, rejoice at the thunder of her hooves. The scent of tilled earth is seasoned with the salt of the marshes, stronger and stronger as we draw closer to the coast. I'll sell her and pay my passage to Ireland as fast as that. I'll be away.

The mare clatters to a halt, so suddenly I only stop myself from tumbling off by hanging on to her ears. She snorts with a sense of a journey completed. The firm track has petered out and we stand at the edge of the marshland, the ground soft with sour water. Today it is calm, very different from the last time I was here. It stretches ahead, flat and dour, cut through

231

with sluggish ditches meandering towards the sea. I pummel her neck.

'Move!' I cry.

She droops her head, nose sniffing the hedgerow for a tasty mouthful. I yank on her mane and she ignores me. I jab my heels into her belly.

'Come on!' She finds a patch of grass that meets her approval and begins to crop, teeth grinding down its sweetness. 'Giddup! Ho! Girl!' I shout, thinking of all the encouraging words I've heard men yell at their beasts.

She pauses in her chewing and I think I have persuaded her: her guts rumble, she lets out a long fart and returns to munching. I kick more and more viciously, punching her head with my fists and tugging her ears over and over. She takes as much notice of me as she would a gnat.

I slide off her back and smack her side, kindly this time. She twists her head and brushes her nose against mine, blowing moist heat into my face. I bend, scoop up a handful of mud, hold it to my face and inhale deeply.

'Smell that? It's not been dug, or ploughed, or planted. They don't want it. They say it's of no use. But it's beautiful. It smells of escape. Don't you see?'

She does not. She's a horse. She sniffs my hand.

'It's safe to walk upon, if that's what you're worried about.' She draws away. 'You won't get lost. I've been here before.' She knows a falsehood when she hears it and flicks her tail in derision. 'Over there . . .' I wave a dripping hand 'is the sea. Take me that far. Then I'll let you go,' I lie.

She continues to graze.

'Please,' I beg. 'Please take me away from here.' One ear twirls as though she might be listening. 'I'll feed you warm bran mash. I'll polish your hooves with butter. I'll groom you with a golden

232

brush set with badger bristle.' She ignores my fairy tales and does not stir her hoof one jot further.

The sky is low, but not dangerous; like a sheet that needs laundering stretched above my head. Wind is bringing rain from the west. It'll be here in under an hour, by the look of the clouds. Something about the weather is sickly, and I shudder despite myself. Birds are gathering overhead. Plovers flash their red beaks, a handful of seagulls crack the air with ugly voices. The skin on the back of my neck prickles.

'Here to tell me of another storm?' I cry. I shake my fist, setting them into a flap. 'Afraid of me?' I scream. 'Good! You've made a dangerous enemy.'

You don't just act like a simpleton, you are that creature, they cackle.

'I'm not a fool!' I yell. 'I am not!'

You want her. You want her.

'I don't!' I wail.

They swirl away, chattering. For all my protests, they are right. I am stupid. I do want her. Everything I have ever known shrieks at me to keep going, to ride and ride until the horse dies beneath me, and then run until I collapse with exhaustion, and then pick myself and run some more and never stop.

I throw myself on to the ground and scream my frustration and anger. I drum my heels, wail until I am wrung empty. I lie there listening to the nothing between my ears. The reeds rattle with my secret, passing the truth from stem to stem: *The Maid is a fool, a fool, a fool. The Maid loves. The Maid loves.*

For the first time, I speak to my fears as one who is not in thrall to them.

'Be quiet,' I say, and the tauntings hiccup to a stop, surprised that I am their master, even if only for a breath. 'I am my own woman,' I say. 'If I love – so be it. *If* I love, that is.'

233

I rinse off the muck in a ditch and climb back on to the horse. Her vast eyes glitter with what looks a lot like amusement. She whickers and stamps her hoof. I cluck at her, tug her mane gently. She turns about and we begin the long trek back to the village.

As soon as I have stabled the mare, I seek Anne out and find her in the house, shelling peas. I take her hand and place it on my breast, over the spot where my heart thumps.

'Are you hungry?' she asks.

I shake my head from side to side. I cannot speak for the pebble lodged in my throat. The mute disguise I have created for the village is accurate, tonight at least. Anne nods in response. I stumble into her arms before she has had a chance to open them to me fully. I am so famished I think I may swallow her in my kisses. But she is hungry also. I cling to her like one who is drowning, and plunge my hand into her body as though the safety I seek is between her legs.

NONE
1349

From Saint Cuthburga to Saint Frithestan

THOMAS OF UPCOTE

The boy found me in the church, pressing grease into the hinges of the window shutters.

'I must speak with Father Thomas. I was told he was here.'

'You have found him,' I said, climbing down the ladder and wiping my hands on my stomach.

The lad did not move from the doorway. 'I have a message. From Father John, of the Staple. He preaches at Saint Petroc's.'

'Yes, yes, I know him.'

The boy shifted his weight from his right foot to his left, and back again.

'So? The message?'

He stared at my pattens, my hose loose about the knee, my oily tunic.

'What then, boy? Has he sent a fool?'

'No, sir. Father. Reverend sir.' He sighed. 'Father John will attend upon you today, after Sext.'

'But that is in a few hours only.'

'That is the message.'

'Will he be alone?'

'No, Father.'

'Then who will be with him?'

'He did not tell me,' he shrugged. 'Gentlemen.'

He put out his hand and would not move until I put a penny into it. He kissed the coin and left without bidding me good day. As he passed through the gate I heard him singing, *There was a fox lived in the wood.* I tried to walk slowly to the house, but was still breathless when I arrived. Anne brought water and I began to clean my hands.

'I need my best shirt and over-tunic,' I said, picking the stickiness from beneath my fingernails. 'John of Pilton will be here this mid-afternoon. And some other gentlemen.'

Anne held the bowl steady. 'Then I will take the girl to the well, sir.'

'No, she will stay. And you also.'

I could not get all the dirt away. It seemed that I moved it from one part of my hand to the other. I rubbed harder.

'Strangers will confound her.'

'They are not strangers to me. They have business here. With her.'

'With her?'

'Hold the bowl still. Can you not see that I am covered in muck up to my wrists?'

'What business?'

'My business. The work of God. And men.'

Anne took the bowl to the window. 'Thomas, what have you done?'

'I have done nothing. I do not need to explain myself.'

She threw the filthy water through the open casement. I heard it splash against earth.

A crowd of boys ran shrieking beside the wagon, announcing its arrival. It was as tawdrily attired as the men within; painted and panelled sides, and a hooped roof of scarlet cloth that bulged and sucked its cheeks in the breeze.

They began their complaints as soon as they climbed down: the dampness of the air, the clenching smoke from the hovels, and Nicholas Fuller the physician the loudest amongst them. He peered into the cup of ale brought up from the brewer's house, sipped at it unwillingly.

I smiled and held my cap, bobbing my head at these insults as I showed them up the stairs into the schoolroom. The light warmed the window frames and filled the room with the smell of flax oil and beeswax.

John showed Nicholas to the largest chair, dancing about his skirts. I knew also William Sneaton, the master of the boys' school, but not the other man, whom they called Walter. None thought to introduce me to him.

'Master John tells us that you boast of a monster pulled from the marshes,' began Nicholas.

I opened my mouth, but the schoolmaster filled the space. 'There was a monster born in Hartland, as I heard tell, that had two snakes growing from its breast, and another from its mouth. Its mother had lain with the Serpent.' He smoothed the long hair on his chin. 'It was at the time of the hunger. Sent by the Devil himself.'

'To confuse us.'

'To turn us from God.'

'I heard this too.'

'I also.'

They tussled for a while to be the first who heard this tale, the tips of their noses sketching circles in the air.

'What happened to the creature?' I asked.

They looked surprised that I could speak. Or dared to.

'I did not hear tell.'

'Nor I.'

'I believe it died; it was ordered to be starved,' said William.

'And the mother?' asked John.

'Stoned for her sin.'

'But the child I have here is no monster,' I said. 'There is no deformity about her.'

'Is she not green? I heard she was green,' said Nicholas.

I lifted my chin. 'She was green. And brown. A multitude of hues when we found her in the marshes.'

'A fish then,' said Walter.

The others turned towards him, nodding agreement. Nicholas coughed into his hand, wiped it against his embroidered tunic.

'Not a fish,' I continued. My heart beat fast, but I placed my hands in a calm arrangement upon my stomach. All would be well. I was convinced of her holiness: they would be too. 'The colours upon her were easily loosened by water and much scrubbing.' I looked from face to face. 'Not the scales of a fish, which we also scrub away, but dirt, revered sirs.'

I watched their faces. Walter smiled and I permitted myself to smile also.

'Dirty,' he said.

Nicholas grunted. 'I heard it on good report that she is a pygmy.' He glared at John. 'Is she small?'

'Only as any girl close to womanhood,' I replied.

'Is she a pygmy then? Did you consider this?' he continued, ignoring me.

'Origen has proved that pygmies are not human,' piped the schoolmaster.

'She is a child, not yet full grown,' I persisted.

'Why does she not tell you whence she came?'

'She does not speak.'

240

'Speech can easily be beaten out of the unwilling,' said William to the others, but not to me.

'She is not unwilling. She makes noises, but they are not English, nor Latin, nor Greek.'

'French then?'

'Not even French. No tongue of men.'

'I heard she grunts and whinnies,' said John.

'Like a beast.'

The word rolled heavily in the space between us and I could not pick up its weight swiftly enough.

'Does she have the head of a dog? I heard of a dog-headed boy born in Bristol,' squeaked William. 'His father sinned grievously, and his children were cursed.'

'They are godless in the north.'

They nodded again; hounds on a hot day that hang out their tongues and droop their muzzles.

'She has the head of a girl,' I said, my voice straining to be heard. 'There is no malformation in her body.'

'I heard tell of a girl with the claws of a crab rather than hands,' began William. Nicholas glared at him, and he quietened. The man Walter spoke to me more politely.

'Can she speak to beasts?'

I selected my words with care. 'It is true that she innocently chooses the company of animals. She lodges in the stable.'

'This is foulness,' rumbled Nicholas. 'Her mother lay with a horse.'

'She does not have any of the features of a horse.'

He did not hear me. 'Who then cast her out to conceal her vileness. That is why she stalls with beasts. She is half beast herself.'

I answered quickly, finding words I did not know I possessed. 'Or perhaps she is sinless: the Holy Brannoc himself yoked

241

stags to the plough, and a wolf became his faithful servant. Holiness, not foulness.'

'Saint Petroc did this too,' said John, very loud, so that all turned to him.

'He did,' I said, and prayed it did not sound like a question. My heart warmed to him for the first time I could remember. They would believe. God would make it so.

'Foulness,' grumbled Nicholas, glaring at John.

'As beasts are to us, so must we appear to God,' sighed William, tugging at the hairs on his chin so fiercely that some came away. He looked at them, wound around his fingers, then shook them onto the floor. The rest of the company grunted, nodded. I waited for quietness to come upon us again.

'I would not claim any holiness for myself, sirs,' I said. 'Not at all. I am a simple parish priest. I do not have the learning you gentlemen possess.' I looked at my knees. 'But I have observed this child. When we found her, she bit and snarled in the company of men. Now she holds herself meekly, and contends no more. At least, not when she is with me, a man of God.'

I did not say, *And also Anne.* Most of all, I did not speak of my vision. I would not influence their own awakening of faith. It was not for me to say she was holy. That was for the Lord. Nicholas removed his cap, flapped it before his face. His cheeks oozed with sweat.

'She does not speak in the tongues of men, and prefers the company of horses. Is that not mark enough of an animal?'

He hawked and emptied his mouth onto the rushes. I would not let myself become angry. *I am as mild as a lamb,* I said privately.

'With God's grace she has been sent to us as a girl child,' I said, and nodded devoutly; saw all heads save Nicholas's nod

242

too. My voice swelled. 'Must we not allow little children to come to the Lord? Did He not teach—'

'Enough talk,' interrupted Nicholas, waving away my protestations. 'We must see this proven. I would examine this creature. I am a man of medicine. I will tell you if she is child of beast or child of man.'

The nodding began afresh. I swallowed air, which lay heavy in my belly.

'I will send for her,' I said, for I dared not leave the room.

I could have fought them. To this moment, more than any other, I would return and be a different man. But I was determined to make them see through my eye of faith, and my words were not sufficient to the task. If the act of looking upon the Maid hastened their belief, then so be it. It was my undoing.

I leaned out of the window and cursed the emptiness of the street. The cart still stood outside the alehouse door. I could smell meat cooking. The cart driver would be enjoying his meal. My mouth filled with water.

'Aline!' I bawled and her face appeared at the window, wet about the mouth. 'Go to my house, I beg you. I pray you see that the girl is brought here.'

'The girl?'

I pushed my head further out of the casement, clinging to the sill.

'Can you not hear me? The Maid,' I hissed. Still she stared at me. 'The Vixen,' I whispered, and rolled my eyes.

Her mouth formed a small *o*, and she bellowed to the room behind her that she must be errand-girl to the priest. There was laughter, smothered none too quickly.

I looked more closely at the wagon. The straw at its bottom was enough for comfort, but dirty. My uncharitable humour noted that the good doctor was not so rich that he could afford fresh rushes for his journey. Or was too lazy to have a care. As I watched, the surface stirred and a rat tumbled from the back of the wagon and hobbled towards the nearest wall. How slowly it moves, I thought. Even the vermin of the Staple are lazy. One of our cats would soon put a finish to it. I felt moist breath on my ear and my blood leapt. Nicholas laid his paw on my shoulder.

'A fine schoolhouse my Lord Bishop has built here,' he said.

'Indeed, sir. We are grateful every day.'

'It is a shame we did not need to chase out any boys to make room for us.' My face glowed. 'Can any read in this place? Save yourself, Father Thomas?'

'We are humble folk,' I chanted.

'Indeed you are.'

He patted me like you would a toothless hound, long past its hunting days. I leaned further out of the window to escape his clutch.

'See: she is brought,' I shouted and gladly, for Anne was approaching, leading the Maid by the hand.

The girl blinked as though the light pricked her eyes. Anne had clothed her in one of her old under-dresses, and the girl rubbed at her thigh, unused to the heavy fabric so close to her skin. I prayed she did not tear it. Prayed that she kept it upon her and did not caper about naked. They must see her for the angelic creature she was.

Their feet creaked the stairs: Anne's tread heavy and slow; the girl's faint, quieter than any child, who are by nature noisy. I pushed the comparison away. She *is* a child, I reminded myself. Sent to me by the Lord. Then they were in the room. The Maid held onto Anne's hand and regarded us steadily.

'Now then,' said Nicholas, and swept across the floor towards the women.

The girl shrivelled into Anne's side.

'Have a care, my good doctor,' I called out. 'She is a maiden, and modest before any man.'

'Yes. So you say,' he said, and sat again, his legs wide open at the knees. 'Woman, bring her to me.'

He coughed, and it turned into a rattling bark. He pounded his chest and spat into his hand, peering at the dark gobbet before smearing it onto his thigh. Anne turned wide eyes towards me. Her cheeks were pale. She bit her lip and made a show of lifting her eyebrows and casting meaningful looks at the place on Nicholas's gown where he wiped the spittle. I frowned at her and remained silent.

'There is nothing to fear, mistress,' said John. 'We are not here to do any harm. We must decide simply if this is a child of man or beast.'

'See,' I said. 'Look upon her. The Maid is clean and whole. Born of woman.'

The physician rubbed his palms against his knees, darkening the wool. 'But she stands before us clothed,' he said. 'Who knows what foulness she may be hiding beneath her wrapper?'

'She hides nothing, sir,' said Anne. 'I have cared for her, bathed and clothed her. I have seen the whole of her.'

Nicholas sweated his hands up and down his thighs. 'I'm sure you have. But am I not the physician here?' He looked about him at the other men, and they smiled into their sleeves.

'Who knows what passes for clean and whole in such a place?' muttered the schoolmaster.

'Let her be stripped,' said Nicholas.

'Let it be so, mistress Anne,' I said, examining the ribbed plaster on the wall.

She knelt beside the girl and whispered words we could not hear, motioning for her to raise her arms so that the dress could be lifted over her head. As she raised the cloth we could see in turn the roughened skin of her knees, the ropes of her thighs, the goat's beard between them, and the pale crescent scratches laddering up her belly to the buds of her new breasts. Then at last her head, the tufts of hair where Anne had shorn her. She stood quietly and looked at us. Not bold, merely curious; tugging at the knots on her head.

I waited. For a miracle. For them to be struck by the evidence of her holiness. The room was quiet, save for our breathing. The only light was that trickling through the thick glass at the windows.

'Turn her.' The doctor's voice was rough.

Anne spoke softly, helped her turn, revealing the wings of her shoulder blades, the rack of her ribs and barely swelling hips, and again, the veil of healed scars and scratches. I did not know why God did not cast a halo of brightness around her. Had I sinned in some new way? Had I displeased the Lord? At last I found my voice.

'See. Did I not say she was whole? The only marks on her are scratches. From the cruelty of men or beasts, I do not know. But she is clearly born of woman, as are we all.'

All save Nicholas nodded in agreement with me, and Anne began to place the dress over the child's head.

'Wait,' said the doctor, and coughed into his hand again. 'She may be hiding her beastly nature within. The Devil tempted Saint Anthony in the form of a female. With teeth in her cunny. I will test her.'

'Nicholas,' began John, quietly.

'It is the only way to be sure,' he said before the rest of the words could be out. 'I have tested many women thus in the Staple.'

He glared at us, to see who would fight against him. We were silent.

246

'You shall not destroy her maidenhead,' said Anne. 'For then how shall things be for her?'

'I have done this many times,' he spoke, and loudly.

'Did you find any teeth?' growled Anne.

He turned upon me, scarlet with choler. 'You keep an unruly house, priest: I do not know who is servant and who is master.'

I said nothing. John stepped forward.

'Let us calm ourselves, gentlemen.' He held his hands up as though about to pray. 'Master Nicholas is a fine physician, and a godly man. Thomas is a gentle and careful priest.' Nicholas grunted. 'There may be no need of fingers. This goodwife vouches for the Maid's virginity, and so it may be. We can search for teeth with our eyes as well as we may with our hands.'

Nicholas remained silent, but the others dropped their chins on to their breasts, grumbling agreement. John turned to Anne.

'Mistress, let the child be seated,' he said. 'Then, if you will, hold her knees open.'

Anne stared at John a moment, then crossed the floor, brushing my sleeve. She did not look at me. I was a bird perched on the sill, waiting for her to shoo me away. She fetched a stool, placed the Maid upon it with great gentleness, speaking quietly all the while, and pushed the scrawny legs apart. Their heads turned to the task. I looked at the floorboards, counting the tiny holes of worms that dined on the wood, and would dine again and again until the floor crumbled and fell under its own weight.

'Will you not examine her also?' said John, close by, voice low so only I could hear. 'Unless this is a sight you have tired of already.'

Any brotherly feeling I held in my heart fled at that moment. In his eyes I saw anger and vengefulness and had no idea why. I looked at the Maid: the teasel straw at the join of her thighs, the lips that parted and showed the smallest of pink tongues. No teeth.

John's voice swelled to the roof-beams. 'I hope I may speak for us all when I say what we have here is proof of womanhood? Our dear brother in Christ, Thomas, has indeed saved a human child from the marshes. Not a beast. Are we satisfied?'

Nicholas would not speak. He watched Anne cover the girl and hold her close, kissing the top of her tangled head. William and the man Walter nodded together.

'Reverend Master Nicholas, are you satisfied? I would have us in agreement.'

'Yes; be with us on this matter,' said the schoolmaster.

Nicholas cleared his throat, and John seized upon the noise. 'So, we are agreed. Good. We have declared her a simple girl, abandoned by some godless farmer. Let it be made public. There is nothing else for us here. There are no wonders. Nothing.'

'Yes, she is a maid.'

'A maid only.'

No! cried the voice of my soul, but the words stayed locked within. The schoolmaster scratched at his backside through his cloak. John looked at me as though I might struggle against his words, but my arms lay heavily at my sides, and I thought them so weighty I might never lift them again. I said nothing of my revelation, of the holy task God had vouchsafed to me, of my unshakeable faith in the Maid's holiness.

I could not understand why she did not reveal herself to them as she did to me. She could blind them with her radiance if she chose. She chose not to. It was not my place to say she was holy. That was for God. This was her fault.

'We will take our leave, Father Thomas, and our grateful thanks for your kind hospitality.'

Blood found my cheeks, for it struck me that I had offered them only ale as they had arrived, and nothing more. The slant of light through the windows showed it was late in the day. I bowed, to hide my shame and confusion.

'Let us go,' snorted Nicholas. 'I have no great taste for a place where mothers abandon their children. I am hungry. You will all dine at my house, I pray you, sirs.'

He drew out a broad piece of cloth from inside his cloak and wiped the whole of his face, which shone with moisture. He hawked into the rag and stared at it. 'See how the very air here is corrupt, and makes me sicken.'

He held it up like a flag, spotted with blood.

None bade me farewell. The room was quickly empty. Anne busied herself with leading the Maid down the narrow staircase, and did not speak a word.

I listened to the commotion as they hauled themselves back on to the cart; the clink of coins in Aline's hand; their loud thanks for her welcoming beer; their sorrow they had not been offered food, for they were sure it would have been as tasty as the drover's report of it. With much shouting and clattering the wagon turned and began the climb back up the hill and the six miles to the Staple.

When I could no longer hear the creak of wheels, nor Nicholas' hoarse coughing, I left the school-loft and found Anne and the Maid on the street. The Maid looked directly at me, head on one side. Her hand lifted itself and found a comfortable place on Anne's shoulder.

'She is no beast.' My voice beat against air.

'Sir, I know,' said Anne. 'I have always known.' She paused. 'And now you have had men come test it out and also find it to be true.'

She turned her face to the Maid: their brows touched. My hand stirred, aching to slap her into looking at me, but I did not let it.

'This was not my doing. You know I speak the truth, mistress.'

249

She set her chin against me, chewing the words before spitting them out.

'Sir, did you labour to bring the test to an end? No. You welcomed their spite into this place. And anything else they brought with them.'

A nail drove its chill point into my belly.

'I do not know what you mean, woman,' I blustered.

'You saw the fever brewing in that man's sweat, yet did nothing. You did not fight against those gentlemen any more than a fowl throttled and plucked for their table.'

'Madam, you speak against me, and against God's laws.'

Her eyes opened and closed. Surely she would be quiet now.

'Is it God's law to use a girl so?'

'The apostle tells us that the husband shall be the head of the wife. That is what I meant.'

'Sir, you are not my husband.'

The Maid looked at me attentively. Her hand rested still upon Anne, neither tightening nor loosening in any way.

'Mistress Anne,' I said, and found my voice light as a boy's, 'I wish it were not so.'

'Passionately I wished the same. This spring. Three months ago, even. No longer. I am a sinful woman, for I am in your house and not a wife. Today I thank God for my sin. I would not be tied to you by God.'

'Anne.' I could say no more.

She led the Maid away and I watched them walk down the street towards the ford. I did not follow. I found my way to the stream beyond the churchyard and waded in up to my knees. Washed and washed myself over and over but still could not make myself clean. I wished to beat myself against a rock, as women do with their linen.

ANNE

As we leave Thomas behind us, I cling to the Maid's hand. Any man observing us – and today we have been observed sufficient for a lifetime – would swear that I lead her. I know better. Without seeming to, she holds me back as though she can tell from the trembling of my limbs that I am near to bolting. So we proceed. I have never walked so slowly, nor needed to.

I have trodden this street many times, but today it is a foreign land, the ford so far off it will take the best part of a day to walk there, surely. The Maid hugs my side so that she is the one who appears afraid. She is the one who has been wounded, yet this past half-hour has cut me open as deep as a knife. My hands shake, and not only in fear.

I am furious.

If she was not hanging on to me so firmly, I would run to the house, *his* house: drag out his bed, his clothes, his books; burn them all and dance round the bonfire screaming songs of conquest. And if he came scampering up the road to see what all the fuss was about, squawking *what a to-do*, I'd pick him up by his greasy shoulders, toss him on top of the heap and watch him sizzle.

I'd invite everyone to warm their hands: Mother, Father, even my sister Cat, the whole village. I'd drag the winter meat down from its hook and feed the folk till they could eat no more. We'd toast bread in the flames, warming chilly fingers and drying out our sodden feet. Thomas would blacken and crisp up like a good bit of roast pork. I'd say, *For once the snail-paced skinflint has sweetened the air around him*, and everyone would laugh.

But I am on the mud track on the way back to Thomas's house. The rain flings itself sideways into my eyes, soaking my delectable picture. It flickers and snuffs out.

'I did not know men could do such things,' I whisper.

The Maid does not reply.

'Have you ever seen anything so . . .' I scrabble for a word, but nothing seems sufficient. 'So vile,' I say eventually.

It does not encompass what I wish to say, not at all. There is no answer.

'Don't you think so? Surely you must think so.'

She is quiet.

'Why won't you speak?' I say miserably. 'Have they terrified speech out of you?'

The realisation that this is precisely what has happened is so awful to bear that I fall to my knees, throw my arms around her hips and bury my face in her belly.

'Oh Lord!' I wail, blotting her shift with my tears. 'Why did they not defile me instead? Holy Brannoc, strike them down! Every one of them, for shaming this girl!'

'Anne,' she hisses. I raise my face to hers. 'Hush.' She glances about us nervously. 'Get up,' she says, speaking in a strange way. I hear the words, but her lips do not move. 'Now.'

'My love?' I gasp, scrambling to my feet. 'You are not struck dumb?'

I wipe my face with my apron. My knees are still trembling.

252

I am crammed full to bursting with feelings – relief, passion, anger – and all of them contending against the other.

'Not here,' she continues, in the same odd way that makes her look as though she is not speaking at all. 'God's Blood, let us get to the stable, then talk.'

I ache to take her hand and dance around the churchyard, but I walk solemnly at her side, through the ford. It is only when the door is closed behind us that I speak.

'You are well!' I shout. 'The Saint be praised for your deliverance!'

She shoves me against the wall, and at first I think she is going to kiss me, in that fierce way of hers I relish so dearly.

'Be quiet, Anne!' she cries, face writhing in fury. 'What was all that carry-on in the street?'

'I was—' I begin.

'Asking me if I was struck dumb? Every eye in every cott was upon us.'

'I saw no—'

'No what? You can't fart in this village without everyone and their dog knowing about it.' She pauses, waiting for the stone to make ripples in the sludge of my mind. 'My whole disguise is convincing people that I'm a halfwit who cannot speak save when God speaks through me. You could've given me away. You did give me away.'

'You worry too much,' I protest.

The words are feeble and roll between us, dry as knuckle-bones in a child's game. I open my mouth to apologise, but she grabs my kerchief where it fastens around my neck, twisting it so violently that the air in my throat is squeezed out.

'Do I?' she hisses.

'Maid,' I wheeze.

'I have been plumbed and prodded. I have only just escaped

having my cunny stretched by that slack-wit's fist while your bastard Thomas stood by, and yet you say I worry too much?'

Stars are sparkling in my eyes. The bellows of my lungs are empty. I pat her fist, rammed under my chin. She ignores me.

'I have spent this quarter-year playing the fool and you risk bringing it to nothing. All it takes is two minutes of caterwauling in front of the church where everyone can see.'

A river is rushing in my ears; I am caught up in its tumbling flood. My arms fall limp. Her wild words swim thicker and thicker and I close my eyes. At that moment the strangle loosens and air dashes into my body. It takes a dozen greedy breaths for the dancing lights to clear. When they do I find myself leaning against the wall and the Maid a long way off, turning over the straw with her toe.

'I hurt you,' she grumbles. 'I am sorry.'

She gives the straw a mighty kick and it sends up a spray of splinters. I rub my neck, cough.

'I was about to say that I am the sorry one,' I say, voice hoarse. 'You are right. I was foolish.'

Her back is to me, shoulders hunched, expecting a blow, a kick, a punch; her body speaking where her lips cannot. I cross the room and stand behind her, fold my arms across her chest and hold her gently, back to belly. She hardens, but does not thrust me away. I place my nose into the crook of her neck and inhale the thick musk of the mare, which has become the Maid's own particular scent.

However, I am neither greedy nor stupid after what she has borne today. I will not press her to further intimacy, although I have learned the rapture it brings. There is a rumble, deep within the well of her body. I do not know if she is purring or warning me off. I continue the light caresses, murmuring forgiveness with each stroke. I think of the cat we had when I

254

was a child, an old mouser who loved me to pet her, eyes shut, ears flattened with delight. So unlike my thin girl, body pricked to run, however sweet my touch.

I am sinking into a delicious half-dream when she pulls away. I jerk awake, and sigh, consoling myself with the thought that at least I held her for a short while. But she is not finished: she grasps my head and hauls me into a kiss of such hunger I think I shall be gobbled up. Her tongue pushes my lips apart, running back and forth against the gate of my teeth. I keep them closed, for I know not what else to do, I am such a fool. She stands back, just far enough to speak.

'Open to me,' she pants.

'Are you sure?' I gulp. 'After what has happened?'

'Never more so.'

I obey her command. She fastens upon me once more, diving into the slippery cave of my mouth. My hands seize her head to hold her steady. We suckle upon each other and I cannot tell who is more desperate to devour the other, nor does it matter: for the first time we are matched in desire, one body fused breast to breast, joined at the mouth.

She draws away once more, cheeks shot with crimson, eyes gleaming. She glances over my shoulder and my heart plummets, for I think she has heard someone approach the stable. I am delightfully mistaken. A smile lifts the corner of her lips; she takes my hand and leads me to the house.

The place sighs its emptiness over us as we enter. She strides to Thomas's room and flings back the door. His bed stands narrow as ever, prim with the linen I have washed and bleached more times than I care to remember, yet never white enough to please. Beneath the window crouches the chest wherein he keeps his books, upon it a plain latten cross. Hooked to the wall at tidy intervals are his tunics, shirts and second-best cote, like so many dark ghosts overlooking him at his devotions.

The Maid struts around the room, pressing her nose to the wall and tutting at some invisible fault in the plasterwork. She swipes a finger along the bedstead, grumbling about dust. She rubs his winter cloak between finger and thumb, muttering, *Poor stuff, very poor indeed,* although I know it is the best piece of wool this side of the Staple. She mimics the self-satisfied bob of his head with such eerie perfection that my laughter is nervous as much as it is delighted.

'Once again you capture him,' I breathe, full of wonder. 'It is as though he is here.'

'I hope not,' she says, and makes a great show of searching for him under the counterpane, behind the door, in the chest and all sorts of drollery; clapping her hand over her mouth in mock fright until I am laughing so hard I have to hold my stomach.

'Come to me, my pretty Anne,' she leers, her voice so much like his in timbre, yet so unlike in word or meaning.

'No,' I say. 'Not that.'

At once, she returns to herself. 'Very well,' she says in her own voice. She flourishes her hands as though chasing moths from the room. 'He is gone from this place.'

'To think I once wanted the snot-nosed, self-loving—' I gasp, the rush of words spilling like water from a jug.

She laughs, so loud and free I realise that what I have said is amusing as well as gloomy. I touch my fingers to my mouth, feel how it turns down at the corners. As I listen to her laughter, I begin to smile. If I can choose to be miserable, I can also choose to be happy. Perhaps I am not chained to my feelings. I can slip free.

It is a dangerous idea. If I can do that, then I might also slip free my moorings to this house, this village, this shire. I might float up to the clouds and ride them east or west; wherever takes my fancy. I might change my name and be an Alison or a Jennet. These thoughts are so frightening that they make me tremble.

'What ails you, Anne?' she asks, leaning her warmth into me.

'I could be – anyone,' I whisper.

'That sounds like a glorious way to be.' She grins, but not unkindly. 'Maybe you can choose anything. And be everything.'

My heart leaps. 'No! That is too terrible. If I can choose to be anything, then where is Anne?'

She laughs again and takes my hand. 'The weather changes. The land looks different from one moment to the next: white with snow, wet with rain, bright with sunshine. But it is the same earth. You are always Anne, constant as that land.'

'Is it that simple?'

'If you wish it,' she says.

I take a steadying breath. 'In that case, I could leave this place.'

'You could. With me.' The room swings around us. 'What do you need now, Anne?'

I swallow. The sound seems excessively loud. *No one but you,* says the voice of my soul. 'I need to sit down,' I say, and smile.

'Come then,' she says.

She points to the bed and raises her eyebrows with wicked intent. My frightened old heart cries *no!* But this new heart beating within me roars *yes!* We race to see who can get there first, pushing and shoving to be the winner. I throw myself onto the mattress and would shout, *I have won!* but its luxurious softness steals my cry of victory clean away. I bounce, testing to see if I can believe the evidence of my own backside.

'It's *feather,*' I gasp.

She hears the wonderment in my voice and starts to snicker. 'What else did you think that sniping cheese-parer would rest his arse upon?' she sneers. 'Surely you knew this.'

It is like sitting on a cloud. I think of my straw palliasse in the outer room.

'He does not allow me in here. Only when I sweep out the rushes, and then he watches.'

'How generous of him to permit you to clean his room!' she cackles.

'I always thought it was to avoid fornication. He lectured me about it often enough. As though the sight of the bed would fill me with such lust that I'd hurl him upon it and seduce him into sin.'

'I notice the glass in this window is whole,' she remarks dryly. 'No nasty draughts in here.'

I survey the room, its quiet comforts. 'Perhaps he was right,' I say. 'Upon this bed I find myself seized with thoughts of passion.'

'Do you indeed?' she answers.

'And fornication,' I growl.

'Oh, mistress Anne!' she breathes. 'How you lead me astray!'

She shoves my shoulder, half in play, half in earnest. I make a great show of toppling backwards, spreading my arms wide.

'I am overthrown,' I say. 'My walls are breached and I lie open to you.'

She smiles, eyes full of dangerous strategies. She pushes my skirt up to my thighs and kneels between; bends over and presses her nose to the quivering spot between my legs. She inhales deeply, raises her head and smacks her lips.

'You smell of bread.'

'Oh. That sounds so – workaday.'

She lowers her head once more and slides her tongue into my cunny.

'You are delicious,' she murmurs.

I have never heard myself so described, having grown to accept myself as unremarkable as an unstirred pond. Nor did I ever think to be touched in this way.

As though she can hear my thoughts, she continues, 'I'll take you over spices and silk any day of the week.'

She smiles with more fondness than I have seen in the whole time she has been here. It is a door opened on to a room of hidden affection. She returns to licking wetness into what is already wet and I writhe with the bliss it brings.

She undoes the lace at my bodice and scoops out my breast, tugging the nipple, already hard and standing upright to meet the bite of her teeth. She browses there awhile, then draws out the other breast and shares her attention between the two, nipping first at one then the other, sending bright threads of delight through my body and straight to my quim.

Her fingers walk the soft skin of my thigh, higher and higher. I have never been so in need of the push of her fingers. She tortures me with slowness, circling, brushing the ready spot between my legs. I climb step by step towards the completion she has wrought in me before, only to have her withdraw at the very moment I need her the most. I am her instrument and she tunes me, plucks me; each string vibrates and hums the sweetest tune. I can do nothing but sing the chorus, *Oh yes. Oh yes.*

Over and over she does this until I am demented with need and can stand the delay no longer. She reads my body clearer than any words I might utter. She presses me further, pushing within me and I soar, my body clasping her fingers and squeezing with the fierce heartbeat of my joy.

I tumble slowly back to earth. I watch the room draw in its walls, the ceiling beams drop into place, the floor come up to meet the bed. Sounds creep in: the creak of her body beside me, the rasp of my breath, the pattering of rain on the window glass. I am gathered into my senses with the lassitude of a drunkard.

I want us to live in this instant and nowhere else. Nothing leading towards this moment or away from it has any significance. Even though I know this fancy of mine is a dream, I have no desire to wake.

I roll over to face her, my elbows sinking into the mattress. She smiles with understanding. I grin in response, trail my fingertips from her scuffed and grazed knee to the hem of her shift, slide my hand beneath and warm myself on the delicate skin of her thigh. There's a rumble at the back of her throat. I proceed with great care, inching closer to the spot where she has wrung pleasure from me, for I wish nothing more than to light that delicious fire in her. But as I draw near she stiffens; the purr becomes a growl until at last she springs away, fast as a cat from a fire. She squats at the head of the bed, legs pulled up, arms wrapped around her bony knees. Her eyes are wide.

'No?' I say.

'No,' she grunts.

I am confused, for her pleasure is as dear as if it were my own. I stretch out my hand, to bridge the gap between us.

'Why?' I ask. 'When the reward is so delightful?'

She shrinks from my touch. 'I derive all the satisfaction I need when I bring delight to you. I watch it in your eyes, feel it in your body. I need no more.'

Her lips clamp together like Cat's babe when he is in a contrary frame of mind and she is trying to feed him.

'Do you think that because I am new to this that I am not capable of pleasuring you?'

'Stop being a fool.' She sees my face fall, stung by her words, and relents a little. Her mouth works up and down. 'Can you not be happy with what we have?' she says, and there is sadness in it.

'I am happy. I would have thought that was clear.'

'Then be content with what I can offer.'

'I do not understand.'

'No. You do not; and you are lucky that it is so.'

The air thickens between us. I know not one whit of her time before now. I have asked, over and over, and all she has given me are grunts and refusals. I have lived my whole life within twenty paces of this house. Who knows where she has been, what she has done. What she has had done to her.

'I am sorry,' I say. 'It is true; I understand nothing. Teach me about yourself so I do.'

'I can't. You'd throw me out.'

'Is that what has happened before?'

'Yes.'

'You are my Maid. I will never do that.'

'You will, whatever you say.'

I want to drag her close and cover her face with kisses, lift away her clothes and continue to sprinkle those kisses across her stomach. But she says nothing more.

'Very well,' I say. 'I shall not argue back and forth. When you are ready, I will listen. Know this.'

My flesh has lost its heat and I am uncomfortable with my nakedness; the way my breasts slide into my armpits. The salty smell from between my legs seems to fill the room, all the way up to the ceiling. I slip my hands through the armholes of my shift and pull it over my head and she watches. I wonder if she will stop me now that I am concealing the flesh that only a few moments ago she declared so delectable. She stares at me as if my body holds as much interest as the stable door. I drag my gown over my head and thrust my arms into the sleeves.

'Here,' I say. 'Help me to tie the laces at my wrist.'

She tugs the ribbons until all fits snugly. The air between us is fragile and could break with the slightest knock.

'I am sorry for my sharpness,' she continues after a long space that I manage not to fill with chatter. 'I permit no one to touch me. Even when I desire it. And I desire it with you.'

My soul swells, aching to cry out, *Then let me!* But some preserving influence stays my tongue.

'This is not your fault,' she says.

I know it is not. But I resist saying so, contenting myself with a small murmur of agreement. It is all I shall get from her today. It will profit me nothing, making a to-do about it, for she is as immovable as Lundy when she sets her mind to it. I sit up and re-braid my hair.

'There has been great sweetness here today,' I say, calmly. 'Let us not spoil it with bitterness. When you are ready to open to me, I will be here.'

'Even if I never do?'

'Even then.'

Thomas continues to shrink into a shadow that passes across the wall of my days, darkening the room but for an instant. The moment passes, he is gone and the day grows bright once more. If he notices the change the Maid has wrought in me, he says nothing. In faith, he remarks on very little: not the food I hurl into his dish nor my long absences. It seems I am become the mistress of my own house. I like the taste of it. It is no lie: I am mistress, and not merely of the house, but of my life. I stand straight and tip up my chin.

I complete my household chores hastily. When Thomas asks for his sheets to be washed I say, *There is linen in the attic room.*

A chest full of it. I stare at him until he turns and goes to collect the ladder. If he notices the unlocked door and the many things disturbed, he does not remark upon it. We grunt *good day* and *good evening* as we pass and I hear the sounds rolling empty in my mouth. I should be grateful for this merciful change in my daily circumstances, but a perverse part of me misses our hurling back and forth of angry words.

I have the sensation of waiting. It is only with the Maid that I feel any semblance of animating breath. She speaks little: rather, she sparks me into flame with her hands and mouth. Her fingers write stories upon the blank page of my flesh till I am illuminated more brightly than the Saint's book chained up in the church, woven into a woman far lovelier than any Sheba.

The idea of leaving the village with her grows stronger with each day, until the notion becomes a wish and the wish swells into desire. Yet it is at odds with my fear of the pestilence lying in wait and ready to spring upon us the moment we step outside the bounds of the village.

It is the Feast of Saint Wulfhilda when I find her in the stable as usual; brushing, combing, and chattering away to the mare as though it can understand her. She nods when I enter, but is busily engaged in feeding the beast a thin gruel, far more water than oats. I twist my apron between my fingers until she pauses and peers at me more intently.

'Out with it,' she says. 'You burn with questions.'

I huff out the breath lying heavy upon my breast. 'How did you stay safe?' I ask. 'Out there. From the pestilence.'

'I am a good dancer,' she says, and laughs with more than a hint of bitterness. She sees my confusion. 'It is nothing. A private joke between Death and myself.'

I chew the inside of my cheek. 'I want to come with you.'

Her eyes widen with something that looks a lot like pleasure. 'But I am afraid,' I add.

'Of course you are. Only a simpleton wouldn't be.' She rubs the mare's nose and sets down the empty bowl. 'Perhaps I have been lucky. But I believe it is more than luck. I have a shield. Against the pestilence.'

'Tell me,' I cry. 'Not just me. You should tell everyone.'

She shrugs. 'I have tried. No one wishes to learn.'

'I do.'

'Then watch,' she says, and that is all she will say.

She rubs the mare's neck, whispering words of a calming nature, much as fell from my lips when she was first given to me after the great storm. I can scarce believe it was but a quarter-year ago. It seems that half my life has been gladdened by her presence. My thoughts meander in this agreeable direction as she pummels the animal's belly with her small fists. The beast snorts, its eyes swimming with a delight I know only too well, for I feel that same animal bliss when she lays her hands upon me.

The Maid's attention does not waver, and for the strangest moment it is as though she is alone with the mare, communing as one creature to another. It is foolishness, yet I am jealous that this animal has captured her attention, leaving none for me. I cough. Her head darts up, wondering if I am warning of Thomas's approach. When she sees I am not, she casts a smile at me. Her smile, the one she keeps for me alone, and I am content once more.

'Now,' she says. 'This is my talisman against the fever. She is ready.'

The mare lifts her tail sideways and lets go a fountain of piss. The Maid makes no attempt to step out of the way: on the contrary, she sticks first her hands and then her arms into the flow. It is the oddest thing I have ever set eyes on, and I have seen some queer things when folk declare themselves cured by the Saint.

'Well, I never did,' I say, for lack of anything better.

She reaches into the manger and draws a sheet from beneath the straw.

'From the attic?' I ask.

She winks. 'From the attic.'

'I did not see you.'

'No, you did not.'

We grin at each other. She holds the sheet under the mare's backside. Just when I think she must be done, she steps under the waterfall herself. The stream dwindles to a feeble trickle, then ceases. She wrings out her hair, and tosses the sheet over a roof-beam.

'You wanted to know my secret. I have shown you.'

She tips her chin, pressing her lips into a thin line as if waiting for me to call her disgusting. I do no such thing.

'I am curious,' I say. 'Not critical,' I add hastily. 'But I must know: why horse piss? You've washed everything in it, and the floor is soaked.'

'The simple answer is that I do not know. No one instructed me. As I told you, I have kept one step ahead of this fever almost a year. I have observed the creep of its shadow. How it hides in ships for sailors to bring onshore.'

She shakes her head as though her ears are full of wasps. She busies herself tearing strips of linen from the edge of the sheet, knuckles white with effort.

'I will not waste time telling you nasty tales. I have watched who and what it touches, and it won't approach horses. Why, I have no idea. Would that I could be a horse, but even my skills won't stretch that far.' She lets loose a laugh, one that dies as soon as it is out. 'Nor can I wrap myself in a horse hide, for they are inconvenient garments. In faith, I cannot afford to *ride* a horse, let alone buy one and skin it. So, I am left with the essence of the beast. While I clothe myself in that, I am safe.'

She hangs the wet rags neatly around the stable wall, where they drip onto the tamped earth floor. She keeps back two and wraps them around her ankles; I follow suit, adding one round each wrist for good measure. However foul the smell, it's a fool who turns down help against disaster. When I am done, I heap a basket with the damp linen.

'Anne?' she asks.

'No point in wasting a moment. I am going straight to my sister,' I say.

'The Staple?' she says.

'Yes, and don't try to argue me out of it,' I declare.

'Would I succeed?' she says.

'No.'

'Then I shall not waste my words.' She places her hands upon my shoulders and pulls me into a kiss.

We do not see him till he is almost within the stable; only the brief darkness of his shadow falling across the door alerts us. We exchange startled looks and I breathe relief that it is Geoffrey and not Thomas.

'Good day, Geoffrey,' I declare. 'Have you brought the Reverend Father one of your fine cheeses?' My words are over-loud, but he does not notice the artifice.

'The Maid. I have—' he begins, falters, and halts.

His eye roves from me to the Maid. I think that she will start playing her idiot part and am surprised when she does not. Instead, she turns very slowly to face the open doorway and takes a step forward. Sunlight strikes her, clothing her with a semblance of gold. Pale yellow liquid drips from the hem of her shift.

With great deliberation she raises her arms and holds them out to Geoffrey, stiffly as though they are made of wood. At first I wonder why she is making such a strange gesture, then I see how the light catches the fine hair on her arms in a quivering halo. Even though I know this is one of her tricks, my breath still gathers tight.

If I am affected, Geoffrey is far more so. His mouth dangles open as though he means to greet us, but no sound emerges. He presses his hands together, wringing them so fiercely I am afraid he might break a finger. I draw in a breath to bid him good day once again and startle him out of his swoon, but the Maid fires a glance at me. She holds her ground, glowing in the sunshine and the smallest part of me wonders if in fact she might truly be sent from God to save us. At the very moment I think she cannot possibly hold his attention any longer, she speaks.

'I know why you are here.'

It is the voice of an angel, so soft it seems to speak for Geoffrey alone and straight to the ear of his soul. He makes a throttled noise and with no further prompting falls to his knees with a thump.

'Maid!' he squawks. 'Dear God and all the saints! Save me!'

He sucks in a hurtling breath and begins to weep, loud and wild as a girl. While he is thus distracted, the Maid catches my eye and tips her head in a meaningful gesture. I see what she needs: the sun is moving across the stable door and taking its light from her. I move out of the way so that she may keep up with its movement, shuffling into the path of its beams. She flicks another glance at the pieces of linen displayed around the stable and nods.

I take one and with a grave expression offer the sopping scrap to Geoffrey. He looks at it and then at me, unsure what he is meant to do. I wait for him to guffaw, *What manner of trickery is this? It is wet through.* But he gapes ardently at the Maid. She smiles and speaks once more with that cunning stillness of her lips.

'Geoffrey. God sends this gift. Take it, and be well.'

'What about my mother? My father? Can they be saved also?'

She heaves out a heavy breath. 'Of course,' she says. 'Mark my words. Tell everyone: sweep the straw from your houses. Soak the floor with the stale of horses. Bind this cloth around you. It will keep you safe.'

'I will tell everyone!' he cries, glowing with a zeal I never thought to see in his dull eyes.

'No!' roars the Maid. 'No,' she adds, with greater serenity. 'Not the priest.'

'Not Father Thomas?' he stutters.

The Maid glances at me and I step forward.

'You heard what the men from the Staple did to our Maid,' I say, and surprise myself with the venom that spills from my tongue. 'That was all the doing of the Reverend Father. Would you have him poke his nose in again?'

Geoffrey gulps. 'No!' he cries, clutching the rag and cradling it to his chest.

The sun has climbed higher and half the Maid's body is in shadow.

'Go,' she says, with force behind the word.

I take his hand. 'Come now, Geoffrey,' I say, raising him up and bustling him out of the stable. 'Would you weary the Maid?'

'No!' he gulps. 'Oh, it is true! Father Thomas said she was sent by God!'

I will not echo the blasphemy, for I know the truth he does

not. I lead him away and it takes far longer than it should, for he is forever twisting his head round to get a last look at the Maid through the stable door, even though she has slipped out of sight.

'She's gone,' he moans disconsolately and I think he might start wailing again.

I had no idea he was such a big booby. By the Saint, Alice can have him with my blessing.

'She has not gone,' I say, with such glib ease I am sure the Maid's skill of invention on the spur of the moment must be rubbing off on me. 'She is praying. For strength,' I add. 'When she gives gifts of healing, it makes her very tired.'

He wipes his nose on his sleeve and sniffs noisily. 'I gave her nothing in return!' he wails. 'I must go back—'

'No, cousin!' I say quickly. I clasp his arm and squeeze it firmly, to reassure him and also to steer him away more swiftly.

'But I must!'

I rack my brains and am struck with inspiration: how I can please the Maid with the thing she most needs. What we need, if we are to be away. It strikes me then, fully. If she goes, I want nothing more than to be with her.

'Next time,' I whisper. 'Bring a coin. That will suffice.'

I accompany him as far as the ford, basket over my arm. He dawdles by the water, eyes singeing holes into the back of my gown as I hasten eastwards to the Staple. I have helped him. I have also helped myself, and the Maid. I did not lie, but what I said felt nothing like any truth I have spoken before. I have set foot into a new country, and it is strange and unsettling.

I've barely crossed the Staple bridge and stepped through the west gate when a lump of mud flies past my ear. I turn and see the little brat that threw it. He stands with his feet apart, sticking out his tongue. His mother scowls at me rather than at him.

'Is this how you treat visitors?' I say, when she shows no sign of chiding him.

'We have no visitors. Nor want them.'

'That's a fine welcome.'

'It's all you'll get. Where are you from?' she asks, with a sharp edge to the question.

'From Brauntone.'

She sniffs and spits on the ground. The child lets out a wheezing sound I realise is a chuckle.

'So you say. But you could be lying. You could have crept in from the east, all full of the fever. That's why we've barred the east gate. There's no one left breathing that way.'

I wrench my coif to one side and show the skin at my throat. 'See? Clean. Unmarked. I've no need to creep.' I wave the basket and she takes a step back, makes the sign of the Cross. 'See this? Full of relics from the Maid of Brauntone herself.'

She tosses her head in a gesture that could mean she cares not one whit for my words, or could be the way a horse jerks its head when alarmed. It comes to me that she lives in fear, and I do not. Such a simple realisation, but it cuts my breath in half. I have spent so long thinking myself hard done by because Thomas is not the man I wanted him to be, because I have no child to call me mama, because I do not dine on fine meats, because of this, because of that. Yet here I stand, free of the terror that crouches in this woman's heart. I straighten my back, burrow my fingers into the basket and pull out a rag.

'For you,' I say.

I don't know why I am being kind to this sourpuss, but since the Maid came to me I have grown in generosity. Her nostrils flare.

'It stinks,' she sneers.

'Take it, don't take it, it makes no odds. But the Maid says it is proof against the fever.'

A few days ago I would have doubted my words. The Maid may be deceitful, fickle and inconstant as water, yet in this there is no falsehood. The woman snatches the linen from my hand and gawps at it. I raise my skirt an inch or two to show where I've bound one round each ankle. She laughs mockingly, but neither does she cast my gift to the ground.

'Give me another,' she snaps. 'One for each leg.'

As she knots them, a gaggle of passers-by stop and stare. Like the woman, they scoff at first, but all the same they want their share. It takes all my strength not to have the basket snatched out of my hands, for there is a panic in these folk I've not seen before.

'Enough. The basket is empty,' I cry, shaking it upside down. 'Wait!' I call as they start to walk away. 'I seek Catherine, wife of Henry. The farrier.'

'I don't know him,' says the surly woman, more kind-hearted now. 'But try by the north gate, up towards Pilton. That's where you'll find the smithies.'

As I turn north, a man dashes to my side and plucks at my sleeve.

'My wife says you have relics from the Maid,' he pants, nodding at my basket.

'They have all gone. Come to Brauntone. There are plenty to be had.' I shake him off and continue.

'Where are you going?' he calls after me.

'To my sister.'

'I know her house.' He rolls his eyes sideways.

'You know my sister?' I ask.

'Of course, of course. Come on.' He does not take his attention from the basket.

'Where does she live?' I say.

'This way. Hurry now.'

'Why should I hurry?'

He glances left to right and right again, head bobbing like a shuttle. I fold my arms.

'What's her name?'

'Who?' he asks, tugging his beard.

'My sister. The one you're taking me to.'

He lets out a squawk and flies at me; or rather flies at the basket and tries to grapple it from my hands. I crack him over the head with it and he crumples to his knees as though I've hit him with an anvil. He sobs, rocking back and forth.

'Please,' he whimpers. 'Please.'

Snot dribbles from his nose, making his beard sticky. I roll back a sleeve, untie the band about my wrist, and give it to him.

'That's all I have.'

I expect him to run off, but he weeps even more wildly, hugging it to his breast like a baby and crying, *Please, please,* over and over. Folk scuttle past as though they cannot see him, just as a stream rushes around a rock in its path without pausing. At the end of the street I turn and he is still there, moaning.

I make my way without further interruptions, asking directions from folk as I go. Despite their suggestions, the streets tangle like a ball of yarn that a cat has got hold of. Thomas's house is the grandest in our village, but shrivels when compared to some of the palaces I see: houses with glass at the windows, doors speckled with iron rivets, fastened with hefty bolts. I wonder what it must be like to live in a place where a man needs to keep his door locked against his neighbour.

The further I walk northwards, the less the buildings puff

themselves out. I am sure I end up walking in circles, for it takes almost as long to find Cat as it did to walk the six miles to the Staple. It is a relief when I find her house, a comfortable-looking place, not overly proud of itself. I stand on the threshold and call her name.

'Sister, it is me!' I shout louder when I get no answer.

There's a thump of something dropped, a cry of irritation. My sister, all right. I step within without needing to duck my head, the lintel is so towering high. Cat dashes into the room, her hair half-braided. She wipes her hands on her skirt with such force it is as though she is angry with them.

'What? Who is it?' she barks.

She squints her eyes and I realise she cannot see my face with the light behind me, so I close the door and step closer.

'Oh,' she says, the furious pout falling away.

'My dearest Cat. Beloved sister,' I exclaim, the words bursting from me with a passion I never felt before.

We fall into each other's arms and I find tears leaping to my eyes. I stick my nose deep into her hair and breathe her in. She hugs me tight, but breaks the embrace before I do and holds me at arm's length.

'Look at you,' she says, eyes bright. 'Look at my little sister. By the Saint, Nan. I did not know you. You are – taller.'

She repeats herself a few more times and I have no desire to stop her, for I cannot remember when I heard her so affectionate. After a while, we become more composed. She draws me to one side, bids me sit and brings a cup of ale. She sits also, taking my hand in hers and squeezing. But I have no desire to prattle about the weather, so I drain the cup, set it down and am all business.

'Is there trouble?' she asks, her face returning to its usual serious self.

I consider the question. There is a world of trouble without, but not the sort she means.

'Mother is well, Father is well,' I say.

She crosses herself. 'Praise the Saint. Praise our Holy Mother Mary. But? I know there is a "but", Nan.'

'Of course there is. It's why I am here. I will not talk of Death in case he hears us, but all the same, I have something for you. It is proof against the fever.'

I reach beneath my skirt and untie the rags around my ankles. I hand them to her and she wrinkles her nose.

'Yes, yes. The smell.' I flap my hand to brush away her objections. 'I would not walk all the way here and all the way back simply to give you some pointless piece of nonsense.'

There is a pause. 'Listen to you. You've changed. Grown up. I like it, Nan. Has Thomas become a man at last?'

'Not a bit of it,' I say and am surprised by the lack of anger in my voice. 'Margret was right about him. Everyone was.' I find myself smiling. 'Thomas is as far from me as Exeter, and a good thing too.'

'I've not seen you for so long. No word. No news.' Her eyes widen. 'I thought you were angry with me. Thought you'd grown too high for your own sister.'

'Never!' I cry. 'The truth of it is that I am not allowed visitors. It is one of Thomas's little ways.'

'Ah. I begin to understand.'

'Yes, I have been foolish.' I clasp my hands around hers. 'Cat. You were right: I was a spoiled and peevish child.'

'Nan—'

I hold up my hand. 'I thought the whole world and everything in it was mine by right. By the Saint, I must have been unbearable.'

'Oh, Nan.'

'My dear sister, I am here to say that I am sorry. With all this death around us – well. Let us say there are more pressing considerations than *Anne wants this* and *Anne wants that*.' I smile to show my lightness of heart. 'I do not wish to fritter away the remainder of my days being selfish. I have made mistakes, not least imagining a life with a priest that was built on clouds. I no longer wish to be that stupid girl. Let us be at peace as I strive to grow into a cleverer woman.'

She begins to cry. The years of bickering ease their burden. I press the linen into her hand.

'Do you believe this will help?' she sniffs.

'I have seen it do its work. I wear it.' I show the remaining band at my wrist.

'Then I shall do so also.'

I am about to say that I must hurry back because Thomas will be moaning for his supper, but the truth is that he is not the one drawing me back to the village. Cat looks about to ask a question, so I get in first to steer us to easier subjects. Although the Maid is not here to eavesdrop, I shall prove that I can keep her secrets.

'Where is your boy?' I ask.

'Asleep. I'd just managed to get him down when you arrived. I dropped a jug and thought it'd set him howling, but he didn't stir. Come.'

She takes my hand and draws me into the solar, the size of Thomas's private room, but so different. Pegs and hooks cover every inch of the wall, hung with a jumble of cloaks, gowns, towels and tunics. The floor is strewn with wooden animals. She bends and retrieves a horse just as I am about to tread on it.

'Careful. You'll break your ankle. By the Saint, I do the same myself ten times a day,' she says cheerfully.

I turn the creature over in my hand. When I tug the string running through it, its tail flaps up and down.

'It is pretty.'

'Father made it. All of them.'

I see my father: broad hands fashioning this tiny beast, down to the curled lip, pricked ears, the hair of the mane picked out with an awl. Her boy sprawls on the mattress, legs flung apart in sleep. Cat leans over, smoothes the hair growing long over his ears. He snuffles but does not wake; chest rising and falling with the rabbit-quick breath of infants.

'I leave the toys scattered on purpose,' says Cat quietly. 'If Death comes in, he'll trip and snap his neck. It is a silly notion.' She turns fierce eyes to me. 'But I would fight Death with my bare hands if he tried to take my son.'

Her kiss when we part is far warmer than that which greeted me. She hugs me to her breast.

'Oh, my dear little Nan,' she gasps, her voice hiccupy. 'Be not so long before you come again.'

We weep like babes, for all that we are full-grown.

'I shall not. I swear it. By the Saint, I swear it.'

It is a promise I am determined to keep.

VIXEN

When the deaths begin, it is like an outpouring of held breath.

'It's Simon. The miller,' says Anne one morning, dashing into the stable. 'His son. The youngest.'

She paces from one side of the stable to the other then back again, fiddling with her kerchief. It looks neat enough to me. Her gaze swims around the walls, the floor. I do not ask what she is talking of, nor do I need to.

'Thomas says it's river-fever,' she continues, and at last she looks at me. 'He won't—'

'No, he won't,' I say, quietly, and watch her anguish fade a little.

She takes a deep breath. 'I must go to them.'

'We will go.'

A smile lifts the corners of her mouth for a moment, but is swallowed quickly. I am half-ready: I've smudged charcoal around my eyes and am draped in one of the good sheets, my head stuck through a hole I snipped in its middle. I spit on my hands and run them through my cropped hair to make it stick out. Anne watches me twist the tangles into points.

'You look like a hedgehog.'

'So?'

'Isn't it a bit much?' She waves her hand, encompassing my head, my blackened eyes, the sheet. 'When you raise your arms it looks like—'

'Wings? I know.'

She presses her lips together. 'The people will think—'

'That I'm an angel?'

'Not exactly. But I fear you take them for fools.' She skewers me with a look. 'Do you?'

I take her hand. 'Anne. When I first showed you my talisman, what did you think?' She lowers her eyes. 'Tell me honestly.'

'I thought it filthy,' she whispers.

'Yes, you did. And rightly too.' She glances up through her eyelashes. 'Do you think I relish this smell? Do you think I'll paddle in horse piss once the Great Dying has run its course?'

'No?' she asks.

'Of course I won't. I'll bathe for a week to get the stink out, for it has soaked me to the bone. Until then – I do not mock the villagers, but they need more persuading than you and will listen to an angel a lot sooner than to a plain lass. The faster they do what I tell them, the more they'll be helped. There is no time to waste on philosophy.'

'Very well,' she says.

She arranges me like Gabriel himself and we go out of the stable on to the street. Anne strides ahead, basketful of rags over one arm. It is not difficult to find the way. The wailing guides us, the sound of grief so unbearable that it can loosen a man's knees and make him lean on the nearest wall to hold himself steady. I have no desire to breathe in that misery, but Anne looks at me sternly.

'Remember, we can help.'

A wattle gate halfway up the street flaps open and the man called Simon is borne out of the hut by two lads, one beneath each armpit as you would do a wounded soldier. He shakes them off and staggers towards Anne. The villagers shrink away, but Anne stands her ground and claps her hands on his shoulders. There is a sucking-in of breath: she touches him despite the stench of fever. He gulps air like a man who has swum up from the depths of a pond.

'Where is she?' he croaks, blinking at Anne. 'The Maid,' he adds. 'If she had been here, my boy might—'

It is time for me to play my part. I gather my courage, step forward and speak.

'People.'

It is a single word, and I speak it quietly, but it cuts through the thicket of babbling. They turn towards me as one and gasp at my outlandish appearance, mouths flopping open. I raise my arms.

'People,' I repeat.

Simon totters in my direction. 'Why were you not here?' he cries. 'My little one. My babe—'

'I am with you now. You should have called me right away,' I add, gruffly.

'Oh, God,' cries Simon and falls back into the arms of the youths, who struggle to bear him upright. 'Protect us now, Maid! Save us!'

'Did you sweep your house free of straw?' I say.

'No,' he whimpers.

'I instructed you. Did I not instruct you?'

'You did!' he wails.

I glower at him for the length of time it would take to drink a cup of ale. Then I turn my eyes upon the rest of them and fix them with the same scorching glance. If cozening won't make them take note, then harsh words will have to do. I find Geoffrey in the shivering herd and scald him with a glare.

'Did I not entrust you with this task? To tell the people?'

Geoffrey hurls himself on to his face, crying, 'Mercy, mercy!'

'Do not deny it!' I shout. 'I warned you!'

'Oh, Maid!' he snivels. 'I tried! They called me a fool!'

There is a pause, and no sound fills it. Even the birds hold their beaks shut. I suck in a strengthening breath.

'You must do this.'

They fall to their knees, muttering contrition and wringing their hands. When I judge they have knelt long enough, I hold up a hand and cut the noise short as fast as a good knife through meat.

'Will you do as I say now?'

'Oh God, yes!' they cry.

I point to Anne, who holds up the basket. 'Take these,' I bark. 'Tie them around the throat of everyone in your house. Ankles, wrists. Sweep the floor as I command you. No straw. Soak the earth with the stale of horses.'

'Horse piss?' quavers a lone voice, and a questioning murmur rumbles through the mob.

I fix the doubter with a grim look. Anne speaks, her voice clear.

'However strange, this is a sovereign tincture. When the children of Israel fled Egypt, they daubed blood on their doors and the Angel of Death passed over. This is your sign. Heed the Maid. Do this and be safe,' she says. 'Or die.'

The people nod with frantic obedience. I distribute the linen, nodding soberly as if they were pieces torn from the Virgin's veil itself. A woman unwraps a slice of bread from her apron and lays it at my feet. I grunt acknowledgement. The next woman removes her kerchief, folds it neatly, and places it along-side. James comes running from the alehouse and presents a jug of ale.

Geoffrey is the first to earn a smile. He lays down a farthing and I beam at him. At this, the whole company scramble forwards, pressing pennies between my toes. I raise my eyebrows at Anne until she grasps my meaning and busies herself shoving them safely into her bodice. Not that that is all she does. She might think I am too busy to notice, but amongst the goings-on, I see her talking to an old woman.

She has been hanging back, chewing her fingers nervously. Anne digs between her breasts, pulls out a coin and presses it into the gnarled hand. As if that is not bad enough, I watch as she retrieves another and adds it to the first. It glitters silver. If I could leap to her side and grab it away, I would.

The old woman gawps at these treasures, then at Anne, showing what remains of her teeth, all four of them, in a broad pink grin. She mumbles a blessing and pats Anne's sleeve with a speckled hand. For the briefest instant I see Anne freeze; but the brown marks are the spatters of age, nothing more.

Then the crone hobbles over and drops a farthing at my feet. The copper coin. Not the silver. When she's done, she totters away, leaning on her stick and peering into her palm at the bright gift Anne gave her. I can do nothing about it but fume.

The folk might have emptied their pockets but they are not finished. One man kisses my foot. Another grabs a fistful of the sheet, then another, pawing and clutching and tugging until it sets me off balance. I throw a glance at Anne and she springs to my side.

'Enough!' she cries. 'Would you injure the Maid?'

They fall back, mumbling penitence.

'Come tomorrow,' I say. 'I shall succour every one.'

'You know where you can find her,' Anne declares. 'Come to the stable.' I squeeze her fingers tightly. 'Bring gifts,' she adds, rather unwillingly for my taste.

281

Anne scoops the offerings into her apron and picks up the pitcher of ale. I stride ahead and the crowd parts, but some follow and will not let go. The cling of fingers sears my arm; I have never wanted to escape the touch of people so fervently. I dive into the sanctuary of the stable and Anne slams the door.

'Leave us!' she cries, her voice swelling with command.

Through the wall I can hear a gabble of apologies. Eventually, the yard grows quiet.

'Are they gone?' I whisper.

'Gone. Quite gone.'

I shudder. 'I cannot stand the touching.'

'I know. Look. They have given us gifts.'

She empties the contents of her bodice and apron onto the dirt. I turn over the pile of offerings with my foot.

'Bread,' I mutter. 'A jug of ale. A kerchief, like we haven't got enough linen already.'

'What's the matter?' she grumbles. 'You're in a foul temper today. What about the money?'

I ignore her and give the jug a kick. It sprays its contents across the floor. The earth drinks it straight away.

'What are you doing?' she says. 'Of all the ungrateful—'

'Me? Ungrateful?' I shove my face close to hers. 'This is rubbish. Rubbish, do you hear me?'

'Maid,' she says, calmly.

I wish she would shout. I wish she would fight. I would know what to do.

'I saw you,' I growl. 'You gave that old witch some money.' I try to make my voice furious, but it comes out as petulance.

'Gammer Kaly? Yes. I gave her a sixpence and a farthing. She gave you the farthing back.'

'By all that is holy – sixpence?'

'She needs the money. She is a widow.'

282

'And will be dead within the week. All of them will be.' I sweep my hands in a circle, encompassing this stable, this village, this manor, shire, land. 'Every single one. Dead. And we'll be propping up six foot of earth unless we get enough money to pay our way through the forest.'

I pause, panting with the effort of my outburst.

She takes a deep breath. 'If you wish me to argue with you, then I shall, although it seems a fearful waste of time and breath. If you wish me to bring money to you, I shall do that also.' She points at the scattered coins on the ground. 'There are plenty left. Look.'

I shake my fist at the roof-beam. 'Plenty? There's barely enough to get us to the Staple. Aren't you listening? We need safe passage through the forest.'

'The forest, the forest. What is the matter with you?'

'Haven't you heard anything I've said? There are dangerous men there.'

'Then we shall pay them.'

'What if they want more than money? What will I give them then?' I shout.

There is silence. She stares at me, a long look that drones its insistence and will not leave me be.

'Maid. What have you done?'

I cannot meet her eye as an equal. I turn to the wall. It is pockmarked with the peepholes Thomas made when he was spying on me. I can't remember when he stopped doing that. I would rather have a hundred men ogle me for an hour than endure one minute of Anne's stare.

'With what did you bargain?' she says to the back of my head.

If I stand completely still, perhaps she will stop asking questions. Perhaps she will go.

'You do not need to say anything,' she sighs.

I want to be small enough to squeeze through the holes in the wattle and daub. Small as a beetle, a spider, a flea. Something to be trampled underfoot. When her hand brushes my shoulder I almost leap through the roof. She twists me round and forces me look at her.

'Tell me one thing,' she says, her expression a strange mixture of iron and honey. 'Is this still your plan?'

I do not ask what she means by plan. I know; she knows.

'No,' I whisper.

'No?' she growls. 'Be sure, Maid. Would you do this thing now?'

'No! By all— No!'

'Good,' she says, very calmly. 'That is all I need to know.'

She turns her attention to the discarded coins, counting them into the empty basket. She picks up the jug, examines it for cracks and, finding none, places it beside the door.

'Anne?' I say. She straightens up and looks at me. 'Aren't you going to shout? Throw me out?'

'No.'

'You aren't going to give me up?'

'No,' she snorts, with something that sounds like humour. It might be contempt. I thought I had the full measure of this woman.

'Why not?' I say, my voice the most insignificant of squeaks.

'Have you learned so little about me?'

I blink at her. 'You forgive me?'

'Yes.'

'How?'

'You were very different when you first came here. I have changed. I believe you have also.'

Never before have I wanted for words; now I seek within my great store and find nothing.

'So,' she continues, with the same fortitude, wiping her hands on her apron. 'We shall not cheat my people out of everything they have. There will be exchange, and fair to boot. I will not be reduced to thieving, even if Death is staring me in the face.'

I stare at her, blood heating my cheeks. The late-morning sun squeezes thin fingers through the breaches in the stable wall and pricks the linen of her kerchief with light. She takes my hand in hers. I feel my throat work as I swallow her words.

'Yes.'

'I am not a fool,' she says, with a great deal more kindness. 'I have no desire to remain here and die. If the world is coming to an end, I shall search for a new one with you.'

I want to pull a face and slip into any one of my hundred disguises, feel the muffle of its cloak. But her hand on mine tethers me to my body and I cannot escape.

'You see me in all my ugliness and still you want me?' I ask.

'I see how you have been twisted into ugliness.'

'This—' I point at my painted face, my outlandish hair 'has protected me, Anne. Being cold, being clever, being anyone but myself. It is a thick coat and has kept me warm and dry all my life, since . . . Since I can remember, and I remember a long way back, even though I wish I could not.'

'Maid. Tell me what you remember. Who you are.'

I look at her, and look at her truly. 'It is difficult, Anne.'

She nods. 'Yes.'

'Soon,' I say. 'I swear. Soon. It is difficult to change, however much I wish to.'

'Do you wish to?'

'With every ounce of my scrawny being. But know this: I shall never give you up. Not to anyone.'

* * *

285

So do we busy ourselves. I do not cheat them out of money. I give them hope. I play their angel, but only as much as is needed to make them listen, and no more. I teach them as I taught Anne. Before this time, I never helped anyone who was not myself, nor ever wanted to.

VESPERS
1349

From Saint Cornelius to Saint Cosmas

THOMAS OF UPCOTE

I went to say the Office, but was so far distracted from my habitual calmness that I was at the church before I realised my feet were unshod. I should have entered confidently, as barefoot as Our Lord Christ. But the recent weeks had rendered me unsure of anything.

I hovered at the door, hand on the gnarled wood. As if in a dream, I saw myself enter, stride to the altar and speak the well-rubbed words, showing off my poverty to the Lord. But what if this was pride? What did it serve if my so-called humility was a lie, leading me directly into sin? Perhaps going into the church barefoot was excessive. I was no penitent. And yet, if I returned to the house and put on my good boots, would that then be vanity?

I hopped up and down in an agony of indecision. In the end I decided to go back and put on my second-best pair of shoes. Thereby I would be neither vain nor proud. My heart wrenched that it had taken me so long to make such a simple decision. God was waiting in the church, tapping his foot. I hurried through the ford and past the stable.

I heard it first, before I saw them.

It was the sound of two women talking, Anne and one other.

The door was ajar and I opened my mouth to cry *halloa* to Anne, for I had not seen her for three days, but some agency held my tongue. Perhaps if I had shouted I would not have discovered them as I did.

Any intention to fetch my shoes was replaced with curiosity. I stood on tiptoe and held my breath, not knowing why I was being so stealthy, nor what I expected to see. Ordinarily, female chatter would not prompt the slightest interest, but this morning the sound prickled with significance and I was drawn to it as surely as a dog is drawn to the scent of a fox.

Anne was saying *yes, yes, yes*, over and over.

The other woman was younger, now that my ear was pressed to the wood and I could make out the lightness in her words. Her voice barely grazed the air, in that shy way maidens often speak. But something in this voice was not shy; not shy at all.

I heard the words *dodderer, cheese-parer, gizzard-neck* and every word declared boldly. Why I did not stride into the stable and demand that Anne return to her duties I do not know. The whole glebe was mine to go where I pleased, but an insistent hand held me back. I breathed softly and listened.

'No, nothing,' said Anne, with an unfamiliar authority.

'You are sure?'

'He does not even notice the dirt beneath his feet,' Anne snorted. 'Dense as a sack of chaff.'

There was a swishing sound of barley stalks chafing against each other when ready to be harvested. I realised it was giggling.

'A sack of beets.'

'A sack of beans.'

'A sack of stones.'

'A sack of mud.'

They traded insults, and with each one this man of whom they spoke grew more deaf, more blind and more estranged from humanity. I should have gone in then and chastised Anne and her companion for their intemperate speech, but I knew what held me in check. It was shame. I was the man they spoke of, and I deserved every word. The laughter continued, and I burned. Then there was a moist sound I did not recognise.

'Oh.' Anne spoke with such passionate release that I knew the stranger had touched her. It was the exhalation of a lover. 'Make haste.'

'Ah yes.'

At this there was silence, far more terrible than words. I wondered what Anne meant by haste. I could bear it no longer: I burst in and found Anne cradling the Vixen to her breast as though nursing a babe. The child – for still I thought her so, I was that much of a fool – had the teat between her lips and was sucking on it.

My mouth was open, I suppose, and I blinked. Of all the sights with which I might have been presented, I did not expect this. Anne gave me a startled look, the print of alarm written in crimson upon both cheeks.

'Mistress!' I cried, throat so dry it was more like the caw of a rook than a human voice.

Anne opened her mouth to speak but nothing came out. We stared at each other, locked in mutual confusion. In her eyes I read fear, shock, slyness: all manner of things I never thought to see. But before I could seize on any of them, the Vixen broke the silence.

She squeaked like a featherless chick tipped from the nest, flapping her paws in the helpless, jerky gesture I had seen so many times before. Her piping grew more terrified and piercing to the ear.

'She is afraid of you, sir,' remarked Anne, regaining her equanimity and hanging on to it.

'How so?'

'Bursting into the stable like that!'

'What are you *doing*?' I blustered, waggling my finger at the Maid.

'Doing?' she echoed, eyes bright with something I did not understand. 'Why, I am comforting her.'

'Comforting?' I said, in disbelief.

'Of course, sir. What else?'

She had recovered her poise with such speed that I began to doubt I had seen her so discomfited. The Maid continued to wave her fingers at me, all the while keening and endeavouring to conceal herself in Anne's armpit. Anne tucked her breast into her bodice and only then it truly struck me that it had been naked the whole time. Blood sprang to my face, and also to that nether part which marked me as a man.

'She is such a child,' Anne said fondly and tickled the girl's nose, which prompted much gurgling and ecstatic rolling of her eyes. 'She may be a woman in her body, but she is an infant in her mind,' she added with remarkable firmness.

As she said this, she fixed her gaze upon my face. Then, very slowly, she let her eyes travel down the length of my body, as though examining me for the first time and finding a stranger. She paused when she reached my belly, lifted her eyebrow at the sign of manhood she found there. After the time it would take to drink a cup of ale, she let her gaze descend to my feet.

'Why, sir,' she said, 'you are unshod.'

Without intending to, I looked down and saw my bare feet. It came as a surprise, for I had quite forgotten. In the preceding few minutes a change had been wrought. I was not sure what it was, but it was as definite as autumn into winter and I was impotent in the face of its inevitable progression.

'Your feet are muddy,' Anne said mildly. 'Shall I fetch a basin of water?'

I gawped as witlessly as the Vixen. 'No,' I croaked eventually. 'I must go and say the Office.'

'Yes, it is the hour.'

She turned her attention back to the girl, bouncing her on her knee, to squeals of idiotic delight. I returned to the church as bare-footed as I came.

Rain streamed off the backs of the men digging at the edge of the village. I thought they might swim, the mud was so thick about their calves. Anne stood at the lip of the trench, watching it gape wider with each spadeful. She was alone. This was so unusual an occurrence that it was as though she had forgotten to put on her gown, for she seemed naked without the Maid at her side.

'Where is the Maid?' I asked, despite myself.

'About,' she grunted and continued to stare into the hole.

'What are they doing?' I shouted.

She crossed her arms over her breasts. 'A pit must be dug. Before there are none left to dig graves, or willing to.'

'What for?'

'For those who will die.'

'We shall not need it. We are saved.'

'Sir, we are not. Not any more.'

'It is almost Michaelmas. We have been preserved all this summer.'

'We have not.'

'We have.' I strove to keep the whine from my voice.

'You choose to ignore what stands before you. And I know why, even if you do not.' She lifted her chin into the downpour. 'There has been a letter from the Bishop.'

'How do you know this?'

'You got it four days ago. Why did you not read it in the church?'

My face grew hot. 'I got a letter, it is true. Do you look into my private business now?'

'I cannot read it, nor do I need to. Any fool knows the seal of the Bishop.'

'The Bishop sends me many letters. How can you tell me what was in this one?'

'It was read out in the Staple, before it was passed to you. They dig a great pit there, beyond the east gate. So we dig here.'

'The Staple is sinful. They will have need of it.'

'Will you disobey the order?'

I raised my fist, but she did not flinch away. 'Will you strike me and deny the Bishop? Beware, sir, that you dishonour your Lord. Tell me I do not speak truth, then hit me as hard as you wish.'

The labourers leaned on their shovels and watched us. One man was wearing a broad linen band around his wrist. He lifted it to his lips, kissed it and touched it to his forehead.

'This pit will not be needed,' I said, loud enough for all to hear. 'We are spared by grace of the Saint and the Maid. Next spring we will laugh and fill it in again.'

Anne lifted her shoulders. Down in the hole they were digging as though they had never paused.

'Give me a spade,' I said to the nearest man. 'I will toil at your side.' The downpour was so thick they could not hear me. 'A spade!' I shrieked.

One of them stopped, ran a paw over his muddy chin. 'We are using them all, Father,' he said. 'There is not one left over.'

I jumped down beside him, grasped the handle. He tugged it away and I stumbled.

'Have some respect,' I shouted. 'I am your priest.'

He put the point of his nose to mine and spoke through his teeth. 'Father Thomas. Reverend Father. Get out of the pit. We have no need of your aid.'

I crawled up the side and onto the bank.

'Surely you can stop now,' I yelled through the thundering water. 'It is the depth of a man with a boy upon his shoulders. I can walk ten paces down one side.'

They did not slow.

'The order from the Bishop is to make it so, and we obey,' shouted one, so spattered about I did not know him. He also wore a strip of pale fabric around his arm.

'Call on me,' I shouted. 'I am here to help you. At all times.'

I turned; Anne was gone. I thought of the Maid. God had sent her to me; she was mine. I must find her. I trudged up the sodden track between the houses but did not see her, so I walked back, calling at each window. The village shrugged its shoulders. Aline's husband James filled the doorframe of his cottage.

'Good day, James. Have you seen the Vix— I mean, the Maid?'

Water trickled down the back of my undershirt.

'No, Father.' His breath was sour with ale, his gaze a fly that would not settle.

'Where is she?' I said, trying to see past his broad arms. Perhaps he was hiding the Maid from me.

'Father, you do not need to come in.'

I pushed him aside, but she was not there. Aline stood beside the hearth, clutching and unclutching the hem of her apron. A small boy lay upon the floor, his ears nipped black. And the smell.

'Why did you not call on me earlier?' I gasped.

Aline's gaze slid across my cloak and to her husband, who wrung the tail of his hood, frowning at his busy fingers.

'It is so quick, Father. He has been sick one morning only.'

'We must pray,' I said, holding my nose against the stink.

'Father, have you no comfort for us?'

'God is our comfort.' My fingers quilled a blessing over their heads as I stumbled backwards out of the door. 'Pray!' I cried.

The rain had slackened to a meagre spitting. I hastened to the stable, found the mare snuffing the air, twitching its tail. The walls gave out the meadow smell of dried horse dung. The floor was swept clean and a pile of hay was neatly stacked in the corner. I raced through the yard and found Anne on the road.

'Where are you going?' I panted.

'To the well,' she said, hefting the pot on to her shoulder.

'I can see that. The Maid is not in the stable.'

'Sir. She goes where God leads her.'

'Indeed. It is time to . . . I am going to . . .' I stuttered. 'Aline's boy is ill.'

'Another?' Her eyes grew wide.

'I do not understand what you mean. It is nothing to concern yourself over.'

'Sir?' The jar slid from her hands to the ground. 'How so?'

'I have just come from there. He has a slight fever, is all.'

Her eyes darted up and down the path. 'I will go to them this day, sir. With your leave.'

'Yes, mistress. If you must,' I sighed. 'You may go.'

'Thank you, sir.'

I watched her dwindle down the track and as I did so she halted, turned, waved. I waved back, started towards the church. But a worm in my soul made me pause and turn again. Anne was a child's toy moving through the drizzle towards the foot of the forest. And, as though she had gathered herself out of the air, the Maid strode beside her, clasping Anne's hand. She held herself straight and tall, nothing like the lame beast she was in my company.

I should not let myself be so affrighted. The Saint would listen, the Maid would return to me and the boy would be healthy by evening. To be sure of it I went to the church, took one of the altar cloths from the vestry and touched it to the shrine. If it was holy comfort the people wanted, then that was what I would give them. My soul grumbled that Anne took the Maid from my side so often. I must chastise her for her selfishness; the Maid was sent to preserve the village, and at my side she must stand. Still, I had the Saint and for now he would suffice.

I found Aline and James huddled over the child. The older lad shrank into the far corner of the room.

'I am here,' I said. 'I have brought comfort. A relic from the Saint himself.'

I lifted up the folded cloth. Their eyes devoured it hopefully. I stepped forwards, trying to ignore the stench that hovered over the boy. He whimpered, 'Mama.'

'Now, lad,' I said to him. 'Be strong and show your father how you are no longer a babe crying for his mother.'

He did not attend to me, and threaded the room with thin wailing.

'You have coddled him into girlishness,' I said to Aline. 'How he whines.'

Aline made a strangled noise and buried her nose in her apron. Her shoulders lifted and fell as though she was laughing. James clenched his fists and shifted his bulk towards me. Aline touched his elbow, and he ebbed away. I laid the cloth over the boy's forehead. He quivered.

'Oh, most saintly Brannoc,' I cried, 'look upon your people. Do not forget us at this time of trial. By the power of your most holy relics, heal this boy, we beseech you. Shine forth with your remarkable wonders. Heal him now.'

Aline and James bent over their babe, waiting for the miracle. I held my breath also, but there was no fluttering of angel wings outside the hut. The child grizzled and I grew weary of it. I began to roll up the cloth.

'Is that all you can offer us?' growled James. 'Where is the Maid?'

'Why did you not bring her?' added Aline, snuffling like a sow. '*She* could help us.'

I shrugged. 'Your lad has a bad cold,' I said.

They stared at me. 'Sir,' said Aline quietly. 'You know what you see before you.'

'It is a mild fever only. I can tell it from his face.'

'Look at his throat, man,' rumbled James. 'The signs are there.'

I did not want to look. I stuck out my chin. 'I will not be ordered about by an ale-wife and her husband. I am your priest. You will call me "sir". Or "Father".' I drew in a deep breath. I should be charitable: they were unlettered serfs. 'I will pray for the boy,' I smiled. 'Call on me in your need. I shall not desert you.'

The boy died in the night, as I heard it. I found James the next day, sitting idle by the stream. The reek of ale was strong. I folded my hands before me.

'How fare you, my son?' I said, and kindly, for I knew his grief must be great. He looked at me briefly, said nothing and lowered his head, gazing at the dawdling water.

'No word of greeting for your priest, James?' I said, placing much tenderness in each word. 'We have all suffered sorrow,' I continued. 'I know your lamentation. But we must put our trust in the Lord, and bear this travail with a good heart. You and Aline have been spared, and your eldest lad. The Lord has blessed you.'

'You are no man of God,' he slurred. 'That boy was barely away from the breast. He had no sin in him.'

'We all bear the sin of Adam.'

'We've always been guilty of that,' he grunted. 'Why now? Why not the time of my father? Or my grandfather?'

'God chooses when He will punish us.'

He twitched his head as though to shake off a horsefly.

'James, my son. You should not take so much ale. It stirs up bile.'

'Drink will fight off the infection. All men know this.'

'Prayer will fight it off, not beer.'

'Did prayer save my son?'

He hauled himself to his feet and staggered off between the houses, wailing like a female. He did not understand. This could not be the pestilence. We would be spared. I had been given a vision. We had the Saint. I had the Maid. *We* had the Maid, I corrected myself.

After Nones I went again to their house to persuade them of my conviction. I was their priest and they must listen. James's shoulders swelled the doorframe.

'Have you come to tell us more about our sins, Father?'

'I have come to pray with you.'

He stepped aside. Over the smell of burning herbs corruption blurred the air.

'It is my Robert,' quaked Aline. 'First the babe, now Robert.'

The elder lad sprawled on the floor, a scrap of linen folded on his brow. It stank of urine.

'What is this?' I said, pointing to the wet rag.

'It is a comfort to the lad,' said Aline. 'See how he sweats.'

'Where is it from? It is sopping with the stale of horses.'

I picked it up. Plain undyed linen cut neatly from a larger piece, a sheet by my reckoning. I rubbed it between thumb and forefinger. Smooth as butter.

James spoke. 'It is nothing, Father. Aline was using it to wipe the sweat from his face, just before you came in.'

I knew he was lying, and still had the strength to fight them.

'I asked where you got it. It is fine quality.'

In the silence I heard the door flap its tongue. Aline's eyes darted over my shoulder. Anne stepped past me and twitched the fabric from my fingers. I was too slow to snatch it back. In a swift movement she pressed it into Aline's hand and it melted away. James dragged off his hood and greeted her. Anne beamed at me.

'You have come to bless this ailing child,' she said loudly, although I stood less than two paces away. 'You are a good priest, Thomas. How benevolently you tend your flock, with no thought for yourself.'

She swept her eyes over Aline and James, widened them. The two of them nodded their heads furiously, cawing, *Yes, Father, bless you Father.*

'Let us then praise God and the Saint for all their blessings,' Anne continued, with the same forcefulness. 'Shall we not do so, sir?'

'Yes, indeed,' said I, there being little else to say.

We prayed. The child coughed and spat. The prayer ended.

'We thank you, sir,' said Anne. 'Prayer is what this child needs. You must go then, and pray for him.'

'Should you not be at—?' I began, and then stopped. The

300

house? The stable? Anne provided the answer before I was able to finish the sentence.

'I will now stay a while and comfort these good people. Unless you have great need of my labour.'

'No, no.'

'You must go to the church. It is almost the hour for Vespers.'

'Yes, indeed,' I muttered.

They stared at me. I blessed the house, blessed the child, then crouched my head out through the door and into the rain. The wicker hurdle slapped into place behind me and the walls sighed their relief. I stood a few moments, listening to the rattling wheeze of the lad through the daub. No other voices. Not prayer, nor anything else.

The whole village held its breath. No child splashed its feet through the puddles, no one beat his pig down the track, or herded his sheep back up it. No cow lowed, no ewe bleated. Yet it seemed I could hear the urgent whisperings of many mouths. I bent my ear to window after window, but heard only the hammering rain.

'The Saint bless and spare us! And the Maid!' I yelled.

I dashed to the church through the pelting rain and clung to the shrine. If I prayed earnestly, perhaps the Saint would turn over in his long sleep, rub his eyes and reach out his hand for me to pull him from his bed. I desired this with a sudden and desperate hunger, yearned for him to see how devout I was, how tightly I clasped my fingers. My words flowed from me as though another man spoke them, his fluting voice a few paces distant. The Saint dozed on. The carved flowers froze in my hands.

'Guide me, Lord,' I moaned. 'Oh, where shall I turn?'

God led me out of the church and to the stable. I held my breath in the heartfelt hope that this time the Maid would be waiting, her kind eyes strengthening me, but it was empty save for the mare. The girl's shift lay over the back of the creature and I pressed my face into its softness to find the scent of her holiness, but coughed on horse piss. Dangling around the stable walls were linen ribbons, hung there by a careful hand.

This was not the work of the Maid. It could not be. This was Anne's doing. I would have none of this superstition. I stepped back, stumbled on the stacked hay, and my heel knocked against hardness. I dragged the straw aside. Water jars, three of them. The liquid was not water, nor beer. I sniffed at it, smelled the urine of horses once again. I kicked them over, one after the other.

The next morning brought a porridge mist, thick enough to stir with a spoon. Slowly, the trees beside the ford pulled themselves away from the fog and the earth resolved itself gradually into familiar hills and hedges. As I made my customary walk around the village to see that all was well with my small flock, I saw an old man labour to unleash his gate from its post. He was shaking, his fingers foolish with the leather strap. I did not know him, but could see he needed help. He heard me approach and turned, face green with the effort: still I did not recognise him.

'Let me help you,' I said.

'I must milk the cow.' He set his teeth against me, and ground the words until they were small. 'The cow needs to be milked.'

Behind the gate there was a deep moan of agreement. I moved to untie the latch.

'No,' he growled, and pushed at my hand. 'You cannot help me.'

'Let me. Please.'

He coughed, and pitch tarred his chin. At last I saw past his strange colour and hunched body.

'But you are Edwin,' I said. 'The bell-ringer. I know you.' He turned his back. 'Why did you not come to the church yesterday? I rang the bell myself.'

'I must milk the cow,' he grunted, fingers trembling.

He pushed the gate away and staggered towards the beast, falling upon her side and embracing her as though she was his mother and he a child who had fallen a long way and ached for comfort. I wanted to say, *What has happened to you?* but I knew the answer. His body shook. At first I took it for a further sign of the fever, but there was a creaking sound, and I knew it for weeping.

'The Peace of Christ be with you,' I said.

'This is your fault, Father,' he rattled. 'You have brought this Great Mortality upon us.'

'Me? Have a care, Edwin. I am your priest.'

'Are you? We don't know what you are. One day you are a labourer, the next a gravedigger. Will you become a pig-drover next, or an ale-wife? We want a priest. Not another farmer. We have enough of them.'

'I am glad to work alongside you good people.'

'We want our Saint honoured.'

'I do this, and more.'

'We want a priest to do it. God does not want to be served by a peasant.'

'I loved you.'

He spoke to the cow. 'We were happy. Sheltered in the cloak of our Holy Saint. Showed him proper respect, and he looked after us. You have spoiled everything.'

'Edwin,' I said.

He ignored me. 'If you're this man of God you say you are,

then you must have had a warning. Kept it to yourself, you did.'

'Come with me,' I begged. 'Ring the bell. I need you by my side.'

'Do not touch me,' he said. 'Go.'

When I returned to the house, Anne was by the hearth, slapping dough into flat rounds.

'Good day, sir,' she said politely, kneading the sticky mess between her fingers.

'Where is the Maid?' I snapped.

She looked up. 'Sir?'

'The Maid!'

She smacked the dough onto the hot stone, where it hissed. 'She is about the village, perhaps at the well. I do not keep her tied to my apron.'

I laid my hand on her shoulder and twisted her so that she faced me. 'I will not have you make relics of the girl's clothes.' I growled. 'False relics.'

She returned her attention to the hearth, flipped over the bread-cake. 'It brings comfort, sir. We have little to comfort us. The people are famished for want of hope.'

'I will not have it. You lead the people into heresy.'

She paused, peered at me closely. 'I do not understand you. You wanted the Maid to perform wonders. Now that she does so, you complain.'

'Not like this . . . this superstitious nonsense.'

She threw her hands into the air. 'So you want everyone to follow your wishes entirely?' I raised my fist. She ignored its threat. 'Sir – tell me truthfully. Do you believe she is sent from the Lord? Or was it all a trick to keep us biddable?'

'How dare you question me?'

'I do dare, sir. And you have not answered my question. Do you believe it?'

'Yes!' I cried. 'Yes! I saw her. In a flood of celestial light! I believe!'

'Do you think you can make something true by saying it loudly?'

'How dare you!'

I struck her; not harshly. She toppled against the hearth-stone, but would not rest.

'Must God ask permission of you how to conduct His miracles?'

This time my fist sent her sprawling. 'Blasphemy! Have you no fear that God will strike you down?' I roared.

'The only one to strike me down is you. And see: I rise again.'

She got to her feet. I took my stick and let it speak my answer: God strengthened my arm, over and over until she was on the floor again, and quiet. She coughed into her palm, licked the blood away.

'I speak the truth,' she said. 'I have seen it. Aline's son sickened yesterday. You saw him. They feared he would follow his younger brother. But he is recovering.'

'Hold your tongue.'

'He was dying until I placed her linen upon his body. It took the pestilence from him. It lay on his face and kept away the corrupted air. If that is heresy, then I will have it.'

I would have beaten her again, but the strength in my arms was dissolved into gruel. The smell of burning flour filled the room. She staggered back to her feet.

'You see – I am not broken. I am not broken by you at all.' She folded her arms and turned away.

'I have not given you leave to go. It is near to Prime and I would eat.' I spoke to the back of her kerchief.

'There is one loaf in the basket. The rest are burned. I am

305

going to Aline's house to share in their thanks,' she said, one hand on the door-frame.

'I thank God for their deliverance,' I cried to her back. 'God is good to us.'

The house withered with the absence of her.

ANNE

I do not think I am important to the life of the house until I take myself away and lodge in the stable. As I grow, the house shrinks and Thomas with it.

The next morning, as I watch Thomas hobbling towards the church for Matins, a lad I do not recognise dances up the path. He does not pause to greet Thomas, but comes directly to me. It is a matter of a minute for him to speak the message. Having delivered the scant words, he skips away with a piece of bread in his fist.

Cat is dead.

I stand at the door, watch the boy chewing with a hearty appetite. I should sweep away the old reeds, for they stink. I should card wool. There is enough of it awaiting my attention. I should make oatcakes. I should grind oatmeal. With sand. No, without sand. That is how it should be done. I think I know how to grind meal. It is very difficult to remember.

My thoughts stagger back to Cat. Her screwed-up nose, the years of sniping, the arguments, the fights. The kiss of peace we gave each other when I saw her only . . . I would give anything to hear . . . My thoughts stutter to a halt. I have nothing to give. I have nothing within me at all.

I should tell my mother. With the thought, guilt flays me raw. I cannot remember when I last sought out my parents' company, last made certain of their health. A chill settles in my belly. I have been caught up in my own little miseries and present pleasures. The Maid has become my whole world. I cringe that I have been so contemptible a daughter. I will visit, I promise myself. As soon as . . . No, now.

I wrap a shawl around my head, scoop up a bundle of rags from the stable and am at their door in moments. When we embrace, they are as warm as they have ever been. My father grasps my shoulders, crushes me to his breast; my mother pats my cheek and calls me her darling babe. I am possessed of an odd sensation that they are standing at a great distance. They smile and speak sweet words, but all I can hear is a humming in my ears, like flies on meat. I tell them about Cat and they weep into my hair.

'Take the rags,' I say, over and over. 'I must go.'

Ma kisses me so hungrily her tears smear my face. I am grateful, for my eyes are dry. At last I am released. The Maid catches me as I stride past the house.

'It is Cat,' I say, before she asks the question. 'She is dead.'

The words should presage tears, but they do not.

'Anne,' she says, and it is all she needs to say. Her eyes are soft. She rests her hand on my arm. I pat it, and continue down the path. She chases after and grasps me, more firmly. 'You cannot be going to the Staple,' she puffs.

'I can.'

'It is too late.'

I open and close my eyes. It is a great effort to accomplish this small task. Speaking is even more wearisome. But she is glaring at me, and wants for an answer. 'To talk to her, yes,' I say. 'But I must say a prayer over her body.'

'There are priests to do that.'

I glare back at her with equal fierceness and she drops her head, cheeks splashed with crimson.

'Don't leave me,' she whispers. 'Don't,' she adds, with venom in the word. It does not sting.

'You cannot sway me on this.'

'It is madness.'

'Yes, it is.' I hear the steadiness in my voice. I had no idea that I possessed this certainty before I opened my lips. 'I know that pestilence infests the Staple. I know it's at our gate and darting in and out when it chooses. But I have to do this.' I place a kiss on each of her sharp cheekbones. 'I shall return.'

I make my way through the ford and past the church. She hugs my steps.

'Swear it,' she says, voice tight.

'I swear by my love for you.'

The air freezes, fast as your nose in a blizzard. Her eyes widen. 'Anne, I cannot – I cannot say—'

Heat sweeps through my belly. 'It matters not what you can say and what you can't. You are my love,' I say, voice warm with remembrance of the delight she has brought both my body and my heart.

'Don't, Anne,' she says despairingly, clapping her hands over her ears. 'You must know that I cannot love you in return.'

'Then I shall love you. You cannot stop me.'

'I can,' she says, but the fire has gone.

I walk along South Street, and at the crossroads take the road up the hill towards the Staple. She keeps pace the whole way.

'There is no point in loving me,' she continues, voice

twanging with misery. 'I am not worth the candle. I will die and you will grieve. Or you will die and I will grieve. It is better my way.'

'To be stone?'

'Yes,' she pouts.

Halfway up the hill, I stop and turn my face to hers. 'I have been a carved statue for too long. Creaking about my daily tasks with a *yes sir, no sir.* Then you came and breathed life into me. I will take that, even if I have it for one day only.'

She stares at me, lips working backwards and forwards. For this one moment in the grind of my days, I burn with the knowledge that I am right. My face glows with the truth I have spoken and she sees it. She makes a tight sound at the back of her throat and drops her chin.

'I am afraid, Anne,' she says, glancing up.

'So am I. But I have everything to return for,' I answer.

I embrace her and continue on my way. At the summit I turn and she is there, waving, a ghost of a smile on her face.

I resolve to make haste, not pausing to greet any folk. I need not worry about distractions, for I pass not one single soul. Each cott along the way has its gate shut tight, its shutters fastened. Yet although the road stretches empty, I have the queerest sensation of being watched, and not by friends. I shake off the clammy feeling and stride forwards.

At the west gate of the Staple I meet two fellows dragging a wagon loaded with a pair of coffins, one long and one short. The men have pulled their hoods so low only their mouths can be seen. I follow the bier, as there is only one place it can be headed, praying for the souls of the unfortunates upon it. Folk scurry past, some crossing themselves, but most sparing not one glance.

I try to imagine the people lying in these boxes, stretched

out with hands folded peacefully, and I cannot. I try to imagine Cat inside the larger, and my recollection falters. I strive to recall her familiar features and fail. Only the most awful of sisters would forget her so quickly.

At last we pass through the east gate and come to the common pit. The men heave the coffins from the wagon; either they are far stronger than they look, or the bodies within are feather-weight, they lift them so easily. Maybe the coffins are empty; maybe I have been tricked. Perhaps this whole pestilence is a joke. No one has died, every grave is untenanted and any moment now, Cat will creep up behind me, place her hands over my eyes and say, *Guess who?* This is the way I thought as a child. No longer.

The men take away the lids, for they are not nailed down, lift out the shrouded corpses and with great gentleness lower them into the pit. Finally, they hurl a few shovels of quicklime over the new guests. Their task completed, they turn the cart and trundle away. I listen to the squeak and rattle of wheels until it is lost in the hum of the town. I survey the ranks of bodies and wonder which one is my sister. Some are half-covered with earth, the bottom of the pit lost in the mud from this morning's rainfall.

Before the time of this pestilence a dead man was laid in a box of his own, a long way off from his fellow. For the first time it strikes me how lonely it is to lie alone with only your-self to talk to, twiddling your bony thumbs while you wait for the angel to blow the last trump. Now everyone is laid shoulder to shoulder.

I comfort myself with the thought that at least Cat does not want for company. Nor, I think, does Adam, for I have heard that no one can count the number of men ploughed into the fields of France. I picture Cat gossiping to the woman laid at her elbow, jaws clack-clacking in immortal conversation; of Adam and his comrades boasting how many pints of beer they will drink when God calls them into His celestial alehouse. The air freshens and I turn my eyes to the sky.

The clouds look set to weep for me. I think of all the mothers here, the children, the brothers and sisters, all the innocents mowed down. Still I do not weep and have no idea why I am so hard-hearted. I feel sorrow; but it is not a mewling, sobbing misery that casts me to the ground. It is far more like anger.

'Anne?'

The voice at my shoulder makes me leap half out of my skin. I whirl about, heart hammering with the conviction that it is Cat I shall see. It is Margret. I try to say her name, but a cough spills from my lips. I do not know I am falling until I am caught in her strong arms.

'Beloved Margret!' I gasp. 'How did you know to find me here?'

'I did not. I come to pray for the souls of the dead. There are so many, I am never done praying.'

I press my face into her shoulder and when I look away there are wet spots upon the fabric. Perhaps I am capable of tears after all.

'Where are their mourners?' I say, my voice wavering.

Margret gazes steadily into the pit and therein I find my answer. 'I heard of your sister's death and came to offer prayers especially. I reckoned no one else would attend.'

'No one?' I echo. I know what she will say, but I must hear all the same.

'Henry went before her, a week ago.'

'And the boy?' I whisper.

'Was the first.'

She does not look at me, and I am grateful. We stand quietly, for there is little more to be said.

'Do you not fear that Death will snatch you, coming here so often?' I ask, after the time it would take to tie the ribbons on my bodice.

'I am not afraid of Death.' She speaks in such a way that I do not doubt her. 'That does not mean that I am not afraid.' She turns her eyes to mine. Her lips work with the effort of holding back words she does not wish to speak, but must spill all the same. 'Anne. My John is a good man.'

'He is.'

'Yet I watch good men stripped of their goodness. John is beset with frightful things, and spiteful folk. Their malice is as contagious as this fever.'

'Do not worry, Margret. You made a fine choice in John. He loves you.'

Margret peruses my face for signs of sarcasm, and when she finds none she smiles at me for the first time in many months.

'I am no longer sure of anything. After Thomas visited us—' She sucks in a breath. 'Straight after, John sent Jack away to Exeter. He tells me it is for safety, but Exeter seethes with the pestilence, so how can it be true? I fear he is ashamed and wishes to place our son out of his sight. As though he can make believe that Jack does not exist, was never born . . .'

She swallows a gobbet of bile and makes a strangled sound. I place my arms around her and hold her steady. I kiss the top of her head, warm through the delicate linen of her kerchief.

'He has taken himself from me,' she wheezes. 'All night he prays and I lie alone, listening to him sob. He is tearing himself into pieces, Anne, and I cannot sew him back together.'

She clings to me, and I rock her until the fit passes over. At last she turns her face to mine. Her eyes are dry, as mine are once more. It is a wonder, that misery can leave women without tears.

'Margret,' I say, and kiss her brow. 'If you have need of me, come straightway. Do not tarry. My door will never be closed against you.'

'*Your* door? What of Thomas?'

I laugh, surprised at the fury in the sound. 'I could tell you such a tale, my sweet! But now is not the time. But I declare in truth: come to me. I am your friend. I always have been.'

'My dear Anne.'

I help her to her feet and we shake out our gowns. I take a deep breath and only now notice the stink of the pit, the buzzing of the flies. I slide my arm through hers.

'Let us walk. I have said my farewells.'

I take a last look to the east, where a line of trees sweeps its cloak across the hills that surround the Staple. The forest lies upon this whole land like a blanket, and all we have managed to do against its hideous smothering is snip small holes in it through which to poke the roofs of our dwellings. All my life I've been warned from straying too far into its depths: boggarts, cut-throats, bottomless pits seething with worms. It's where the Maid says we must go. Not so long ago, I'd have thought her a piskie come to steal me away under the hill. A small part of me wonders if she still is.

I hug Margret close to my side and feel her warmth through my sleeve. We walk back through the town towards the church. Once again I notice the emptiness of the streets: no children at play, no women leaning against their doorposts to gather the latest news. The few we do meet hurry past without a word of greeting. One woman gazes out of her window, and I shout, 'Halloa!' but she stares through me. Her face is blank as a dish of milk: no curiosity, no anger, no animating force at all.

'The place has changed,' I remark, as we arrive at the west gate.

'Everything has changed,' mutters Margret. 'Go quickly home. Do not tarry along the way.'

'I've no mind to do so.'

'Good.'

I take her hand. 'Margret,' I say. 'I was cruel to you when we spoke last.'

'Anne, you do not need to—'

'I do. Thomas is everything you said he'd be, and more. It would take a day to list his faults; but I am burdened with my own, so I shall leave it at that. What is important is that you were right. I chose pride and greed over friendship, and for that I am sorry.'

She regards me levelly. 'By the Saint, Anne. How grown you are.'

'Cat said the same thing.' My heart clenches its fist. 'I have lost her,' I croak. 'But I have found you.'

She lays her hand upon my shoulder. I lean into the caress, hungry for forgiveness, knowing that in a moment she will withdraw and be gone. But she does no such thing. Rather, she slides her fingers along my shoulder, slips under my coif and brushes the trembling skin of my throat. She lays her other hand upon my cheek and tips my face to hers.

'Beloved cousin,' she says, a light in her eyes I do not recognise.

'Margret?' I breathe.

She nods in answer to a question I do not know I have asked. 'Yes. John loves me. But I do not think it will be enough.'

I do not understand. I am still so new to love that I believe it is stronger than anything, perhaps even death. I am wrong about love, but right also.

* * *

I return to find the house grown even more lost. The hearth is cold. At some point the wind has blown through the room and scattered the ashes in a dusty shawl. The floor is half-bare, for I never finished the task of clearing out the straw. It is mouldier than when I left it and mushes beneath my feet. There is another smell, that of dead mice and worse. A pot leans against the hearthstone, a rough crust of pottage at the bottom.

Surely I have not kept away for so long. I search for the broom and find it leaning against the outer wall, bristles still wet from the last shower. I shake off the raindrops and labour for half an hour sweeping the old reeds out of the door. I try to set fire to the heap, but they are so damp they will not take. Just when I think I've coaxed a small flame to life, it starts to drizzle.

I go back inside to wait out the shower. It is only when Thomas rises from the bench that I see him. I am sure he was not there before.

'Mistress,' he says, with a dignity he strives to wrap tight about him.

He looks towards a spot over my right shoulder. I turn my head to see who is behind me, but the room is empty. I never before noticed quite how much he speaks through his nose, like a pipe on which he is endeavouring to blow a bright tune.

'The house gladdens to see you,' he squeaks, his eyes focused on somewhere far away. 'It pleases me also.'

'Thomas . . .'

He winces at the sound of his name. His body is grown too pinched for his clothes, his over-tunic hanging from his shoulders like an empty sack. His chin is a mess of poorly cropped stubble, as though he has taken a meat-knife to it.

'Yes. The house rejoices,' he adds, with such hopefulness I

cannot decide if I want to weep at the sorry way he misses me, or kick him across the room.

'You are thin, sir,' I remark.

He whisks his fingers, as though a gnat is bothering him. 'I am well, God be thanked.'

'God be thanked,' I mutter.

For all his starved appearance, his eyes burn with the same devouring fire I saw when he delivered his sermon on Queen Sheba, so many lifetimes ago I cannot count them. Once I was drawn to that brightness: now I see a hunger that sucks the life out of all it touches. It gives no warmth, drawing the heat of others into its maw so that all who fall into its circle are sucked empty as old wineskins. I shudder at the ghastly image.

'Sir,' I say through clenched teeth. 'You are unshaven. I shall tend to you.'

I hear the false cheer in my voice, slathered thinly over disgust. Without being told, I realise it is very important that he should not know I feel this. Thomas is foolish, priggish, pitiful, proud. Never before have I thought of him as dangerous.

He hops around like an excited boy, fetching the knife, the bowl, the oil. As usual, I grumble a little. As usual, he chides me and counsels obedience. Anyone observing would think our household the same as ever. Only the Maid might notice the rigor of my fingers about the handle of the razor, the forced gaiety of my humming as I sharpen the blade on the whetstone. I have learned more from her than I think.

He drags the bench from the wall and seats himself expectantly. Once I would have found this an intimate act, and marvelled at the closeness of his body to mine. Now he is as arousing as a broken cartwheel. I swipe oil on to his chin and throat to soften the coarse hair and thereby hasten my task as much as possible.

'By the Saint, sir,' I remark. 'Your beard grows in quickly. My brother could go four days before he had as much to show.'

At the mention of Adam my thoughts fly straightaway to Cat. I should tell Thomas that she is dead. But I do not, and am not entirely sure why.

'You do not often speak of your brother.'

I close the door to that part of my soul and lock it tight. 'No, I do not, sir.'

'He was a fine man?'

'He was. The finest.'

I test the blade against my thumb until I am satisfied it is sharp enough. I press the heel of my hand upon his right temple, pull the skin taut and lay the razor on the topmost part of his cheek, beneath the eye. Of a sudden, I am in no hurry. He holds his breath, waiting for me to commence. I draw the blade downwards, biting my lower lip with concentration. I look everywhere but into his eyes. I am close enough to feel the fur of his breath on my face.

'You are indeed tough-bristled,' I say, for lack of anything better. I turn aside to wipe the blade against the napkin laid over my shoulder. 'I mean no disrespect, sir.'

'I take none, mistress.'

I mumble thanks. 'Turn your head,' I command, and he obeys. I scrape his other cheek. 'Thomas, you should shave more often,' I chide. 'It is like trimming a gorse bush.'

He laughs. It is such an unexpected sound.

'Are you well, Thomas?'

'Am I merry so rarely?' he asks.

My eyes must show the answer. 'You have more important matters to attend to,' I mutter. 'You are a man of God.'

'I was amused at the thought of you trying to prune gorse with a shaving-razor,' he answers.

'Indeed,' I murmur. 'That would be a fine mess.'

I place two fingers beneath the tip of his chin, push it high enough to get at the straggling hairs beneath and place the knife against the knob of his Adam's apple. Once more, I pause. I am aware of his breath coming and going in time to my own, the peppery smell of it, how my fingers are clenched around the bone handle. I have a sharp knife in my hand.

'Is there something amiss?' His voice strangles due to his odd position. I feel the nervous thump of his heart against metal.

'Not at all, sir. I was merely wondering where to shave next.'

I place my hand across his mouth and hold him still; drag the blade down his throat with the rasp of a wood-chisel. It is a cold day: the doors of the house are closed and the room is quiet save for the scratch of the blade and my breathing, full of concentration. I draw the knife across his skin. The moist warmth of his lips swells against my fingers.

Outside I can hear passers-by; too far and too faint to make out their words, but women, chattering as they pass on their way to the well and back again. Louder, quieter, louder again they go back and forth. It is only when he mumbles, 'Mistress?' through my fingers that I fly back into my body and realise how far I have strayed. I let him lower his chin and he peers at me.

'I am such a sleepy-head,' I say, and smile.

He smiles back, and it is as though he has struck me across the face.

'I will shave your head now, sir,' I say with firm efficiency.

'Anne.' He grabs my wrist.

'No!' I cry, in answer to a question he did not speak and I do not wish to hear.

'What has happened to us?'

319

'Us? There is no *us*. There never has been,' I growl.

'Once you wished it so.'

'No,' I moan. I will not let him cozen me, not now.

'Will you not smile at me, Anne?'

I blink at the sound of my name on his tongue. I would have taken delight in it, but long ago. I tremble as though the air is venomous, writhe to free myself from his grasp. He hangs on.

'Let me go,' I say as calmly as I can manage. 'I must shave the spot on your head.'

'The tonsure,' he corrects me.

'Yes, yes. The *tonsure*,' I snap. 'Whatever it's called, I must shave it.'

'Anne,' he says again. 'It can wait a moment.'

'It can't.' I struggle so mightily that my kerchief slips to my shoulders, uncovering my braids. 'You are staring at me,' I gasp.

'Your hair is beautiful.'

'What? Why are you speaking so strangely, Thomas?'

'I remark upon the truth, simply.'

'Thomas, what is the matter with you?'

'Anne—'

With my free hand I brandish the razor under his nose. 'Stop it. Will you let me finish shaving you or won't you?'

'Anne, wait.'

I let out a cry of frustration and hurl the blade to the floor. It skims through the reeds and strikes the wall.

'It is too late,' I declare.

'It is not.'

'It is! For everything!' I shout. 'Why will you not see what is before you, Thomas?'

'There is nothing before me, save your troublesome self,' he mutters.

'Oh, be quiet for once, Thomas. People are *dying*. Surely you are not blind to that.'

'Not in this village.'

'Yes; in this village.'

'No.'

I throw up my hands. 'Are we going to say *yes no yes no* like children? We are past games.'

'The pestilence will pass over us. We are protected by the Maid. And the Saint.' His voice wobbles and I seize the uncertainty.

'Are we? You do not believe it any longer.'

'I do!' he quavers. 'So should you, if you wish to live!'

'I am a long way past belief.'

He looks so stunned I swear I could tip him over like a ninepin.

'How dare you speak such blasphemy!' he splutters. 'I am a man of God!'

'Oh, hold your tongue. That tired old saw is as threadbare as a beggar's blanket. You are not this man of God you claim to be, Thomas. You are a fool.'

I wait for him to strike me. He blinks; his jaw works back and forth, lips pursed as though ready to spit out a refutation. He says nothing. His hands stay clamped to his sides. I watch a while, waiting for him to stalk off in the direction of the church, but he does not stir. His eyes squeeze shut, spring open. I wonder if he can see me any more, he is so taken out of himself.

Far away, very far indeed it seems, the church bell begins to chime its tuneless melody. I gasp my relief and do not care if he notices.

'You must go. It is the hour for the Divine Office.'

A shadow sweeps across the floor. I turn to see the Maid

standing in the doorway. Such a thin creature, yet she blocks the light. My head jerks towards her and my heart soars to the sky.

'Maid!' I shout. She gives me a curious look, counselling caution. 'I must go,' I say, far too loudly for this cramped room. 'The Maid has need of me.'

'Can she not wait?' Thomas whimpers, clutching my sleeve-ties.

'She is hungry.' I dash from the room, leaving him with a fistful of torn ribbons.

'My tonsure!' he shouts, but I am gone far beyond the reach of his commands.

I leap into her arms, heaping her face with kisses, caring not one whit if the whole world and the Bishop are spying upon us. Thomas is forgotten, the half-swept room is forgotten and I do not remark upon it until much later, when neither Thomas nor myself care overmuch for diligent housekeeping.

She helps me drag the basket to the orchard and we set about filling it with fruit. Or rather I pick, for she bores swiftly and wanders about between the trees, sniffing the air. The first apple comes away with a neat twist of my hand, and the second. Each one I touch drops and I think myself very lucky to have such a faultless crop, all ready on the same day.

Maybe this perfection is what prompts me to pause. I examine the next apple more closely before dropping it into the basket to join its fellows. It seems firm enough when I squeeze. I hold it to my ear and shake: I ought to hear a faint rattle of seeds, but there is no sound. The skin is unblemished, with no sign of burrowing insects, but around the stem is a dark spot the size of a thumbprint.

I give the stalk a tug and it comes away with a wet pop, followed by the slight but unmistakable odour of rot. I take the paring knife from my bodice and slice the apple in half. The core drools with sloppy mulch. I take another from the pile and cut it open, revealing the same mess. I take a third: it is so far gone that corruption has infected the flesh to within a hair's-breadth of the skin.

I test every fruit in the basket, tugging the stems. Almost all come away with the same telltale softness. Out of the twenty-four I have picked, seventeen are fit only for swine. The whole tree delivers sixteen apples I consider sound. The remainder tumble around me in a deceitful carpet of red and green, beautiful to the eye and poisonous at the heart. Even the pigs will turn up their snouts.

I move to the next tree. It is a different variety, tart even when ripe. The first two apples are unmarked and I am much cheered. Perhaps only the other tree was blighted. I chide myself for being cast down so quickly. The shadow of the pestilence makes us fear the worst at every turn.

I pluck with a good heart, shaking each and hearing the loose seeds rattle. After five, I reach one that is quiet. *Perhaps it is simply not ready*, I counsel myself and hear the emptiness of my hope. I cut it open grudgingly, for I do not wish to see what I know I will find.

It is the same tale. Its heart is mud. As I watch, a maggot lifts its head out of the sludge, disturbed in its gluttony. I drop the vile thing with a squeal as if it has stung me. I am skittish as a child who jumps at every little thing. At this rate, I will be lucky to collect two baskets of sound fruit from the entire orchard.

'Anne?'

The voice is so close that I think a demon has crawled into

my ear. I shriek again. When I turn, it is the Maid. She gives a half-smile.

'You're afraid of your own shadow,' she remarks.

'You crept up on me,' I pout.

'You're jumping about like a cat on a fire.' She jerks her head at the tree. 'What's afoot?'

'The apples are rotten. Near enough the whole crop,' I say. 'If this orchard is a model for the county, there'll be no fruit left by Christmas-tide.'

'And no one left to eat them,' she says carelessly, picking up one of the blemished fruits and hurling it at the nearest tree. It explodes wetly.

'We could take the sound ones,' I say, hoping to divert the conversation in a more pleasant direction. 'When we go.'

'There's no point. They're too heavy. Best stick with salt pork, cheese and bread. As much as we can carry. I don't know why you're bothering picking them.'

'Because there are still bellies to fill in this village. If we do not want them, there are plenty who do.' She shrugs, but helps to haul the basket to the stable all the same. 'We can distribute them to the people when they come for fresh rags.'

'You are ever generous,' she says.

I bed the apples upon straw for safekeeping while she fetches armfuls of the driest stalks from the back of the byre. I observe the easy way she moves, how her hair has grown over her ears and makes her look far more like a woman and less like a girl.

'How old *are* you?' I ask.

Her face slams down its shutters. 'I don't know,' she snaps and spins around so that I cannot see her expression. 'Old enough to know what I want. And that's an end to questions.'

'You are angry that I ask?'

'If a pole of beans gets no water and no light, it grows stunted. If it grows at all,' she grunts.

'That is not an answer.'

She takes an apple, holds it to the light and, satisfied that it is whole, polishes it against her thigh.

'Why do you need to know?' she mumbles, rubbing.

'Because I know nothing about you. And I wish to. Is that so terrible?'

'You know all I can give.' She digs her teeth into the skin and munches, slowly.

'Rubbish. You promised an end to games. I know you can play a hundred different parts. I want to see you.'

Bite by bite, she gulps down the fruit, pips, stalk and all. When she has done so, she licks her fingers. Only then does she look me in the eye.

'You really want to know?'

'Yes.'

'If I speak, I cannot take back the words. They will be out, and no power on this earth will be able to fold them away again.'

'I know,' I say.

'And what if you feel disgust? If you hate me?'

'I shall not.'

'What if you do not believe me? There is a lot to swallow.'

One hard winter when I was young, Adam snapped an icicle off the eaves and dropped it down the back of my shift. I remember how loudly I squealed. I do not make a sound now, but feel the same chill.

'Tell me.'

She takes a breath and begins. It is the breath that divides our time before and our time after. She reveals such things as I did not think could exist in this world, her voice matter-of-fact, as

325

though she is describing a pot of peas, each as dull and unremarkable as the last.

'First, there was my mother,' she says. 'Was she my mother? She was the woman who was there as I grew, the only one I remember. I used to comfort myself with stories that I could not be her daughter: no mother would permit the acts wrought upon me. It was bad enough that my lullaby from the cradle was how much she did not want me. Far worse was her other song of "Daddy's come a-hunting".

'I had many fathers, and each as bad as the last. When they tired of her sagging delights and left her snoring, they would start on me. Until she found out. It was the only time she ever surprised me: I thought I'd earn a beating, but her eyes lit up like beacons. It was time for me to put bread into our bellies, she said. She was tired of filling the mouth of a greedy bitch like me who did nothing from morning to night but eat, shit, and sleep.

'I told myself I had been stolen from my true dam, who was scouring the earth for me, weeping for the theft of her own babe. One day the door would fly open, she would gather me into her arms and the hell in which I burned would be forgotten. But these were children's tales and melted like butter on a gridiron.

'Every moment I could, I sat at the door and peered into the faces of passers-by, for one of them might be her. It was never for very long: the one who called herself Ma hauled me back inside, announcing, "Girl. You are needed." And it would begin again.

'Vile acts are rarely new. Cruel folk are not inventive and the acts inflicted upon me were no different to those inflicted on girls since Eve crawled out of Adam's side. Girls are taught from the womb that they are filthy, sinful, disgusting, worthless meat. So was I treated.

'When I bled, and cried, she beat the tears out of me. Threatened me with death if I dared to cry again. I believed her because mothers do not lie. She told me to smile and simper and do what I was told. So I smiled and I simpered, and the men came and the men went: black-toothed, black-hearted, drunken, vicious, sticky-mouthed, herring-breathed. I earned us bread and beer besides. I was small for my age and there are men who like it so.

'I grew clever. I learned how to send myself away from my body. First, I hovered near the door, watching the child in the straw and what was being done. It was too close, too much to bear. So I learned how to leave the house and sit in the gutter, continue my vigil for my true mother.

'It was not far enough. I learned to fly above the houses, up and up until I could see our huddle of hovels, the river that bent round the town like a long wet arm, cradling the folk within. Higher still I soared, until all I could hear was the rushing of air in my ears.

'I looked down upon the land, far below. Around the city crouched the forest. The houses looked so helpless against the dark surge of trees, like a tide poised to crash and swallow the whole lot of them, every last man and woman, good or bad. I rejoiced, as much as my broken soul could rejoice, and prayed for the trees to lift up their roots and crush every single one.'

The Maid breathes heavily, and pauses. I breathe also. I do not touch her, however much I wish to clasp her to my breast. I know it would neither help, nor be welcome. I have watched people kiss away tears, not out of any desire to comfort but rather to make the noise cease. I do not want her to think I am one of those people. Then she begins again.

'More childish dreams. I always fell back into my body. The cottage still stood, the straw still reeked and my mother was counting the coins she had been given for the use of me. When I was alone at last, I wept. I don't know if it was from the pain, for I never managed to shut that out, or because I had to return to my body, or because there was never going to be any rescue.'

At last she stops talking. Not, I think, because her story is finished, but because she has said all she can for today. I lay my hand upon the straw between us where she can see it and know I am with her.

She shrugs. 'So there you have it. I was born, I suffered, I ran, I grew hard and cold, I came here.'

There is nothing I can say. But I cannot leave this silence between us: it could be taken for the silence of disbelief, of fear, of revulsion. I look at her small face, so full of defiance.

'Thank you,' I say.

'Thank you?' she repeats.

'For telling me. It was difficult to hear. But far more difficult to speak, I think.'

'I am sorry. I have made you miserable.'

She raises her hand to my face and it comes away wet. She licks my salt from her fingers.

'Anyone would weep, to hear such cruelty,' I say. 'That, or be made of stone.'

'I am stone then, for I do not weep.'

I blow my nose on my apron. 'You are not. Your stone is the wall you have built around yourself. Stone walls are an excellent remedy against enemies.'

She gives me a look that is half wonder that I see it, and half anger to have been so easily discovered.

'Is that what you want?' she snaps. 'To breach me, leave me defenceless?'

'I want nothing if you do not want it first yourself.'

She throws me that look again, although this time wonder

is battling powerfully against rage and doing well. Her mouth opens. There is a crackling from the back of her throat, as of twigs burning. At first I think speech has deserted her and she is being transformed into the witless girl we all thought she was at the start.

'My love?' I murmur.

Her face twists, the sound grows louder, and she lets out a throttled yelp. It might be *no*; I cannot tell. Then she jumps to her feet and is away and I watch her grow smaller and smaller along the track towards the forest. The part of my soul that was left me after Adam died quits my body and races after her.

VIXEN

I run without seeing where my feet are heading and am deep into the forest before I stop and it breaks out of me.

At last, I weep: for everyone I've lied to, stolen from, sneered at, tricked, cheated, crushed, kicked, used, fucked, run from, spat on. I vomit out my hatred and watch it coil at my feet, slick as an eel. Then I retch some more.

When I am emptied of remorse, I find what's left of myself at the bottom of the well: I am a lump of wizened meat with snapped teeth and broken claws, shrinking, black and shit-filled. This ugly monster stirs, unglues an eye and squeals. I weep for it also. It is a long time before I am done.

I rub the heels of my hands into my eyes until green stars blur my vision. If I was the same creature of a quarter-year ago, I would keep running and not stop. I would find a new village, a new Thomas, a new Anne. But there is no other Anne, and I am not the same woman. There is only one place I wish to be.

I turn and pick my way back through the trees towards the village, and it is only by chance that I come upon the ruins of Knot-Beard's camp. Their fire is cold, the ashes wet and half-covered with earth, the hearthstones scattered. They have not been here for days, perhaps weeks. I tell myself they have been captured. But I know the truth: it was not the Sheriff who caught up with them. On one of their farming raids they found more than food. The pestilence snatched them away. I shall not see them again.

Above my head a magpie sets up a *clack-clacking*. It sounds uncommonly like Death rattling His jaws as He laughs at the joke: I've been saving money to pay men long gone. I could have run away weeks ago.

I stop at the well and wash my face in the cistern. I wait for the water to settle and peer at my reflection. I look the same and yet am different; not that I am sure what I looked like before.

I find her in the stable, soaking rags and folding them neatly to distribute to the villagers. It makes my heart clench, my breath halt. She looks up as my shadow fills the doorway. Neither of us says a word. I hold out my hand. She rises, approaches. I lead her to the back, where the hay is heaped for winter forage and I draw her down on top of me. I cannot say *love*. It is a foreign tongue and I do not know if I will ever be able to speak it. But I can say her name, and I do so softly.

'Anne.'

I kiss her face with the same gentleness. I hope she can hear the words I cannot say in the touch of my mouth and hands. She says nothing, still, and I am grateful. I draw her hand between my legs and hold it there. At first she does not move.

'Yes?' she asks.

'Yes,' I say, and close my eyes.

'Keep your eyes open, my love,' she murmurs. 'Know it is Anne who touches you and makes your body sing.'

She moves her fingers, slowly at first and my belly lifts into the caress. Despite the sweetness that trembles my body,

331

I do not cry out her name, nor tumble the stable walls with shrieking.

'Am I too quiet?' I whisper.

'You are who you are, which is all I wish. I need no fancy show to dazzle my ears.'

I watch as she tends to the desires of my body and those of her heart; see my pleasure bloom in her eyes, hear her breath catch in tune and rhythm with mine. As the joy begins to mount, I am struck with a sudden terror that I will fly away, as I have always done. I look into her eyes and they hold me steady. I ascend, not out of myself but into a shuddering brightness. Delight seethes through my flesh and bursts my body into light and I am in that light and of that light and—

I may not draw down the sun and stars, but I fall further than I thought possible into the rapture of another's touch. Afterwards, I lie against the warmth of her body and could not run even if I wanted to, not that I want to at all. Gradually I gather myself together, not into the hardness of stone but something far more malleable. I run my hands over my limbs. It would not surprise me to find I am a different shape, just as beeswax forms to the shape of a new mould.

'What are you doing?' she asks drowsily.

'I feel different,' I say. 'I wonder if some great alteration has been wrought while we have been lying here.'

'Perhaps you *are* changed.'

She gazes at me with the tenderness I have seen before, but even that is changed. She is in possession of herself. I should like that also, and not merely to be in possession of clever disguises.

'You are right, Anne. All those masquerades – they were better than being my own vile self. They were my protection.

332

I have played so many parts that I am unsure where they end and I begin. They are become as much a part of me as my own skin. Who am I if I strip them all away?'

'You are this woman, lying beside me. You are my beloved.'

I chew the flesh on the inside of my cheek. 'You say you love me.'

'I do not say it. I live it. I breathe it. That is far more than words.'

'How can I know?' I say.

I hear my voice, so small I wonder if I am still a child. Perhaps all the years between my childhood and now are a dream, and in a moment I shall be shaken awake and find . . . No. I speak again, voice so husky it could be the scratching of the paddles when she is carding wool.

'I will try to be myself, Anne. I wish to try.' I swallow, past the anger, past the fear. 'I am yours.' It is a terrifying confession. 'I cannot promise,' I say, more boldly, for breaking promises is what I am used to. 'I promise nothing.'

For the first time in my life I have stopped running. It may mean death, but I was never more alive.

COMPLINE
1349

From Saint Justina to Saint Wilfrid

THOMAS OF UPCOTE

I instructed my legs carry me to the house, but they were unwilling. My heels scuffed the bare floor. I had not spread new rushes. I would only have to replace them. I wondered why Anne had bothered, every week. Then I remembered how I commanded her to do so. How I commanded her to wash my linen. How many tasks I bade her do, and every single one of them meaningless.

The wind had picked up and was casting rain through the windows, so I shuttered them and secured the door. I wandered to the kitchen, to the solar and back again to the main room. It was cold and the hearth gaped, waiting to be filled with wood. I went again to the kitchen. A half-loaf lay on the shelf, furred with mould. I could not sit. I could not stand still. Neither could I lie down. I had no desire to be there, but there was nowhere else to go. I spent the day in uneasy wanderings, never settling in one place for more than a few moments.

I was so caught up in the swirl of my own thoughts that I did not see the light coming from the stable until I was almost upon it. At first I thought a sheaf of straw had caught fire within. The door was open, but blocked by men with backs turned. I knocked one upon the shoulder, and he jumped.

'Oh, it's you, Father,' he announced, very loudly.

There was a sudden quietness, which only then made me realise there had been sound before.

'God's blessing on you this evening,' I said. 'You are Adam the carter, are you not?'

'I am not,' he answered, and crossed his arms. I could not see past him.

'This is my stable,' I whined.

'Let him through, brother,' said Anne's voice.

At once his face unfolded into a smile and he stood aside. The smell of damp wool buffeted me first, then I saw the source of the brightness: a half-circle of candle-stubs pressed into the dirt and potsherds filled with mutton fat, wicks spitting. The dust was speckled, as though light rain had fallen upon it. On this side of the flames huddled the men, women and children of my flock. Beyond the candles sat Anne and the Maid, the light quivering against their faces.

A man stood, pushed back his hood and stepped to the edge of the marked space. He placed a small parcel on the ground.

'It is a knife,' he said. 'A good one. My son's.'

The mob sucked him back and a female was next, with a jug.

'Milk,' she said. 'I boiled it as commanded. I pray you send back the pitcher.'

Anne nodded thanks. I watched as bread was offered, then a piece of green cheese, a boiled egg, coins, a slice of standing pottage. The Maid's arms were heaped with scraps of wool, linen and homespun russet, and these she sifted through her fingers. Occasionally she paused at a rag that caught her eye, lifted it to her face and kissed it. Each time she did so, a gasp escaped one of the people crouched about her.

See! She kisses mine!

And mine also!

338

And mine!

Anne put her hand behind the bundle of hay that was her seat and drew out a leather bucket covered with rush matting. She placed it between the girl's feet and took away the lid. The Maid cast a smile across our candlelit faces. A voice sputtered out, 'Oh, good Maid!' and fell into weeping. The girl's gaze hovered in the direction of the sound until it was comforted into quiet snuffling. Then, piece by piece, she dipped the strips into the bucket, leaned out of the circle and placed each into the hand of its owner.

Thank you, Maid; thank you, Maid babbled the people. They swayed like cornstalks, tying the rags around their ankles and tugging down their clothes to cover them. At last her arms were empty. She patted her hands together.

'It is finished,' said Anne.

The Maid swept her eyes over each in turn, and at last fixed upon me. Everyone in the stable followed suit, and stared. I felt blood flame in my cheeks, and knew it for wrath that Anne indulged these fools in such heathen fiddle-faddle.

'Hold fast to your faith in the Lord!' I cried. 'You must believe!'

There were a few raised eyebrows, wearied agreements. One man close by muttered, 'Yes, yes, we've heard that one before.' I glared: he held my stern gaze unflinchingly. I was first to look away, but only because I had more important things to attend to than play a staring game. The Maid would never commit these acts alone. I seethed that Anne used her so.

'We must keep faith in the Maid!' I added.

Ah, yes! They replied, with greater passion. *Our Maid!* They nodded at each other, sighing *the Maid, the Maid,* the words rippling back and forth with many signs of the Cross and touching of ribbons at throat, wrist and ankle.

'You must believe in her holiness! Sent from God to protect us from the pestilence!'

'Of course we do, Father!' declared a woman.

'What makes you think we do not?' said another.

'She is our own dear Maid!'

I found some courage. 'I will not have this – blasphemy. You must turn to God for comfort.'

'Where was God when my baby died?' a man asked. 'Where were you? If it wasn't for the Maid, my son would have perished.'

'But this is idolatry!' I blustered, waggling my hand. 'A show for peasants to gawp at.'

I got no further, for they crowded upon me so thick I thought the air would be stolen from my mouth. Hefty shoulder touched hefty shoulder and even though I stood on tiptoe, I could not see the Maid through the mass of bodies.

'Peasants?' growled the man I thought was the carter.

I cudgelled my brains to serve up his name, and by some miracle was obeyed. 'You are James!' I said, and heard the desperation in my squeak.

He ignored me. 'The Maid looks after us right enough, so she does.'

'Don't tell us how to treat our blessed Maid.'

'We've heard what the Staple men did to her,' sneered a female with beer sweltering her breath. 'You brought them down upon us.'

'Me?' My voice quailed with disbelief. I wished it could have been fury.

'They brought the pestilence in with them. Because you stood by.'

Despite the heat in the stable, my body grew cold. 'They did not touch her!' I cried.

'If a man let that happen to my daughter, I'd – priest or no priest.'

'How do we know he's a priest?' piped up a woman. 'How do we really know the Bishop sent him?'

There was an unpleasant muttering, as they considered this question.

'So, whoever you say you are, you keep your paws off the Maid,' growled James. 'She's ours, not yours.'

'No!' I shrieked 'The Maid is mine! She is, she is!'

I hurled myself at them, but could not break through the wall of flesh. A man grabbed me by the throat and shoved me away.

'How dare you!' I spluttered, rubbing my neck.

I knew the truth. I had seen it: the Maid, bright as the sun, sent to me as a sign of God's bounty. I would not lose their respect. I was their priest. They would kneel. They would pray. The force of my will would make it so. The force of God's will, I corrected myself. They would cleave to my words. God's words. The two were the same thing. The Maid would never desert me, never. The people would believe.

Even though you no longer believe it yourself, said the voice of my soul.

'No!' I shrieked, and the world grew dark.

'Reverend Father, are you well?'

A woman's face hovered over mine, pale and bloated as a corpse rising from a pond. I could not understand why I was lying flat on my back.

'What?' I shouted. There was a fearsome buzzing in my ears. 'Why are there wasps? Get them away!'

'Father Thomas?' she repeated.

I knew her face. Aline, that was it. Aline: a contentious drunkard. I hoped I had not spoken out loud, but her expression of concern did not alter and I reasoned that I had managed to hold my tongue.

'What do you want?' I whined, holding my hands before my face to defend me from blows, which did not come.

It was all I could do not to hold my nose. The stench of ale, mixed with womanish odours, rolled off her in a sick tide. A man's face appeared at her shoulder. His name danced out of reach. Once I would have sworn it was William my steward, but was sure of nothing tonight. Names, names, names. I did not know why I bothered with them. Hubert, James, James, Hubert. All were fodder and the Lord would fork us into the common pit sooner or later.

'Let me help you, Father,' the man grunted and not unpleasantly, which seemed a great wonder.

What kindness have you ever shown him? My soul's memory offered nothing. I felt close to weeping. His hands slipped beneath my shoulders and he hefted me upright with as little difficulty as a bag of peas. He patted straw from my gown.

'Upsy-daisy, Father,' he cooed, in the way you might to a child who has tripped and fallen.

The woman gave a small smile that barely lifted the corner of her mouth and patted me on the shoulder. 'There now. Right as rain, aren't we?'

I peered at her again. Her eyes bore a great emptiness and I knew that a calamity had fallen upon her house. It had to be death, for there was nothing else on people's minds; but who had died, I could not recall.

'The Lord comfort you in your loss,' I croaked.

She glanced at the man. Their eyes met but they said only, 'Bless you, Father.' My feet were unsteady and my knees loosened once more.

'Let me help you, Father.'

'Don't touch me!' I screamed. 'Help me, Anne!' I wailed, and by God's grace she spoke.

'People, enough!' she said. 'Let the Reverend Father depart in peace. I am sure he needs to go to the church. It is high time we were all about our business, isn't it?'

My head bobbed wildly. The bodies drew away and air rushed back into my lungs. Every face smiled sweetly, as though I had dreamed the past few moments. The Maid gaped her mouth exceedingly wide and yawned. Anne smiled and raised her hand in what might have been a blessing, or a gesture of farewell. The folk gathered themselves together and made their way out with many a polite *goodnight Father*. I mumbled *goodnight* in response, for it seemed strange to stay silent.

As soon as the place was empty the Maid leapt up, seemingly not tired at all, and began to sweep the floor with a fistful of haystalks. She then took the bucket and sprinkled droplets until all was wetted. Afterwards, she scooped the liquid over herself, rubbing furiously from ankle to calf to thigh, briskly, as if all must be done in a great hurry. She then lifted up her shift and Anne stood before me.

'Will you allow the Maid no modesty, Father Thomas?'

'Of course, yes,' I stammered.

She stood so close I could smell the tang of lavender in her hair. She stared at me boldly, and tipped her head to one side.

'Well then, Father. We will say our own goodnight to you.'

'Anne,' I said, my voice breaking like a boy's. 'You cannot use the girl so.'

'I do not. If anyone has used her, it is you, sir.'

'She is mine.'

'She is no one's.'

'God sent her to me.'

'Ah, your convenient God. The one you no longer believe in.'

'You cannot take her from me.'

'I do not. She comes freely.' At this, she looked at the Maid, smiling warmly. The Maid returned the smile.

'She is all I have,' I whispered. 'Anne. Come back. To the house. Both of you. Things will be different. I promise.'

She looked at me for a long while without answering, as though considering a particularly intricate conundrum.

'Thomas,' she said, when I thought the silence could not possibly continue any longer. 'You are not listening. You never have. It is too late. I told you this.'

'No!' I howled, and flew at her. I thought only to sweep the Maid into my arms and bear her away from the stable, but found my hands upon Anne's shoulders, slamming her against the wall. 'You cannot have her!'

I shoved harder, seized with a sudden desire to break her. I felt teeth in the back of my neck, small hands clawing at my face, but ignored the pain. I struck out with my free hand and knocked the Maid off my back; heard the thump of her body hit the floor.

'You bitch,' I hissed, to Anne or the girl I did not know. 'I hurt you: see, I can hurt you.'

At the words, Anne broke into laughter and would not stop until I struck her. She paused only to touch her hand to her chin, then continued to laugh until tears ran down the side of her nose. The Maid crept across the floor on all fours and wriggled into her skirts.

'You do not frighten me,' Anne glowered, voice steady. 'If you could have bent before this, maybe you would not have broken. You are a snapped branch, Thomas.'

'No,' I moaned, my fury wilted.

'I said goodnight. Go. Or would you have me call back the fine men of your parish and tell them how you threaten us?'

I had no words to say. I fell out of the stable and went to the church. The vestry smelled of damp. I peeled off my cloak and sat in shirt and hose, listening to the leisurely trickle of water behind the wooden press, observing the seep of dark patches upon the plaster. A diligent priest would repair the cracked roof-tiles that allowed rain to enter and mildew the books. I wondered where I might find such a fine man.

I knew that I was cold, and should put on my priestly robes and say the Office, but the dripping held me in a daze. Somehow I believed I must wait for it to stop before I was permitted to stir. It was trying to tell me something. There was some message, if only I was not too stupid to reckon it out. I waited for the length of time it takes to drink a jug of beer, and still did not understand.

There was a great emptiness in the centre of me, as of my innards stolen away. I ached with the loss of them: a hollow man rattling with the words of a God who had turned away His face. He had vouchsafed the Maid into my care, only to take her away. He had sent Anne to my house, and she was no longer mine either. I did not know where I had erred. I could not bear this desolation. I went into the altar and knelt before the Cross.

'Oh, Christ, forgive my sins. Restore my faith. Restore Anne. Restore the Maid,' I whimpered. 'I am lonely.'

I felt no answering Kiss of Peace. I banged my brow against the stone, thumping harder, harder. With each crack I cried out: 'I beg you, restore my faith. Let me believe again.' The Cross remained a lump of brass. After a while I discovered that my tears had ceased. I became aware of how much my knees ached, so I stood, hands dangling. I did not know what to do with them if God did not want them pressed together in prayer.

I returned to the house. In the outer room, Anne's mattress

sprawled next to the door, as if it was endeavouring to escape. Hurled on top was one of her under-dresses, a tangle of blue kersey. I smoothed out the wrinkles, laid myself upon it and pressed my cheek against its breast. There was the faintest trace of her sweat at the armpits. I took the sleeve between my lips, sucked on the linen, and closed my eyes.

When I next opened them, the room was bright. The emptiness had not gone from me, and I cast about, thinking how I might fill myself. I remembered how I felt when I saw the icon. God was in it, and in me. Maybe it was not faith: maybe it was only my own desires and longings that flared up so brightly that day in the Staple. But I wanted that certainty again.

If I prayed to the Virgin, that most merciful of mothers, surely She would restore my faith. I did not want to live without it. I could not live without it. If God were still my Master and Lord, then He would show Himself in the icon. That was as far as my reasoning took me, for my mind worked exceedingly slowly, and I did not wish to cudgel my brains into consideration of other eventualities.

I decided to walk, rather than take the mare: there was no haste, for the hours of the day hung about me weightily. For once it was not raining. This late sun was too late to save the harvest, which had long rotted in the ear, but served to give the muck a firm crust. I strode eastwards with something near to a good will. I did not meet one man upon the road, and was thankful.

Spiders' webs shone in the early light, and nettles drooped with their burden of pearls. In the hedge I heard the gem-like piping of a goldfinch. Small rivers glittered down each side of the track and the brightness of God's glory stirred a tiny flame within my breast.

But in a breath the sky was slate, the cloud impenetrable. At last I arrived in Ashford. The windows stood unshuttered as before, but this time there was no scurrying of folk rushing to hide. The air was heavy with flies. I thumped my stick hard upon the ground.

'Good day, I say to you!' I shouted.

As I looked about more closely, I saw there was no smoke, although it was too cold to be without a fire. I pushed my head through the nearest door, calling out greetings. The hut was empty: no bundled clothes, no food, no pots, not even a knife.

The next hut was the same: nothing but the stink of rotten straw. And the next, and the next. I could not understand where the people had gone. Then I heard a deep grunting in one of the hovels. I rushed towards the noise, for I thought it a man in pain. The stink of corruption slapped me as I ducked inside, and I held my hand to my mouth. In the far corner of the room a sow was rooting in a mound of filth, teats swinging. As I blocked the light she raised her head and let forth a violent squeal, and I fell backwards out of the door.

A tangle of dogs burst out from behind one of the huts, pursuing a cur with a chicken between its teeth. As they saw me, all stopped, the ones at the rear slamming into the backsides of their fellows. The leader tipped its head, swaying the dead bird back and forth. His tail quivered.

'Here, boy,' I clucked. 'Here.'

I held out my hand, rubbing thumb and fingers together. The beast's tail fell, its lips writhed, and a deep rumble stewed in his throat. His brothers followed the example, setting up a whining and flashing their teeth, taking slow and slinking steps, paw over paw towards me. I waved my staff and the big dog shook his head, spraying feathers. The snapping and growling swelled.

I stepped forward, yelling and swiping at them with my stick.

347

At once they showed their tails and ran, disappearing around the side of the nearest dwelling. The leader paused, dipped its rump to the earth and pushed out a coiling turd. Without taking its eye from me, it stood, and with its hind legs kicked the shit in my direction.

I hurried gratefully into the Staple. It could not have been more changed. The bustling thoroughfares were vacant save for an occasional person hastening along, bent under the force of a gale I could not feel. The streets were strewn with clutter, as though the houses had belched it out overnight: a brass bucket, almost new; a well-stitched boot, missing its pair; a baker's tray, still half-laden with loaves.

Outside the church was a straggle of people, each man standing a long way off from his fellow. I strode to the front without having to shove, for everyone moved aside as I passed, and came face to face with people from my village. We stared at each other.

'Good day,' I said at last. 'God's blessings upon you all.' I heard the waver in my voice.

'Indeed, Father, it is a good day,' muttered one of them.

His mouth set into a hard line, for what trifling insult I knew not, nor had any desire to. These peasants took offence for the most unaccountable reasons. The woman at his elbow tugged her kerchief across her nose. I raised my hand in blessing and they took a few steps back. I wondered if they thought I was about to strike them. The clouds curdled over our heads and it began to drizzle. Wetness found its way up my sleeve. I lowered my arm, there being no good reason why I should continue with the benediction. At last the doors in the south porch were opened and I tottered forwards. No one pushed, unwilling to so much as brush against his neighbour's coat.

Inside, I pummelled my eyes at the sudden black, darker

even than my previous visit. As I grew used to it, I saw the cause: heavy blankets were nailed across each window. I looked about for the image of Mary, but it had been hidden. My heart hungered for Her. I concealed myself on the north side of the nave, beneath a dim painting of Saint Petroc and the miraculous shower of fish.

There was a sound of shushing. John appeared from the dusk behind the altar, flanked by two boys with lit tapers. They stopped at the chancel steps, faces ruddied by the candle flames. John then climbed up onto a wooden platform newly built there. He stood so high that even I, cowering at the back, could see him clearly from the knees up. Then he raised his arms.

'Let us see Her! Where is She?' screeched someone, man or woman I could not tell. 'Do not keep Her from us!'

John licked his upper lip. 'Do you dare threaten the Virgin?' he growled. 'Who are you to demand that She smile upon you?'

The same voice cracked, 'Oh, forgive me; forgive me, Mary,' and collapsed into sobbing.

'You have come here today to seek the healing power of Mary.' John's voice quietened to a whisper. We held our breath. 'We ache for Her. We yearn for our Blessed Mother. But God holds Her away from us.'

'Dear God, no!' howled a man.

'It is because of sin.' John dropped his chin onto the gleaming gold of his cope. 'I do not stand before you as one who is sinless. I am the greatest sinner of all. I am mired in sin.'

No!

Not you!

He balled his hand into a fist and brought it crashing on to his breastbone. A female shrieked, as though it was she who was beaten.

'O God! I am a sinner!' John wailed, most grievously.

As his tears flowed, so did ours for our own sins. I hated myself for it; knew I was a fish with a worm dangled before it, foolish to gulp so hungrily at the hook. But my teeth ground, and my tears fell. Then a voice spoke out from the twilight above our heads; a fatherly voice that had not been bawling along with the rest of us.

'How have you sinned?' it asked.

All about me bones cracked as folk twisted their necks to right and left to seek out whence came the words.

'I shall not lie,' moaned John. 'I cannot lie. This is my sin.'

He pointed his finger towards the vestry door. Across it swagged a curtain: at once it bellied out like a female heavy with child, and a woman stumbled into the church. She was looking over her shoulder, so I could see only part of her cheek. But I knew her at once: Margret. The meagre congregation shrank away, clearing a space twenty paces wide.

John's voice soared again. 'Did God not bid priests to be chaste? Were we not commanded to be as clean as Christ?'

He let the silence hang over us for the time it would take to drink a small cup of beer.

'Dearly beloved; I have offended both God and all of you; the faithful. I took Margret to my house and used her as my wife. I confess this doing was detestable before the face of God, and I am heartily sore.'

Margret writhed against the curtain at her back. A lock of hair crept out from under her cap. Her breath was marvellously loud.

'How can I lead you to cleanness when I have polluted myself? How can I show you the face of the Virgin when I have turned my own back on holy virginity?'

None spoke. We had no good answers.

'O God, I beg you to forgive my most grievous fault. O

350

brothers and sisters, bear witness to my pledge. I will sin no more. I will cast out my sin.' He shouted at Margret. 'Tempt me not. Be gone, woman, and sin no more.'

The space around Margret widened further. A gob of spittle splashed at her feet. John's voice grew at once gentle.

'She lives in the hope of forgiveness, as do I. Did not our Lord spare the woman taken in adultery?'

'I am not tender-hearted like the Lord,' hissed a man a few steps to my right, and his neighbours groused their assent.

Margret shrivelled into the door arch, but the stone did not open up and shelter her. Her fingers scrabbled behind the curtain and I heard the rattle of a handle.

'Be careful you do no sin against this wretched female,' John called. 'Did Christ not say, only the sinless may cast a stone? It is for God to decide who will be punished and who will be spared. It is not for us. I tell you now, let her go in peace and humbly seek the mercy of God.'

Hinges squealed: a hand slipped out from behind the curtain and shoved hard. Margret staggered forwards. I saw fists clench; felt my own hands tighten with hatred. She took one step, then two, then raced to the south door. No one touched her.

'Turn now to God!' shouted John. 'Come to security. Come to forgiveness. May the Lord forgive us and heal us. Look, we beseech you, on your people prostrate before your mercy.'

Here he swept his arm down like a threshing flail and the gathering, as one body, dropped to the floor and kissed the stone.

'Hear us, O God our Salvation! Hear the intercession of Mary!'

'O Mary!' shrieked one soul.

'Yes, Mary! O Holy Virgin,' I cried out too, made bold or mad I do not know.

351

I could not understand why She was kept from us so long. My whole body trembled with the desire to see Her. My faith would return with just one glimpse. I craved it. As if in answer, there was a glowing at John's back, as though the sun rose behind him. A host of lit tapers floated down the chancel, and at their heart two men carried a wrapped shape, staggering a little beneath its weight. I gasped. She was come amongst us at last.

'O Holy Mother, look upon us now!'

The men manoeuvred their burden to the top of the steps. John gripped the edge of the covering-sheet and gave a mighty tug. Her face smiled, sorrowfully. I waited for the rapture. It would come; now. All my doubts would be made certainties; every question would be answered, and I would be filled again. I held my breath. Held it longer.

Nothing happened. I hammered my eyes into Mary's face. *Come, Mother. Take me to you. Please.* I could not understand: I was begging most humbly. All I desired was to feel the Lord in my soul once more. Was I so distasteful to God?

John's voice boomed. 'As you have cured the sick a hundred times, cure us. Say to the scourging angel, *Now hold your hand.* O heal us, and snatch us from our ruin.'

Men and women writhed upon the floor like the grubs that swarm in the belly of a dead cow. Did God want this sign from me before He would show Himself? I threw myself on the ground and rolled around, yowled as loud as the rest of them. After a while I felt foolish, and got to my feet.

John was not finished. 'See how we mourn,' he bawled. 'Drenched in tears, weeping for our vices, stained as we are in sin. Are we not stained?'

A roar of agreement was torn from every throat but mine. My breath came steadily, my head cleared of the choking fume I had endured for many weeks. I looked around, marvelling at

352

the people rolling on the floor. John's gaze fell upon me, and his eyes shone with recognition. I waited for him to shout a greeting, call me to join him on the dais. He stretched out his hand. I believe I smiled.

'We are all mired in sin. Are we not, Brother?'

Faces turned in my direction, curious to see if this new person would be more entertaining than Margret. I heard my name hissed softly, echoing round the walls.

'I have not sinned,' I said.

John drew his brows together. 'Do you not also keep a woman, and you a priest?'

'She keeps my house only.'

I heard sniggers of disbelief, and realised that a space was growing around me, as it did for Margret.

'Do you not fear that God will punish you?'

'But there is no sin,' I whined.

John ignored me, his voice thunderous. He was no longer speaking to me, but to the whole gathering.

'You took an innocent into your house and corrupted her. You could have spared her, but did not. Do you not care if the wrath of God falls upon her head? I am being merciful to Margret. I accept my grievous fault. I would rather put her away than condemn her to hell for my sin.'

'But I am chaste,' I insisted. 'Let God strike me down if I speak a lie.'

'Do you presume to command God?' he snarled, to a chorus of indignant gasps. 'You, who sneer at sinners, coming into our homes and feigning holiness; you, who conceal your own sin!'

Eyes singed holes in my cloak. The only home I had visited was his.

'I feign nothing—' I began.

'Behold this man!' John interrupted. 'This priest to a peasant saint. A saint who spent his life with swine. Can a pig be holy? See the true holiness that blesses *this* church. Turn now to Our Holy Mother and only true Protector.'

He flourished his arm at the icon, and every head swivelled towards it. All about me the people howled, *Mary, Mother, Mary,* over and over until I thought She must bend down from Heaven with Her fingers in Her ears and tell us to hold our tongues. There was nothing more I could say. But I would not let them see me angry: I knew the truth of my chastity.

When I emerged from the cave of the church I had to shade my eyes from the glare. Coming into such a dazzle should have afforded me hope but only gave me a headache. The light cast itself upon the town and, as if for the first time, I saw the deserted houses, the filth piled in the unswept streets, smelled the unmistakable stench of putrefaction. The stink of the Great Mortality.

'No,' I said, to whom I did not know, for I stood alone. *No.* My soul squeezed its eyes shut, clapped its hand over its nose.

A man staggered by, a shrouded body over his shoulder. He tripped over a spit-iron in his path and went down on one knee. Without thinking, I stretched out my hand to aid him. His head jerked upwards, a mix of surprise and hope on his face, dark spots on his throat. My hand hovered in the air between us. Then I folded my fingers back into the palm. I took a step back, and another. His eyes clouded over; then he heaved himself upright and clumped away with his burden.

I wrapped my hood about my face and fled.

The early twilight of autumn was falling as I reached the village. I was seized with a dread of going back to the house where all served to remind me of what I had lost. Nor did I wish to go to the church. My feet bore me to the churchyard. I stretched myself on the ground, and stared into the dark bowl of the heavens.

It had stopped raining: the wind had unbuttoned the coat of clouds and the moon shone half its breast through the gap. The world tilted suddenly and it was only by holding firmly on to the grass that I did not tumble into the sky. The stars reeled; I reeled with them. We gazed into each other a long time; a lifespan, it seemed. I thought of the tale of Old Man Hob, how he fell asleep one night and woke up a hundred years later. I knew the truth: he did not sleep. He looked at the stars like me. It was simple. I understood what had to be done to bring the Maid back into my keeping.

ANNE

I find her in the stable two days after the feast of Saint Osith. She cowers behind the hay-stooks, legs drawn up in a tight parcel.

'Sister?' I say and stretch out my hand.

She withers from my touch, knees scrabbling against the floor; twists her face, baring broken teeth. Spittle flecks her chin. She lifts a trembling hand to shade her eyes.

'Anne?' she croaks. 'Do you not know me?'

It is only then that I recognise her. 'Margret?' I gasp.

'I am Margret. I was Margret, you might say.'

I look over the whole of her body, from head to foot. This cannot be my beloved friend. The bodice of her gown is torn, one breast uncovered. At first I think the pestilence is upon her, for her skin blooms with dark swellings, but after a moment I know these are from the hand of man. Many men. She pulls back what remains of her sleeve, showing the thumb-marks on her upper arm, fresh bruises laid over older.

'You are safe now.' I am unable to think of anything else to say.

She turns to the wall and makes a strange noise with her tongue. I lower myself to her side and open my arms wide.

After long consideration, she crawls within their circle and lays her cheek over my heart.

'Are you hungry?' I ask.

She shakes her head, a gesture so tiny I barely see it.

'How have you eaten?' I say.

She takes a shuddering breath and begins to speak, the words spilling from her as though unstoppered from some foul pitcher.

'I cannot count the houses standing empty.' Her eyes flare, then shrink into dark specks. 'There was bread within one, bite-marks still upon it. Salt pork in another. The wells have not run dry.'

She hesitates.

'Margret. You need not tell me if the telling pains you.'

'I fear it will pain you, rather.'

I kiss the top of her head. 'Nothing you can say will make me love you less than I do at this very minute,' I murmur.

She takes in a quaking breath. 'At first, men found me. So I moved by night. Men still found me, but fewer, and I cared less. I discovered that I did not desire death. So I smeared ashes on my breasts and neck and they thought me plague-ridden, and ran.' She smiles at some sharp memory. 'So, cousin. We both live. God spares us still.'

'I am glad you are here. I only wish you had come sooner.'

She makes a whimpering sound. 'I doubted you would want me, after John denounced me before the people.'

'I would always want you,' I say fiercely.

'I know that now.'

The Maid and I tend to her bruises, the Maid helping silently, unsure of trusting Margret, however much I tell her it is safe. Towards evening I pass Thomas in the yard while I am carrying a dish of hot porray to feed the three of us. I stride straight past as though I have not seen him. He hops at my heels.

'I will not permit this harlot in my house!' he squawks.

'Who?' I ask innocently.

'Do not think to bewilder me, woman!' he squeals.

'She's not in your house. She's in the stable,' I reply, and continue walking.

He grabs my arm and I almost drop the bowl. 'Attend to me, woman,' he growls.

'Oh, hold your tongue,' I snap, shaking off his hand. 'You and your harlot this and harlot that. We could all be dead in a week and here you are quacking like a duck with a broken wing.'

He continues to bounce at my side. He does not follow me into the stable, but hovers at the door, squinting at the shadows.

'Leave us be, Thomas.'

'I will not permit this.'

'Will you not?' I declare. '"When I was hungry, you fed me. When I was naked, you clothed me." Remember? Christ said it, and that's how things shall be while I am housekeeper.'

Margret appears and smiles. 'You should be a preacher, Anne.'

A strangled sound comes out of Thomas's mouth. 'You!' he squawks. 'You have turned Anne's mind!'

'By the Saint, Thomas,' I declare. 'She's been here for less time than it takes to boil a cabbage.'

'I will not—' he cries.

Margret steps forward and presses her nose to his. Any further words he thought to spit out are swallowed with a gulp.

'Not one word from you,' she says, coldly. 'You are to blame for this. You were a guest in our house, yet whined and wheedled at John, sowing a seed of fear in his heart, wherein it grew. We were happy before you.'

Thomas's mouth hangs open; his eyes open and close. I am

not sure if he can see her, or me, or anything else around him. After the time it would take to unbraid my hair, he retreats across the stable-yard, walking backwards the whole way.

The following morning, I find Margret standing in the orchard, staring at a space between the apple trees. A basket lies at her feet.

'It's hardly worth picking them,' I say cheerfully, for I do not want her to think I am unappreciative of her efforts.

I peer into the basket. She has filled it with rotten fruit, as though she cannot tell the good from the bad. There are broad patches of sweat soaking through her kirtle and over-dress.

'You should rest, Margret,' I remark. 'The labour has marked you.'

'I wish to be useful.'

'You are more than useful. You are my friend.'

She raises one arm and looks at the creeping wetness. 'Perhaps you are right. I am tired. I will rest.'

She turns and walks unsteadily towards the house. I try to coax her back to the stable, for I want no more contentiousness with Thomas than is absolutely necessary. But she is like one half-asleep and does not pause until she is through the great door. Only then does she halt, gazing about as though she has never seen a house before.

'My fingers prick me, Anne.' She squints at them, swallows hard on some tight lump. 'Do you not find it cold?'

'No, Margret. It is a warm day for this late in the year. The shutters stand open and let in the sunshine. It is a gift we have waited for: see.'

I point out the dust motes wandering on the slanting shafts of light. She will not look, but turns her hand over and inspects its back; lifts it and places it under her coif, against her neck.

'I am so very tired,' she barks, and falls.

'Margret?' I grasp her arm.

'Let me rest. Do not touch me, Anne. I am sick.'

'No!' I cry. She mews, deep in her throat, and cramps into a tight bundle. 'Let me help you,' I say, stroking her shoulder.

I place my hands under her armpits to lift her and feel heat rolling from her flesh. She does not struggle, the air whistling in and out of her throat. It is only then I understand.

'Oh, my Margret,' I moan, rocking her back and forth.

I squeeze her hard, and a cough claws its way out. She pulls away and covers her mouth with her hand.

'Let me lie down,' she gasps. 'I must. Let me lie down, for the love of God.'

'Yes, yes. Let me help you.'

I raise her, most tenderly, and help her to Thomas's bed, for I will not have my most darling friend lie upon anything less. I make the bolster comfortable behind her head, smooth the sheet, shake out the coverlet. She kicks off her wooden pattens and lowers herself carefully.

'Anne,' she croaks and fixes her eyes upon me, so dark I could fall into them and never find my way out again. 'You must not stay here. You know what this is.'

I squeeze her hand, gently, for every touch makes her wince.

'I know, Margret. But I shall not leave you.'

'Please. Do not be foolish. What does my flesh tell you?' she whimpers, clutching at the sheet. 'I cannot do this to you.'

I have no answer, other than to drag a stool to the side of the bed and seat myself upon it. She twists her head aside, eyes brimming with liquid. Her tongue sucks against the roof of her mouth.

'I cannot swallow,' she wheezes. 'There is a fist pressing into my neck.' She scrabbles at the fastenings of her kerchief. 'I am so hot.'

360

Her fingers fumble so that I have to loosen her coif, and lift it away. There is a sprinkling of crimson below her left ear, as though blood is bubbling to the surface. I place my fingers against her neck and feel the small hardness of a dried pea lodged there.

'And here also,' she says, pulling down the front of her bodice to show her breasts, smudged with scarlet flowers.

'Do not leave me, Margret,' I whimper.

'Anne, my love. It is too late. Pray I am taken quickly.'

She stiffens suddenly, straining to hold her head as far away from her as she can.

'What is it? What is happening?' I cry.

She leans forward and retches mightily, labouring to force out some piece of vile matter. At last she spits on to her skirt: it is a furious red. She falls back against the pillow, sweating with this great travail. The tip of her tongue picks its way across her upper lip.

'You are thirsty. Let me fetch you some water.'

I dash to the kitchen. The stone ewer is dry and draped with a spider's web. I stick my head out of the door.

'Maid!' I yell, loud as I can.

There is no answering cry. I snatch a jug and run to the gate; look up and down the silent street. It is a long way to the well and I do not wish to leave Margret alone. I shake my head. It seems to be full of bees. Then I see the Maid, coming out of the stable, and rubbing sleep from her eyes.

'Get me some water!' I shriek, stumbling into the yard. 'Margret is sick.'

'Sick? Is it—?'

'What else?' I say, shoving the pitcher in her direction. Each step I take towards her, she takes two backwards. 'Maid. Bring some of your rags. Now.'

361

'It's too late for that.'

'It can't be!'

'It is. Get out of the house, Anne,' she says. 'Now.'

'No. She is my friend.'

I take another step but she is away from me as quick as breath. I race after her, but it is useless. I start for the well, but am only a few yards along the track when I remember there is water in the church, and clean too.

I expect to find Thomas whining to the Lord, but am mistaken. For once the place is empty. The font squats in the half-darkness. I wipe my nose on the end of my sleeve and set to winching up the heavy cover. The basin is three-quarters full. I say a quick prayer of thanks to God for letting me take the holy water. The words catch in my throat.

'Oh God,' I cry. 'Help me.'

I find myself on my knees without knowing how I got there. I look at the wall. The saints gaze down in mercy, arms heaped with keys, wheels, arrows, flowers and all the instruments of their passion.

'Preserve my beloved friend,' I beg. 'Heal her.'

I think of the last time Margret and I were here; how we stood on this same spot and laughed at the garish paintings. The Virgin Mary catches my eye and glares at my impertinence.

'I was a child!' I shout. 'I did not mean . . . I did not know . . .'

I raise my eyes to the Doom painted above the chancel arch where Christ sits in judgement, good souls to his right and evildoers to his left. I wring my hands.

'You took Adam. You took Cat,' I wail. 'Please don't take her; not Margret.' My nose dribbles snot. It drips off my chin and on to the flagstones. 'She did no sin but love. She's my friend. My only childhood friend left.'

I have never prayed so wildly, never in my life. I pray for miracles, for mercy, to keep Margret by me. I beg the Saint to intercede. I call on the Virgin, on the Saint, on the whole host of holy men and women. My prayer threads upwards until it is lost in the rafters, no louder than the mew of a hungry kitten.

'She's all I have left of this life,' I weep. 'Please.'

Christ stares at a point far beyond this land set in its rocky sea. The paint on his face is peeling. There is a brown patch where rain has crept down the plaster. Pieces of his halo have fallen away. I get to my feet and wipe my face on my apron.

When I return to the house, Margret is staring at the wall. When I lay my hand upon her neck I find the lump grown to the size of a pigeon's egg. I fill a cup and hold it to her mouth.

'Drink some of this,' I say. 'It is blessed. It will heal you.'

I manage to get some of the water through the chinks between her teeth, but most drizzles down her chin and onto her breasts. I do not care. *If it is holy it will heal where it falls,* I reason. She nods thanks and I think she seems calmer.

Then her jaw sets rigid, her teeth grind against each other, and a corrupt stink buffets me as her bowels loosen. She moans with shame, but she can barely take in enough air to cry out. I loosen her dress and peel it away, uncovering flesh stained with the pestilence.

I find linen in the chest at the foot of the bed, sop it in the water and wipe her as clean as I can. I hold her over Thomas's chamber pot while she empties herself again, the urine falling away from her thick, bunched together like looped string. Thomas's bed is now so fouled that I carry her to mine. She is as light as a stack of kindling.

All the pestilence within her seethes to the surface of her skin, like scum rising to the surface of a pond. The swellings breed so fast I have the strangest fancy that I can see them grow, gorging themselves upon her flesh until they are the size of goose eggs, crowding about the dark hair at the join of her thighs.

Every scrap of common sense I have ever possessed commands me to flee. But I stay. When night draws sky and earth together, I take a taper from Thomas's store, a fine one stored for the Easter vigil. I light it and kneel at the side of the bed. I thumb a sign of the Cross on her forehead and whisper, 'All things will be well; all manner of things will be well.' I will not leave her side.

I am woken by a rumbling in my left ear, like that of a pot set to boil. I jerk back to wakefulness, not knowing straightaway where I am. The flickering shadows resolve themselves and I see that it is not long before dawn. The thundering comes from Margret's breast, where I fell asleep. She is breathing with diffi-culty, the swellings in her throat so great that they block the easy passage of air.

Her hair is wild from the night's conflict, so I fetch my comb and tease it through the knots. It is a scrap of bone carved with tiny birds, given to me by my mother when I came to this house. When was that? It is so long ago I cannot bring it to my recollection.

Her curls tangle in the teeth, but I am patient and gentle, and after the first few moments she does not wince, nor try to drag herself away. By the time the sun is up I am finished, and her hair spreads thinly over the pillow.

I blow out the candle. She fouls herself again; but this time is not ashamed, so far is she caught up in the fever. I wash her carefully as before, but this time there is nowhere to lay her but on the floor, which I do, making a mattress of sorts from all the rushes I can sweep together. I try to feed her a little more water, but her jaw is clamped tight. The boils are now the size of an onion.

So the day unravels. I lose count of the hours, so distracted are my thoughts. The sun climbs towards its highest point in the sky, which in this season is barely to skim the top of the hill. I watch the light come, I watch it go, and I watch Margret in the hours that slide in between. The Maid does not come. Thomas does not come. No one comes at all.

Presently it grows so dark that I turn my attention from her to light the candle again for a second night's vigil. At that moment she bends double, as though a beast has sunk its fangs into her belly. She stretches her mouth wide and lets loose a long scream.

'Oh My Lady! Where are you? Why will you not come?'

'I am here, Margret,' I say.

I don't know if she is able to hear me. Her eyes sink back into her head like those of a fox. Slowly, her arms and legs spread out in the shape of the Cross of the holy apostle Andrew, her whole body frantic in its battle against the sickness. She tries to vomit, but there is nothing left to spew up. She is wrung empty as a leather sack. She cries, she shrieks, she squeals: then her shrieks are snuffed out and the room aches with a silence that is far more terrible.

I hang on to her, hoping my touch might anchor her to life, but she is gone deep into the vale of Death. I cradle her to my breast and will not let her fall, not even when the skin on my own arms begins to blister and my head fumes. I pull open my bodice and see the scabs that crust my own breasts, like hazelnuts in size and colour.

'Margret,' I say, although she cannot hear. 'Soon I shall join you. Wait. I am racing to catch up. I am only a little way behind.'

I think, soon I will die and we shall be together. I shall see Cat, and Adam. Nothing on this earth will be of any significance. The room tilts suddenly and I join the company of the rushes on the floor. I am in the grasp of the pestilence, and it squeezes me so hard that I fall out of my wits.

I hurt cruelly. I am cold: I am hot. My legs are water. I hear the dashing of feet along stone: they rush away from me, then towards, then away again. I cannot make them stop. The floor sways beneath me and I cling to it for fear I might fall.

I swim upwards through thick pond weed, break the surface of the fever to find a dog panting in my ear. After the time it takes to card a piece of fleece I realise it is my own breath, close and loud. My cheek scratches against straw. The room begins to draw itself together from a soup of blurred shapes into sharpness and colour, and I set about the task of remembering why I am stretched out upon a pile of rotten hay-stalks.

Without turning my head, for it hurts too much to do that, I can see a hearth at the centre of the floor, next to it a long bench. I can see its underside: how the wood is crudely planed where no one can remark upon it, how rough the dowels that clutch side to back. The dim light gumming the surfaces of all about me indicates an early hour. I think, *I must set the porray to cook*, and remember I am a housekeeper.

Then I wonder how I might stand up and sort the peas, for it seems I have shrunk entirely into my head. Heavy fingers lie close to my nose. I think they might be mine, but am not sure. I am not sure of anything. I urge myself to stir and the hand moves, which seems a great marvel. Nothing about this body is familiar.

I lie there a long time, curious at each new sensation as though I have only been birthed this morning. By and by, I grow used to the hand before me, and at last accept it as my own. Next, I discover my left shoulder tingling with pins and needles, smell the reeking breath fluttering between my teeth.

As the light swells into day I swell into myself. I am suddenly aware that I am thirsty, and hungry. I have a great desire to eat an apple, one picked too early, green and sour to the taste. I roll carefully onto my back and examine the roof beams above me. I lift my arm: it obeys me.

Where the sleeve falls back I uncover scabs, dry enough to pick away. I have fought the pestilence and I have won. I wonder if this is what a miracle feels like. I feel much the same Anne as yesterday, except my head hurts more than I think possible. I want to tell someone about this mystery. The Maid will want to know. And Margret: I must tell her. At last I manage to sit up and see her, a few feet distant.

But it is not Margret; it cannot be. This woman has straw in the place of hair, hobnails for teeth. Her mouth stretches wide, tongue grey as a sheep's. I struggle to her side, try to push the slug of a thing back into the mouth, but it will not fit. Surely Margret's teeth are not that yellow. The jaw will not stay closed until I set a piece of wood from the dead fire beneath the chin. My breathing quickens. She is my friend. I love her. As I lick my upper lip, I taste salt. I cannot look upon this body: Margret has fled its shell.

I topple about the room on legs unsteady as a calf straight from the cow. I stagger into the outer room, leaning first on the wainscot-bench, then on the table, set on its trestles ready for an evening meal no one will eat. The house seems strangely large, the furniture unfamiliar. The walls are hung with an abundance of brass pots, frying pans, sieves, plates of pewter, plates of iron, dressing-knives, flesh-hooks, pot-hooks, spit-irons, fire-shovels, tongs, trivets, strainers, candlesticks, spoons, ale-stands and leather bottles. Things, things, and not one of them of any use. I could leave them today. I could walk away from everything and not look back, not once.

I make my way to the outer door and lean on the frame; watch the sun edge itself across the sky, dipping behind clouds as it proceeds on its steady way. I cannot stand for long, and have to sit. I think I will not sleep again, but as soon as I lie down I am swept from this place into the orchard, beneath a tree so mightily burdened with fat and perfect fruit that the branches droop their arms about me, almost to the ground.

Through the leaves I see Margret skip past, her step light as a girl's. I raise my hand to pluck at her sleeve, but twigs cling to my dress and hold me back. I cannot reach her. She dances up the path, towards the forest. I fight against the tree, but it will not let me follow.

'Margret!' I cry.

She turns one last time and waves, smiling.

VIXEN

As Anne labours within, I stand without. The house squats like a toad, the stink of the pestilence oozing through the thatch in such a choking cloud that I cannot approach any closer than the gate. Thomas appears at my side. He is as much of a coward as me, and stops at the gate also. He champs his jaws together for a few moments as if trying to reach a decision, then gets to his knees.

'We must pray,' he announces. I stare at him. His eyes harden. 'You must. You may be a beast, but you will kneel. Now.'

I stay where I am. His eyes melt into desperation.

'Please. Do this. You are sent from God. If you pray with me, you can save Anne. You can.'

I snort. Surely he cannot be that benighted. Not now. But it seems he is, for he continues his warbling.

'You are an angel,' he whinnies. 'You showed yourself to me once, remember? Let me see that brightness again. Please.'

I don't know if I have finally had enough of his empty clatter, or if I am also made witless with the dread of what is happening to Anne.

'Be quiet!' I shriek. 'For once, will you hold your flapping tongue!'

The day sucks in its breath. He looks around as though I am a wooden poppet and somewhere behind my back a trickster is throwing his voice like men do at fairs.

'Who speaks?' he says, squinting.

'It's me, you dog turd.' His face wipes clear of all expression and for one delicious moment he has nothing to say. I fill the space. 'Yes,' I say. 'Your Holy Maid is not an idiot after all.'

'But the Maid can't speak,' he protests. 'What manner of devilry is this?'

'Haven't you worked it out yet?' I cry, waving my hands at him. 'Surely you cannot be that stupid.'

He gawps, lower lip drooping.

'Yes,' I sigh. 'You are. You have heard me speak; but your desire to have me mute and miraculous was greater than the good sense God gave you.'

I watch the slow light of comprehension creep across his features.

'Why didn't you say anything before?' he whispers.

I lick my lips. 'And show myself to be nothing but some plain runaway? I'd have been flogged into the sea.'

'You could have spoken to me.'

'You? You spoke around and above me, never to me. I spoke to Anne. I am hers. She told me what a fool you were, how hungry for miracles. Not that I needed telling.'

He gulps, eyes blinking. There is a pause and it goes on far too long. I know it and he knows it too.

'I believe!' he cries. 'You are holy!'

'I am not. You're not convincing anyone. Not any more.'

His lips wrestle one against the other, as though his mouth is full of bile and he must needs spit it out, but dare not for some pointless sense of propriety.

'God cannot have meant for this,' he says eventually.

'Oh, hold your tongue.'

'How dare you!' he cries. His mouth curls into an unpleasant shape, like a bit of shoe leather left in the rain and dried by the fire too quickly. 'I shall . . .' he stutters. 'I shall tell the people what you are!'

This time I cannot hold in the laughter. 'They know what I am.'

'They know?'

'And love me for it. I am saving their lives, which is a lot more than you are doing. They care nothing for you. Every word you speak is a turd floating in their beer. The people are mine. Anne is mine. We are leaving. I know ways through the forest you cannot follow.'

There is another pause, where he opens and closes his eyes over and over.

'No. I forbid it!' he squeals.

'You forbid it?' I scoff. 'Words, words. You are full of them, you old bellows. How do you plan to make your word law?'

'I shall denounce you to the Bishop! Those men will come back from the Staple and then we'll see who's the master. They got a good look up you last time. Next time they won't stop with their eyes!'

I laugh. 'I do not fear them, nor any man. Soldier or saint, you all want this.' I step forward so quickly his eyes broaden with alarm. Before he can shrink away, I grab his paw and press it to my breast. I'm as flat as a boy, but he grasps my meaning clear enough. 'You called me Vixen?' I hiss. '*You're* the dogs: slavering, sniffing . . .' My words snag in my throat.

'I never touched you,' he croaks. 'Never a finger. Not you, not Anne, not any creature.'

'But you want to, don't you?'

With my free hand I grasp the root and branch between his

thighs. He is soft as a new cheese. I let him go and he sinks to his knees, pummelling his fists into his eyes.

'No. It is fornication,' he squeaks. 'You are a maid. I am a man of—'

I tip back my head and crow with fierce delight. 'You can't even say it any more, can you? You stupid, tiny man. You understand nothing. God has deserted you. You are a speck of dirt on a flea's backside. A maggot in a speck of dirt on a flea's backside.'

It is mean-minded and vindictive and I know it. I should hold my tongue. In my head I hear Anne's voice; how she would counsel caution, how a cornered beast is more dangerous than it looks. But fear and cowardice have dragged me far away from good sense. I am not just. He is not one of the many men and women who have hurt me. This man saved me from the mob; for that reason alone I should be merciful. I am anything but. I have stored up a lifetime of anger and upon his head I heap its slurry, railing, screeching, howling. I wait for him to grit his teeth and give blow for blow: but his face collapses in on itself, eyes wet as whelks.

'You are not worth insulting. A man should fight back. A man would fight back.'

He makes wheezing noises and I realise he is weeping.

'Anne,' he moans, rocking back and forth. 'All she wanted . . . I pushed . . . No . . .'

He manages few words between the gulping breaths, but all the same I hear the passion, the loss, the remorse, the misery. I hear his love for Anne. How his God swept away any chance of happiness with her. How he has been warped into this threadbare sack of bones. It should make me kind. I should hold out my hand and speak tenderly to this unhappy man. But I am new to kindness and am afraid that if I show him any, I might squander my whole stock.

It is my great, my only error.

I watch myself taunt him and do not like what I see: a cruel girl sneering at a wretch stripped bare of everything. Anne would chide me, and with good reason. Anne would judge neither of us. Anne would comfort him, and me, and I would grow strong enough to be generous. But Anne is within, showing a bravery of which I am not capable. She is dying, clasping the hand of her dying friend. We two cowards stand outside, circling each other like dogs, snarling and snapping: each of us chained to the spot, unable to leave, yet unable to go inside and help.

It strikes me at last: if Anne is dead, then I would rather join her than stay here. I leave Thomas wailing in the dirt.

I take only one step over the threshold before I am halfway back out, gripped in terror. The house bloats with the stink of death. Lying on a heap of foetid straw on one side of the room is Margret, chin propped shut with a lump of firewood, tongue pointing stiffly at the roof. Then I see Anne, stretched out on the floor beneath the bench. Despite my fear, I kneel and take her hand. I expect it to be cold, but she is warm and life flutters within.

'Anne!' I cry. 'I am sorry. I am here. Now.'

I pour a cup of water from the half-filled jug and, nestling her head upon my lap, feed her small sips. Her lips move, slowly at first and then more hungrily as she takes greater and greater gulps. Her eyes open, and she sees me. Very slowly she smiles, as though it is a profound effort to do so.

'Anne,' I repeat. 'I thought you dead.'

'No, I am alive,' she says, astonished at the discovery of this simple truth. 'I had the fever, but did not die.'

The story seems too marvellous to believe; perhaps soon she might start to talk of men with eyes in their bellies, ears hanging to their knees.

'It is a miracle,' I say.

'Is it?' she whispers. 'I am not sure I believe in them.'

'Margret—' I begin.

'Yes,' says Anne, and speaks the words that affright me still. 'She is dead.'

I heat a pot of peas upon the hearth and make a poor job of it, but I claim no skills as a cook. It is hot, and that is sufficient. She manages a few mouthfuls with an appetite that both surprises and delights before she lays down her spoon. The afternoon hangs silently between us.

'I am a coward,' I whisper in a shrivelled voice.

'Are you?' she wheezes. 'If I hated everyone who was a coward, then I should have to hate myself.'

'You forgive me?'

'Of course I do.' She pauses, gathering her wits together as though they have strayed. 'Do you think I would rather have you brave and dead? If you had stayed with me, you would have caught the fever also. You stayed away. I am happy, for you are alive.'

I brush my forehead against hers. 'Thank you,' I whisper.

'Thomas is still outside, I take it?'

'Yes.' I grimace with the memory of my malice.

'What is it?' she asks.

'I told him we are leaving,' I mutter.

The blood in my stomach grows cold. She sighs and closes her eyes briefly.

'Then it is too dangerous to stay.' She tries to stand, clasps the side of her head, lets out a groan and her knees buckle. I catch her, and she seats herself carefully on the bench. 'But we are going nowhere today.' She surveys the ruined house. 'Save to the stable. I have had my fill of death.'

'What of Margret?' I nod towards the body of her friend, stretched out on the far side of the room.

'We must bury her. Will you help?'

I lower my eyes. I have been cowardly. I will be so no longer. 'Yes.'

I fetch a sheet from the attic and Anne winds Margret in its folds. I carry the shrouded body over my shoulder. Anne totters at my side, leaning on one of Thomas's discarded staves. We place her in the common pit. For once, the rain holds itself away, the low sun heaving itself across the sky.

'Let her lie comfortably,' says Anne. 'Shoulder to shoulder with friends.'

'Friends? I thought—'

She smiles. 'After we are gone, I believe all enmity is shaken out of us. That is the meaning of love, as my poor wits reckon it. How very peaceable God's kingdom will be.'

I cast a spadeful of earth onto the corpse and we say our final prayers.

'There is no more business to be done here,' she declares. 'It is time to go.'

I know she does not mean to the stable, but a lot further. She turns her face to mine. Thomas is even more of a fool than I thought. All his gabbling about there being a light around my head, when right in front of him was a woman lit with such brilliance that I almost need to shade my eyes. I nod my answer, for words are lacking.

'We will take what we need.'

'We shall,' I answer.

'And no more, for we are not thieves.'

'No,' I agree.

'We shall leave the people with your knowledge. They will live, or . . . Either way, we must be gone, must we not?'

'Yes.'

'I never thought I'd leave. I thought I'd be too frightened to quit the village. Now I've changed my mind and it is as easy as changing my kerchief.' She shudders, as though someone has poured a dish of ice water down the back of her gown. 'There's no surety that we will live. Perhaps I am your undoing. Perhaps you should have stayed cold and hard, and run away at the start.'

I clasp her hand.

'Maybe once upon a time, Anne. I railed against this prison, as I thought it. It has become my liberation. I cannot explain, but I am no longer afraid.'

She looks at me, face bright with fear and something else besides. It is strength, shining far brighter than the weak sun above our heads. We return to the house, but only to collect the food and garments we shall need on our journey, for Anne declares this is the last time she will step through this door. In the stable, we wash Death's reek from our bodies and replace it with the comforting odour of horse piss.

'Good,' she announces, with finality in her voice. 'We are ready.'

'We are.'

'I wonder,' she says, looking at her finger-ends. 'Is there anything – or anyone – I should fear on our journey through the forest?'

'There is no danger. From any man.'

'No?'

I know of whom she speaks. A flame of blood springs into my face with the memory of that betrayal.

'No. A greater force than the law of this world has swept them away.'

'Good,' she sighs, on an outrush of breath. 'I do not believe I have the vigour to fight another battle just yet.'

A smile lights her features, casting its warmth upon me also.

That last night, I do not sleep. Anne closes her eyes and is lost to dreams, for her travail against Death has exhausted her. Perhaps we should wait a few more days – but I shake my head free of this nonsense and keep my vigil. I think of how she has changed; how we have wrought these changes in ourselves and each other.

She sleeps so heavily that she barely seems to breathe. At one point I am so convinced that she has gone to join Margret that I place my ear to her mouth. I am not satisfied until I feel the goose-down of breath on my cheek. I lay my hand on her unbound hair and she stirs. I am afraid that I have woken her, but she wrinkles her nose at the straw tickling it, turns over and sleeps again.

I look around at the stable. It is battered, and smells of horse urine. The walls leak wind, the thatch is busy with insects. There is the constant sound of the door squeaking in the breeze and distant thunder from the mare's insides. It is not home: I would not know home if I walked into it with both eyes open wide. But I will remember this place tomorrow and the day after, and it will be a sweet remembrance.

Not that I shall find it difficult to quit. My heart beats firm as a hammer on an anvil. I am ready for the morning. It will be easy. Before this, everything was set about with insurmountable difficulties. Anne makes everything possible. We are free. I taste the sea between my teeth.

NOCTURNS
1349

The Feast of Saint Edward the Confessor

THOMAS OF UPCOTE

My old self would have gone to the stable once more to beg them to stay. I would never be so craven again. I was growing crafty. If they wished to scorn me, refute me, humiliate me in front of my flock, so be it. They were engaged in a dangerous game, and I would beat them. To do so I would be a different man, a cunning man.

I went to the house, breath hanging on the air before me. I closed my eyes to the filthy ruin of the bed and instead watched my hands dress me in two pairs of hose, three shirts, my thickest tunic, my cassock, my cloak over all, and my strongest boots, as though for a long journey. The wind mouthed at the window shutters.

My feet were then directed along the road leading west out of the village, with much noisy stamping of my heels, punching of my staff into the dust, and greetings cried to the few souls who peered at me from their windows. I even begged a piece of horse-bread, declaring it was to sustain me. *I go to tell Father John of the death of his troublesome woman.* I almost giggled at how easily I fooled them into thinking I was starting out for the Staple. As I chewed, the ice of my appetite cracked and I gobbled in earnest.

381

I climbed the hill towards Heanton until I reached the bend that would take me out of sight of any person watching. Then I stopped. Waited. When I was satisfied that I could hear no pursuing footsteps, I cut across the rough ground, concealing myself behind bushes and trees until I came to a spot from where I could look down at my stable yard.

The two females were standing there, bundled up for a long journey; the Vixen wearing more clothes than I had ever seen her in, her head covered by one of my old caps. I did not understand why she was dressed as a man. It was against Scripture. She pounded the dirt with her feet, slapping her arms about herself. I did not know why she was making such a fuss: I could not feel the cold at all. Anne tipped a draught of ale down her throat and I licked my lips as thirst pricked me.

Men and women stood about, and as I watched, more and more joined the gathering until it seemed the whole village surrounded them. They knelt at the feet of the Maid, presenting offerings: from this distance it looked like money. *Thirty pieces of silver*, I thought. She nodded thanks and passed them to Anne, who put everything into a sack. Then she raised her hand in blessing, and my stomach griped with disgust at the blasphemy.

Anne's mouth opened and closed: she was too far for me to hear, but I understood clear enough. A man pointed up the track, nodding his head until the tail of his hood flew about. Others joined in, miming the thumping of my staff, my waddle, my devouring of the bread. Threads of laughter drifted up the hill.

When it seemed they could find no further sport in me, Anne swung the bag onto her shoulder and took the Vixen's hand, leading her out of the yard. I did not need to observe any longer to guess where they were headed.

382

I circled the village, keeping my head low. Crisp clouds illuminated a blue sky and the air tightened my breast. A dry winter at the end of a rainy year. This world was topsy-turvy. Knees creaking, I scrambled down an ill-used track on the far side of the hill that would bring me to the foot of the forest. I felt so different, I wondered if my name was still Thomas. I spoke it aloud. 'Thomas.' The sound clicked and whistled against the back of my teeth. Perhaps I would take a new name.

I began to count off all the names I knew, beginning with those I remembered from the calendar of the saints, and this took me to the well. Frost ringed the pool, giving it a cloudy fringe of spilled milk. As I stared into the water I heard the sound of approaching feet, and leapt for the cover of the undergrowth, hugging myself small.

There was a bout of coughing and I realised that I had run so swiftly I had arrived ahead of them. They passed by, the Vixen hawking and spitting into the bushes I hid behind. Next, the splash and bubble of a water bag being filled, the murmur of Anne's voice. Although I could not see her, I could not mistake it. I held my breath. It would not do to be discovered now.

After they had drunk their fill, I heard them shuffle up the path into the trees. I was wary, and trod cautiously between the bushes to each side of the track, glad for the softness underfoot: any cracklings and rustlings were gulped up by the forest.

All trees were stripped, save for a few leaves dangling limp as scraps of flayed hide. There was ivy winding underfoot, the brightness of holly. The wind breathed as softly as did I. It seemed the earth and I were in one accord at last. I marvelled that I had not understood it before. But I did not scourge myself: I was far beyond beatings.

383

I paused before each wonder: a worm struggling in the leaf-mould, a snail pebbled shut against the frost in the crook of a branch, a tree shelved with broad trenchers of orange fungus, a tiny new sapling. A rook hung out its ragged cry above, and its mate threw back a response. The trunks were licked green with mossy tongues, and I found myself rubbing my hands over their bark.

The beeches gave way to oak, then beech again. The path shrank to a thread between a tangle of browning nettles and elder heavy with shrivelled berries. On a whim I grabbed a handful from the nearest bush and squeezed them until my hand purpled with late juice. I was running my tongue over its sweetness, when without announcement I stood on the muddy lip of a broad pool.

At least, I thought it a pond at first, for it did not purl like moving water. Then I saw a twig carried by on its surface. I was startled at how clear it was; for although it moved, it crawled so sluggishly that it did not stir up any silt. The bed of the stream was rippled like sand at low tide. I could see the branches above reflected below. I gazed at them a long time.

Then I heard breathing. Felt small, light fingers upon the base of my neck. They gave me the tiniest push. I rocked forward onto the balls of my feet; rocked back. I turned round: nothing but trees. The skin on my left palm pricked with the claw of some beast drawn across it. I lifted it to my nose, expecting to see blood drawn, but the liquid there was the juice of berries. My shoulders clamped together and it took all my strength not to run.

When at last I was gathered back into myself, I was afraid that I had lost the trail, and raced forward until I came to a clearing twenty paces across. At its centre stood a charcoal-burner's stack, tumbled in upon itself. Next to the heap of fallen logs were the

384

figures of Anne and the Vixen. I crouched in the shadows and spied on them through the twigs. The Maid was sniffing at the charcoal. She stretched out her foot and touched the edge of the pile, drawing it back straightway, hopping up and down and muttering *ow, ow ow*.

Then Anne screamed. She grabbed the Maid's wrist and hauled her away, jabbing her thumb over her shoulder. Not at me, but at some other horror. As soon as they were gone I approached the clearing. The whole pile of charcoal had been consumed into ash, the fire out, but I could still feel heat swelling from the base. I kicked at it and it crumbled into greyness, releasing the sweet perfume of burned timber.

Then I saw what had so frightened Anne: the body of a charcoal-burner, toppled sideways off his stool. The marks of the pestilence were clear: on the side of his rough-shaven skull the scabs were angry and red, creamy at the edges. His lips were rolled back over his teeth; he looked for the world like a man grinning at a jest so merry it made him fall off his seat.

Anne was making such a clamour that it was a simple thing to follow. At last she ceased her row and mindless chatter replaced it. A voice deep within wondered if she had changed her mind and was trying to persuade the Maid to return to the village, but I dismissed it as foolishness. Anne was lost to me. Lost to God.

I found them resting in a space made by a fallen tree. They huddled on the bench of its trunk, Anne leaning against the Vixen and stroking her cheek. The midday sun was low, the light wet upon the leaves. Something crashed away to the right, setting birds in a scramble for the sky. Anne waved her arms about and screamed. But the Maid laid her hand upon her and she was still. The girl stiffened, nose quivering. Then she loosened, slapping the flat of her hands against her thigh, wheezing delight as she mimed a branch falling. The laughter of the two women curled about the clearing.

When they had finished, they untied the mouth of the sack and drew out apples, meat and bread. Pushed the food into their faces, chewing so noisily the sound carried to where I knelt. My stomach squealed, and I was glad to be many paces distant.

Anne wiped her fingers on her skirt and muttered something to the Vixen, hauling herself to her feet. She strode between the trees, peering into the bushes at my right. Surely I had not been found out. Then she lifted her kirtle, breathed out heavily, and squatted. First I heard the stream of piss, then smelled the warm odour of shit. There was a rustling as she plucked dock leaves with which to wipe herself.

A twig snapped under my shoe. She jerked her head sideways and saw me. For what seemed like hours, we stared at each other. Then, with great leisure, she stood, arranged her skirt, and smiled.

'I thought you might follow. Leave us be, Thomas.'

'I can still save you!' I squeaked. 'You have been ensnared by the demon!'

'So, first she was an angel, now she is a demon? I wish you'd make up your mind.'

I heard a voice cry out, 'Anne?' My head swung back to the clearing. The Vixen was rising very slowly from her haunches, looking directly at the spot where Anne had gone.

'Anne? What is happening?'

I held my finger to my lips. 'Don't answer. Come with me,' I whispered. 'We can go home.'

'What home?' she snorted.

'You are my Anne. My wife.'

I believe I saw her eyes soften for the smallest instant; then

386

she was stone. 'I do not belong to you, Thomas. I never did. How many times must I say it?'

'Anne!' cried the Vixen, louder this time, and I heard the crash of feet through the undergrowth.

But these were the footsteps of no earthly female: rather, I heard the rasping of hellish claws. I grabbed Anne's hand to take her away and save her from the clutches of this demon, but she struggled, yelling, 'Help, help, I am here!' however much I urged her to be quiet. She was so unruly that I had to strike her with my stick. It was done purely to calm her. She paused a moment, gasped, swung sideways and dropped to the ground.

I watched where she lay slumbering peacefully. The side of her head sparkled wetly. I examined the tip of my stave: hair was glued to it. My heart tapped out a polite rhythm in my breast, air ebbed and flowed gently in and out of my nostrils. But oh, how my soul flared. With the blow, God had come back to me.

I marvelled that it had taken so long to see my way back to Him. All the time He had simply wanted me to exercise governance over troublesome females. Nothing about this had been difficult. I had not understood; but now it was done, I felt His grace flood back.

'Anne!' came the shriek again, much closer. There was the swishing of a beast trampling through bushes and the Vixen was on me in an instant: tugging my hair, clawing at my eyes. One talon hooked in the corner of my mouth and pulled it into a half-smile; teeth shredded my ear. But its efforts were paltry, like a gnat trying to bring down a bull.

'Does Satan not try me with a more ferocious adversary?' I laughed. 'If that is all you have in your army, then I have nothing to fear.'

I hurled the demon aside, but it was on me again straightaway.

It could not hurt me, but it was bothersome. I ploughed through the trees, trying to dislodge it, but it clung to me as tight as a tick on a ram, sucking away my patience. I reached up, grasped its hair and cast it to the ground, knocking the wind out of its lungs.

It squirmed in the dirt, choking. I took the opportunity God had granted, dealt it a blow with my staff and it moved no longer. I took it by the wrist and dragged it through the trees, its toes scraping the dirt. I had work to do and I needed to be out of the shadows.

When I was done, I would return and rouse Anne from her slumber. Perhaps I would dare to wake her with a kiss. I giggled at the playful notion. It was not a pleasant sound, so I reminded myself that priests do not giggle. Was I still a priest? It was difficult to remember. I shook away such complicated thoughts. God's plan was written clearly in my soul: I would not be turned aside. I looked up; saw sunlight dancing on the tips of the furthest branches. I sang as I entered the clearing.

> Thy mercy is great unto the heavens,
> Thy truth unto the clouds.
> Be Thou exalted, oh God:
> Let Thy glory be above all the earth.

When the psalm was done, I looked at the Vixen lying at my feet. Its right arm was twisted oddly. Its eyes cracked open and shone at me, breath harsh between gritted teeth. It was not dead. It did not matter.

'Hush now,' I cooed.

For answer, it made a deep gargling and spat at me. 'You piece of shit,' it rasped. 'Will you never shut up?'

It tried to rise, shrieked with the pain of some broken part of itself. I watched the face contort in agony; waited for its breathing to slow down.

'What have you done to Anne?' it moaned. 'She did nothing to you.'

'Oh, but she did. She took you away. I could not permit that. The Lord gave you to me. You are mine. To do with as He commands.'

It made a noise that may have been merriment; I could not tell. 'Still the idiot,' the voice rasped. '*Mine, mine, mine,*' it whined, in a cruel imitation of my voice. 'You never had her. You never had me. You have nothing.'

'Be quiet.'

'I was hers.' Her face wrangled into something I realised was a smile.

'I said, be quiet!'

I shook my fist. It made the throttled sound again and this time I knew it for laughter.

'Or what? What can you possibly do to me that has not already been done?'

I raised my foot and brought it down on its shoulder. It let out such a cry that the rooks were sent flapping.

'You see?' I sneered. 'I have dominion over you.'

'You empty little man.' The fiend drew in a wincing breath. 'Know this and let it haunt you until you dare stand before God. Anne loved me.' It grinned, teeth bathed in blood. 'Me. Under your roof. And I loved her. Hear me? All the love under God's heaven and none of it for you.'

'No.'

I clapped my hands over my ears but the words leaked through.

'Anne!' it shrieked. 'If you can hear me, know this! I love you!'

Would it never be done with its babbling? This was the Devil speaking. I lifted my foot and stamped down again, harder, and felt something give. Suddenly the forest was filled with wild squalling. I looked around to discover where the sound might be coming from: October was early to be slaughtering pigs for winter. It was most curious.

The Vixen's mouth gaped so wide I could see the glistening dangle of flesh at the back. The screech was issuing from there. I slapped my forehead. Of course, how foolish of me. This was the demon fleeing the innocent body of the Maid. But enough of this racket. I would not be steered away from my task. God's task. I tore away the end of my sleeve and stopped up its mouth.

I needed a blessing to cast out the evil spirit. The Lord placed words on my tongue and I shouted them to the sky, clamped my hand over its lips, pinched its nose between thumb and forefinger and watched its eyes bloom. At last it grew limp. A worm of dark blood crawled from its nostril. After a while, I took my hands away. As the demon left the body of the Maid, so did all the contentiousness. She lay quietly at the heart of the forest, peaceful as the angel I had always known she was. I knelt and offered a prayer of thanks that the Lord had given her back to me. My own bright Maid, at last.

I stripped away the boyish garments, for they were an offence to both God and man. I unrolled the leather strap from about my waist and bound her wrists to her ankles, as men do with lambs. My fingers were never cleverer. It was as though I had been waiting all my life to do this beautiful thing for the Lord. I was God's vessel. *Do not be afraid,* said my soul.

The time had come to anoint her. I had no oil, but spittle would suffice. I licked my thumb, signed a cross on her forehead and suddenly there was a light about her head, just as when she first came to me. As I marvelled, the world fell into a drowse, the forest silent. So, this was the peace at the heart of God. I had sought it for years in my church and had found it here, beneath a vault of trees.

The trees shrank away and I was tossed backwards onto the ground. In my mind, I was lying on my back and looking at the stars. I was standing on the road to the Staple, before I saw the icon. I was welcoming Anne into my house for the first time. I was crouching under the Bishop's hand at my ordination. I was reeling under the force of my father's fists. I was chewing my mother's dugs. I was a seed planted in my mother's belly. I was in all places at once.

I gazed up at shreds of sky peeping through the branches, and knew myself once again in the forest. I heard the cracking of boughs as though the trees were closing in upon me, arching their vast arms above my head, roots lifted to crush my bones into leaf-mould. Then it occurred to me that this snapping was Anne being dragged through the undergrowth by the Devil, enraged at being cast out from the Maid. I sprang to my feet. If Satan thought he could take Anne away from me and into the hell-mouth, he was mistaken.

'Give Anne back to me!' I cried. 'You can't have her!'

I crashed through the bushes in pursuit, but the Devil played tricks on my ears. First, I heard his feet crunching twigs to my left, then to my right, then behind me. I swung about, expecting to come face to face with him, but he danced away and all I saw was a flicker at the corner of my eye that could have been his tail. I spun in faster and faster circles to catch a glimpse, but all I succeeded in doing was making myself dizzy.

'Show yourself!' I yelled, and was answered by the cawing of carrion crows. I knew it was Satan speaking through the filthy birds, and that they were laughing at me, every last one. 'You can't fool me! I am a man of God!' I screamed.

The cackling grew in cruelty and vehemence. I would not let these phantasms divert me from my path. To hear the better, I scraped my hair behind my ears. It had grown long since Anne – my mind stuttered. I felt the undertow of treacherous thoughts and pushed them away.

'Dear God, deliver me!' I cried. 'Deliver me to do your work!'

Perhaps He heard me, for at once the forest held its hundred tongues. There, straight ahead, I heard a twig snap. I raced in pursuit, knew I was on the right scent, for the scuffling grew more desperate the closer I approached.

'You'll not escape me!' I exulted. 'Anne is mine!'

I could not see her, but the rustling in the bushes made it easy to track her down, clear as the clang of a bell draws men to prayer. I was so near I could smell her fear. I tipped up my chin and howled to God.

> O conqueror of Moab!
> I grind my boot on Edom.
> I shout in triumph over the Philistines!

I stretched out my hand. One more step and I would have her. I took that last step and slammed into a vast oak. I shook my head. It was not there before. The Devil must have planted it in my path.

'Let me pass!' I screeched, pounding my fists against the bark. 'Please!' I begged. 'I must have— I must save Anne,' I gulped. 'Don't you see?'

I grasped the trunk between my fists and shook it. My knuckles bled, skin ripped from my hands, blood running to my wrist. I might as well have tried to empty the sea with a spoon for all the good it did.

I scrambled to the right side of the oak, raced forwards and straight into the arms of a blackthorn. It gripped me tight; spines spearing my tunic, piercing the flesh of my arms and breast, and holding me fast. I tried to move my head, but the thorns would not let go of my hair. They pricked my cheek in a warning to hold still. I felt a tear of blood well up and trickle down my chin.

'Let me go,' I croaked. 'I beg you.'

I wept salt: it joined the other wetnesses upon my face. Helpless, I listened to the rustling of undergrowth grow fainter as Anne was carried away, away and out of my life.

I was not aware how much time passed. I drowsed a little, for I was very tired from my day's labour. The next thing I knew was that the blackthorn had released me and I was lying on a heap of brambles. The sun sent its beams from a much lower point in the sky.

I stood up carefully. I was scratched and torn, but the forest had not defeated me. I looked around. The trees had drawn back into their proper places. I picked my way back to the clearing. It was not difficult because all my thrashing and stamping had beaten a path clear enough for a simpleton to follow.

I half-expected the Maid to have been spirited away by some celestial agency, reasoning that if Anne had been dragged off by a demon, then the Maid would surely have been lifted to heaven. But she was awaiting my return and had not stirred by as much as a quarter-inch. I was so grateful that I fell to my knees, never minding how grazed they were.

'Oh God! You have spared me!' I cried. 'You have spared my flock!' I corrected myself hastily, hoping He did not notice.

I would carry her back to the village. She would continue

to heal us. God had charged me with this task and I would not shirk. With no further delay, I wrapped her in my cloak. The skin on my palms was tight. I licked the stain.

The sun was almost gone. I straightened up, hefted her onto my shoulders. She weighed little, as do the holiest of God's creatures. My over-shirt was bloody, so God guided me back to the charcoal-burner's clearing, where I laid it on the embers and placed the men's garments alongside. I watched them smoulder, their charred threads mingling. Even bare-chested, I felt no chill.

The last crumb of daylight illuminated my path out of darkening forest, but I needed no candle to find my way, for I bore the Maid's radiance in my soul. Deep amongst the trees a vixen screamed out her heat, demanding a dog-fox to ram her plump with pups. The creature I carried upon my back was Vixen no longer.

Steam hovered over the pool at the foot of the well. I laid down the parcel of the Maid's body, knelt and plunged my head into the water. I pulled straight back out, convinced that someone was waiting to leap upon me and steal my burden. Nothing stirred. I wetted my arms to the elbow; washed first one half of my face, then the other, not taking my eyes from my bundle.

The track to the village was deserted. I was beginning to think the whole world emptied out save for me, when I met a man with a heap of sticks on his back.

'Good evening, Father,' he said.

'Am I your father?' I asked. I did not know him.

'Father Thomas?'

'You know me?' It was a wondrous thing.

He stared at the load I carried. 'You shouldn't carry such a weight yourself. Let me help you.'

'No.' I must have shouted, for he stepped back. 'No,' I repeated, gently.

'You have brought us a new marvel from the Staple?'

'The Staple?' I wished he would stop staring.

'You went there this morning.' His eyes grew narrow. I fought to make sense of his words.

'Yes. Indeed. The Staple,' I coughed, trying to hide the Maid behind me. It was too dark for him to see clearly.

'Are you well, Father? You are wearing no shirt,' he said.

'I am not cold. I am going to the church to tend to the relics of the Saint. We have need of intercession at this time of trial.'

The man crossed himself, muttering agreement.

'You may leave now,' I said. 'I am on God's business.'

I hastened to the church, fighting the urge to turn about and find him watching me. I ran up the nave to the shrine, grasped the handle of the great iron chest and watched my hands drag it out as easily as if it had been a basket of logs. I took the brass cross from the altar and used it to prise up the lid.

At the bottom of the box was a swirl of grit the colour of mud. Lumps the shape of turnips floated in the muck. I pushed my hands into the stickiness and swept one up, but it dissolved into corruption. I had planned to lift out the Saint's bones and wrap them. There was nothing here to wrap.

I wiped my palms but could not rid myself of the filth. I could not permit the reliquary chest to remain soiled with this disgusting mess, not when I had such a pearl to place within. I rinsed it out with water from the font, wiping it dry with a festival cope. It was the end of the old world. Time to begin afresh. New saints. New miracles. God's protection would remain with us as long as the Maid's relics lay here. I unrolled my cloak and laid it like a blanket at the bottom of the box, arranged the body neatly on top and locked her in her new home.

It was Vespers. I went to the treasury and dressed myself for the greatest of feast days, lit tapers, filled the roof with incense. I strode through the chancel and my voice rose to the rafters, stronger than I had heard it in months.

Listen, O daughter!
The Lord is enthralled by your beauty.
With gladness and rejoicing you are brought:
You shall enter into the place of the Lord.
Therefore shall the people praise you for ever and ever.

I roared the words as though for the first time, my soul soaring high, leading me up the steps and to the altar. Everything was burnished with gold. I raised my hands and glorified my Lord. What I did was not my will; it was God's. I obeyed. God had returned to me, in pomp and splendour. I was His servant; I could be nothing else.

Tonight I stood alone in the church. But tomorrow the people would come, and the miracles would begin again. No one would die. The pestilence would be defeated – not that it was ever here. Rumours and tittle-tattle. This was my miracle. It was accomplished.

VIXEN

It is such a hot day when I leave the forest, sweat rolling from my limbs, my need for this place rolling away with it. My body is escaping me. No one can mend me now.

Death is waiting, crouched on a branch. He grins fit to burst, stretching out scabby arms to carry me off into His kingdom. But as His talons brush me, they crumble; as do His hands, wrists, elbows: the whole rattlebag shivers into dust. I spent my whole life running and it was from a bogey, a scarecrow, a raw-head-and-bloody-bones tale I told to scare myself.

But there is no time to ponder the mystery. Laughing at this great joke, I make my way through the trees or, rather, upon them: by some marvellous agency I hop to the topmost branches without so much as snagging my sleeve on a twig. I dance upon the leaves, bending them less than does a squirrel, skipping west past the patchwork of the Great Field, the dull spread of the marshes, the humped dunes. Even the sea looks small, it is so far below.

There is a heavy sound, of a gate banging in the wind. I pause, look back and see a woman, wringing her hands and weeping. She starts to follow, but I tell her she cannot come where I am going.

'I will wait for you at the threshold,' I cry.

I lean earthwards to kiss her on the mouth one last time, but am barely able to brush her lips, I am being swept along so fast. Above my head, the sky is falling in the shape of vast snowflakes, tumbling thicker with each step until my vision blurs and I think all the angels in heaven must be shedding their feathers.

I shout, 'My love!' but my voice is lost in this gentle blizzard.

It is time to go. I set my eyes forwards and slip over the threshold of the world. The sky is muffled in gathering whiteness and I am going faster and faster until I am running so swiftly my feet leave the treetops and I fly into the snowstorm.

NUNC DIMITTIS

ANNE

When I come to, I open my eyes and find branches spreading their arms above me, the sky in pieces between them. There is a wet place on my head. When I touch my fingers to it, they come away red, which almost makes me swoon again. But I am made of tougher clay than the woman I once was and will not slip into another faint. I dig my fingernails into the flesh of my palms and the pain ropes me to the quay of consciousness.

I lie in the brambles, listening to the sigh of insects, worms champing the earth beneath my head. Everything that I call Anne is seeping out of the side of my head. *I will be part of this earth soon*, I think. It is peaceful. Pleasant, even. Perhaps it would not be so terrible to sleep awhile. I close my eyes.

'Anne!'

Her scream startles me awake.

'Know this! I love you!'

I raise my head to discover why she is shrieking and the sudden movement drives a nail between my eyes. I yelp, fall back gasping. The sounds of her agony will not let off. I must know, must help her. I lift my pounding head slowly, wincingly, and this time am able to see through the trees to where she lies. I wish I could not. Of all the terrible things I have witnessed, I would wash this from my memory.

He works his will upon her, steady at his labour until she is broken and cries out no more. She is gone somewhere far beyond my reach and I know with grim certainty that he will do the same to me unless I get away. I have no desire to follow the Maid into darkness. I can no longer help her, but I can help myself.

I gulp down my groans. Despite my unwillingness to quit this soft couch of leaves, I raise my head with great care. The branches above sway with far more force than merely wind flowing through them. I try to stand, but the ground swings to and fro, a rough sea in which I cannot swim. I decide to remain on my knees.

Very slowly, with as little sound as possible, I haul myself along on my elbows, puffing and gasping at the wrenching in my brow. I crawl through the undergrowth, away from him, away from her. With the grind of each inch, his roaring and yammering grows more and more distant.

I leave behind the last remnants of the old Anne, knocked out of my brains for ever with the swipe of his stick. If there are thorns, I do not feel their pricking. When I examine my hands afterwards, I find them stuck with spines, thick-set as hobnails on the sole of an old clog. I crawl until I can hear him no longer. Then, at last, I permit myself to fall, and sleep.

When I wake, it is to searing brightness. At first I think I have died and am standing before the brilliance of God, but it is simple sunlight slicing through the trees.

I am afraid, for I seem to be hemmed in by tree trunks from which I see no escape. By small degrees my fear dissipates. I

402

look afresh and see the trees are stretching strong branches that shelter me from harm. I let myself be cradled, mothered into comfort. The forest floor is soft as a breast, with a deep coverlet of leaves.

I thrust my hands into the cushion of leaf-mould, sift it through my fingers. Each leaf is nourishment for the small beasts of the forest, who in turn feed the greater beasts, who in turn feed men. My head swims in contemplation of this marvellous chain of being. Yet men stamp upon them, kick them out of the way as if they are nothing. I wonder if we are not poorer for the loss of a single leaf, each as lovely as the cast-off wing of a small brown angel.

I scoop up a heap and toss them into the air. They fall in a damp pattering, full of the aroma of decay that is not dying but the promise of rebirth next spring. I hurl more and more, in an unruly storm. Each leaf is a woman, a million of us, tramped into dirt. We bud, we fruit and, when we can bud no more, we serve no further purpose. After our brief harvest, we are raked into heaps for burning. I see the face of the earth swept clear of our dappled light, our softness. A barren world scraped bare and dry, lacking the thick mulch of our abundance.

I smile. I am become quite the philosopher.

I get to my feet, shake out my dirty gown, squint at the angle of the sun, reckon the best path and strike north through the trees. The bracken underfoot is black with the old year, a carpet of moss spreading its carpet. Lichen veils the trees, stiff with fungus so tough a maid could seat herself. Toadstools lift their blotched crowns, a cuckoo-pint pokes up its knobbled cock of crimson seeds.

I pick my way through brambles, heavy with wizened berries. I sigh, for it is long past Michaelmas and they have the Devil in them. I am a dozen steps further on before I stop, arrested by the nonsense that has just passed through my head. I crouch, pluck the berries and cram them into my mouth. If the Devil's in them, I can't taste him.

I browse bush after bush, stuffing myself until my hands are purple. *A most royal colour*, I think. At this, there comes to my ears a strange sound, rough and cracked, and I realise I am laughing.

Half a day on, I come upon a treasure chest of beech nuts, too deep into the forest for pigs to find. I feast till I can eat no more. A prudent housekeeper would fill her kerchief with some to eat later. The idea makes me laugh again, louder than the first time. I like the sound far more than I like the idea of being prudent, and walk on unladen.

This dead year is coming to its end. There is no surety that the next place I go will be kind, but it will be away from the village and its particular madness. This pestilence is a tide, and like the sea it will draw back. When it does so, it will leave a land scraped clean. Some of us will lie gasping, wet through, but still living. I am one of them.

If I live, and I shall live, I shall build me a life. It stretches before me, granted in answer to a prayer I did not know I had spoken. I shall live that life like the gift it is, and waste neither it nor myself. I am my own woman. I like her. She has stories to tell, and all of them are interesting.

My old life is flickering in the eye of memory, enchanting but as insubstantial as the leap of flames in a fire. I see that Anne: her dowdy hair and dowdy mind, her sulks, her suck-a-thumb. I look upon her as a stranger, yet I do not hate her. I have tasted enough hatred to last several lifetimes and will dine on it no more. That Anne was as soft as a fist of dough, and the mould I was given was narrow and fit me unhappily. I chafed against its sides, although I hardly knew it at the time.

I am grown now. Yet I have the strangest notion that I am not done with growing, nor shall be for as long as I walk this earth, and perhaps the next. I shall find a different name to wear, one which fits my new soul. I do not know what that name is, but it will come to me in its own good time.

The Maid would be proud of me, I think. She lit the flame of my lamp, but I am the one who tends it and keeps it bright. At night I close my eyes and she is there, leaning on the doorpost of my dreams, arms folded, head tipped to one side, giving me that slow smile I so rarely saw in life. Now she is gone to a more peaceful place, she smiles all of the time and I am right glad of it. I would she were with me still – but when I say this to her she lays her hand over my heart and it pounds so mightily I fear it will burst out of its cage. She shakes her head, grinning all the while, and I wake up, crying out.

It is like that for a long time. I do not stop wanting her, but I begin to understand the shake of her head, why she presses her hand to my heart to show that mine still beats, whereas hers is still. And also, I believe, to show that she gave herself to me as much as she could. However small a portion, it is enough.

I pass through the village once, many years later, with my mistress. She is a fine lady and has a great affection for the saints. Being possessed of money from her various husbands – God rest and preserve them all – she makes many pilgrimages and takes me with her. It is my opinion that she's prompted by curiosity and an eagerness for life rather than piety for dead men, but I keep some opinions to myself.

I see him, from far off. Despite his wrinkled face and cowering step, I'd know him anywhere. Children hide their

405

faces, not brave enough to jeer. Men shudder as he passes, like dogs shaking off water. I pull my kerchief over my nose, but he staggers past like a man half-blind or half-drunk, hand patting the air as though affrighted by what is before him. He seems collapsed in upon himself; a man sucked dry by the leeches of his sins. I wish him no ill. I wish him nothing at all.

I watch him go and wonder what my life might have been if I had let him pass on the Saint's Day all those years ago. I am surprised to discover I feel not one scrap of regret. If I had not gone to his house, I would not have met the Maid and my life would be immeasurably poorer. Not to say shorter.

I take a turn around the churchyard and find it scattered with strangers. I ask who tends the alehouse and hear an unfamiliar name. Likewise with bell-ringer, miller, steward, reeve: all are young folk with no memory of who came before them. It is a village with no old men, save Thomas. With a griping in my belly I make my way up the street to my father's cottage. It stands empty, the thatch fallen in on one side so that the door is blocked. My mistress finds me there.

'There is no holiness in this place,' she declares. 'What say you, Nan?'

She is the only one I permit to address me thus. 'It is a tumbledown place,' I reply.

'Like so much of this land,' she sighs. 'Before the Great Dying this was quite the place to come on pilgrimage.'

'So I have heard, mistress,' I reply.

'I have a nose for saints and there are none lying here,' she says. 'The villagers say that the Saint climbed out of his shrine one night and walked into the forest. He deserted the village because of some great sin, although no one knows what.'

'Well,' I say. 'That is indeed a wonder, mistress.'

'Are you done?' she asks softly, for she is a kind woman.

'I am done,' I reply. 'I have no desire to stay.'
She takes my hand and we take our leave.

I had the first word. I never thought to have the last. I cut my
own path through this halting, hobbling, half-empty land. I am
not broken. Not by men, certainly: their cruelty has not undone
me. Not by God, for all Thomas's ravings about sin. I am not
struck down by Death, although he has sopped his bread in my
dish and drunk from my cup. I never thought to be merry again,
but the heart heals in its own time and not to our promptings.
I stand straight and stride through this world. I dance over hills,
through valleys, along beaches; treading light upon the sand,
carrying the small bright lamp of my star.